PRAISE FOR

LION HEART

'To read one of Ben Kane's **astonishingly well-researched**, bestselling novels is to know that you are, historically speaking, in safe hands'
Elizabeth Buchan, *Daily Mail*

'This is a **stunningly visual and powerful** read: Kane's power of description is **second to none** . . . Perfect for anyone who is suffering from *Game of Thrones* withdrawal symptoms'
Helena Gumley-Mason, *The Lady*

'**Fans of battle-heavy historical fiction will, justly, adore *Clash of Empires*.** With its rounded historical characters and **fascinating** historical setting, it deserves a wider audience'
Antonia Senior, *The Times*

'**Grabs you from the start and never lets go**. Thrilling action combines with historical authenticity to summon up a whole world in a sweeping tale of politics and war. **A triumph!**'
Harry Sidebottom, author of the *The Last Hour*

'The word **epic** is overused to describe books, but with *Clash of Empires* it fits like a gladius in its scabbard. What Kane does, with such mastery, is place the big story – Rome vs Greece – in the background, while making this a story about ordinary men caught up in world-defining events. In short, **I haven't enjoyed a book this much for ages. There aren't many writers today who could take on this story and do it well. There might be none who could do it better than Ben Kane**'
Giles Kristian, author of *Lancelot*

BEN KANE is one of the most hard-working and successful historical writers in the industry. His third book, *The Road to Rome*, was a *Sunday Times* number four bestseller, and almost every title since has been a top ten bestseller. Born in Kenya, Kane moved to Ireland at the age of seven. After qualifying as a veterinarian, he worked in small animal practice and during the terrible Foot and Mouth Disease outbreak in 2001. Despite his veterinary career, he retained a deep love of history; this led him to begin writing.

His first novel, *The Forgotten Legion*, was published in 2008; since then he has written five series of Roman novels. Kane lives in Somerset with his wife and two children.

LION HEART

BEN KANE

ORION

An Orion paperback

First published in Great Britain in 2020
by Orion Fiction,
This paperback edition published in 2021
by Orion Fiction,
an imprint of The Orion Publishing Group Ltd.,
Carmelite House, 50 Victoria Embankment
London EC4Y 0DZ

An Hachette UK Company

1 3 5 7 9 10 8 6 4 2

A CIP catalogue record for this book is
available from the British Library.

ISBN (Paperback) 978 1 4091 7349 6

Typeset by Input Data Services Ltd, Somerset

Printed and bound in Great Britain by Clays Ltd, Elcograf S.p.A.

MIX
Paper from
responsible sources
FSC® C104740
FSC
www.fsc.org

www.orionbooks.co.uk

For Joe Schmidt, rugby coach extraordinaire, with deepest respect.

Despite the disappointment of Japan, you and your legacy will long be remembered by Irish rugby fans. I wish you every happiness and success for the future, and if I have the good fortune to meet you one day, the drinks are on me!
(P.S. A more suitable book title to dedicate to you, I cannot think of.)

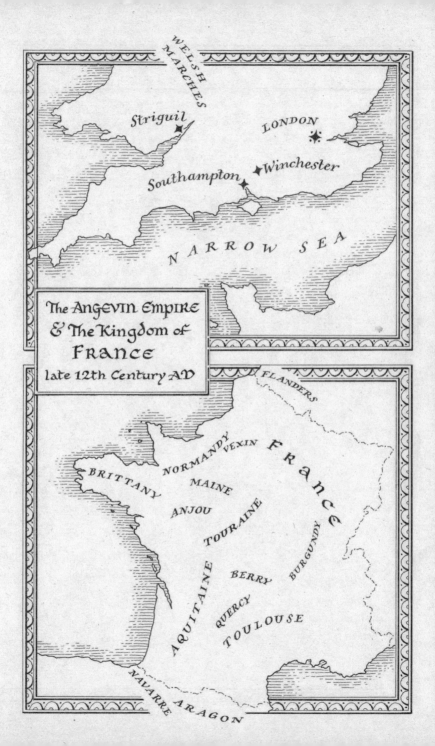

The Angevin Empire
& The Kingdom of
FRANCE
late 12th Century AD

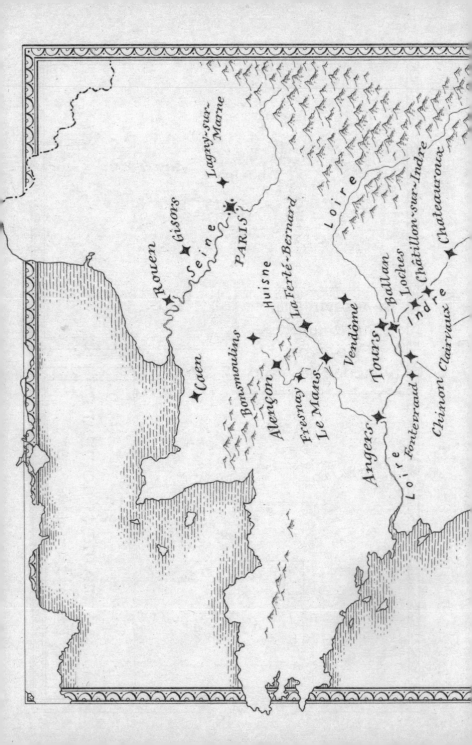

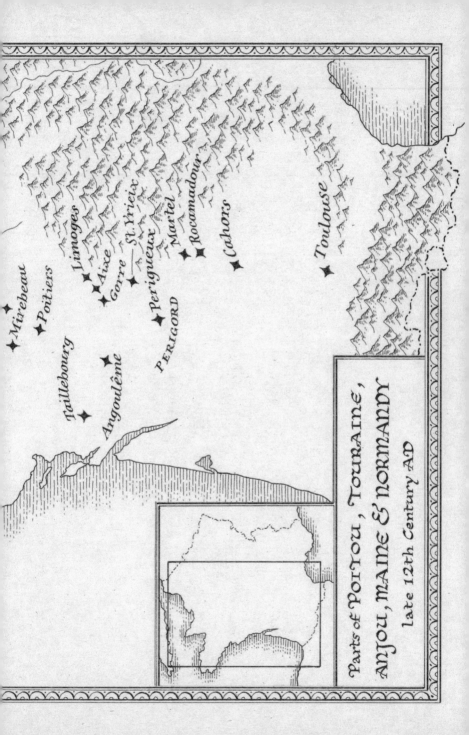

Mirebeau

Poitiers

Taillebourg

Angoulême

Limoges

Aixe

Gorre

St.Yrieix

Perigueux

PERIGORD

Martel

Rocamadour

Cahors

Toulouse

Parts of POITOU, TOURAINE,
ANJOU, MAINE & NORMANDY
late 12th Century AD

List of Characters

(Those marked * are recorded in history.)

Ferdia Ó Catháin/Rufus, an Irish noble from north Leinster.

At Striguil:
Robert FitzAldelm, 'Boots and Fists', knight.
Richard de Clare, Earl of Pembroke (deceased).*
Aoife, his widow.*
Isabelle, their daughter.*
Gilbert, their son and heir.*
Rhys, orphan Welsh boy.
Hugo, Walter, Reginald and Bogo, squires.
Big Mary, washerwoman.
FitzWarin, knight, and friend of Robert FitzAldelm.
Gilbert de Lysle, messenger for Duke Richard.
Guy FitzAldelm, knight, and brother to Robert FitzAldelm.

House of Anjou and its associates:
Henry II, king of England and Anjou.*
Alienor (Eleanor) of Aquitaine, his wife.*
Henry, the Young King, oldest surviving son of Henry II.*
Richard, Duke of Aquitaine and second son of Henry II.*
Geoffrey, Count of Brittany and third son of Henry II.*
John, 'Lackland', youngest son of Henry II.*
Matilda*, one of Henry's daughters, married to Heinrich der Löwe*,
    former Duke of Saxony and Bavaria.
Alienor, Juvette, maidservants to Matilda.
Beatrice, maidservant to Queen Alienor.
Geoffrey, bastard son to Henry II, and his chancellor.*

Geoffrey de Brûlon, knight.*
Maurice de Craon, knight.*
Hawise of Gloucester, bride of Prince John.*

Richard's household:
André de Chauvigny, knight and cousin to Duke Richard.*
John de Beaumont, knight.
John de Mandeville, Louis, 'Weasel' John, squires.
Philip, squire and friend to Rufus.
Owain ap Gruffydd, Welsh knight.
Richard de Drune, English man-at-arms.

The Young King's household:
William Marshal, knight.*
Adam d'Yquebeuf, knight.*
Thomas de Coulonces, knight.*
Baldwin de Béthune, knight.*
Simon de Marisco, knight.*
Heloise of Kendal, ward of William Marshal.*
Joscelin, squire to William Marshal.
Jean d'Earley, squire to William Marshal.*

Other characters:
Philippe Capet*, king of France, and son of King Louis* (deceased).
Bertran de Born, troubadour.*
Count Vulgrin Taillefer of Angoulême.*
Matilda, his daughter.*
William and Adémar Taillefer, Vulgrin's brothers.*
Count Aimar of Limoges, their half-brother.*
Philippe, Count of Flanders.*
William des Barres, one of Philippe's knights.*
Count Raymond of Toulouse.*
Count Hugh of Burgundy.*
Peter Seillan, close advisor to Count Raymond.*

PROLOGUE

History remembers the great. The kings and emperors, the popes. Ordinary men such as you and I go nameless to our graves. No archbishops celebrate our funerals, no magnificent tombs preserve our final resting places. Yet some of us were there, when the fates of kingdoms hung in the balance, when battles that seemed lost were turned on their heads. Ever forgotten by the monkish scribes and the historians, we helped the mighty on their paths to glory and eternal renown.

White-haired and bent-backed I may be now, but in my day I wielded a sword with the best of men. All Christendom knows of Richard, king of England, Duke of Normandy, Count of Brittany and Anjou – the Lionheart. Precious few have heard of his knight Rufus, and even fewer of Ferdia Ó Catháin. This troubles me not. I did not serve Richard for wealth or fame. Loyalty made me his man, and his man I am still, although he has been dead these thirty years, God rest his soul.

My eyesight dims, my muscles weaken. Wearing mail and riding a destrier was once a delight; now I am grateful to shuffle to the bench outside the door and warm my bones in the sun. Death will come for me, if not this winter, then the next. I will be ready, but I pray the monks have time enough to record my tale, such as it is, before my last breath leaves me.

Three score years and ten is a greater span than better men have had. My life has been rich. I have known true love's exquisite joy, where many have not. I was there, heart swelling, to hold my new-born sons, and my daughter. I had brothers-in-arms who were closer to me than my real brothers ever were. Sorrow entered my life more than once, and tragedy too; these are but trials sent by the Divine to test us. All a man can do is shoulder his load once more, and carry on.

They say that God moves in mysterious ways, and it is certainly true of my path. From a little-known part of Ireland I came to England, where I fell into the service of the greatest warrior of the age – Richard Coeur de Lion. Together we besieged castles, and fought dozens of battles. I bled, I killed for Richard. I am not proud to say I murdered for him too. I confessed those sins, but in my heart, I am unrepentant. God forgive me, I would kill those men again if I had the strength.

I shall continue, else we shall be debating my soul as the sun sets. I was there when Richard met his father Henry for the last time; I stood in Westminster Abbey when he was crowned. I came close to dying in Cyprus, saving his queen. At Arsuf, we fought side by side and defeated Saladin; not long after, we marched almost to the gates of Jerusalem. When Richard was betrayed on his journey back from the Holy Land, the king and I shared a dungeon. I helped him reclaim what was his from his dog of a brother, John. He too is as dead as Richard, and by God's grace roasting in Hell.

But I have raced on, and almost told the tale's ending before its start. It may have struck you as odd, reader, to learn of an Irishman serving the English king. The saints be thanked that my father died without knowing. Did I ever regret it? Now and again perhaps, but once given, an oath is sacred, and the bond of comradeship that is forged in war is unbreakable. Perhaps I make no sense. Forgive an old man's wandering.

Let us go back half a century, and start the tale anew . . .

PART ONE: 1179

CHAPTER I

Ten years had passed since the treacherous former king of Leinster, Diarmait MacMurchada, had invited the English into Ireland. Their conquest was by no means complete, but the grey foreigners, as we called them, had the upper hand. The proof of this lay not just with the strip of territory they held along the east coast, but the fealty offered to the English monarch Henry by many of the Irish provincial kings. Four years prior, a hammer blow to our hopes had been struck when King Ruairidh of Connacht had also pledged his allegiance.

My father was a minor nobleman in northern Leinster, and after Diarmait made an alliance with the English, he had offered his loyalty to Ruairidh. Furious with what he regarded as Ruairidh's betrayal, Father took the inconceivable step of joining with the king of Ulster, long our enemy but still unconquered by the invaders. His choice was an ill-considered one. When the enemy came ravaging, Ulster did not answer our call. We fought bravely, but our lands were soon overrun.

Taken hostage for the good behaviour of my family, I was sent to Dublin. From there I travelled in a sturdy cog east and south over the sea, to the cloud-ridden Welsh coast, the length of which was dotted with castles. Cover a land in such strongholds, I thought grimly, and the locals, with nowhere to go, will be forced into a final stand as my own family had been. Again I saw the English knights' charge in my mind, an unstoppable wave that had shattered our light-armed warriors.

Our voyage came to an end in sight of England, at the stronghold they call Striguil. Home to the de Clare family, it sits on a bluff overlooking the River Wye, and was the largest castle I had ever seen. A mighty rectangular tower, it was surrounded by a palisade that snaked across the summit of the hill. Beyond that, on every side but that which gave onto the Wye, I would discover, lay a defensive ditch. I did not let it show, but I was impressed. If this was the ancestral home of an earl, King Henry's donjon must be remarkable indeed. The English weren't just expert at fighting, I thought, they were master builders too. My fears that Ireland's chieftains and kings would never drive the invaders into the sea returned. I quelled them, for it seemed that if I gave in to *that* despair, my own situation would become altogether worse. Dream of defeating the English in my own land, and the miseries heaped upon me could somehow be borne.

Nineteen years old, taller than most, mop-haired and raw-boned, full of the arrogance of youth, I spoke little French that day, and not a word of English. Since being handed into captivity by my stony-faced father, I had endured a difficult time. Taking his parting words to heart – 'Give in only if you must. Do only what you have to.' – I had refused to obey any commands. On the first day, I called the brutish knight into whose charge I had been given a flea-infested dog, adding that his mother worked in the back alleys of Dublin. I had not considered the consequences. Some of the crew were Irish, and, intimidated by the knight, translated what I had said.

My insults that first day earned me a hiding, and my mulish carrying-on thereafter earned no respect, just more beatings and short rations. I look back now, and wonder at my bull-headed behaviour and more, my short-sightedness. By the end of the voyage I was old friends with the knight's boots and fists. Forever burning with rage and humiliation, I would have tipped him into the brine, or worse if I had laid hands to a weapon. And yet despite my youthful bravado, I had wits to know that such an act would have seen me follow him to the ocean floor, and so I buried my hatred for what I hoped was another day.

'Rufus.'

Still unused to the name my captor had given me – unable, or more likely, I thought darkly, unwilling to try mastering my own of Ferdia – I paid no heed. My eyes were fixed on the figures standing on the wooden jetty below the castle. It seemed that word of our arrival had landed before us. I had no idea who might greet us off the ship, but it would not be Richard de Clare, the Earl of Pembroke, one of the chief nobles who had invaded Ireland. He was dead, praise God. Even when he was living, the earl would not have deigned to watch the arrival of a captive such as I. Nor would his wife, the countess Aoife, in residence here since his passing. Reputed to be a great beauty, I had nightly conjured pleasant fantasies about her to take my mind from the thinness of my blanket, and the hardness of the deck.

'Rufus, you dog!' Boots and Fists – my nickname for Robert Fitz-Aldelm, the block-headed knight in charge of our party – sounded angry.

He caught my attention at last. I recognised 'Rufus'; I knew what *chien* meant. I am as high born as you, I thought with contempt. My ribs were still hurting from his last attack, and yet stubborn to the last, I kept my gaze locked on the close-to jetty, and my mind on Aoife. Daughter of Diarmait MacMurchada, the king of Leinster, widow of Richard de Clare, she would be the mistress of my fate.

'Rufus!'

I did not hear.

A ball of agony exploded in my head; my vision blurred. The force of the blow sent me reeling sideways, into one of the crew. He shoved me away with an oath, and weak-kneed, I fell to the deck. Boots and Fists laid into me with his usual energy, careful as always not to kick me in the face. Sly as a fox he was, mindful that those above him would not sanction the punishments he had been doling out since we had sailed from Dublin.

'Areste!' The voice was reedy, but full of command. A girl's voice.

I knew that French word as well: it meant 'stop'.

My heart hammered. No more kicks landed.

The girl spoke again, an angry question. I did not understand.

Boots and Fists moved further away as he answered. His tone was respectful yet sullen. I could not make out the words.

Light-headed still, I opened my eyes, taking in the sideways view. A line of iron nail heads. Gaps in the planking. Below, scummy water, several fingers' depth of which occupied the space under the deck. The whiff of piss – despite the captain's rules, some men did not like urinating over the side – and rotten food. Boots and shoes moved about; the former worn by the men-at-arms, the latter by the callous-handed crew. A coil of rope. The bottoms of barrels that held water, mead and salted pork.

Boots and Fists had not come back. Deciding that it might be safe to get up, I eased into a sitting position. Darts of pain came from my belly and back, from my arms and legs. I tried to feel grateful that the only part of me he had missed – apart from my head – was my groin. I cast a glance at Boots and Fists, who was talking yet to the girl on the jetty. We had come in alongside it now, and men with thick ropes were making the ship fast. Standing, gripping the vessel's side to steady myself, I was astonished to see she was a mere child. Clad in a mulberry gown and over it, a dark green cloak edged with silver braid, she was perhaps six years of age. Long tresses of red hair, a lighter shade than my own, framed an oval, serious face.

Her grey-eyed gaze fell on me. For some reason, I suspected she was Richard and Aoife's daughter. What she was doing here alone was beyond me. I dipped my head, a show of respect I did not feel, and met her stare once more.

'Are you hurt?' she asked.

I gaped. The girl had addressed me not in French, but my own tongue.

'Mother says that it is impolite to let your mouth hang open. If nothing else, flies will go in.'

I closed my jaw, feeling foolish, and managed, 'My apologies. I did not expect to hear Irish here.'

'Mother insists that we learn it. "You may be half-English," she says, "but you are also half-Irish."'

My gut had been right. I pulled a smile. 'Your mother sounds like a wise woman. To answer your question, I do not think he broke any bones.' I wanted to glare at Boots and Fists, who I sensed was doing his best to understand, but thought it wiser not to. 'My thanks for intervening.'

A little nod.

She was a small child, but there was a gravity to her. It was no surprise, I decided, given her breeding.

'What is your name?'

'Ferdia Ó Catháin.'

To my surprise, she pronounced my family name correctly, the 'c' hard, the 't' silent, and the rest of the word like 'hoyn'. Her mother was proud of her Irish roots, I thought with a flash of pleasure.

Boots and Fists growled something in French. I understood only 'Rufus'.

'He says they call you Rufus.' The girl cocked her head. 'I can see why.'

I raised a hand to my head, amused despite my pain. 'Mother used to say that the fairies dangled me by the heels in a pot of madder to give

8

me such red hair. They must have done it for a shorter time with you.'

The girl's serious manner vanished, and she laughed. 'I shall also call you Rufus!' She must have seen something in my face; her expression changed. 'Unless you had rather I did not?'

Once more Boots and Fists interrupted. Despite my lack of French, it was clear that he wanted me off the ship. The men-at-arms were already on the jetty, taking the shields and leather-wrapped bundles of weapons passed to them by the crew.

Ignoring the discomfort it caused, I swung a leg over the side and eased myself onto the dock. Boots and Fists followed. He pointed to the path that led through a scattering of houses to the base of the palisade, and again spoke in French.

Curse it, I thought. I shall have to learn their tongue, or my life will be impossible. 'He wants me to go up?' I asked the girl.

'Yes.' Her previous air of command had waned; it was if she knew that her power was limited. She could stop my beating, but not my destiny as a captive.

I resisted the first dig in the back that Boots and Fists gave me. 'What is your name?'

'Isabelle!' The voice – a woman's – came from somewhere behind the palisade. It was shrill, and unhappy. 'Is-a-belle!'

An impish smile. 'Isabelle. Isabelle de Clare.'

My instinct had been right. I dipped my head a second time, more willingly, for the girl's heart was in the right place. Lowering my voice so the Irishmen among the crew could not hear, I said, 'I owe you my thanks, for stopping that amadán from kicking me to a pulp.'

She giggled. 'Careful what you call FitzAldelm. He might speak some Irish.'

'He does not understand a word.' Confident that I would soon be dining in the great hall, I half turned. 'Do you, amadán?'

Boots and Fists – FitzAldelm – scowled, and gave me a shove.

'See?' I said, my cockiness growing.

'Isabelle!' The voice had risen to a harridan's screech.

'That is my nurse. I had best go,' she said, rolling her eyes. Picking up her skirts so they did not trail in the mud, she sped up the path ahead of us. 'Farewell, Rufus!'

'Farewell, my lady,' I cried.

It was the first time I had not resented someone addressing me so.

My pleasure was brief.

Boots and Fists gave me an almighty dunt in the behind. I nearly fell on my face. Picking myself up, my ears full of curses, I began to climb. Passing through the gate that led into the castle, Isabelle did not see.

I almost called after her, but full sure that my ill-treatment would soon be a thing of the past, I held my peace. If Aoife was a just woman, I decided, Boots and Fists might even be punished for what he had done.

Reaching the gate, which had already been closed, I looked up at the top of the palisade. Three men's height it must have been, close enough to see the sentry leering at me, but sufficient distance upward to realise that taking the place by storm would be a lackwit's errand.

'Ouvre la porte!' demanded Boots and Fists angrily.

Open the door, I thought. Remember those words.

Impatient, Boots and Fists stepped past me and rapped on the timbers with his fist. Sturdily built, it was still the weak spot in this part of the defences, and yet in the event of an attack, the garrison would empty pots of heated sand on the attackers' heads while arrows rained down from the rampart.

The door creaked open, revealing a soldier in a gambeson and hauberk. Plainly a soldier several rungs down the ladder of command, he endured Boots and Fists' haranguing without complaint. A question was asked. I heard the name 'Eva', the French for Aoife. Giving me a curious glance, the soldier replied with a shake of his head.

I had no time to dwell on the significance of this, for Boots and Fists shoved me in the back, indicating I should enter.

I had been inside a bailey – the word given by the English to the space inside a castle's defences – but never one so large. An irregular rectangle, open at the centre to the skies, it was bordered on one side by the two-storey stone keep with its attached kitchen and storage houses. The other sides, formed by the palisade, had at their base slope-roofed buildings I took to be barracks, stables and the like. The place was crowded, but scarcely a person paid me any heed.

A smith in a leather apron bent over a horse's foot, hammer poised to drive another nail into the shoe he had been fashioning. At the beast's head, a youth in a ragged tunic and torn hose gripped the bridle, at the same time picking his nose with his free hand. From the back of a cart, a heavyset man heaved down bulging sacks of vegetables to a second. Out of an empty stable came a rat catcher, pushing his one-wheeled pole. He was followed by several scrawny cats, attention fixed on the half dozen rodents hanging from it by their tails. A group of men-at-arms lounged by the timber-built well, passing a costrel of wine to and fro, and eyeing the young maidservant who was pulling up a bucket from the depths.

The air was rich with smells; horse manure, wood smoke and baking bread. The last made my belly rumble, and I thought with longing of hot-from-the-oven wheaten loaf, slathered in butter and honey. Tortured, for my recent diet had been a world apart from that, I shoved the image away.

'Ceste direction.' Boots and Fists pointed over my shoulder at a door in the basement of the keep.

I caught a tone of urgency in his voice; the hefty push that followed confirmed it.

A woman's voice carried from above, its tone both annoyed and reprimanding. My eyes rose to the staircase that led from ground level to the highly ornamented doorway in the keep's wall. A diminutive shape – Isabelle, recognisable by her green cloak – had reached the top, where an amply figured woman stood. By her wagging finger and continuous carping, she was Isabelle's nurse.

I longed for Isabelle to turn and see me, and raise a friendly hand. Again I almost called out, but Boots and Fists pre-empted me with a stinging cuff that saw me bite my lip. Sure that something was wrong now, I searched the bailey for someone of high rank, the steward, or one of the knights, but could see no one. I dragged my feet, but it made no difference. Soon we had reached the ominous-looking door, and after he had opened it with a heavy iron key, I was forced into the dark, damp space beyond.

I peered about, eyes adjusting to the gloom. Timber pillars thicker than a man stood a dozen paces apart, supporting the floor of what was probably the great hall above. Doors lined the walls on either side. I judged them to be a mixture of granaries, storerooms and prison cells, and my suspicion about the last was borne out when Boots and Fists prodded me towards a doorway that gaped like the mouth of a tomb. I stopped dead. I was no king's offspring like Aoife, but nor was I a felon. I deserved better quarters than this.

Mouth opening to protest, I turned towards Boots and Fists.

He had been waiting for his chance. Up flew his right fist, circled as I discovered later with a heavy loop of iron, to take me under the chin. I never felt myself hit the floor.

CHAPTER II

What shall I say of the terrible period that followed? In truth, I lost count of how long I spent in that hellhole. At the time, it seemed an eternity; I was told afterwards it had been more than a sennight. With just a thin woollen blanket between me and the beaten earth floor, I was constantly cold. I would even wager that the chill rivalled that of the windswept monastery on Holy Island I had heard about from monks. To warm my bones, I would pace the cell, which was six steps by six. From the door to the back wall I walked, first with fingers outstretched to avoid collision with the stones, and then, confidence growing, with both hands gripping my shoulder-wrapped blanket.

Total darkness was my world. The passage of the hours was marked only by the arrival of a man-at-arms with food and beer. I had no idea when these visits were, but my growling belly told me it was perhaps once a day. Far less often, one of my gaolers would come to replace my overflowing bucket with another.

During these brief contacts, a dim light would seep from the external door beyond, into the basement and thence into my cell. Almost blinded, but desperate to be allowed out, I first greeted the guards with indignant protests that I was not supposed to be here, that while a hostage, I was still a nobleman. Whether they understood my abominable mixture of Irish and French, I could not tell; they either laughed or said nothing in reply. I soon learned to hold my tongue, because after several attempts, Boots and Fists paid a visit.

Placing a torch in a bracket by the door, he had a man-at-arms stand with a ready sword in case I should resist, and proceeded to kick me black and blue. Although I burned to fight back, taking my chances against two opponents, I knew it to be an attempt doomed to failure. Curling into a ball, I told myself that it was better to have a life, bloodied and starving, than a slow dungeon-death from a gut-stabbing.

He came back the next time a guard brought food, and repeated the beating. He had learned that the word amadán meant 'fool' then, presumably from one of the Irish crewmen, and was in a complete rage. A kick to the head sent me spiralling into blackness. I have no idea how long he laid into my unconscious form, but when I awoke, I had never been in so much pain. Needles darted into me with each breath, revealing that a couple of ribs were cracked. Blood caked my face. I had lost a front tooth, and my belly felt as if the smith from the bailey outside had been hammering away on it for an hour. By the saints, Boots and Fists knew how to make a man hurt.

I learned my lesson from those hidings. From that juncture, the sound of approaching footsteps made me retreat to the cell's back wall, and wait for the door to creak open. Wary as a wild beast, I would watch as the bowl and cup were placed on the floor. Only when total blackness had again descended would I scuttle on all fours – aye, like a starving dog – to devour the meagre rations I had been left.

Alone in the dark, beaten within an inch of my life, chilled to the marrow and ravenous with hunger, I came close to losing my sanity. Prayer helped at first, but when it went unanswered day after day, night after night, I lost hope. Monks will be familiar with fasting and solitude, but they have never languished in a dungeon. Never been deprived of light until the merest hint of sun sears your eyes like a lightning bolt. Have never suffered Boots and Fists' expert attention.

Abandoning prayer, I took myself to my home in Ireland, picturing it in an attempt to remove myself from the misery of that cell. I have not yet spoken of my childhood home, Cairlinn. At the northern extremity of Leinster, it sits on the southern shore of a long, narrow inlet, on the opposite side of which is Ulster. A steep mountain lowers at the settlement's back. Sliabh Feá, we called it – the English would say 'Shlee-uv Fay'. Many a fine summer's day I reclined on the summit with my friends, our chests heaving from the race up, staring over the narrow strip of water that separated Cairlinn from Ulster. As men, my friends and I boasted, we would raid north for cattle, as our fathers and grandfathers had done. The clans of Ulster had always been our enemies, or so the stories went.

Memories helped for a time. I would sit against the cell wall, blanket wrapped tight around me, and imagine my father's big hands, calloused and broken-nailed, yet also gentle, showing me how to grip a sword. Mother, frowning with concentration, teaching my younger sister to embroider. The skylark's call above Sliabh Feá on a hot summer's day. The tantalising smell of mackerel, caught in the bay, frying in butter, or that of bread, fresh from the oven. Women and men dancing around the great fires on the longest night of the year. Bealtaine, we call it; the English know it as Beltane. Winter nights perched by the fire, storms raging outside, and the bard weaving tales of love and betrayal, friendship and enmity, war and death. My name Ferdia comes from the legendary *Táin*, a story told by firesides in Ireland this thousand years and more. 'Toyne' would be as close to the word as English tongues could manage.

I had not seen much of life then. My store of memories ran dry after only a short time. I tried to relive them again, but the misery of my situation grew too much. Briefly unmanned, I shed bitter tears, railing in my head against the injustice done to me. I tried praying to God, but He made no reply. Rage replaced my sorrow, and uncaring who might hear, I beat on the door until the skin of my hands was ripped and bleeding. No one answered, no one came. I was going to die here, it seemed. Despair and exhaustion overcame me, and I slumped to the floor. Before long, in spite of the cold and my aching heart, I had drifted off.

I woke with a start to a rasping sound by my ear. Scrambling to my feet as the bolt scraped back entirely, I shuffled further from the door. My guts roiled; scarce three hours had passed since I had wolfed down my last meal. Boots and Fists had come back, I decided. To my surprise, I felt my own fists bunch. Images filled my mind. His ugly face contorted in fear. My punches bursting his nose like an overripe plum. Screams, cries for mercy filling the cell – his, not mine.

The door opened. Torchlight spilled along the floor.

I took a deep breath. Boots and Fists was about to get the surprise of his life. If by some miracle my attack succeeded, the man-at-arms who always accompanied my tormentor would probably end it with his blade. If I failed, I would receive a beating like none of those that had gone before. The first result would see me dead, the second maimed.

I no longer cared.

'Welcome, FitzAldelm,' I croaked. I slid my feet apart the way my father had taught me, and raised my fists.

'Ferdia Ó Catháin?' asked a piping voice.

Confusion gripped me. In the doorway I made out two small shapes, one a shade taller than the other, and behind them, a large one. 'Yes?' I answered.

'See, Gilbert? I was not making it up,' cried a voice in Irish.

Shocked, I recognised it as that of Isabelle.

The large figure shifted about, and said something in French. A man, he did not sound happy.

Isabelle's retort was sharp; the man fell silent. 'You have been cruelly treated, Rufus,' she said to me.

Gilbert interrupted, the way small children do. 'Rufus? I thought you said he was called Ferdia.'

'I have red hair,' I explained. 'Some people call me Rufus.'

'I like that name,' said Gilbert.

'Hush,' ordered Isabelle. 'I tried to free you, Rufus, but the guard will not listen to me. When my mother hears what has happened, she will be furious.'

Aoife has not yet returned, I thought, my newly risen hopes sinking. 'Where is she?'

'Somewhere on the coast, visiting my little brother's castles.'

'I have almost a score in Wales,' announced Gilbert with childish pride. 'And more in England and Ireland.'

'That is a lot,' I said, thinking of my father's small stronghold, one that would never have been mine, thanks to my older brothers. Oddly, Isabelle was in a similar position. Despite being the elder of the two, she would not inherit the de Clare lands, because sons took precedence over daughters. I made a half bow towards Gilbert. 'So you are the Lord of Pembroke.'

'I am.'

'It is an honour to meet you, my lord.'

Gilbert turned to Isabelle, demanding, 'Who is he again?'

'I *told* you. An Irish nobleman who has been sent to Striguil as a hostage, and he should not be locked up like this.'

'What is a hostage?'

They are so young, I thought. Isabelle was perhaps six, and Gilbert only three or four. That the pair had managed to reach me was a marvel, yet to obtain my freedom remained beyond them.

'Quiet, Gilbert, and let me think,' chided Isabelle.

'When will your mother return?' I asked.

'Two days, or three.'

It was not forever, but I dreaded the thought of Boots and Fists' reaction when he heard of my visitors. 'Does the seneschal know I am here, or any knights of the mesnie?'

The man with the children spoke again to Isabelle, his tone still respectful, yet more insistent.

She stamped her foot. 'I cannot stay, Ferdia. Nor can I free you – I am sorry.' Her voice was anguished.

'It is not your fault, my lady,' I said, trying to sound nonchalant. 'Are you hungry?'

'Famished.'

'Food shall be sent to you, and wine.' She retreated, taking Gilbert by the hand, and allowing the guard to shut me in once more.

I could not help myself. 'And FitzAldelm, my lady?'

The door thumped shut; the bolt slid across.

Through the timbers, Isabelle said, 'He will not come back before my mother returns. I swear it.'

In the darkness, a long sigh of relief escaped me.

In the event, my incarceration lasted another day and night. To my relief, there was no sign of Boots and Fists during this time. On the last morning, wakened from a fitful sleep, I paced my cell in an attempt to take my mind from the cold and my still growling belly. Isabelle had been as good as her word, but the leek pottage that had been delivered, and the venison stew and fresh bread that came after, were long gone. I had licked the wooden bowls clean already, and was wondering if I should check them again when noises from the bailey caught my attention.

Men shouted, and horses' hooves clattered. Even through the thick walls, I could sense the excitement. Someone important had arrived. I prayed as I had not done for days. Let it be Aoife, God, I beg you.

His answer came sooner than I had hoped.

Several men-at-arms arrived, and opening my cell door, led me out to the bailey. They did not lay a hand on me, as I emerged, blinking, wary, into bright sunlight. Lank-haired, foul-smelling, my clothes stained, I must have resembled a wild beast. More than one person curled their lip, and I threw back hate-filled glances. If I had had a sword, I would have cut down every man in sight. I considered trying to seize a blade, but alone, unarmoured, I would provide the men-at-arms in their heavy gambesons with perhaps a few moments' sport. Like the tile cover that keeps a fire lighting overnight, I decided, I would batten down my hatred for another day.

'Do you speak French?' The voice was nasal, imperious.

My head turned. A short, officious-looking man in a sleeveless, belted tunic of fine blue wool had come down the stairs from the great hall's entrance. I did not recognise him, but by the cut of his clothes and arrogant manner, took him to be the steward. 'A little,' I replied.

Bizarrely taking this to mean I was fluent, he chattered away in French. The few words I understood were 'Eva', 'filthy', and 'bath'. He pointed to a building beside the smithy, where I had seen the horse being shod a lifetime before. Assuming he meant I was in no state to meet the countess Aoife, and that I should have a bath, I lifted one arm, and mimed scrubbing under first it, then the other. A stiff nod was his reply.

'And after?' I ventured in French.

'Wait.' The steward spoke to the men-at-arms, and disappeared back up the same staircase.

An order in French, and a push from one of the men-at-arms. I did as I was bid, and walked to what turned out to be the servants' quarters. In the first room, I found a wooden bathing tub, two-thirds full of warm water. I could have cried. Rarely have I shed my clothing so fast, even when a woman has been involved.

Clambering into the water with a groan of pleasure, I ducked my head under and came up still smiling. With the men-at-arms remaining outside, the lone witness of my joy was a servant, who, expressionless, offered me a bar of soap. It was not the expensive kind from Castile I grew used to later in life, but the usual soft bar made from mutton fat, wood ash and soda. At that moment, however, it seemed more precious than a lump of gold.

Clean, my hair washed, I climbed out and took the rough linen cloth presented me by the servant. Drying myself, I thanked him in French. A little surprised to receive any acknowledgement, he bobbed his head. A set of plain but good quality clothing had been laid out on top of a wooden chest; on the floor was a new pair of low-cut boots. I indicated my own braies, tunic and hose, lying in a heap. The only word of the servant's reply that made any sense was 'fu', fire. Thoughts of meeting the countess Aoife filled my mind; I cared not what happened to them, and waved an indifferent hand.

Emerging, I found the steward waiting for me. He looked me up and down, and sniffed. I wanted to box his ears, but remembering how my antagonising of Boots and Fists had ended, pretended not to notice. Meek as a lamb going to the slaughter, my hopes rising with every step, I followed him. Two men-at-arms lumbered behind us, all brawny arms, unshaven chins and hard stares.

Straight up the staircase led, to the great hall. We entered one end of the huge space, and I had to hide my amazement. My father's hall had not been large in comparison to the king of Leinster's, an impressive building, but this dwarfed both. Curved trusses of wood, thick as a man, supported the high ceiling along the length of the room. Patches of bright blue sky were framed in the arched windows to left and right – there was no need today for the candles in the wall-mounted sconces. Below the windows hung embroidered tapestries, their colours rich against the dull cream of the plaster.

Curious, I glanced about me. Cloth-covered tables and long benches, those used for meals, were arranged against the end wall. Watched by a hawk-eyed chamberlain, servants were polishing silver cups. A youth swept up dirty rushes; a second scattered fresh ones on the wooden floor that had been the roof of my cell. So close, and yet so far, I thought. The two places were worlds apart.

A touch at my elbow. I smiled an apology at the steward. He did not return the gesture, but indicated I should follow him. I obeyed, the heavy tread of the men-at-arms at my back an unpleasant reminder of my yet precarious situation.

I walked the length of the chamber as household knights, clerks and servants watched sidelong, muttering to one another behind their hands. Most stares were inquisitive or neutral, but many were un-friendly, even hostile. I wondered what stories had been told about me since my arrival, and spread as round-the-fire gossip. Boots and Fists would have been spinning a tale of lies and deceit, that was certain. If he had the countess Aoife's ear, I was about to fall from the frying pan into the fire. My fear resurged. Isabelle liked me, but the opinion of a child, even one who ranked so high, seldom counted for much. Thanks to Boots and Fists, her mother's mind might already be decided that I was a dangerous savage who needed caging.

I felt the weight of someone's gaze, and turning my head, saw none other than Boots and Fists in the midst of half a dozen knights. He leered, and said something to his companions, who laughed. Tough-looking men, my eye was caught by one with an odd haircut, a barbering that had left the back of his head bald, with the shearline angling down to his ears. A puckered scar marked his chin.

Angered by the knights' contempt, worried by Boots and Fists' confidence, but willing to give nothing away, I acted as if I had not seen. Dry-mouthed, heart thumping, I followed the steward to a low dais upon which sat two elegant high-backed chairs. Both were empty. Behind them, a floor-to-ceiling partition formed the division between the hall and what were presumably the countess's private quarters.

Hearing children on the other side of the screen, I pricked my ears. A woman spoke. A girl's voice – Isabelle's – rose in protest. The woman spoke again, sharply. Silence followed. My fear rose another notch. I steeled my resolve, and offered a prayer to God. All would be well, I told myself.

With a warning glance that told me to stay where I was, the steward padded to a door set into the partition. He knocked. A woman an-swered, and he entered, closing it behind him. He soon returned, and by the now-familiar up-down look of scorn he gave me, I judged the countess would not be long after him.

The door opened. A figure appeared, followed by three maids. The steward announced Aoife's arrival in French. Silence fell, everyone turned to face the dais. I knew better than to stare, but could not help myself.

At that time, Aoife had seen thirty-one summers. In theory, she was past her prime, but the woman that sat before me took my youthful breath away. All thoughts of her as an enemy vanished like morning mist. I drank her in. A long gown of green silk shimmered as she moved, and set off the dark red of her hair, which was held back by a delicate net of jewelled gold. A belt of the same precious metal encir-cled her slender waist, and a blood-red ruby gleamed from a brooch at her breast.

An indignant *pssst*, and I tore my gaze from Aoife. With furious gestures, the steward was indicating I should bow. Mortified, I bent from the waist, and said in Irish, 'A thousand apologies, my lady.'

'Do they no longer teach manners in Ireland?' Aoife also spoke in Irish. Her tone was light, but there was metal beneath.

Embarrassed, and praying that she had not seen my lust, I bowed again. Behind me, I heard titters. '*Chien*,' said a voice. 'Irish dog,' said another. My cheeks crimson now, I replied, 'They did, my lady, and I forgot them entirely. Forgive me, I beg you.'

Her smile reached her eyes, which were a dazzling green. 'You are forgiven. If what I have been told is true, 'tis no wonder if courtly behaviour was not to the forefront of your mind.'

Unsure of what best to say, I made no reply.

'You are Ferdia Ó Catháin, of Cairlinn in Leinster, given into the custody of my son as a guarantee for your father's good behaviour.'

'Yes, my lady.'

'Will the promise be honoured?'

Startled, I remembered my father's entreaty, that I should never bend the knee to the English. 'I will not either,' he had said, winking. Seeing my worry, he had continued, 'Never fear. I will be careful to present a loyal face to the local garrison – in order that you should remain unharmed – but there are ways and means to fight the enemy. Well-spent silver can purchase many things. Weapons, armour, and men to use them.' Another wink. 'I will say no more, for fear you might let something slip.'

'Well?' demanded Aoife.

'Your pardon, my lady. I was thinking of my family.' Pleased to see her expression soften, I went on, 'My father is a man of his word.'

'And you?'

Surprised by her directness, my honour pricked, I stuck out my chin, and said, 'I am also, my lady. I swore not to escape in Ireland; I repeat that pledge to you now, before God and all His saints.'

Aoife seemed satisfied. 'I understand that in my absence you were incarcerated in a cell below us.' She tapped the point of her slipper on the dais for emphasis.

'Aye, my lady. I was freed not an hour since.'

'I have been told that the knight Robert FitzAldelm mistreated you. That he beat you.' She repeated her words in French, and as shocked gasps rose, cast a glance down the room towards Boots and Fists.

Isabelle *had* spoken to her mother, I decided.

'Is it true?' Now her green eyes bore down on me.

He did it more than once, I wanted to say, but I could feel Boots and Fists' gaze burning a hole in the back of my tunic. Striguil was to be my home, I thought, and my only friend thus far was Isabelle. Her exalted existence would ensure that our paths rarely crossed, and despite her friendship, she was yet a child. I would meet Boots and Fists daily, however, and I had no doubt that he had friends and allies aplenty. Chances were that he already planned to make my life a misery. Condemn him in public, and I risked a knife between the ribs in the dark of the night.

I made my decision. 'There was an altercation on the ship as we came up the river, my lady. I was rude to FitzAldelm, and when he admonished me, I raised my hand to him.' It seemed likely that something akin to this would have been Boots and Fists' story. That was my hope. 'He responded as any knight would, and Lady Isabelle happened to witness it.'

Aoife's brow furrowed, but she gave no indication of disbelieving my story. 'And after that – when you were in the cell?' She stared at me, and though it was impossible, I felt as if she could see under my tunic and hose to the bruises that covered my body.

'The food was poor, my lady, but I can complain about nothing else.' I gave her what I hoped was a winning smile.

Whether she saw through my lie, I could not tell, but her full lips curled with amusement. 'It was wrong of FitzAldelm to imprison you so, but understandable in the circumstances perhaps.'

'Yes, my lady,' I lied, thinking, God grant me revenge. I will show Boots and Fists what a beating means.

'You shall sleep in the hall henceforth, and dine here also. I may call on you from time to time. Other than with my children, I rarely have occasion to speak Irish.'

'It would be an honour, my lady,' I replied, delighted.

'You shall learn French as well.'

'Yes, my lady.' I bowed, hoping that the worst was behind me.

CHAPTER III

The inside of the stable was warm and clammy. Sweat ran from my brow as I worked into a far corner with my shovel, searching for dung that had thus far eluded me. I found only a rat, which darted away before I could split it in two. I whistled for Patch, the head groom's terrier, but there was no answer. I cursed the wretched dog, never there when needed, and returned my attention to the beaten earth floor. Deciding it was sufficiently clean, I took up my brush and began to sweep the result of my labours, a pile of dirty straw and manure, towards the door.

Half a year had gone by since my arrival at Striguil. Full summer had arrived, and with it, sweltering weather. After my audience with Aoife, I had been set to work with the squires who looked after the household knights. Serving no one in particular, I was made to toil for all, an unfair burden I could do little about. A good number of the squires were civil enough, and after a period during which I kept my head down and complained little, welcomed me into their company. The two with whom I had most in common were Hugo and Walter. Hugo was lean and tough, and his fair skin and freckled face could have marked him as an Irishman. Walter was his opposite, with a sallow complexion and dark hair. Slight of frame, but wiry as a hunting dog, he was friend to everyone.

Eager not to lose physical condition, nor my skill with weapons, I trained with the pair at every opportunity. In padded gambesons or in full mail – borrowed, of course – I battered at them while they did the same to me. We wrestled, and boxed, and swore at one another, as young men do. I trained with a wooden sword and shield, honing my skills against the pell, a man-high stake driven into the ground. There was time also to ride at the quintain, first with the mocking laughter of those watching in my ears, and then, as I improved, with a few encouraging shouts.

Of the rest of the squires, I can say that they did not abuse me overmuch, but there were some who went out of their way to take advantage. At breakfast that morning, one of the worst offenders, a lantern-jawed dolt by the name of Bogo who fancied himself a knight already, had ordered me to clean out the stables – a task upon that occasion which should have been his.

To argue would have given Bogo and his cronies precisely the opportunity they were looking for. I had fought back the first time they had attacked me, and even knocked two down before I was overwhelmed. After the confrontation, nursing a black eye and split lip, I had come to the sour-as-sloes realisation that staying out of trouble was the best policy. I could not fight every man in Striguil. Nor, to my chagrin, could I harm Boots and Fists. A knight, his person was inviolable to the likes of me. Henceforth, I had decided, I would avoid him like the plague, and choose my other battles. 'Fight when you can win,' my father had often said. 'Otherwise walk away. Only a fool would not.'

And so, ignoring the smirks of Bogo and his friends, I had stitched my lip and gone to find the broom and shovel. I had set to, eager to finish the task quickly, for the day's warmth made toiling inside the humid stables pure torture. My work would not end when I was done. There were two horses to be curried, saddles and bridles that needed cleaning, and after that, a set of armour to be polished. By the time I finished, the knights' supper would be ready. Only after helping to serve that would I be free to come and go.

In these baking temperatures, that meant larking about in the shallows of the River Wye. A delightful escape from the heat, there I could also hold my own. Confident in the water thanks to a childhood by the sea, I was well capable of holding another squire's head under for longer than was pleasant. Pushing the heaped straw outside, I thought, let Bogo come within reach and I will teach him a lesson.

A voice broke into my reverie. 'What a stink!'

'Lady Isabelle,' I said, looking up with a smile. No one else addressed me in Irish. 'I take it you do not want to help?'

She frowned. 'That would be beneath me.'

I laughed and proffered the broom. 'It is honest labour. Come, try it.'

'No!' Losing a little of her confidence, she hugged her doll and retreated a step.

'I jest, my lady,' I said, switching to French. It was a habit between us on the rare occasions we had to talk, a way for me to practise the language other than during the tiresome lessons I received from one of the chaplain's clerks. 'It would not be seemly.'

She pouted. 'That is what Mother says when I ask to use a bow, as Gilbert does.'

'Boys learn archery, girls do not.' And yet an apple does not fall far from the tree, I decided. I had been in Striguil long enough to know that Aoife was strong-willed and independent-minded. Her daughter was no different.

'It is not fair.'

Nor is it that I am a hostage here, I thought bitterly. Out loud, I said, 'However, it is the way of the world.' Seeing her disappointment, and recalling her frequent visits to the mews, I added, 'You can hunt a hawk when you are older. Does that not appeal?'

A sigh. 'The falconer says it will be years before I have the strength.'

'Then you need to be patient, my lady.' I wanted to add, 'As I must.' Like her, I would have to bide my time. Eventually, I would see Ireland again, and with God's help, my family as well.

'You sound like Nurse, or the chaplain. Or my mother,' she said, scowling.

I made an apologetic gesture. 'Adults often sound the same to children.'

'Isabelle!' The familiar screech rang out.

'Can you teach me?'

I cast a wary look about, and whispered, 'Archery?'

'Yes.'

I imagined the countess's reaction, or that of Boots and Fists. 'I would like nothing better, my lady, but my life is not worth it.'

'I thought you were my friend!'

'I am, my lady,' I protested, but she had stormed off.

'Upsetting the Lady Isabelle?' sneered a familiar voice. 'Is that how you amuse yourself, amadán?'

'It is not,' I said curtly, shielding my eyes from the sun, the better to see Boots and Fists riding across the bailey, one of his cronies alongside.

Since I had been freed from the cell, an odd truce had risen between us. Both of us loathed the other, but I dared not seek revenge and he seemed content – mostly – to respect my status as a noble hostage.

As he drew near, I saw that the sides of both horses were white with lathered sweat. Despite my hatred of FitzAldelm, I felt a grudging respect. While the other knights of the mesnie took their ease in the coolness of the great hall, reciting poetry, or listening to the minstrel pluck tunes on his lute, he and his friend had been practising at the quintain. Jealousy pricked me next. For someone newly introduced to the sport, I was not bad, but he was devilish good. Pit us against each other in a tourney, and there would be one victor. Like as not, his companion, the man with the odd haircut, would do the same to me.

'See to my horse.' Flinging the reins in my direction, FitzAldelm slid to the ground with an easy grace.

'And mine.' The second knight – FitzWarin was his name – had a little more manners, handing me the reins.

The pair strode away without a backward glance.

I ought to have been grateful that FitzAldelm had not taunted me further, or struck me, as he sometimes still did when I was not quick to obey. All I felt, however, was a burning desire to beat his face to bloody ruin.

I decided to hurt FitzAldelm the only way I could: by subterfuge. It would have been easy to injure his horse, the dumb, faithful beast, but the thought turned my stomach. Besides, the finger of blame would point at me straightaway. Here I was, with it in my care. No, I decided, there had to be another way. Loosening the girths and removing the saddles, I led the horses to the water trough. Standing by as they drank greedily, I racked my brain as I had these past months for ways to strike at FitzAldelm without being caught.

My gaze fell upon one of the Welsh washerwomen across the yard. Hard-working, red-knuckled matrons with a bawdy sense of humour and sharp tongues, I saw them every day. I was no retiring virgin even then, but their lewd suggestions, offered mock-seriously, often turned my cheeks red.

They say that often we cannot see what is in front of us, and realising it, I laughed to myself. Big Mary it was that day who had the hot and unpleasant task of soaking dirty sheets and tablecloths in a solution of wood ash and caustic. Broad in the beam, none-too-blessed with intelligence, she was also one of those with a soft spot for me. Once I had finished with the horses, I sauntered over.

'You seem warm, Mary.' Welsh was similar enough to Irish that I could converse in it.

Looking up from her wooden vat, she gave me a lustful wink. 'Not as warm as I would be with you astride me, young Rufus.'

I gave her my best attempt at a seductive smile.

She wiped a strand of hair from her sticky forehead and muttered, 'Come by my cot tonight, and I will tup you 'til dawn.' Her meaty hand reached for my groin.

I eased away, terrified, but managing to give her a wink. 'You are a vixen and no mistake, Mary. Come, are you thirsty?'

She licked her lips. 'Parched, I am.'

'I will fetch you a mug of beer.'

'God bless you, lad,' she said, beaming.

Making for the pantry, I began to whistle.

My plan took time to bear fruit, but that did not trouble me. I had waited six months already; a short while longer was of little consequence. As a wise man once said, revenge is a dish best eaten cold. I sought out Big Mary more than once, making our encounters seem as if by chance. Resisting her physical advances with a combination of flattery and swift feet, I won her confidence; the chicken and raisin pastries stolen from the kitchen increased her goodwill.

When I explained sadly that my sheets were infested with bedbugs – more so than any of the other squires – she almost fell over her bunioned feet in an attempt to help. It was a brazen lie, but she had no idea. A daily soaking in caustic would do it, Big Mary told me, and with the hot weather, drying my sheet each day would be simple. I filled her ears with praise, and planted an occasional peck on her reddened cheeks, managing to escape with only my arse pinched.

She had no idea that my real intent while in her company was access to the knights' clothing, and more specifically, to FitzAldelm's. She had no inkling either that for several evenings, I had wandered through the fields where the countess's cattle grazed. Seeking out the trees under which the beasts sheltered in the heat of the day, I searched the trunks for evidence of scratching. I even managed to wrestle a small, affected calf to the ground while its mother was drinking from the river, and collect what I needed. Anyone who has worked with oxen recognises the leprosy-like condition that can affect many young stock, covering their faces in thick, crusty scales. Leprosy it is not, thank God. People who work with such beasts do not succumb to that hideous disease, but they can develop red, itchy patches on their hands and arms. Therein lay my plan.

While Big Mary sweated over her trough of washing, I slyly filled FitzAldelm's fresh-laundered, dry clothing with the skin scrapings and scabs I had found. Then, patient as a wolf watching an injured deer, I waited. There was no longer any need to seek out Big Mary. To keep her sweet, I explained that my ever-rarer visits were due to sheer exhaustion from my labours. Luckily for me, the household knights had been training hard – rumour had it that an important visitor would soon arrive – and the squires were busier than ever, caring for their masters' horses, polishing armour and honing nicks from sword blades.

I look back at that time, and smile at my callowness. Obsessed with FitzAldelm, thinking of little beyond Striguil's walls, I had no notion that my life was about to change forever. I was to meet a prince. A mighty warrior. A man who would rule not just England, but Normandy and Brittany, Anjou and Aquitaine. Who would lead an army to the Holy Land, almost to the gates of holy Jerusalem itself.

Richard Coeur de Lion.

The news broke a sennight after I had tampered with FitzAldelm's garments. Brought by a messenger first to Aoife in the great hall, it spread through the castle like a fire in a hay barn. Richard, second son of King Henry, had landed on the south coast of England, and at some point in the coming month, would visit Striguil. From that point on, nobody could talk about anything else. I had had little reason to know anything about Richard before then. Intrigued by the prospect of a royal visitor so close in age to my own, I learned fast.

Installed as Duke of Aquitaine by his father at fourteen, he had been campaigning there since the age of seventeen, five years prior. Despite his tender age, one of the knights recounted, he had spent his first summer attacking and taking the strongly built castle of Castillon-sur-Agen.

His success had not prevented trouble the following spring, that of the year of our Lord, 1175. Rebellious by nature, resentful of their new overlord, the nobles of Aquitaine had formed an alliance against Richard. Undeterred, he recruited large numbers of Brabançon mercenaries, and set about bringing the rebels to heel. For much of the following three years, he waged war throughout Aquitaine. There had been a few setbacks, most notably at Pons, but the strongholds of St Maigrin, Limoges, Châteauneuf, Moulineuf, Angoulême, Dax, Bayonne and St Pierre had all fallen to the warlike duke.

The unfamiliar, musical French names stirred my imagination, and the depth and breadth of his campaign mightily impressed me. Ignorant then of the mud and gore, the shit and piss, and the stink of rotting flesh that go hand in hand with a siege, I imagined myself in the duke's army, winning fame and renown. Each time my dreams ran away with me, my conscience would intervene. Richard is an enemy, it would carp, like everyone in this cursed land. Stung, I would admonish myself and remember my father as my lord, the man to whom I owed my loyalty. Foreign wars meant nothing. Only the struggle in Ireland counted. If the opportunity presented itself, I decided, I would learn how a castle could be taken. That would prove useful upon my return.

Despite my best efforts, I enjoyed the tales of Richard's exploits. It seemed that no stronghold could withstand him. Battle-hungry, he was often to be found in the thick of the fighting. According to Gilbert de Lysle, the messenger who had brought word of his impending visit, his crowning glory had come about a month before. Thanks to his knowledge and the fact that he would soon depart, de Lysle was in much demand. Everyone from the chaplain and his clerks to the knights, squires and pages wanted to hear him speak. It was no surprise then that de Lysle, a pleasant, balding type with little between his ears, had scarcely been sober since delivering his message to the countess.

I heard the tale of Taillebourg on the second evening after the dramatic news about Richard had flashed around Striguil. Persuaded after a late supper to share more of what he knew, de Lysle settled down amidst the cushions filling a window seat in the great hall. An eager-faced audience formed around him, knights, officials and even the steward himself. Squires and pages hung around on the fringes. Servants lingered at their jobs, their ears pricked. Keen not to miss a word, I had armed myself with a jug of wine and worked my way to stand by his right elbow. I saw the angry glances that Bogo and his cronies threw me, and cared not. Once de Lysle had realised I was there, he held out his arm every time the level in his cup dropped below the halfway point.

'Tell us of Taillebourg,' urged FitzAldelm to a chorus of approval.

De Lysle made no answer. His cheeks were flushed. There were wine stains on his doublet too, but he was alive to the fact that every person in the room was waiting for him to speak. He drank deep, and nodded his thanks as I darted in with the jug.

'Ah, Taillebourg,' he said.

'Were you there?' asked FitzWarin.

'I was,' said de Lysle.

Excited mutters.

'An impregnable fortress it is, standing on a huge outcrop over the River Charente, with sheer rock faces on three sides. The last side is more strongly fortified than any castle I have seen.'

'I have seen Taillebourg,' announced FitzAldelm self-importantly. He paused to scratch at his neck, raising my hopes that the scabs had done their work, and continued, 'An army could dash itself to pieces off the walls, and only a bird could reach the tops of the cliffs upon which it sits.' Catching de Lysle's glare, he fell silent.

'As I was saying,' de Lysle went on grandly, '*I* was at the siege. Taillebourg belonged to Geoffrey de Rancon, an ally of the count of Angoulême, a noble who had already submitted to Richard's rule. Strong-minded as all those from Aquitaine, Geoffrey refused to bend the knee. He must have been confident, for his castle of Pons had recently withstood Richard's four-month siege; Taillebourg was a more forbidding prospect. So formidable are its defences that it had never been attacked.' Draining his cup again, he held it out for a refill.

I was quick to oblige.

'Richard likes to grasp the nettle, though. God's bones, but he is a leader! Leaving Pons, we took a number of small castles before marching on to Taillebourg. Hearing of our advance, the inhabitants of the surrounding countryside fled to the castle. They watched in dismay from the battlements as we burned their farms, cut down their vines and emptied their barns.' A loud slurp, and a satisfied chuckle. 'How they must have hated us, in our camp that lay close to their walls, and the only gate into Taillebourg. They had no idea of Richard's purpose, of his orders to make merry, to sing and to carry on. Our sole intention was to annoy the garrison. Offering a carefree appearance, we were in fact ready for battle, and when the enraged defenders burst in force from the sally gate, they got a rude surprise. We drove them back—'

FitzAldelm, who had looked annoyed since de Lysle's rebuke, curled his lip. Again he scratched at the base of his neck. 'We? Did you take part in the fighting?'

His cronies chuckled.

'A figure of speech, good sir. I am no warrior, but a humble servant of Duke Richard's,' said de Lysle, unperturbed. Even as FitzAldelm issued a retort, he added, 'Did you fight at Taillebourg?'

Short of brains though he was, de Lysle knew like everyone present that FitzAldelm had been at Striguil. I swear the laughter that followed lifted to the roof. Unable to conceal my mirth, and increasingly sure that my handiwork with his underclothes had borne fruit, I buried my face in the shoulder of my tunic. My attempt was in vain; I caught FitzAldelm staring daggers at me a moment later.

As the clamour died away, de Lysle resumed his story. Black-browed, furious, nonetheless FitzAldelm did not interrupt again.

We listened, rapt, to the rest of the tale. How Richard's soldiers had driven back the defenders with such fierceness that they had taken the gate. Although many of the enemy managed to regain the citadel, the majority of their supplies had fallen into Richard's hands. Demoralised, the garrison surrendered. The shock of Taillebourg's fall was huge. Geoffrey de Rancon surrendered Pons without further resistance.

'After years of unrest, peace was restored to Aquitaine in the space of a few months,' said de Lysle grandly. He raised his cup high, uncaring of the wine that slopped down his arm, and cried, 'Thanks to Richard, *Coeur de Lion*!'

Ah, the fickleness of youth. Carried away by the tale, forgetting my enmity with the English crown, I confess that I roared as loudly as the rest.

CHAPTER IV

I have no idea what hour it was when my bladder woke me. A faint tinge of light was visible around the shuttered windows, but darkness yet reigned in the great hall. The air was close, fuggy, laden with the smells of wine and farts. Snores echoed. Straw rustled as men turned in their sleep. Caught deep in a dream, a dog whimpered and twitched. Lying on my tick, close to the draughty doorway that led to the bailey, I considered my options. I could last until dawn before venturing to the garderobe in the yard, but the increasing twinges from my lower belly meant finding sleep would prove difficult. Louts like Bogo thought nothing of pissing in a quiet corner, but since arriving at Striguil I had thus far refrained. Better to go outside, I decided with a sigh.

Leaning up on an elbow, I was reaching for my boots when a sound halted me. My eyes roved the room, seeking the source of the noise, which had seemed furtive. No sleeper's incoherent mumble, no whistling snore, nor had it been the deliberate, ponderous clambering to one's feet of the still drunk. The sound came again, and this time I spied its maker – a darker shadow than the surroundings – creeping towards me. I lay back down, terrified that my pounding heart would give me away. Scarce daring to breathe, I waited until I heard the footsteps go outside. Then, lacing my boots, I padded across the floor, avoiding my fellow squires and the boards that creaked.

At the door I listened, worried there might still be someone the other side of the threshold. Hearing nothing, I risked a glance into the quiet-as-a-graveyard bailey. It was brighter there than inside the hall, but dawn was a good distance away. Not a soul was stirring. Perched atop a barrel by the kitchen door, one of the resident cats regarded me with suspicion. I paid it no heed. Disappointed to have lost my quarry so easily, I had decided to empty my bladder when a flicker of movement by the stables caught my eye.

I turned my head, glimpsing a man's back as he vanished inside. He was clad in a dark tunic, but beyond that, I could not say. More curious than suspicious, I padded down the stairs to the nearby garderobe. My call of nature answered, anxious to regain the comfort of my pallet before the day and its attendant toil began, I had all but forgotten the man I had shadowed. That was, until I heard footsteps outside.

Frozen to the spot, sure I was about to be found out, I felt an intense relief as the man came not into the garderobe but made for the stairs and the great hall. Disappointment savaged me a heartbeat later, for I had not a clue to the identity of the stable-visiting figure. An ear to the timbers, I tried to discern how far up the staircase he was. The task was impossible. I could barely hear a thing. To have any chance of recognising the man, I would have to go outside and risk being seen. Curiosity triumphed over fear; I stuck my head round the garderobe door.

Although the man was two-thirds the way up, I would have known FitzAldelm at three times the distance. No one in Striguil had a block-head quite like him. Suspicion flared bright in my mind now. Pallet and sleep discarded in favour of a search of the stable, I exited the garderobe. In my haste, I caught the door with the point of my shoulder. It opened wide, and only a deaf man could have missed the screech of the rusty hinges.

Praying that FitzAldelm, who had entered the great hall, had somehow not heard, I hurtled across the yard and into the hay barn. I clambered to the top of the largest stack, where I lay, panting and terrified. As I waited, the cock began to crow. I heard nothing outside, however, and began to hope that I had escaped.

Then, movement without. Footsteps. Fear gripped me. It was Fitz-Aldelm – it had to be. I dared not look over the edge of the hay. If he entered the barn, he would spy me in an instant.

It is uncanny how a man can tell when someone's eyes are on him. Listening still for FitzAldelm, I turned my head. Not six paces from me, also at the top of the stack, lay one of the parentless Welsh urchins who lived in and around the castle. Most people had no time for them, but I had never lashed out or thrown taunts the way I had seen Bogo and his sneering cronies do.

Beady-eyed, black as a Moor with dirt, the urchin had sticks for arms and legs, and was about eight or nine years old. No doubt he had been watching since I had come running into the barn. His mouth opened.

Boots scraped off the earthen floor.

Sure it was FitzAldelm, fearful the boy would give me away, I placed a finger to my lips, praying the urgency in my gaze was clear.

The urchin saw something, for he stayed mute.

The footsteps below paced to and fro. FitzAldelm's voice muttered, 'Where is the cursed ladder?'

The mongrel is going to check up here, I thought. A cold sweat broke out on my forehead. Discovery would see FitzAldelm assume I was the one who had caused the door hinges to screech. *That* would make him think I had seen whatever he had done in the stable. I steeled myself for a struggle I would lose, for FitzAldelm was never without his dagger, while I was unarmed.

A rustle. I looked, and my heart gave a great leap of fright. Even if I had wanted to, I could not have stopped what happened next. Sliding his bony arse over the hay, the urchin perched on the edge for a heartbeat, and dropped to the floor below.

Sure that I was undone, that he planned to betray me in the hope of a reward, I threw up a plea to God and all His saints. Remembering then my never-answered prayers when the grey foreigners had attacked our lands, I felt my hopes fade. I closed my eyes and waited for the boy to do his worst. When FitzAldelm realised I was atop the haystack, he would summon me down for a brutal retribution.

'Hiding up there, were you?' FitzAldelm's voice, his Welsh accent as bad as his Irish.

'No, sir.'

A slap. A cry.

'Were you spying on me?'

'No, sir!'

Another blow. A cry, soon muffled.

'Do not lie to me, boy. What did you see?'

'Nothing, sir. I saw nothing!' cried the urchin, his voice cracking.

'You had best not have. Mention this even to a soul, and I will see you at the bottom of the Wye.'

A short silence, then the sound of quiet sobbing, and footsteps leaving the barn.

Delighted with my luck, I wormed my way to the edge of the hay an inch at a time. Of FitzAldelm there was no sign. Below me, I made out the shape of the urchin, hunched against the base of the stack. Quietly, keeping an eye on the door, I eased down beside him. 'He's gone,' I said in Welsh.

There was no reply.

'You did not tell him I was here. I am grateful.'

Again, no response.

'A silver penny is yours by way of thanks,' I said.

A pair of beady eyes, full of tears, came up to meet mine. Two.

Staring at his outstretched grubby paw, I chuckled. 'My purse is in the great hall.' I pictured the baker, who would soon be taking bread from the ovens, and asked, 'Are you hungry?'

The urchin nodded.

Half-starved you are, I thought. 'How does a fresh loaf sound?'

The first hint of a smile. 'I like honey.'

'I will get you that as well,' I promised. 'But not a word to Fitz-Aldelm, eh?'

'He is a bad man,' said the urchin, scowling.

'So he is,' I agreed, content that the boy would keep silent. Promising to return with the pennies and the bread, I made my way to the barn's entrance. To my relief, there was no sign of FitzAldelm, just a couple of yawning men-at-arms on their way to the garderobe. The sky over the eastern wall was rosy-pink. Dawn had arrived; before long the bailey would come alive. Bakers and washerwomen, servants and stable boys would all appear. If there was ever a moment for me to see what FitzAldelm had been up to, it was now.

Luck was on my side, for the door he had entered still lay a little ajar. I crept inside. My nostrils filled with rich smells: horses, leather, grease. Perhaps two dozen saddles rested on wall-mounted wooden supports. Innumerable bridles and bits hung from hooks; neatly folded caparisons and saddle blankets were piled beneath. A work shelf lined the wall, covered in tools. There were knives of every type: short-, long-, curve-, half-moon-bladed. Pincers. Tongs. Awls. Pliers.

Everything appeared as it always did.

I cast about, swearing under my breath, aware that I had little chance of discovering FitzAldelm's work. Mayhap he had done nothing at all, I thought, but discounted the notion with my next breath.

He was fond of his sleep; he would not have come in here without purpose.

In the dim light, I sought for his saddle, but soon after, wary of the increasing sounds of activity from the bailey, I had to abandon the stable altogether. Downhearted, for I had risked much and learned nothing, I went to fetch the urchin's silver pennies.

He seemed surprised upon my return. To be so distrustful, the poor mite must receive short shrift from almost everyone, I decided. The coins vanished into a fold of his ragged tunic, and he ate the still-hot loaf and honey with the speed of a hungry hound. Licking his fingers clean, he eyed me with an expression that was, if not trustful, at least less wary than before. He had long black hair, and a sharp, intelligent face.

If the dirt was washed off, I thought, he would be halfway to decent-looking. 'What is your name?' I asked.

'Rhys. And yours?'

'Ferdia.' An idea struck me. 'Can you do something for me?'

Suspicion flared bright in his eyes. 'Depends. What?'

'That knight – the one who came into the barn. I want you keep an eye on him. See where he goes, who he meets with.'

'What is in it for me?'

'Fresh bread every morning. A silver penny if you bring me anything worthwhile.'

He considered my offer with the solemnness of a lord about to pass sentence on a criminal, and then stuck out his hand. Nausea tickled my gullet to see how clean his fresh-licked fingers were in comparison to his palm, but I could not refuse for fear of offence. We shook.

I went in search of my own breakfast in better spirits. Small and puny though the urchin was, it felt as if I had accepted the fealty of my first liege man.

Several days passed. Rhys proved to be an adept spy; I now knew that FitzAldelm liked to frequent not just the tavern in the nearby settlement favoured by the other knights, but also a squalid, rundown establishment in the stews on the road north. He went there to see a whore whose services, if the cries from her room were to be believed, included whipping and other depredations.

Embarrassed – never having heard of such things – I was mortified to be responsible for Rhys having listened to them. To my astonishment, he seemed entirely unperturbed. 'I have seen worse,' he declared. Aye, the poor child. Nine years old he was, but in ways, going on three times that age.

Despite my newly acquired knowledge of FitzAldelm, I remained ignorant of the purpose of his early morning visit to the stables. I had gone back before dawn the following day, my intent to search the place again. Discovered by one of the grooms, come seeking a hoof pick, I had escaped suspicion with a similar tale, but it would have been foolish to try again. Even the rumour of being light-handed risked losing the countess Aoife's goodwill, upon which my very life rested.

I resigned myself to never knowing the truth. It was enough that my deposition of cattle scabs in FitzAldelm's garments had worked. Red, scaly lesions marked his neck and his right wrist, and glancing sidelong down the great hall one morning as he rose from his pallet to get dressed, I knew that his torso was similarly affected. According to Rhys, he had visited several quacks in search of a cure. Happily, none of their creams or potions had thus far provided much relief: every time I saw him, he was scratching or rubbing at himself.

Wary of his fury should he discover my involvement, I buried my delight at his discomfort deeper than a miser stores his gold. One day, I told myself, I would do worse to him, but what I had done would suffice for now.

The messenger de Lysle was still at Striguil. His departure had been delayed by a fever, according to the gossipy chirugeon, but we squires agreed that he was more likely to be suffering the effect of his over-indulgences. 'The wine sack', we had dubbed him. Our suspicions were confirmed when I went to ask after his health and found him sitting in a window seat, pale-faced, but with a cup in hand, and clearly enjoying the ladies' singing emanating from Aoife's quarters. De Lysle was a likeable type, and remembered my ever-ready jug the night he had recounted the tale of the siege of Taillebourg. When I asked about the king, de Lysle was happy to answer.

I, a proud Irishman, cared nothing for Henry of Anjou, but if I was ever to help my father throw the English off our land, it would benefit me to understand the man in whose name the grey foreigners fought. Until this point, I had remained largely ignorant of Henry. I knew he had ruled England, Wales and swathes of land over the Narrow Sea for more than a quarter of a century; my father had described him as a strong-willed, crafty individual, to be feared and mistrusted in equal measure. Mightily fond of the hunt, he also spoke half the tongues of Europe. This was the extent of my knowledge. De Lysle soon changed that, waxing lyrical about Henry. I learned of the king's intelligence, good education and his astute politics. Dominating the Capetian rulers of France, first Louis and then his son Philippe, had been one of his greatest achievements.

Henry had also shown skill on a visit to Ireland some years prior, I remembered. Wary of de Clare and his kind gaining too much power, alive to the danger of the still warlike provincial kings, he had arrived with an army in tow. Before long, he had achieved the almost-impossible, winning oaths of fealty from the Irish leaders, and the allegiance of de Clare. From that point onward, Dublin and the largest towns had belonged to Henry, and Ulster aside, the entire land had acknowledged him as its rightful monarch.

De Lysle smiled at me, and smiling back, I thought, he is not my king. Nor that of my father and brothers.

Tolling bells from the nearby abbey announced that sext was upon us. De Lysle heaved himself to his feet. 'I can tarry no longer,' he declared. 'Few lords or ladies are as generous as the countess. Stay another night, and I swear I will be pickled.'

I laughed. Thanking de Lysle, and promising to see him off, I took my leave.

Thinking of the friendly messenger riding out the gate, and on to another castle, there to bring word of Duke Richard's arrival, I stopped dead in my tracks. A loud curse distracted me – a cook was on the stairs behind me, carrying a stack of dirty pans, and had almost dropped the lot. After I had apologised and let him past, I gave my idea some consideration. It did not take long to draw a damning conclusion.

Humiliated by de Lysle the night we had heard about Taillebourg, FitzAldelm had gone to the stables to tamper with the messenger's tack. I was *sure* of it. Hastening to the bailey with Rhys, I sought out the groom who cared for de Lysle's horse. Deferring to my superior rank, he showed me the beast's saddle, bridle and reins. My hunch proved correct. A neat cut had been made on the inside of the girth band. Not enough to be noticed by a groom as he readied the horse, but of sufficient depth to ensure that the leather would part once a rider's weight bore down on it.

There was no question of my doing nothing. Fail to act, and the innocent de Lysle would be maimed or killed. Change his saddle, and he would notice; indeed the blame might fall on me when his own was examined. But one choice remained. Ordering the shocked groom to silence, and Rhys as well, I sought out de Lysle. He had just taken his leave of the countess, but his ready smile faltered at my news; we went together to examine the girth.

'This is murderous work,' said de Lysle, his amiable face turned stern.

'Aye, sir,' I replied, dreading the question that would follow.

'Who did this?'

I was a terrible liar then. I still am. I coughed, and took an interest in my boots.

'Hellfire, boy!'

I glanced at the groom, who was listening in with all his might, and de Lysle took my meaning. With a jerk of his head, he dismissed the man, before pinning me with a harder gaze than I would have thought possible. 'Tell me.'

I whispered FitzAldelm's name, and when de Lysle looked blank, explained who he was.

'You are sure?'

I related my tale. The shadow creeping through the great hall. The garderobe. Peering up the stair, recognising FitzAldelm. How the hinges had screeched, and lastly, what had happened in the hay barn.

'And this is the truth?' de Lysle asked.

'I swear it, sir.'

'Sadly, your word is no proof of the man's guilt.'

Who else would have reason to do it? I thought, but instead I said, 'No proof at all, sir, which is why I implore you not to tell the countess.'

'I must say *something*. I am the duke's messenger.' De Lysle puffed out his chest. 'A member of the royal court!'

'I did not actually see him cut the girth, sir. I cannot prove it, and FitzAldelm will say I saw someone else in the bailey. That it could not have been him. It will be my word against his, sir, an anointed knight versus an Irish savage. The countess likes me, but I cannot see her believing me over FitzAldelm. Even if we dragged Rhys in front of her, his evidence, such as it is, provides no proof either.'

'You have a point,' de Lysle muttered. 'I do not want to look the fool in front of the countess.'

'And I have to live in Striguil, sir,' I said, thinking of FitzAldelm's reaction when he heard the charge against him. At the first opportunity, he would hunt down the unsuspecting Rhys. Tough though he was, the boy would crumble before Boots and Fists' assault, and then knowing of my presence in the hay barn, the whoreson would come for me.

'Even if FitzAldelm does not realise it was me who told you, sir, he'll suspect I had a hand in it. He will see me dead.' Speaking the words, I felt my gut roil. Just a few years later, I would have fought FitzAldelm any way he wanted, and been confident of beating him, but that summer, I was still young and relatively inexperienced.

'Surely not. As you say, the man is a sworn knight.'

I spilled out the miserable tale of my voyage from Ireland and imprisonment beneath the great hall, taking care to embroider FitzAldelm's brutality towards me. I held a hand to my ribs, which had been broken, and pulled back my top lip that de Lysle might see the gap where once a tooth had been. 'He's a brute, sir. An evil man,' I finished. 'I beg you to hold your peace.'

De Lysle said nothing, but I could sense he was wavering.

I threw caution to the wind. 'Supposing you do not name Fitz-Aldelm, sir, when you tell the countess. She is a kind and just lady. Rest assured, she will leave no stone unturned in her attempts to find the criminal.' Even as de Lysle gave a half-satisfied nod, I continued, 'And the finger of blame will be pointed at the groom.'

Into the face of de Lysle's unhappiness, I added, '*He* is innocent, of that I am sure, sir. I have never seen a man more shocked than when I found the cut in the girth.'

De Lysle harrumphed, but his resolve was weakening further, and I said, pointing to a fine saddle perched on one of the top wall mounts, 'Take that as a replacement, sir. Its owner is dead, and no one has claimed it these six months gone.' My claim was not a complete lie. The saddle belonged to a mesnie knight who had gone on crusade; he would not need it for at least one to two years, if he survived. By the time he returned to notice its disappearance, I hoped to be long gone from Striguil.

I thanked God as de Lysle accepted my suggestion. In truth, he might have acted as he did only because his 'new' saddle was a great deal better than his own worn one. I cared not. My next concern was the groom, but *his* lips were soon sealed by the awareness – explained with care by me – of the consequences that might follow if knowledge of the damaged girth became more widely known. Terrified, he had sworn his silence, and accepted with pathetic gratitude the two silver pennies I handed over in addition.

Under the pretence of asking more about Henry and his sons, but in reality to watch over de Lysle in case his intentions changed, I remained with him until he took his leave. I watched from the battlements over the main gate as the messenger rode away. He turned to look back, and seeing my wave, lifted a hand in farewell. Falling back to his new saddle, his fingers glanced over the costrel of wine I had pressed into his care a short time before. Purloined by Rhys from the cellar, it was a fine vintage.

Deviousness is not a trait I like in others, still less in myself. If I had not acted as I had in this instance, however, my tale would have come to an abrupt end, for FitzAldelm was a murderous dog.

CHAPTER V

Music and laughter carried from the keep on the muggy afternoon air, reaching me on the tilting ground, which lay close to the Wye. The river slid past, a polished band of silver. Now and again, a fish leaped for a fly, shattering the mirrored surface. Although it was late in the day, and the sun was low on the horizon, it was baking hot.

I pretended to pay the clamour no heed, but I longed to be back in the bailey, or better, in the great hall. Duke Richard and his company had arrived not long since, and all of Striguil was abuzz with excitement. Despite my interest in the royal visitor, I had been given the perfect opportunity to train at the quintain. Apart from Rhys, the tilting ground was abandoned. Every knight and squire in the castle was doing his best to catch a sight of Richard, or to listen in on his conversation with the countess Aoife and her ladies.

Even among the squires, competition was fierce to serve at table. My lowly position meant I would get nowhere near the duke, and so, burying my disappointment, I decided to seize the chance given me. It was in my mind to learn English ways, that I might defeat the grey foreigners in Ireland. If I was ever to reach the level of skill possessed by a knight, I had to be able to joust, and seldom enough it was that I had the tilting ground to myself. Saddling my favourite mount, a solid chestnut belonging to my friend Walter, I had ordered a reluctant Rhys to accompany me.

Too short to reach the quintain's cross bar, he was using a small barrel to reach up and hook a circle of woven reeds in place each time I charged past and added one to my lance. Thus far, I had four, but it had taken several attempts to spear the most recent addition, because on my instruction, Rhys was using ever smaller rings.

When he had replaced the ring, Rhys waved. Relieved to have no audience, annoyed by my failures, I squeezed the horse's chest with my thighs the instant that he had pulled the barrel clear. Well-trained, the chestnut sprang into a gallop. I fixed my gaze on the circle of woven reeds, and as we drew nearer, directed the lance tip straight at it. My effort was in vain, whether due to the sweat stinging my eyes, or through error of judgement, I cannot remember. I thundered by, leaving the ring hanging from the cross bar.

'You almost hit it, sir,' piped Rhys as I rode back.

'Nearly never bulled a cow,' I replied, irritably repeating the old herdsman's saying.

Reaching the end of the tilting yard, I whispered a quick prayer and wheeled my horse back towards the quintain. Faithful heart that he was, the chestnut responded with a will, pounding the dusty earth towards the target.

I missed again.

Frustrated but undeterred, I kept at it. On my fourth attempt, I succeeded. Jubilant, I raised my lance high, letting the ring slide down to join the others.

'Shall I hook another one on, sir?' Rhys was already rolling the barrel into place.

'Let us have a rest.' My mind was on the water bag I had left by the stack of lances. Heated by the sun, it would taste of leather and grease even more than normal, but I was too thirsty to care.

Rhys came running. He took the reins, proficient as any squire, as I slid from the chestnut's back. I laid the lance down with the rest, and patted him on the head. 'You must be parched.'

'Aye, sir.' He waited, like a faithful dog, until I had slaked my thirst, and then, upending the double-stitched bag, drank and drank until I thought he would burst.

Smelling the water, the chestnut whickered.

Pricked by my conscience – we had been there for perhaps two hours – I said, 'Let us take the horse to the river. And you must be hungry.'

Rhys's eyes lit up. 'Starving, sir!'

'Like a bottomless pit, you are,' I said, but kindly. I had grown fond of the boy, if I admitted it. I had also come to value him. Unremarkable enough to escape notice, eagle-eyed, he was also possessed of a sharp wit. Thanks to him, I knew castle rumour sooner than most. 'First to the Wye, and after, back to the keep. Fine food there will be aplenty, what with the duke's visit, eh?'

Rhys did not answer.

Surprised, I noticed his gaze was fixed on something behind me. I turned.

'What have we here?' sneered a familiar voice.

'FitzAldelm,' I said, working to keep my tone civil. 'Practice at the quintain, that is all.'

'Steal the horse, did you?'

The baseless accusation filled me with rage, but I replied calmly, 'I did not. Walter lets me use it by times.'

'Walter? Guzzleguts, you mean.' A snide laugh.

My friend was a good trencherman, but I was damned if I would agree with FitzAldelm. I said nothing.

'I take it you are practising now so people cannot see how bad you are?' He regarded his companions, a group of mesnie knights, who duly chuckled.

'Something like that,' I said, keen to avoid trouble, but suspecting that no matter what I tried, it was about to find me. Deciding that the chestnut could drink from the bailey trough rather than the river, I took up the reins. 'Come, Rhys.'

'There is no need to go on our account,' said FitzAldelm, striding to meet us. Clad in gambeson and hauberk, he had a pot helm under his right arm. The buckler hanging from a long strap over his back and his sword were final proof that he, FitzWarin and the rest of his companions, similarly armed, were here to practise.

An alarm jangled in my head, letting the significance of this pass me by. With no need for armour while I trained, I was wearing just tunic and hose. 'By your leave,' I said, trying to lead the chestnut around FitzAldelm.

He blocked my path, smiling. Hair black as a raven's wing, with prominent cheekbones, he possessed an imperious stare that I was ill-equipped to counter. 'By your leave,' I said again.

He ignored my request, and said, 'A master now at the quintain, I am sure, you must be in need of work with sword and shield.'

Weary, hungry, I did not see his trap. I indicated my sweat-stained clothing, and replied without thinking, 'I am not dressed for it.'

'We can soon change that,' crowed FitzAldelm.

My heart sank as one of his grinning companions, a squat lump of a man two hands shorter than I, stripped off his belt, hauberk and gambeson.

I made no move towards the garments, nor the helmet, shield and sword that were being piled on top.

'Dress yourself,' ordered FitzAldelm, pointing a toe.

I hesitated, fully aware that I had not the skill to beat him.

His companions were quick to comment. 'Coward,' said FitzWarin. 'Pisshose,' added another.

The words were like slaps to the face. Do not listen, I told myself, but my fists were bunching.

Rhys tugged at my sleeve, whispering, 'Let us away, sir.'

'Ten silver pennies that if we cut the Irish dog open, his liver is a fine shade of yellow,' announced FitzAldelm.

The cruel laughter that followed saw a red mist descend over me. Shrugging off Rhys's grasp, I was halfway to the squat knight's gear before FitzAldelm even realised.

'Ah. He has a little spine, perhaps.' FitzAldelm watched as I tugged the sweaty, ripe-smelling gambeson over my head, chuckling when it reached only to my waist.

Noticing the knights' mocking smiles, I realised that this had been their intention all along. The hauberk was also too short, but the helmet with its sheepskin arming cap fitted me well. The shield was decent, and the sword serviceable. Long, straight, and double-edged with a sharp point, its hilt was bound with buckskin. I glanced at the hard faces of FitzAldelm and his companions, and decided not to ask about the leather coverings sometimes used to cover blades in practice sessions. Fear tickled my belly, I am not ashamed to say, for there was little chance of emerging unscathed from this encounter. Perhaps God even intended me to die here, I thought, regretting my loss of control.

'Ready?' demanded FitzAldelm.

Ignoring him, I said in Welsh to Rhys, 'Return to the keep. Feed and water the horse, and take yourself to the kitchen. The cook will feed you, on my instruction.'

FitzAldelm's attention moved for the first time to Rhys. It was plain he recognised the boy, but I was grateful to see nothing more. Ignorant of our meeting in the hay barn, there was no reason for him to suspect that our involvement had begun the morning he had tampered with de Lysle's saddle girth.

'Piss off,' said FitzAldelm.

'Go on,' I urged.

Like a little fighting cock, Rhys stood his ground.

Unable to make him leave, and concerned that one of the other knights would round on him, I cried, 'Ready!'

Everyone's attention returned to me.

With FitzAldelm's cronies in a rough circle around us, and Rhys just a few paces further away, we began.

I had grown up using the battle-axe, a fearsome weapon adopted from the Vikings. I had also had training in use of the sword, however, and since my arrival at Striguil, spent good amounts of time sparring with my fellow squires, but I was no knight. FitzAldelm was about twenty-five, which meant he had been handling a sword for at least fifteen years. Knowing thus from the outset that I faced defeat and possibly serious injury, I opted for a battering ram-type attack. Therein, I decided, lay my only hope.

My assault took FitzAldelm by surprise. Driving forward, I hammered a mighty blow onto his shield and came close to knocking him over with my charge. For years after, I would have given everything in my possession to have succeeded. Eventually, however, I came to the conclusion that my life might have taken a different road if I had, and realising that, put it down to experience.

FitzAldelm retreated, swaying with the impact, and I had no difficulty in ducking beneath his ill-aimed retaliatory swing. I sprang at him again, somehow landing a decent strike on his helmet. He staggered back another step, and my heart leaped. Sweet Jesu, I knew nothing then. Thinking the battle was won, I threw a triumphant look at Rhys. Rather than smile, his face twisted with fear. Too late, I turned back to FitzAldelm.

An immense force struck the left side of my helmet. Every bell in Christendom rang in that confined space at the same instant, deafening me. My vision blurred; my jaw snapped shut. I felt my knees give way, and the ground came up to meet me with sickening speed. Winded, my head spinning, I lay there, helpless as a babe and anticipating the agony of FitzAldelm's sword striking wherever he chose. Used only to the no-rules bouts I had grown up with, and FitzAldelm's previous beatings, I expected him to finish the contest without delay.

'Get up.' His muffled voice seemed to come from a long way off.

Nausea bathed me as I lifted my head. FitzAldelm stood perhaps half a dozen paces away, sword and shield at the ready. He made no move towards me. Convinced that he would attack while I was defenceless, I scrabbled about for my own blade. The solid feel of its hilt beneath my trembling fingers provided little comfort, but I was not ready to give in. Dizzy, wanting to vomit, I clambered to my feet.

FitzAldelm was on me like a wolf attacking a sheep. He must have landed three blows before I managed even one, a poor effort that would not have halted a child. I lunged again, and with a contemptuous laugh, he stepped out of reach. I went after him, but he swept around me faster than I could react, and struck me on the back of one leg. To my good fortune, he used the flat of the blade, else my hamstring would have been shorn in two. Nonetheless, the pain was intense – almost as bad as the maniac smith pounding away in my skull. Sheer bloody-mindedness kept me standing at this juncture, that, and my blade, which I had jammed point first into the earth.

FitzAldelm aimed his sword at the slit in my helmet. 'Yield.'

I glared back at him. Sick to my stomach, my head yet whirling, I could not have fought off Rhys. 'I will not,' I muttered.

'Yield!' cried FitzAldelm, advancing.

'Yield, sir.' Rhys's pleading voice. 'He will kill you else.'

Young fool that I was, I decided that it was better to die than to suffer the shame of defeat. I dragged my sword from the earth and raised it towards FitzAldelm. 'Amadán,' I grated.

With a snarl of fury, he swept forward.

Unable to lift my shield, I prepared to meet my God.

'Hold!'

I barely heard the shouted command. Surprised to be breathing, I gazed in confusion at FitzAldelm. Gripping the hilt of his sword, he had fallen to one knee and bowed his head. 'Sire,' he said.

I turned, too fast. My head spun like a child's top. Spots danced at the edge of my vision, and I fell, catching sight of a tall figure in a russet tunic.

I knew no more.

I wish I could say that my first meeting with Duke Richard had been a dignified affair. Instead, it was as I spluttered and coughed, drenched by a pail of water fetched from the river. I found myself lying on my back. A ring of faces stared down at me: a worried-looking Rhys, a stony-eyed FitzAldelm, the squat brute whose gear I had used, Fitz-Warin and several men I did not recognise. One, clad in a fine russet tunic, had reddish-gold hair and intense blue eyes. This, I decided, had to be the duke. De Lysle had often waxed lyrical about his mane of hair.

'You return to the land of the living.' His tone held a mixture of concern and amusement.

'Y-yes, sire,' I replied. Wary, intimidated despite myself, I knew not what to say next, so said nothing.

'Can you stand?'

'I think so, sire.'

He held out a hand and with one powerful movement, drew me to my feet. On that hot summer day, I was taller than most – and yet Richard towered over me. Long-limbed, powerfully built, he was a veritable giant. He wore no sword, but a well-used bollock dagger hung from his leather belt.

My father's instruction forgotten, I bowed my head and dropped to one shaking knee. 'Sire.'

'Rise,' the duke ordered. 'Else you will end up on your back again.'

Everyone laughed, even Rhys.

'Sire.' I took no offence, for there was no malice in Richard's tone.

'What do they call you?'

'Rufus, sire.'

His lips twitched. 'You are well-named.'

'I was born Ferdia Ó Catháin, sire,' adding by way of explanation, 'I am Irish.'

'I guessed you were no native French speaker. How came you to Striguil?'

'I am a hostage, sire.'

'Ah, one of the savage Irish!' Richard said, half-mockingly.

I bit down on the instant rush of anger. 'Sire.'

'The Irish are mighty warriors, or so they say.'

I made a face. 'I did not fare well just now, sire.'

'Indeed.' The duke's attention moved to FitzAldelm, who, thinking the duke was acknowledging his victory, smirked. His grin faded, however, as Richard snapped, 'Your name and rank?'

'FitzAldelm, sire, knight of the mesnie.'

'Is this man Ferdia – Rufus – your squire?'

'No, sire.'

'I am glad to hear it, for you would be no kind of knight to furnish him with such poor gear.' Richard indicated my borrowed gambeson and hauberk. 'They are far too small.'

Sensing the ground shift, FitzAldelm's expression grew guarded.

'It is customary for knights to train with each other, not to practise with hostages. What, then, was your purpose in fighting Rufus?' Richard had sensed something of what had gone on. Driven by the strong sense of right and wrong I would come to know well in later years, he would have continued his interrogation until the truth emerged had FitzAldelm not answered as he did.

'Being Irish, the lad has little skill, sire. I offered to teach him a few moves, nothing more.' FitzAldelm attempted a casual shrug.

'What say you?' Richard demanded of me.

My decision had already been made. FitzAldelm was a dangerous enemy, and I would never forget that. Far better to say nothing, I decided, than to seem weak or afraid before the duke.

'It is as he says, sire,' I replied, nodding at FitzAldelm. 'We were training, and it got a little out of hand. God be thanked, I have taken no serious hurt.'

Richard's blue eyes roved from me to my enemy, and then to the others who had been present. FitzAldelm's companions nodded earnestly. It was fortunate that the duke's gaze did not fall upon Rhys. Too young to realise the reasoning behind my lie, he was bright red with indignation. I gave him a sharp look, and he subsided.

'There is more to this than meets the eye, but I have not the patience to find out more.' Staring at FitzAldelm, Richard said, 'Treat the countess's hostages with more care in future. Had I not arrived, Rufus's soul would be halfway to Heaven. Think what might have happened when that news travelled to Ireland. The countess would not be best pleased that an uprising was caused by the heavy-handedness of one of her own men.'

FitzAldelm muttered an apology, but I saw the murderous expression he threw at me as the duke spoke again.

'You had best learn some skill with a blade, Rufus, else you will make no kind of a knight.'

'Yes, sire,' I said, flushing like a youth caught staring at a lady's bosom, and hating myself for it.

Richard walked away, clapping for attention. 'Let us to our purpose. I am told that some among you wish to join my household. Show me why I should accept your fealty.'

My attention shifted. More than a score of mesnie knights were here, dressed for combat. FitzAldelm and his cronies had come early, to prepare. Now they were all about to set upon each other as the duke watched. I stripped off the hauberk and gambeson, and returned them to the squat knight. It was time for Rhys and I to leave; there was no place for us here.

Remember Cairlinn, I thought, as we trudged the dusty path back to the keep. The English are the enemy. Richard is the enemy.

I warred with myself every step of the way, for the other half of me wanted only to prove my worth to the Duke of Aquitaine.

CHAPTER VI

It was early evening, and with our duties complete, a large group of squires had gone down to the riverbank. The unusual prolonged period of hot weather meant that this had become the norm, an event to be anticipated while scrubbing at hauberks with sand or cleaning out stables. We lay on the sun-warmed grass, supping from costrels of wine and batting away flies. There was much bragging of exploits in the stews, and even more ribald laughter, and suggestions that lies were being spun. Tall stories were also told about hunting and drinking. A lot of the talk concerned Duke Richard too, for he had spent several days recruiting Welsh archers for his army in Aquitaine.

Being somewhat of an outsider still, I sat at the edge of the throng, participating little.

'They say the duke will take twenty knights with him when he leaves.' Hugo, one of the squires I considered a friend, lobbed a stone into the air. A distant splash announced its entering the Wye.

'So they say. Which means the same number of squires will accompany them.' Bogo could not have sounded more self-satisfied. Like FitzAldelm, his master was among those already chosen, and he lost no opportunity in reminding everyone of it. 'Ah, the glory and riches that will present themselves over the Narrow Sea! Those, and the wine. And the women.'

'You have no success with women in Striguil. Apart from whores, that is,' Hugo threw in. 'Why should your luck be any different in Aquitaine?'

Bogo made an obscene gesture at Hugo as the insults and hoots of amusement rained down.

I paid no heed, and instead fell to brooding. There was no question of my leaving with Duke Richard. The countess would never grant permission, and to leave without consent risked retaliation against my family. Even as I harboured dreams of riding to glory in Aquitaine with the other squires, guilt tore at me for entertaining the disloyal thought of taking service with the king's son. I was supposed to be planning my return to Ireland and a campaign against the English invaders. Bitterness soon crept in. It was common for hostages to spend three to five years in captivity, sometimes even longer.

There was more. When taking leave of my father, I had not appreciated that his resistance – even if conducted in a manner that kept the blame off his shoulders – would ensure that I stayed in Striguil. No lord in their right mind allowed a hostage to return to lands simmering with unrest. If my family ever rose in revolt, Aoife might order my execution. The practice was commonplace among Irish kings – the High King Ruairidh had lost two of his sons in this fashion. I told myself my father was wily enough not to be caught rebelling against his overlord, that Aoife was kind-hearted; she would not have me murdered in cold blood.

The harsh realisation was that my destiny remained here. Life was not terrible, I told myself, and it would improve when FitzAldelm left. I could train on the tilting ground to my heart's content, and hunt in the forests over the river. An attractive tavern wench in the stews liked my red hair; I had hopes of pleasurable nights spent in her company. My education in French continued apace; I could even write it a little. Now and again, I managed to spend time with Isabelle, a delightful child. Nonetheless, discontent filled me. Striguil was not my home. There were no bars, yet I lived in a gaol. I was minded of the falcons in the castle mews. Fierce, beautiful birds, they hunted only when their masters allowed, and always had to return to the gauntleted fist and the hood, and after, confinement.

I chewed at my left thumbnail, a habit when I was unhappy, or worried. My gaze wandered over the group. Bogo was gesticulating, boasting about the French knights he would take captive at tourneys. His loud descriptions of the resulting ransoms, and the women who would fall into his bed after, bored me to tears. Hugo made a face that showed he was of the same mind, and passed me his costrel.

The wine was warm, but not unpleasantly so, and better than the usual vinegar we squires were given. After three long pulls, I felt Hugo dig me in the ribs.

'No more, you dog!'

I took a final, sly drink and handed it back.

Hugo raised and lowered the much lighter costrel, and shot me a look. 'Tomorrow evening,' he declared, 'you are supplying the wine.'

'That was my intention all along.'

He snorted and lay back down, draping an arm across his eyes to shield against the still-bright sunlight shafting in from the west.

Bogo continued to hold forth, but some squires had decided to try their luck catching fish. Poles and lines at the ready, they ambled down to the bank where the water slid, smooth and glistening. My attention moved past them to the other side, over rushes growing in thick clumps and the grassy bank above, to the treeline. Beech and birches mingled, their dark green summer-heavy foliage hanging almost to the ground.

I knew the place well. Much of the far bank was wooded all the way to the Severn estuary. Because it lay in Wales, the land was not subject to the harsh forest laws, which could see a man caught hunting blinded or even castrated. I often went over with Rhys in a coracle, with my bow and arrows. We would return empty-handed perhaps half the time, but the rest saw us jubilant, carrying rabbits and birds. Once I had brought down a wild boar. Christ Jesus, but I thought my back would break carrying it to the boat. Even Bogo had been friendly that night, as the rich smell of roasting meat filled the great hall.

A horn sounded atop the palisade. Once, twice, thrice it blew. The signal meant nothing to my ear, but the way Hugo leaped up had me on my feet as well.

'What is it?'

'The gates are to be closed,' said Hugo, frowning. 'We had best get back.'

There was no denying the nervous edge to the squires' excitement as we hurried away from the riverbank. Wild theories about the reason for the horn's sounding flashed to and fro. Richard had again risen against his father, and seized control of Striguil. Plague had broken out in the stews. The local Welsh, peaceful these past three years, were rebelling.

The gate was still open when we reached it. Although I had no reason to be afraid, I felt relief to enter the bailey. Inside, however, chaos reigned. Horses were being saddled by nervous grooms. Knights, dressed for war, paced about, one instant in deep conversation with their fellows, and the next calling for their mounts. Watched over by a grim-faced serjeant, men-at-arms were assembling close to the gate. Archers were gathered by the armoury, from the doorway of which bows and sheaves of arrows were being handed out.

'What in God's name is going on?' I asked Hugo.

'Your guess is as good as mine.'

Our group broke up as knights, seeing their squires, bellowed to be attended. Hugo ran off with a muttered farewell. Having no master to care for, I was left at a loose end. I caught the attention of a passing man-at-arms. 'Are we to be attacked?'

'Mayhap,' was the curt reply.

'By the Welsh?'

'Aye. The castle at Usk has been besieged. A patrol is to be sent out, and Duke Richard will lead the rest of us there on the morrow.'

I had been to Usk once, with the countess. It lay less than a day's ride to the west; if my memory served, it had been seized by the Welsh some years before, but since retaken by its owner, a lord who paid fealty to Aoife's son Gilbert. Now it seemed that the natives had had enough of the English yoke. I took heart. A century had passed since William had crossed the Narrow Sea from Normandy, but still the Welsh would not submit.

A moment later, Hugo came hurrying over with Walter's name on his lips, and I cursed myself for not having remembered. Our friend had ridden away some days prior with his master, a mesnie knight, on business for the countess.

Usk was one of the castles they were to visit.

That evening Richard held a council of war in the great hall. Tall and handsome, long-limbed and athletic, he possessed a magnetism that had everyone within earshot listening to his deep voice. He strode back and forth, laying out his plan. I can admit to falling under his spell a little more.

I was standing with the other squires behind the long tables that had been set up for the countess's knights and Richard's. Among the latter were some of his most trusted companions, men such as André de Chauvigny, his cousin, a much-vaunted soldier. As long as we kept our masters' cups filled, we were free to observe the goings-on. Attended by her ladies, refraining from wine, Aoife sat on the low dais at the end of the hall and listened attentively. Beside her, the chair intended for

Richard remained empty: he was too energetic to stay seated for long.

Once I might have raised my eyebrows at Aoife's presence. Even in Ireland, where noblewomen had more of a hand in ruling, they did not involve themselves with war. I do not think either that she attended because Gilbert – thanks to his extreme youth – could not. No, the countess was cut from different cloth to most of her sex.

First we heard the account of the messenger sent from Usk. Early that morning, a large band of Welshmen had attacked the village beside the castle, setting fire to houses and murdering the inhabitants. Although the marauders had been prevented from taking the keep, some of the garrison had been killed. The castle was surrounded and the Welsh seemed set to starve out the defenders.

'Are such treacherous attacks common, my lady?' Richard asked Aoife. 'News of the Welsh Marches seldom reaches Aquitaine.'

'Usk was lost and retaken some years ago, sire, but there has been peace since. This attack has come from nowhere.'

'And to nowhere it will be sent again,' cried Richard. 'The Welsh must be punished.'

Cups banged off the tables. Shouts of 'Duke Richard!' and 'De Clare!' rose to the smoke-stained rafters.

I joined in, but half-heartedly. The Welsh were no enemies of mine.

Sensing my lack of enthusiasm, Hugo rounded on me. 'What about Walter?'

'He might not be at Usk,' I protested. 'God willing, he is nowhere near the place.'

'Yes, but he *could* be inside. The poor wretch might even be dead,' Hugo shot back.

Confused, conflicted, I stared after him as he hurried to attend his master. The chances of Walter being dead were slim, I told myself, but it was undeniable that he might be at Usk castle. If it fell, he would be murdered without hesitation. That grim realisation decided me.

I would join Richard's force by hook or by crook.

Hugo proved a willing accomplice to my plan, lending me his spare, much-repaired gambeson, and a kite shield that had seen better days. A stolen costrel of wine and a silver penny saw me lent a sword and an old segmented helmet from the armoury. Like Hugo, I had no hauberk. Finding a horse proved tricky, until an encounter in the bailey the next morning with an excited Isabelle – come to watch the preparations – saw me provided, at her instruction, with a sturdy cob. It was smaller than I needed, but I was grateful just to have a mount.

So much was going on that Hugo and I were invisible as we made our preparations. The bailey was full of baggage wains and horses, waggoneers, knights, squires, men-at-arms and archers. The only people who might have interfered were the countess – who was nowhere to be seen – Bogo and FitzAldelm. Fortunately for me, both of the latter had been sent out in advance of the main force, their task along with a half a dozen others to ride the road towards Usk, scouting for danger. I suppose the remaining squires might have objected to my presence, but they did not, thank Christ.

Readying an army, even a small one, takes time, and sext had rung before Duke Richard led us through the gate. He rode at the front with André de Chauvigny and the rest of his knights, and half the mesnie from Striguil. In all, he had thirty-five knights at his back. The squires came after, with half a hundred archers and the same number of men-at-arms following. A score of laden-down wagons trundled at the back, guarded by a mixed force of bowmen and foot soldiers.

It was another beautiful day. The sun beat down from an azure sky; not a cloud was in sight, and the air was still. I was already sweating heavily, from sheer excitement rather than being over-hot. I was scared for Walter, but I was exhilarated at the thought of battle. I drank in the smell of sweat and oil, of leather and horses. The shouts and commands. A burst of song from amid the knights. The blessings of a roadside priest, and the lewd offers made by a couple of whores, come to see us off. Wagon wheels creaked, dogs barked. Gangs of boys pretended to be English or Welsh as they ran alongside, hitting one another with lances made from sticks.

I turned to look back, and spied Rhys at the top of the palisade. I raised a hand in farewell, and he pretended not to see.

Hugo noticed. 'Is he still angry?'

'Spitting mad,' I said, grinning. 'Swore he would kill ten Welshmen at least if I let him come.' There was no conflict in the boy's mind about fighting his own; ever it has been so with mankind.

'He reminds me of Patch,' said Hugo.

'You are not wrong,' I agreed with a laugh. The head groom's dog was a typical terrier. Combative and stubborn, it thought itself many times bigger than its actual size.

We rode.

It is about fifteen miles from Striguil to Usk, a few less as the crow flies. I hesitate to call the route we travelled a road. It was scarce more than a cart track, narrow and unpaved. Deep-rutted, but because of the fine weather, thankfully free of the usual mud, it ran straight in places, while in others, it twisted and bent like a serpent. Forest marched along on both sides, interspersed with areas of scrubby heather and gorse.

Along the smoother sections we riders made better progress. Breaks opened in the column between us and the foot soldiers, and between them and the wagons. Wise leader that he was, Richard regularly ordered a halt so the army maintained its cohesion. To leave a gap invited attack, in particular against the vulnerable, slow-moving baggage train.

We spied him now and again as we rode, but always at a distance. I burned to ride among his knights in their shining mail, but of course had to be content among the squires. I craned my neck to spy the duke at bends in the track, or when the vanguard climbed a hill we had yet to reach. Opportunity finally presented itself when, during one of the halts, the squires decided to check that their masters had all they needed. In truth, it was their excuse to get close to the duke as well – everyone wanted to be around him – and I was not about to be left out. Ignoring Hugo's warning that FitzAldelm's patrol might return at any time, and that I would be undone, I eased my cob in behind his and followed.

The reason for the halt became clear as we neared the duke and his knights. A babbling stream ran close to the left of the track, a perfect place to water the horses. Richard had gone first, as was his right. Now he observed as the knights took turns to lead their mounts to the stream. Seeing this, the squires hurried to help. As the one without a master, I was left in charge of their horses. Frustrated, I watched the duke talking with several knights, perhaps twenty paces from me. Sunlight winked off their hauberks and the mail hose that protected their legs.

Until this point, I had been concerned with riding to Usk. Now, far from Striguil's palisade, and gazing on the armoured figures of the duke and his companions, I became aware of my own lack of protection. Thoughts of Welsh spears and arrows sent tickles of fear up and down my spine. Annoyed, because Irish warriors did not wear mail, and nor did most squires, I told myself that the Welsh would flee at the first sight of Richard's knights.

I think the same presumption was in everyone's mind, for no attention was being paid to the opposite side of the stream, and the trees that stood there. Content that the mounts were in the care of their squires, the knights were mopping brows, supping from replenished water bags, and conversing amongst themselves. The squires were busy leading horses up and down the bank. Only I, tasked with holding reins, was free to stare where I pleased. In truth my attention had been on Duke Richard, and so it was chance that took my eyes over the swift-flowing water.

Horror filled me. Between the trees, stealing like brown wraiths, I saw dozens of figures. Clad in dark tunics and hose, or bare-legged, they carried spears or bows. Many had round shields; perhaps a quarter had helmets. Even as I filled my lungs to shout the alarm, a volley of arrows came. Aimed at the mounts, upwards of a score and a half of which were packed into a small area, it could not miss. I dragged my gaze from that impending horror, and realised the attack was to come in two waves. The archers were spreading out in a loose line, and between them came the spearmen. The arrows of the first were meant to cause panic, while the second would sweep in amid the confusion and terror. Hugo, whose back was to the enemy, was one of the closest to the stream, and oblivious to the mortal danger he was in.

I do not remember dropping the reins. All I recall is the sprint to the bank, shield slapping off my back, and my bellows that we were under attack. 'Hugo!' I shouted. 'Hugo!'

He heard, and so did two others. All three had their shields, God be thanked, or they would have been feathered like birds by the falling arrows.

It was a close-run thing; we reached the shallows just as the Welsh spearmen charged across in a welter of spray and blood-curdling screams. In unison, we lowered our shields, which had been over our heads against the arrows, and formed a tiny wall. Out came our swords.

'For the Duke!' cried Hugo.

The two others echoed his cry; I roared insults in Irish.

I remember terrible squealing from the wounded horses as the spearmen came at us. Better armed we might have been, with our kite shields and helmets, but we were outnumbered by a good margin. Soon, I decided, we would be blade-slashed corpses. Bile rushed up my throat; I wanted to run. Unwilling to show myself as a yellow-livered coward, I locked my knees.

Afterwards, I laughed at how close I had come to dying in a nameless stream, fighting men who wanted to kill *my* enemies, the English. In those bloody few moments, however, I knew only ball-tightening fear and a frantic struggle for survival. Mad with battle rage, the first Welshmen charged straight at us. Shoulders almost touching, shields close together, we braced for the impact, ducked beneath the wildly stabbing spears, and thrust our right arms forward. Four Welshmen died in perhaps two heartbeats. Seeing their fate, the next men tried desperately to slow down, but the weight of the crowd drove them on. We slew or wounded another four.

The Welsh advance came to a juddering halt. Men screamed, and toppled into the stream. Bodies formed little dams. The water ran red. A shield floated away, turning idly. Men bellowed in French. In Welsh. Hooves pounded as horses fled the slaughter. Arrows shot overhead. Relief bathed me, for the archers were not aiming at us. The spearmen split into three groups, one to engage us head on, the others to flank us and attack the main part of our force.

Hugo took charge, ordering us to place our backs against each other. Formed into a tiny square, we prepared to die as best we could. Hugo faced the stream. I was on his left shoulder, looking back towards Striguil. I had time to wish myself behind its palisade, and then the Welsh swarmed in, from every side.

The rest of the fight is a blur. I remember the brown-pegged teeth of one man I killed, and the high-pitched scream of another. I can still taste the fear as my blade caught in a Welshman's shield. He drove his spear at me, and I twisted, but the point ripped open my right cheek. I bear the scar to this day. The Welshman laughed as I cried out, but then his shield sundered. I freed my blade, and planted it in his chest. A brutal dunt from my shield sent him backwards. Blood gouted as my sword slid from his flesh, and God forgive me, I exulted.

To my astonishment, the next Welshman fled rather than fight me.

I soon understood his reason. A huge mailed figure came charging past us, down the slope, towards the stream. It was Richard, helmetless, and a dozen paces ahead of his knights.

My spirits soared as the Welsh broke and ran.

I do not think the duke even managed to bloody his sword.

It was over.

I twisted around. 'Hugo?'

'I am here.' Red-faced, sweating, my friend grinned back at me. I have rarely been so glad. My heart twisted an instant later, however, for one of the others would never see Usk, let alone Striguil. He lay on top of a Welshman, motionless, covered in gore. Reginald, the fourth of our number, was uninjured. We exchanged jerky nods, aware that ours had been the narrowest of escapes.

'The duke,' muttered Hugo, and I turned.

As one, we bent our knees to the bloody mud. 'Sire.'

'Rise.' Richard's voice was warm. 'I would look on the men who halted the Welsh attack.'

We stood.

Recognition flared in Richard's eyes. In a surprised tone, he said, 'It is you – the Irishman. Rufus?'

I flushed. 'Yes, sire.'

'Does the countess know you are here?' Richard made a dismissive gesture. 'It matters not. I am right glad you are. It was you who cried the alarm, was it not?'

'Yes, sire.' I was conscious of men gathering behind the duke.

'We are in your debt.' Our attention turned to the slope above us, which was littered with dead, wounded and dying horses. Of the uninjured, there was no sign. They would be scattered across half of Wales. 'But for you,' Richard continued, 'our losses would have been grievous not just in horses, but in men.'

'I only shouted and ran to the water's edge, sire,' I protested.

'You did well,' said Richard, clasping my shoulder.

'Thank you, sire,' I croaked, mouth as dry as a long-empty wine butt.

'I declare you are as poorly dressed as the last time we met. That gambeson looks as if mice have been sleeping in it, and your helm resembles one my grandfather might have worn.'

Chuckles came from behind the duke; I heard Hugo choke back a

60

snort. Puce with mortification, I stammered, 'They are borrowed, sire.'

I heard laughter, and ashamed, I hung my head.

'Keep yourself alive until we return to Striguil, and a hauberk will be yours – small recompense for your bravery,' said Richard. He threw a look at Hugo and Reginald. 'You shall not go unrewarded either.'

As we filled the air with thanks, I caught sour glances from a few knights – cronies of FitzAldelm – but I cared not.

Richard had acknowledged my bravery.

CHAPTER VII

Lesser men might have retreated after such an attack, but Richard's resolve to relieve Usk seemed strengthened, and this despite the fact that there was no sign of FitzAldelm and his conroi. Rather than continue the day's march, we set up our tents by the stream. Strong pickets were set up around the encampment. Led by the duke himself, a group of archers and men-at-arms disappeared into the forest on the far bank, their task to see that the enemy had truly gone. They came back, unsuccessful, as light from the falling sun splintered through the trees, painting everything an ominous orange-red.

Soon after, I had the first inkling of how ruthless Richard could be. Nine Welshmen had been taken prisoner. No one gave the wounded among them any treatment, nor even a sup of water; they had been roped together to await the duke's return. Pronouncing the nine traitors to the crown, he ordered them strung up from a nearby oak. Stony-faced, he watched as his sentence was carried out.

I mentioned my distaste for the executions to Hugo. He did not like it either, but as he said, the Welshmen would have done the same or worse to us if the situation had been reversed. He was right, and I hardened my heart. I thought of Walter, whose fate was yet unknown, and imagined what I would do to anyone who had harmed him.

Perhaps a dozen horses were recaptured by nightfall. The rest, including those belonging to the squires, had scattered to the winds. Welsh arrows had seen twenty slain or hurt badly enough to need their throats slit. Another five would recover, but play no further part in our mission. Our men were unused to horseflesh, and so Richard strode from fire to fire, explaining it was better eaten than it was allowed to rot, or worse still, left behind for the Welsh.

Despite his cheerful manner, and the small number of casualties, a muted air hung over the camp. We retired to our blankets early. Despite my weariness, sleep evaded me. I started up at every sound, imagining Welshmen creeping between the tents, daggers in hands. When I managed to shove that dark picture away, I was taunted by images of engorged faces, protruding tongues, and eyeballs that seemed about to pop from their sockets. Hanging was a bad death, I decided, asking God to spare me that end.

It was late indeed when tiredness overcame me, because I awoke red-eyed and irritable. My temper did not improve through the morning as, reduced to walking by my lack of a mount, I trudged with Hugo and the rest along the dusty track to Usk. With Richard, de Chauvigny and the pick of his knights riding the only horses, every squire and many knights were in the same situation. The knowledge helped my mood not at all. I cursed the Welsh, and the hot sun, and the clouds of biting flies that swarmed around us. When the conroi containing FitzAldelm materialised from the heat haze, missing a quarter of their number, I cursed to see that my enemy was not among the dead. They brought news of another ambush, but nothing about Usk, or Walter, and I cursed again.

The remainder of the sortie to relieve the besieged castle was uneventful, save for one thing. It came last, sinking deep.

Lack of mounts or no, the Welshmen surrounding Usk took one look at us and fled. There was no pursuit, on Richard's orders. He did not want to risk the loss of any more horses. Trumpets rang out from the battlements in celebration of our arrival, and the flame-blackened gates of the palisade creaked open. As the cheering garrison emerged, Hugo and I stared, desperate to spy Walter.

We saw neither him nor his master. Trying not to worry, we told ourselves that the pair had not reached Usk, that they were at another of the strongholds on their list.

Usk's commander was a florid-cheeked barrel of a knight called, fittingly, le Grand. Giving loud praise to God, he presented himself to Richard. Knee bent, grateful thanks offered, he at once led the duke to a part of the ditch close by the gate.

My ears rang with Richard's shout of rage.

Along with half a hundred others, we hurried to join him.

Our friend and his master sprawled at the bottom of the ditch, naked as the day they were born. Bruises and bloody cuts covered every inch of their shockingly white bodies. Walter lay on his back, a horrified expression twisting his amiable features. He was missing his sword hand, but the indignities he had been subjected to did not end there. His groin was a scarlet ruin, and I realised with horror that he had been gelded. So, evidently, had his master.

'God's legs, the Welsh shall pay for this!' Richard snarled.

I savagely palmed my tears away. I thought of the men who had been executed the previous day, and wished we had done worse to them.

I did not know it then, but I had taken my first steps to becoming Richard's man.

Three days later, we returned towards Striguil on the same track. The stink from the hanged men filled our nostrils a mile before the mighty oak came into sight. The corpses were already bloated; the crows had taken their eyes. The feet of several had been torn at and gnawed by wild beasts. I was not the only one who retched as we tramped past, weary and over-hot. At least Walter lay in a grave, I decided. He and his master had been buried together; stitched linen sheets protecting us from the horrors done to them. I would not forget, however. Watching shovelfuls of earth land with soft, final thuds on the shape that had been my friend, I made a solemn oath to kill any Welshmen who came within reach of my blade.

Opportunity had not presented itself. Before leaving for Striguil, we had marched along this track and that one, seeking those who had attacked Usk. Slogged our way up and down bracken-covered hills. Waded, knee deep, through bog. Crossed and recrossed streams. We were burned by the sun, eaten alive by midges, hungry, thirsty and above all, angry. Our efforts were in vain. The Welsh were gone. Vanished. Like wolves driven from a flock by the shepherd and his dogs, they had slipped away into the forests and hills.

Richard suffered with us too. True, he had ridden rather than walked, but he spent as long in the search as we did. After two frustrating days, during which not a single Welshman had been found, he had ordered us back to Striguil. The harvest was not yet on us, and supplies were running low. To remain in the field endangered his men's lives, and with little to gain, it was wisest to return whence we had come. There had been time for a brief visit to Walter's final resting place, the swearing of an oath of vengeance, and a sad farewell.

Ah, the hot, impetuous blood of youth. I meant every word of the promise I uttered over Walter's grave, indeed I would have attacked any man who called me a liar. And yet the oath was never fulfilled, because those who slew him were not brought to justice. It was bitter medicine to swallow, and in my righteous, naïve fury, I did not realise the valuable lesson contained therein. Years would pass before I came to see that oftentimes, God's workings remain a mystery. To rage against them, to hold grudges, achieves nothing, except to eat one from within. Reach an acceptance of Divine will, and a man can stay sane when the killer of a brother-in-arms goes free, or he who was treacherous remains unpunished.

In my grief, I had forgotten that my reception at Striguil might be chilly. I realised it soon enough. Within moments of our arrival in the bailey, I was spotted by the steward. A summons to the great hall arrived, delivered by a haughty clerk who looked on with disapproval as I ruffled a grinning Rhys's hair and promised to tell him all later.

'Have I time to change?' I asked. In addition to the ill-laid repair stitches and sweat stains, my borrowed gambeson was spotted with blood.

The clerk gazed down his nose at me, and said, 'The countess wishes you to attend her *now*.'

I wanted to shove his head into the water trough, but not wanting to add to the punishments that my unsanctioned departure might have already heaped on me, I smoothed my features and followed.

I saw Isabelle first, seated in a sunny window bay, attended by one of Aoife's ladies. Spying me, she leaped up with a happy cry and discarded her embroidery. She accompanied us towards the far end of the hall, disregarding both the lady's call to come back, and the clerk's unhappy expression. She peered at the tell-tale marks on my gambeson, and then at my cheeks. 'Are you unharmed?'

'I am, my lady.' Remembering poor Walter, I added, 'Thank God.'

She put on a severe face. 'It was wrong to leave without my mother's permission.'

If I had asked, she would not have granted it, I thought. 'I was worried about Walter.'

Concern filled Isabelle's gaze, and she looked towards the entrance. 'You found him, I hope. Is he without?'

Christ and all His Saints, I thought. She has no idea. Richard was still in the bailey; Aoife herself had not heard our news.

'Ferdia?' There was a high note in her voice.

'He's dead, my lady,' I said gently. 'Slain.'

A little gasp of horror. 'Dead?'

'Yes, my lady,' I said, adding the lie, 'He had a quick end.'

Isabelle's hand rose to her mouth; tears welled in her eyes. She stopped, letting us walk on ahead. Wanting to comfort her, I half turned, but the clerk's elbow reminded me that more important business awaited.

I was ordered to stand by the dais while the clerk vanished into the countess's quarters. This sharp reminder of my status – I had never been behind the partition – deflated my mood further. What seemed like a considerable time passed before Aoife emerged. Dressed in a flowing blue gown, a golden mesh covering her hair, she radiated beauty and authority. There was no acknowledgement, however, and the instant she had seated herself, her green eyes bore down on me, unblinking and angry.

Eager to make the best of the situation, I made a deep bow. 'My lady.'

'Where have you been?' Aoife spoke in French, something she had never done in our previous conversations.

Unsure how to answer, for both of us knew precisely, I swallowed.

'Well?' Her voice cracked like a whip.

I muttered, 'With the duke, my lady.'

'Are you hurt?' Like Isabelle, her attention was drawn to the marks on the gambeson.

'No, my lady. That blood is . . . Welsh.' If she was relieved, I could not tell.

'To leave as you did broke your word.'

Shame warmed my cheeks; I studied my boots. 'Yes, my lady. I am sorry.'

'At first I thought you had run back to Ireland.'

I looked up. 'I would not have—'

'Do not interrupt!' Little pricks of colour marked Aoife's cheeks; she was very angry indeed. 'The duke has relieved the siege of Usk?'

'Yes, my lady. The Welsh fled upon our arrival.' Wondering if I was to furnish a full description of the expedition, I opened my mouth, but a glare silenced me. I was given no chance to explain my reasons for joining the duke's force either, or to mention his acknowledgement of my bravery.

Feeling about ten years old, with my father about to beat me, I listened as Aoife laid out my punishment. I was not allowed to leave the castle until further notice. No visits to the village, the stews, or the abbey. Even the tilting ground was forbidden. There were to be no lessons in French. Each morning, I was to attend the steward, who would set me a list of tasks for the day.

I bore these burdens in silence, hating the approving nods of the clerk, who had reappeared to stand behind the countess.

The cruellest blow came last, as it often does.

'You are not to speak with the Lady Isabelle under any circumstances.'

Stricken, my eyes shot up to meet Aoife's, which still sparked with fury.

'Do you understand?' She grated the words at me.

The protest died in my throat. 'Yes, my lady.'

'Fail to abide by these conditions, and I will have you thrown in a cell. You already know what that is like.'

'I do, my lady,' I answered, unpleasant memories spilling past my mind's eye.

'That will be all.' A jerk of her chin dismissed me.

Again I bowed low, and, with the clerk once more beside me, took my leave.

Isabelle had heard every word. She watched, mute, miserable-looking, as I passed by. I gave her a glance that said 'We are still friends', but with the clerk at my back, dared not speak.

The bailey was not far – perhaps two hundred paces – but the walk dragged as if it had been ten miles. As we emerged, it seemed that everyone was staring. The man-at-arms on the stairs, and the grooms by the stable door. The mesnie knights drinking wine, and the carpenter with a load of planks on one shoulder. Later, I would laugh at my innocence. Isabelle's pronouncement had changed my world irrevocably, but apart from Isabelle, Rhys and my two friends among the squires, no one in all of Striguil knew or cared.

Not long after dawn the following day, my spirits still low, I ventured into the kitchen in search of my usual warm loaf. I found a hive of activity. Cooks chopping, stirring, preparing. Red-handed butchers carrying joints of meat. Fires roared in both hearths, tended by sweating servants. In one a fallow deer roasted on a spit; in the other was a fatted calf. Wicker cages held live fowl; tethered by their necks to the leg of a table were several geese. On the work benches lay hares and rabbits, snipe, larks and a heron. Tantalising aromas wafted from the ovens: bread, and, if I was not mistaken, pastries. I could smell spices too – ingredients I had first encountered in Striguil – cinnamon and cloves.

There were no loaves in the usual place. I hung about, trying to be inconspicuous, but in reality just getting in the way. Shooed from one spot to another, glared at whenever my wandering fingers strayed too close to this pan of steaming frumenty or that bowl of chicken and saffron stew, I edged closer to the door, deciding that I would have to wait until food was carried up to the great hall.

At length, one of the cooks took pity on me. A kindly Welshman, stout and red-faced, he often told me I looked like his son, an archer in King Henry's army. 'Ho, Irishman!' he cried. 'Hungry?'

'Of course!'

'We are busier than busy, as you can see,' he said, but beckoned, nonetheless.

Belly rumbling, I obeyed. 'Is this all for dinner?' The countess was to hold a feast in honour of Richard's successful relief of Usk castle.

'It is. "No expense to be spared," I was told. "It isn't every day that one of the king's sons rides to war on Striguil's account."' He pulled aside a cloth under which lay rows of small, fresh-baked pies. 'Beef and onion,' he said. 'Help yourself.'

I took one, then, encouraged by the cook, a second.

'I was sorry to hear about young Walter.'

Mouth full, I nodded. Swallowing, I said, 'He had a bad death.'

'I heard they—' With a grimace, the cook made a chopping motion towards his groin.

'They did.'

'It is wicked. Wicked!'

We both shook our heads, and inwardly, I lamented that the patrols to be sent out by the countess would ride without me. All I could do was pray that Walter's murderers were caught, a request I judged held slim chance of being answered.

A shouted question carried through the din, and the cook stirred. 'Had enough?' He laughed as I seized yet another pie. 'Now begone, ere the steward comes in. He would bend my ear, and yours.'

I rolled my eyes, hating the reminder of my new situation, which the steward had been quick to take advantage of. He had kept me running errands until late the previous night. After a time, I had realised that many were unnecessary, but still raw from Aoife's tongue-lashing, I had obeyed without question.

Such was to be my existence for the foreseeable future, I told myself. A beast of burden. A drudge. A prisoner, trapped inside Striguil.

I could not have given a fig for the upcoming banquet.

Despite myself, I was eventually drawn in by the growing air of excitement in the castle. Sext, the hour the feast was due to begin, was almost on us. My improving mood was due in no small part to the wine I had slyly consumed with Hugo. Charged with overseeing the transport of wine from the cellar to the buttery, he had roped me in to help. Surrounded by cask upon wooden cask, with only the gutter of rush dips to light our way, we found the barrels marked for use by the butler, and set the half dozen manservants to rolling them outside. The instant we were alone, Hugo, the rogue, produced an empty costrel. I needed little encouragement to hold it as he deftly tapped a barrel. We had time for several swallows each, and a toast to poor Walter, before the servants returned for their next loads. Thereafter, we had to find reason to enter the tack room – where the costrel had been hidden – but with the entire castle thronged with servants going about their tasks, this was easily done.

Encased by a warm glow, I had worked uncomplaining through the humiliating jobs set me by the steward – carrying his ledger as he made his rounds, taking messages to the butler, the head cook and so on. Summoned to meet with the countess not long before the feast, he had accepted my suggestion of helping the other squires as they served their masters.

'I will have my eye on you,' he warned, hurrying off.

'Póg mo hóin,' I muttered in Irish. 'Kiss my arse.'

After a quick visit to the garderobe, and a last sup of wine to fortify myself, I made my way to the great hall. Well it was that I had changed into my finest tunic that morning, for the rolled blankets and spare clothing belonging to the knights and squires that lay along the walls every day were nowhere to be seen. Fresh rushes and sweet-smelling herbs covered the floor. Cloth-covered trestles filled the hall, right to the dais at the end, where a long table faced all the rest. From the ceiling hung two great banners, the first that of the de Clare family, and alongside it, the Angevin lions, vivid gold against a red background.

Attracted by the wine on offer, good numbers of knights from the mesnie and Richard's household were already seated. Through the loud hum of conversation came the distinctive notes of a harp. I slipped past the gaggle of servants and joined Hugo at his position along the side wall. Pouring wine whenever it was needed, we amused ourselves by quietly arguing over which knights would get drunkest, and whether any of the serving wenches were interested in us. We decided on Fitz-Aldelm and one of his cronies for the former, and concluded with regret that the sharp looks meeting our lustful stares meant we would have no luck with the latter.

When the countess and Richard emerged from her private quarters, there was a great scraping of benches as the guests stood. Applause broke out; I joined in with gusto, for the duke was a fine leader and a brave warrior.

The feast that followed was the grandest I had ever seen. Course followed course. In addition to the usual soups and stews, and roasted meats, the servants carried out platters with extravagant dishes. Venison in a bitter sauce, capon and chicken served with orange, and last of all, the swan. A royal bird, it had been encased with gold foil in honour of Richard.

Again my position, that of squire without a knight, came to my advantage. I did not have stand close behind my master, ready to hold a joint of meat just so as he cut it, or arrange plates of food to his liking. Hugo had to replace a trencher sodden with too much sauce, but not I. Aware that the keen-eyed steward, patrolling the hall, would be watching, I kept a jug of wine to hand, and saw to it that the nearest knights' cups were always brimming.

My stomach growled throughout. I made do with an occasional untouched morsel swiped from plates removed from the table by the servants, and told myself that Hugo and I could eat our fill later on. There would be leftovers aplenty.

With the last course cleared away, bowls of water and cloths were carried to the tables by the squires that the guests might wash their hands. I had the bad luck to lay mine down beside FitzAldelm, who, with an evil sideways glance, laid hold of his bone-handled table knife. I affected not to notice, but the fleeting encounter was unsettling. Until the moment he left with the duke, I had to be on my guard.

Hugo had seen nothing. His attention was on the dais at the end of the hall. Following his gaze, I forgot my fears. Richard was getting to his feet.

A rippling silence travelled the room. Someone coughed. Quiet again fell.

Richard bore no crown, but he looked every part the duke, every inch the king's son. A gilded belt encircled his waist, a bright contrast to the muted purple of his fine tunic. His beard glistened with oil, his curls had been combed back. Silver goblet held high, he toasted Aoife, who acknowledged his words with a graceful dip of her chin.

'I thank the countess for her hospitality. She has spared no expense, has done everything in her power to ensure that our visit to Striguil has been a pleasant one.' Again Richard saluted Aoife. 'The countess!'

'The countess!' cried de Chauvigny.

Benches scraped backward. Men rose to their feet, cups held aloft, echoing his toast.

Still resentful of my punishment, I made a pretence of joining in.

'Many of you were with me on the march to Usk,' Richard went on. 'It was unfortunate that not everything went according to plan, but the castle was saved, and the Welsh driven off. Would that I could stay and lead the hunt for the savages who were responsible, but a summons from my lord father has arrived. The countess informs me, however, that no stone shall be left unturned, no rathole go unsearched.'

More cheering broke out.

Richard waited until the clamour was abating. 'On the road to Usk, the Welsh slaughter would have been a deal worse but for the actions of four brave men.'

I shot Hugo an incredulous look. Wrapped in misery after Aoife's tongue-lashing, I had forgotten about the duke's promise.

'Squires all, they stemmed the Welsh attack when it threatened to become a flood. It grieves me that one was slain, but the others survived. I would recognise their bravery. Where are they?' Richard's gaze roved over the tables and seated knights, to those of us behind. 'Come forward!'

Exhilarated yet hesitant, I turned to Hugo, who gave me a great shove in the back. 'We cannot keep the duke waiting,' he hissed.

Every eye in the hall was on us as we made our way towards the dais. Reginald, who had been serving on the opposite side of the room, joined us before we reached Richard. A quick glance told me that Hugo and Reginald were as nervous as I, yet it gave me scant comfort. We walked the last distance with measured pace and then, as if we had practised the move a hundred times, each dropped to one knee.

'Sire,' we chorused.

'Rise.' Richard's command was warm. Raising his voice that everyone might hear, he cried, 'Squires they may be, but these three men are not short of courage. The countess is fortunate to count them part of her mesnie.'

Aoife answered with a smile. Because I was watching for it, I was perhaps the only one to see the glitter of annoyance in her eyes – directed at me.

To Reginald, Richard gave a fine dagger in a silver-chased sheath, and to a beaming Hugo, a new domed helmet with a fitted face-mask. Both also received a purse of silver pennies. The duke left me until last, which increased my excitement and nervousness in equal measure.

'Rufus,' said Richard next. A wry look. 'I should address you as Ferdia, I suppose, but Rufus suits you.'

'Call me Rufus, sire,' I said, pleased to feel none of the resentment I had felt when the likes of FitzAldelm used the name.

'The countess tells me that you left Striguil without leave.'

My heart sank. Sure that I was about to receive more punishment rather than the rewards my friends had been given, I nodded. 'I did, sire.'

'You are Irish. This was not your fight.'

I met Richard's gaze as best I could. 'It was not, sire, but I thought my friend Walter might be at Usk. I was worried about him, and wanted to help.'

'Walter?' Richard frowned. 'Was that not the name of the squire in the ditch, God rest his soul?'

'It was, sire.' My mind filled with the sight of my poor friend, naked and mutilated.

'And so it became your quarrel in the end.'

'Yes, sire.' I felt an odd mixture of pride, that I had done my best for Walter, and shame, that I had not been able to save him, and guilt, because I had fought alongside men who were, in effect, my enemies. A conflict broke out in my head, one I had long denied. Decent though they were, Hugo and Reginald were English. I should hate them, I told myself, darting a sideways look at both. I got grins in reply, and instead of glaring, I smiled back, feeling no hatred, but rather a sense of comradeship.

I raised my head to find Richard watching me with knowing eyes.

'It is a powerful thing, the bond forged in battle. Strong as steel it is, and as unyielding. Men will lay down their lives for a brother-in-arms without even thinking.' He paused and added, 'Is that something you would do for these squires beside you, Rufus?'

'Yes, sire,' I said, thinking how my father would have disowned me on the instant for honouring Englishmen so, but unable to lie.

Richard looked pleased. 'It is plain in your face.' He clicked his fingers, and a servant appeared. Taking the hauberk he was offered, the duke stepped forward. 'This is well-used, Rufus, but remains serviceable. Accept it with my thanks for what you did at the stream. It was bravely done.'

The short sleeves on the coat of mail in Richard's hands revealed its age, as did the shiny, repaired sections on the chest and belly. Nonetheless, the gift was princely, its value immense. To me it seemed finer than a king's gold crown.

'Thank you, sire,' I said hoarsely, accepting the shirt. A purse of silver pennies was next. Again I expressed my gratitude. By its weight, I would be able to buy my own horse. These were royal gifts indeed.

'You shall have to practise in the bailey, for the nonce at least.' Amusement rippled in Richard's voice, and I saw him turn briefly to Aoife, who pretended not to notice.

'Yes, sire.' In my head, I hoped he might ask the countess for an easing of my punishment, but I knew better than to ask. Bowing my head, I stepped back to join Hugo and Reginald. We bowed, and retreated the expected distance before turning to make our way back to our previous positions.

Ah, the arrogance of youth. Passing FitzAldelm, I caught his sour gaze. Not for him the acknowledgement of the king's son, the Duke of Aquitaine, I thought, nor the valuable gift of armour. Lifting the heavy mail that he might see it, I sneered, knowing that in the midst of the feast, my enemy could do nothing.

FitzAldelm's brows lowered, and he mouthed a curse at me.

I walked on, feeling as if I had just unhorsed him at a tournament.

Late that night, the celebrations were still continuing. Aoife had long since retired, but Richard, de Chauvigny and a score of others remained at table, drinking and singing. A number of mesnie knights had joined them, for the most part those who would leave with the duke. Hugo's master had retired a while before, however, which had allowed him to find me and Reginald at the back of the hall. There we made good inroads into the countess's wine, and ran over our meeting with Richard time and again. Reginald did his best to hide his jealousy at the gifts I had received, but Hugo, ever good-hearted, owlishly repeated that I was the one to have sounded the alarm, and faced the Welsh first, so I deserved the greater prize.

Embarrassed, I countered his argument with my own, that he and Reginald had fought as bravely as I, and come as near to death, but Hugo would have none of it. On the fourth or fifth occasion, I gave up trying. Drunker than I, he had reached the stage of not hearing anyone else's opinion. Clapping him on the shoulder, I pointed a finger at the door. 'Garderobe.' I heard the slur in my own voice. 'Garderobe.'

Call of nature answered, I decided to clear my head atop the palisade. Up the ladder I clambered. With luck, Hugo would have stopped singing my praises by the time I got back. Like as not, I decided wryly, I would find him fast asleep. The appeal of my own blankets was growing strong.

There was no one to be seen on the walkway, which did not surprise me. The men-at-arms and archers had held their own celebration in the bailey; by the remains of a large fire below, a few crouched shapes were still visible. I turned away and leaned against the wooden rampart, grateful for its solidity, and with a pang of longing for home, peered over the river to the north-west. Would I ever return to Cairlinn? Would I see my parents and brothers again this side of Heaven?

Sadness took me, for I had no idea.

Boots scraped on the ladder, and I glanced over my shoulder.

A head appeared, helmetless, so it was not a sentry returning from the garderobe. Maybe it was Hugo, I thought, brightening. He would understand my desire to see my family again. Sent to Striguil to train as a squire, he had not seen his own for years.

'Hugo?' I asked.

'Eh?' The figure stood up, a burly, heavier frame than my friend. 'Who's that?'

My spirits sank, recognising the newcomer as FitzWarin. What unhappy chance had brought him up here, I did not know, or want to find out. I shuffled back from the top of the ladder.

'God's bones, you are a Welshman come to murder us.'

Stung, not wanting the alarm to be sounded and I blamed for it, I retorted hotly, 'I am no Welshman!'

A mocking laugh. 'I would recognise that awful accent at a mile, Rufus. You mongrel Irish seem unable to master any French.'

'Can you speak my tongue?' I shot back.

This time, a snort. 'Why would I want to?' FitzWarin came closer, filling the air between us with the smell of wine and sweat. 'Once, perhaps, it was the language of saints and scholars. Now it is spoken by the likes of you, a savage who barely knows how to wipe his own arse.'

My hatred of his kind came surging back. Yet fuzzy-headed from drinking all evening, I struggled for a blade-sharp response. Finding none, I spat at his feet instead. 'English bastard,' I said, careful to pronounce the French just so.

Drunk or no, FitzWarin was on me in a heartbeat. His large hands grappled for my throat. I reached up, trying to break the grip, but weaker than he, I could not prevent his fingers from wrapping around my neck. We stared at each other, close as lovers, his face twisted with anger and mine already swelling. He squeezed tighter, grimacing with effort.

A light-headed feeling washed over me. Soon I would lose consciousness. FitzWarin was going to kill me, I thought, stars exploding at the edges of my vision, and I had never even donned the hauberk given me by Richard.

It is odd the things that go through a man's mind when he is close to death.

Also strange is the burning will to survive that can emerge from the shadows.

I brought my knee up into FitzWarin's groin with all the strength I could muster. The sharp exhalation that followed and the slight weakening of his grip spurred me on. I did it twice more, at last connecting fully with his balls. He let go, and staggered back, letting me suck in a breath of air. Despite the pain radiating from my bruised throat, it was one of the sweetest I have ever drawn.

A muttered curse dragged my head up. Fear swelled my heart; if I admit it, I came close to panic. FitzWarin was not done with me. In he came, muscled arms reaching out again. My right hand dropped to my belt, searching for a dagger that was not there: I had left it on the table after cutting a hunk of cheese.

By rights, I should have died then. FitzWarin was twice my weight and a lot stronger than I. He closed with me, and I ducked down, trying to escape his grasping fingers. His upper body struck the palisade with some force, and with a loud crack, a section of it broke. Carried by his own momentum, he toppled off the walkway, almost taking me with him.

Fallen to my knees, I twisted around to see. A great hole gaped in the timbers. Of FitzWarin, there was no sign. As I listened, a meaty thump came from the riverbank far below. Disbelief filled me, and if I confess it, a wave of pleasure. The brute was dead. No one could survive a fall of that distance.

A heartbeat later, a shouted question carried from further down the walkway. Bile rushed up my throat; I came close to vomiting. A sentry had heard. He would catch me in the act, as it were, and I would be blamed for FitzWarin's death. The punishments heaped on me by the countess would be as nothing to what I could expect in return for murder.

My prayers were answered then, for the sentry was a good distance away. He did not spy me as I crept down the ladder like a red-handed killer. The few men in the bailey did not see me re-enter the great hall either, and those within who were still waking were so drunk they did not even realise I had been gone. Finding Rhys, curled up like a pup in my usual spot close to the back wall, I wrapped myself in my blankets and lay down. My heart pounded as I listened for the sentry.

He arrived soon after, and his news sent a large group outside, where, I presumed, they climbed to the ramparts. I dared not follow, so instead lay, feeling a mixture of panic that I might yet be found out, and exhilaration that I had one enemy less in Striguil. A little time passed. Apart from the snores of those around me, the great hall was peaceful.

Warmed by my blankets, belly full of wine, I nodded off.

I dreamed of FitzWarin, his great paws clutching at my throat.

Loud voices dragged me awake. I started, just managing not to throw myself into a sitting position and give away the fact that I was awake. Mouth dry with fear, sure that I was about to be seized and interrogated, I lay still as a corpse.

'What was his name?' By the tone of Richard's voice, he was walking.

'FitzWarin, sire,' replied FitzAldelm.

'He was to accompany the royal household?'

'Yes, sire. He was a good knight.'

'A poor way to end then, eh? Leaning on the palisade, only for a section of rotten wood to break beneath him.'

'At least it was swift, sire.'

'Let us raise a cup to his memory,' said Richard.

Their voices faded away.

Sure now that my role in FitzWarin's death had gone unnoticed, I felt the tension ease from my shoulders.

Surprised to find Rhys's gaze on me – he must have been woken by the noise – I placed a finger to my lips. He nodded, and closed his eyes again. Even if he realised I had been outside, and suspected my involvement, he would not say a word. As for FitzWarin, I felt not a trace of guilt.

Other deeds of mine will require a reckoning with God, but not that one.

PART TWO: 1182-1183

CHAPTER VIII

The year was well underway; spring was in the air, and the tourney season had begun. William Marshal was bored, however. Standing in the Young King's grand tent at Lagny-sur-Marne, a short distance from Paris, he stood by as the armourers summoned by his master offered their wares. At thirty-five, Marshal was eight years older than the Young King, but as he watched Henry oohing and aahing over the military kit, the age gap felt twice as big. If it was not weapons and armour, Marshal decided, it was clothing or jewellery. Well and good it was for the heir to the throne to have an interest in such fripperies, but affairs of state were more suitable subjects. That was not the Young King's way. It had ever been since Marshal had first entered his service, twelve years earlier. A man could not have everything, Marshal told himself. His master had charisma, generosity and a kind heart, all fine qualities. Nonetheless, his thoughts soon circled back to more serious matters.

Henry had tried to school his heir in statesmanship. At fifteen, the Young King had held the throne for a time while his father was absent, but more interested in the good life than the running of the kingdom, had been little more than a cipher. Six years prior, when sent to help his brother Richard during a war in Aquitaine, he had arrived late and departed before the hostilities were over. If these had been the only occasions, thought Marshal, the mark of a growing youth, it might not have been of concern, but the list was endless. Of recent times, Henry asked little of his eldest son, which fuelled the Young King's sense of injustice. In his mind, he had nothing of what was rightfully his, while Richard and Geoffrey already had lands and territories to call their own. Whenever the Young King chanced to spend time with the youthful French monarch, Philippe Capet, he came away with his grievances whetted even keener. It was a well-worn theme, with no end in sight.

Marshal's attention returned to the display, a fine one, he decided. Oiled and burnished until they shone, new styled helmets with face-masks sat side by side on cloth-covered trestles. There were hauberks with aventail fastenings at the neck, a design gaining favour among younger knights, and swords and daggers by the dozen. Kite shields, carefully painted with the Angevin lions, had been arrayed in neat lines against the tent wall.

The Young King picked up a sword and sighted down the blade. At once its maker, a smith with a new tunic that ill-suited his work-roughened hands, began to extol its qualities. 'See, sire? I have inscribed your name there.' The smith's calloused forefinger traced a line along the steel close to the hilt.

The Young King peered closer, and a huge smile split his handsome face. Tall, broad-shouldered, and with thick brown hair, he resembled a younger incarnation of his father, and a more amiable version of his younger brother Richard.

'Henry, the Young King, conqueror of every foe!' he cried.

The smith bobbed his head. 'I thought as you might like that wording, it being the truth, sire.'

It was a patent lie, but the Young King puffed out his chest, and pleased, glanced at his nearest companions, Adam d'Yquebeuf and Thomas de Coulonces, who were quick to utter agreement. Marshal knew himself to be a better fighter than his master, and it served no purpose to say otherwise, or to object to his rivals' presence. From minor baronial families, they had somehow weaselled their way into his master's favours. Marshal gave away none of his irritation. Years in service to Henry's heir meant he was a master at concealing his emotions. When the Young King's gaze reached him, he inclined his head in apparent approbation.

Ordering the inscribed sword, along with a matching dagger and scabbards for both, the Young King moved on to the next table, leaving the smith beaming from ear to ear. D'Yquebeuf and de Coulonces followed at his heels, like a pair of hungry hunting dogs.

The next vendor, an armourer known to Marshal, watched with keen eyes as the Young King tried on first one helm and then another. Pleased by his customer's approving comments, he cleared his throat and mentioned an outstanding debt, the result of a previous commission.

'Begging your pardon for even mentioning it, sire,' said the armourer. 'But six month ago, it were.'

The Young King's pleasant expression vanished; he waved a dismissive hand. 'I am the king's son. You will be paid in due course.'

'Thank you, sire.' Although d'Yquebeuf and de Coulonces were hovering threateningly, the armourer tried again. 'If I might ask for some of the monies before you take yon helmet . . .'

'Christ on the cross!' thundered the Young King as the armourer quailed. 'Am I always to be plagued by money-grabbers? Will!'

Marshal moved swiftly to join his master. Of average height, he had a wiry, muscular build, and a confident manner. He wore his hair short, in the old fashion, and beneath a long nose, sported a moustache, unusual for the time. 'Sire?'

'Deal with this fellow, will you?' The Young King's voice grew muffled as he settled a flat-topped helm with a face-mask over his head. 'What about this one?'

'It suits you well, Hal,' said Marshal, using the informal name given to the heir by his family and friends. He threw a warning glance at d'Yquebeuf and de Coulonces, who backed away a step and muttered to the armourer, 'How much does the Young King owe?'

The sum mentioned, two full marks, was sizeable. Nonetheless, Marshal promised the debt would be paid within the day. Whether he would recover the money was unclear. Extravagant taste meant that the heir to the throne lived far beyond even the sizeable means granted him, and as one of the Young King's closest companions, Marshal often footed the bill. Repayments were sporadic. He kept a tally, naturally, and told himself that when his master took the throne, the debt would be cleared. That, he decided ruthlessly, or one of the highest posts in the land would be his. Suitable reward for long years of faithful service was his right.

Feet stamped in acknowledgement just outside. The Young King paid no heed. He was admiring a kite shield on which the Angevin lions' eyes had been picked out with shards of glass. The armourer claimed they would reflect the sun and blind the enemy.

Marshal recognised a salute when he heard one. Making for the entrance, he arrived just as Count Geoffrey of Brittany, the Young King's second brother, ducked his head and came in. Not quite as tall as either Henry or Richard, he nevertheless towered over most men. His good looks were marred by a semi-permanent sneer, which deepened as he recognised Marshal.

'Welcome, sire.' Marshal dropped to one knee, his dislike of Geoffrey masked as efficiently as ever. 'We were not expecting you.'

'Good. I wanted to surprise my brother.' Geoffrey's gaze moved on, taking in the Young King, who had still not seen him. 'There he is, the magpie, in search of more gewgaws.'

'He needs a new helmet for the tourney, sire,' said Marshal, annoyed despite himself. Geoffrey's tastes were similar to the Young King, as his squirrel fur-lined, gilt-braided green cloak and jewelled belt clasp showed.

'Of course he does,' Geoffrey threw over his shoulder. 'Brother!'

Marshal climbed to his feet, fighting back anger. Everyone else in the royal family allowed him to stand after making obeisance. Not Geoffrey, the oily tongued snake. Not a flicker of emotion reached Marshal's face, however. In the Young King's court, like any other, a man had always to be on guard. Men like d'Yquebeuf and de Coulonces, even now fawning at Geoffrey's approach, were not to be trusted either. Although they had served the Young King almost as long as Marshal, there had never been any love lost between the three.

Baldwin de Béthune, who had just entered, was a reliable comrade. Sharp-eyed and a consummate horseman, he and Marshal were as close as brothers. 'There is trouble brewing, or I am no judge,' he whispered to Marshal with a nod at Geoffrey.

'And precious little we can do about it,' replied Marshal.

The Young King's expression was wary as he greeted Geoffrey, but his mood was lightened by his brother's declaration to join with him in the forthcoming tourney, which was being held by Philippe of France.

'No one on the field shall stand before us,' the Young King declared.

'Nor shall they,' said Geoffrey, leaning closer. 'But defeating French knights is not my only reason for visiting.'

The Young King, who had finally tired of examining weapons and equipment, gave him a sharp glance. 'Speak.' Seeing Geoffrey's questioning look at those around them, in particular the armourers, he said, 'These companions of mine I trust with my life, but I sense your meaning. It would be wiser to talk where there are fewer pricked ears.'

His own interest aroused, Marshal was glad to walk behind the Young King as he left the tent with his brother. He ignored the spiteful

84

stares cast after him by d'Yquebeuf and de Coulonces, who had not been invited. De Béthune stayed to examine the weapons, but one of Geoffrey's knights, a slim young man with receding hair and piercing blue eyes, paced alongside Marshal.

'Owain ap Gruffydd, sir,' he said in a low voice. 'And you are William Marshal.'

Marshal's smile was wry; he was used to this. 'Correct. My apologies, sir, but I do not know you.'

'That would not be surprising, sir, for I have only recently joined Count Geoffrey's mesnie.'

'By your name, you are from Wales,' said Marshal, intrigued. 'Yet there are few Welsh noble families who serve the house of Anjou. Most tend to threaten rebellion, or actually engage in it.'

Owain made a face. 'You speak the truth, sir. My own father was killed fighting the king a decade ago. I was taken hostage for the good behaviour of my elder brother, the heir, and sent to the king's court at Oxford. Count Geoffrey saw me training on the tourney ground there during his last visit, and asked that I enter his mesnie. His lord father gave me leave, and so here I stand.' A pleasant grin.

Marshal took an instant liking to Owain, who seemed a straightforward character. Aged about twenty-one or -two, he had spent much of his life in the English court; like as not, he regarded himself as half an Englishman. Checking that the Young King and Geoffrey were not listening – they were deep in conversation – Marshal murmured, 'How do you find his service?'

'How do you find the Young King's?'

A plain speaker, thought Marshal, a little surprised, and not stupid either. He shrugged. 'It can be trying, I admit, and sometimes unpleasant things have to be done. All things considered, however, I am content. And you?'

'Thus far, I have no complaints, sir.'

'Do you know why the count has come here? It is not for the tourney.'

Owain looked a little discomfited. 'I have some inkling, sir, but I have been asked to do nothing unchivalrous.'

He likes this business as little as I, Marshal decided, taking to Owain even more. 'Nor I,' he said. 'Let us hope it stays that way.'

Although the tourney would not start until the next day, the large camp was a hive of activity. Horses were having shoes renewed. Pages ran to and fro on errands. Perched on stools, squires polished bridles and headgear, or sharpened weapons. Watched by a group of their fellows, a pair of fully armoured knights went at each other on foot in a practice bout as fierce as the real thing.

The Young King and Geoffrey talked briefly of their mother Queen Alienor, who had been incarcerated by the king since her involvement with a previous revolt against him. Geoffrey had received a letter from her a sennight prior, but seemed little concerned about replying. The Young King declared he had not written to her in six months. Marshal's heart twinged – he himself held Alienor in high regard, having served her for a short time before entering the Young King's mesnie. Selfish curs, the pair of them, he decided.

'You have ever been my favourite brother,' said Geoffrey to the Young King.

Delight blossomed on the Young King's face. 'And you mine.'

'We do not see each other often enough. That shall change.'

The Young King's smile grew broader. 'These words are music to my ears.'

Geoffrey could persuade the Pope to bless Lucifer, thought Marshal. He no more means what he has said than the sky is green.

'Have you seen Richard?' asked the Young King.

Geoffrey snorted. 'I have not, for months, and I am the better for it. Even if I had ridden to Aquitaine, he is far too busy to receive visitors. The nobles there remain unhappy with his rule. Rebellion constantly threatens.'

'Ever it has been so. He subdues one fire only for another to flare up, much as a peasant tries to quench the flames in his burning thatch.'

'The soldier prince, they call our brother,' said Geoffrey, his gaze sliding to the Young King. 'I heard him mention it himself.'

Geoffrey prepared that shaft ere he arrived, thought Marshal, as the Young King flushed. 'Prince of the tourneys' was one of the names *he* was known by in France, but there could be no doubt which of the two was preferable.

'Yet I am the heir to the throne!' The Young King's voice was thick with emotion. 'The man who will lead armies to battle, even to the Holy Land!'

'You are, Hal, and right glad I am of it.' Geoffrey continued, 'Richard has always been big-headed. Like as not, he invented the name himself.'

'Aye.' The Young King packed the word with loathing. 'He needs his wings clipped. To be reminded of his position.'

'Nothing would make me happier.'

'Papa also needs to be taught a lesson, for not treating me as I deserve. He has also treated you ill, brother.'

'It is true,' said Geoffrey with a pout.

'Richard first. How shall it be done?'

'I have made a start,' Geoffrey confided. 'Have you heard of Bertran de Born?'

The Young King glowered. 'The troubadour? I am not over fond of him.'

Marshal knew why. De Born had used one of his sirventes, satirical songs, to mock the Young King for his lack of martial fervour. It was an insult that had sunk deep.

'Try to set aside your ill will, Hal. He is not just skilful with lute and quill,' said Geoffrey. 'He also has the ear of many barons in Aquitaine.'

The Young King scowled, and Geoffrey rested a hand on his arm. 'These are men who could be useful to us, and they are no friends of Richard.'

Seeing something in Geoffrey's eyes, the Young King cried, 'By God, you have already been dealing with him.'

'Better than that.' Geoffrey's smile was like that of a cat presented with a bowl of cream. 'He is here with me, that he might talk to *you.*'

'He must apologise first.'

'That goes without saying.'

The Young King nodded. 'Very well.'

'Let us to my tent. De Born is waiting there, and he has much to say.'

You son of perdition, thought Marshal. He did not trust Geoffrey as far as he could throw him. Nor did he like the sound of what he had just heard. Owain also looked unhappy. To connive and deal with rebel nobles against their own brother was a betrayal of the lowest kind. It could not be called treason, for it was not aimed at Henry, but it felt the same. And he, as servant to the Young King, was about to be dragged into the mire, willing or no.

Some hours later, Marshal was still in Geoffrey's tent. Erected with impressive speed, it was furnished in similar fashion to the Young King's.

Fresh-cut grass on the floor. A large bed with embroidered bolsters, silken sheets and a bearskin cover, and at its foot, an ornate iron storage chest. Geoffrey's hauberk hung from a stand; the helmet was perched on top, and the rest of his equipment piled at the base. A long table with a bench on either side filled much of the open space; it was at this the Young King, Geoffrey and Bertran de Born sat, heads bent together and cups of wine in hand.

They were all friends now, but it had not been so at the start. The Young King had stalked in, haughty as could be, and threatened to have the troubadour whipped. De Born had countered with a stinging remark. It had taken all of Geoffrey's skill to pour oil on the troubled waters, and a sincere apology from de Born, to ensure that peace was restored.

Positioned close to the entrance with de Béthune and Owain, the latter honourably doing his best not to listen in, Marshal was close enough to eavesdrop.

De Born explained how as a troubadour, he was welcomed by everyone from powerful barons to the constables of castles and the holders of minor fiefs. Through him, the nobles fomenting unrest in Aquitaine had a long reach indeed. And yet it seemed his efforts thus far had seen poor results.

At one point, de Born had declared, with dramatic strumming of his lute, 'I am making a sirvente against the cowardly barons, and you will never again hear me speak of them, for I have broken a thousand spurs in them without being able to make a single one run or even trot.'

The duke's ruthlessness in quelling previous rebellions appeared to have had a lasting effect, Marshal decided. Deep down, he was glad. Richard was not his master, but if all of Aquitaine rose up, even the king would not be able to bring the matter under control. Henry's realm would be weakened by the loss of such a swathe of territory, and it was France that would benefit. The king's relations with Philippe were currently cordial, but they could not be relied on.

Furthermore, de Born appeared convinced that with a little more effort, his labours would soon bear fruit.

'Can Hal not see how this meddling might affect him later?' Marshal whispered.

De Béthune shook his head. 'I know not. If there are still problems in Aquitaine when he takes the throne, Philippe will exploit them to the hilt.'

Hearing Geoffrey's voice, Marshal listened in again.

'In Limousin and Périgord, however,' said Geoffrey, with a meaningful look at the Young King, 'men who have risen against the house of Anjou before continue to hold deep grudges.'

'I am glad to say this is true.' Another flourish of the strings from de Born.

'Men like the Taillefers, brothers to the Count of Angoulême who died last year, are most unhappy,' Geoffrey went on. 'Richard has declared himself guardian of the Count's young daughter Matilda, when according to local custom, it is they who should have taken her into their care.'

'I would not be so unjust,' said the Young King. 'Nor so greedy.' As guardian of the child, Richard would collect and keep the profits from her large estates.

Geoffrey nodded. 'It is not in your nature, sire. Know that the Taillefers are not alone. Count Aimar of Limoges and the Count of Périgord would rejoice if you and I were to aid their cause.'

'They would willingly call you Duke of Aquitaine, sire,' added de Born. With a glance at Geoffrey, he said, 'I am told that King Philippe would recognise your title as well, sire. Are you not married to his sister already?'

This can only end in tears, thought Marshal. A glance at de Béthune showed he was of the same mind.

But Geoffrey's guile and silken way with words – aided and abetted by the equally persuasive de Born – soon saw the Young King hauled in like a salmon in a net.

Marshal was not over-surprised. His master had been deeply jealous these many years of Richard's position as Duke of Aquitaine, not to say his martial prowess and leadership abilities. Now the Young King had been presented with what seemed a God-given opportunity, with minimal initial risks and huge potential. Provide de Born with the monies to begin his work, and the royal brothers could sit back and see if their seeds fell on fertile soil.

The Young King appeared blind to the possible sequela, that his father's entire realm was also in danger. Few things affected his loyalty to his master, thought Marshal, but this was one of them.

De Béthune was quick to agree. 'Geoffrey is about to open Pandora's box.'

'And he cares not,' replied Marshal, frowning. 'I am minded of a malicious child, amused by chaos, even when it threatens the world around him.'

Like that, his mind was made up. To act was not a betrayal of the Young King, in the sense that his master would not be directly harmed. In the long run, he would even benefit. Marshal whispered his suggestion to de Béthune, who looked a little shocked, but agreed. He felt eyes on him, and realised that Owain was watching.

'Have you been listening?' asked Marshal.

Owain looked away.

'Well?'

'I have.'

'Like you what you heard?'

Owain met his gaze again. 'No.'

'Nor I,' hissed Marshal.

'There is little – nothing – we can do.'

Ah, but there is, Marshal thought, with a glance at de Béthune.

Richard shall know of this.

CHAPTER IX

A skein of lambswool clouds drifted over the Wye. The air was fresh and clean, and high above, a lark trilled. On the far bank of the river, the budding trees were bright with new leaf. In the nearby paddock, lush with spring grass, lambs bleated, and were answered by their mothers. Guided by a sturdy drover, four oxen pulled a plough in a neighbouring field. Mud covered the tilting ground, but that had not deterred Hugo, Reginald and I. Hard weather over the winter, including months of lying snow, had seen us confined to the bailey for our training. Now at last we could take turns riding at one another, and practise against the quintain.

Nigh on three full years had gone by since Duke Richard's visit to Striguil. To my great fortune, FitzWarin's death had been put down as an unfortunate accident. With Robert FitzAldelm and the majority of his cronies gone soon after, and Bogo with them, my life had become pleasant. True, I had had to endure the countess's punishments after Usk, but they had lasted only a season. Impressed by my obedience to the nagging steward – and in my mind, worn out by Isabelle's pleading – Aoife eased my restrictions in one fell swoop. Terrified that I would lose my freedom again, I stayed out of trouble from that juncture onward.

I had also set to training as never before. No longer did I have to rely on my friends' goodwill for a mount. Purchasing a destrier, a war horse, was still beyond me, but Richard's silver pennies allowed me to buy a solid rouncy. No great judge of horseflesh, I had bought him with Hugo's help. A spirited beast with a tidy, well-muscled chest and fine-contoured hindquarters, I named him Liath Macha, after the grey that had pulled the chariot of Cúchulainn, best friend of my namesake Ferdia. God and all His Saints, but I loved that horse. A more faithful beast no man could ask for.

There had also been enough in the duke's purse for a gambeson, pot helmet and shield, as well as a sword of my own, and with the last few coins, a tunic, shoes and dagger for Rhys. These last gave me as much pleasure as buying Liath Macha. Eyes bright with tears, gripping the knife as if it had been solid gold, Rhys had sworn himself my man to the end of his days. Already impressed by his fierce loyalty, and his dedication to whatever task he was set, I solemnly accepted his oath. A handspan taller than he had been, and a little less scrawny, Rhys went everywhere I went. Now he was in his usual place, by the quintain.

Hugo, Reginald and I were nearing the end of the competition that rounded off our training sessions. Hugo or Reginald tended to win most of the bouts, with Hugo having a slight edge. I languished in last place, but my successes were increasing, at what seemed a snail's pace. Despite this, I loved every moment. There is nothing quite like sitting astride a galloping war horse. And if riding down a rush ring target makes the heart race, I was to discover a charge at the enemy plucks it from his chest and places it, pounding, in his mouth.

That day one final tilt remained for each of us. Two points in the lead, Hugo's confidence had grown; he sat on his horse, poised, sure of victory. Reginald, whose best hope was to come joint second with me, had a face like a dried prune.

I could have whistled to Rhys. He would have 'accidentally' fallen to the ground as Hugo's horse neared the cross bar and the ring. Rhys was a master at shamming injuries. If it meant I would win, he would willingly hobble about for a few days afterwards to complete the deception.

No, I decided. Better to lose than win by cheating.

To hesitate would let my nerves at me again. I couched my lance, took aim and urged Liath Macha at the quintain. Together we thundered over the ground, man and horse working as one. I took the ring so cleanly it might have been as big across as a large plate. Reaching my friends, I dangled it in front of Hugo. 'Beat that, my friend,' I said, beaming.

To my delight, he did not.

Reginald struck well, almost allowing him to catch Hugo, but the victory was mine.

My friends congratulated me, and I grinned until my cheeks hurt. All was well with the world, I thought. The skill of riding with a lance seemed to be mine at last. I could fight in mail too, afoot or on Liath

Macha, and win more than I lost. Hugo and Reginald were solid friends, men whom I would shed my blood for. Rhys, loyal as a hound, was dear to me as family.

Family.

A pang of homesickness hit, followed by another of guilt.

I thought of my mother and father, and my brothers, whom I had not seen or heard from in three years.

And like that, God laughed. Or perhaps it was Lucifer, playing with me.

'A ship!'

The sentry's shout turned my head towards the Wye.

A sail marked with the de Clare colours was visible, moving slowly towards the same dock I had arrived on. In itself, the boat was unremarkable. Vessels like it arrived several times a month, carrying cargo and messages from the countess's castles along the coast. Only on occasion did they sail from Ireland. More interested in the wine I was due from my friends, and the platters of roasted meat served in my favourite inn, I put the ship from my mind.

Upon our return to the bailey, we unsaddled and watered our horses before giving them a good rub down. Hugo and Reginald had to care for their masters' mounts then, whereas I, still without a knight to serve, leaned against the stable wall and watched. It was customary for me to pass sarcastic remarks about the quality of their toil, and for them to suggest rudely that I stop lazing about like a wastrel and help. The banter was loud, and verging on bawdy. So young men, and even those a great deal older, act in company.

'Mother says it is ill-mannered to use such words.'

I turned to find Isabelle approaching. She was dressed in a gown of blue wool; fine leather shoes clad her feet. Cradled in one arm, she carried her latest acquisition, a tiny black and white kitten. More than a little embarrassed, hoping she had not heard the worst of it, I muttered, 'The countess is correct. Forgive me, my lady.'

She gave me an impish grin. 'I have listened in on far worse. The smith has a foul tongue; so too does the woodward.'

I chuckled, for she was right. 'Is your mother aware of your familiarity with these oaths?'

A withering look. 'Of course not.'

Changing the subject, I asked, 'Have you a name for the kitten yet?'

'My brother wants to call it Gilbert.' She paused, before adding indignantly, 'After himself.'

I smiled, for the name was also a common one for cats. 'But you do not.'

'No! He is mine, not my brother's.' She gave the kitten a loving stroke, and it answered with a purr remarkable for a creature of its diminutive size. 'I cannot decide between "Little Meow" and "Little Paws".'

'If he meows like he purrs, you had best call him "Big Meow",' I said.

'No.' Isabelle's self-confidence was even greater than when I had first met her.

'As you say, my lady, he is yours to name,' I said, reaching down to tickle under the kitten's chin. 'I am sure whatever your choice, it will suit him well.'

'Where is the steward?' The question was strident, the voice unknown to me.

We turned.

Through the main gate came striding a black-haired, good-looking man in a fur-trimmed, dark green mantle, and under it, a close-fitting crimson tunic. Long hose covered his legs; a sword and dagger swung from his belt. Perhaps a score and a half years old, he had the self-assured carriage of a knight. This was confirmed by the corpulent squire who hurried two paces to his rear. I had never seen either before, but something about the knight was familiar to me. I could not put my finger on it.

'Who is he?' asked Isabelle.

'I have no idea, my lady,' I answered, but then it came to me. 'A boat has just docked at the jetty. Mayhap he was aboard.'

'He seems in a terrible hurry.'

With the steward as yet nowhere to be seen, the new arrival's gaze had fallen on Hugo. Beckoning, the knight spoke a few words, and pointed to the great hall. Straining my ears, I caught the words 'the countess'.

Without as much as a glance at me or Reginald, Hugo clattered up the steps.

'I am going to see what is going on,' Isabelle declared, and followed.

It was not for me to run after her – whatever news the knight carried was likely to be for the steward and the countess alone – so I curbed my curiosity, and waited to hear what Hugo had to say on his return. I cast sidelong glances at the knight, who was pacing to and fro, all the while staring up at the hall. At length, I realised that what had caught my attention was his block-like head. I studied him more closely, recognising other features: the raven-black hair, and the prominent cheekbones. This was a relation of FitzAldelm's, I decided. A cousin, or more likely, an elder brother, and by the look of him, just as arrogant.

Hugo soon returned. Whatever he said was enough for the knight to take the stairs two at a time. His squire stayed behind.

Hugo came back to where Reginald and I were standing, announcing before we could ask, 'He is meeting with the countess. Some news from Ireland, it seems.'

My mind was still fixed on his identity. 'Is he a FitzAldelm?'

Hugo nodded. 'He is brother to your friend. Guy is his name.'

There was no reason for me to fear Boots and Fists' brother, yet my skin crawled. 'It must be pressing for him to seek her out with such urgency.'

'I heard nothing. The countess dismissed me the instant I had announced him. I would have lingered by the door, but the steward arrived. I had to walk away.' Hugo looked a little crestfallen.

'We shall find out if it is important. And if not?' Reginald shrugged. 'Wine is more on my mind, I can tell you.'

'We had best feed these horses then,' said Hugo, laying hold of a pitchfork. 'Let us to it.'

I joined my friends, for Liath Macha also needed his hay. They japed and carried on as they toiled, but my mind was churning like a mill wheel. News of the goings-on in Ireland reached me for the most part from crew members off the boats. Rare indeed was it that they had anything of worth to tell. Their information was pure tavern talk: reports of battles from Munster to Connacht to Leinster, and overblown accounts of intrigue between English lords and the Irish kings. I had long since decided that the tales had been jumbled and twisted by so many tellings that a man had no way of deciding what was truth and what fabrication.

The information FitzAldelm's brother carried seemed altogether different.

It would have nothing to do with me, I told myself. There was no reason on God's earth that it should, and yet unease plucked at me the way a dog worries a meaty bone.

I heard Isabelle calling me. There was an anxious note to her voice; she sounded on the verge of tears. Assuming that she had lost her kitten or something of that kind, I set down my pitchfork and left the stable, ready to lend my help.

She came down the stairs at breakneck speed. 'Ferdia!'

I hurried over. 'Where is Little Meow, my lady?'

She frowned. 'I left him with Gilbert.'

'Oh,' I said, feeling a little foolish. 'In that case, what has you hurrying so?'

'There has been a rebellion. And a big battle. Men have been killed.'

My fear surged, hovering over me like a great winged beast. 'Slow down, my lady. Where?'

'In Ireland. In Leinster.'

'Leinster is a big kingdom, my lady,' I said in a bluff tone.

'Rufus!' The summons came from the top of the steps.

My eyes lifted. The steward was watching me, his expression severe. In itself, that meant nothing, for the man possessed the humour of a stone, but combined with Guy FitzAldelm's urgency and Isabelle's upset, it signified much more.

'North Leinster,' said Isabelle in a whisper. 'Cairlinn.'

Blood draining from my face, I glanced down at her. 'Cairlinn?'

She nodded, and bless her, reached out to squeeze my hand.

'RUFUS!'

Giving Isabelle a sickly smile, I walked towards the stairs. My vision tunnelled. I remember the creak of the timber as I climbed, and the rough feel of the bannister. The jerk of the steward's chin, commanding me to follow, and his refusal to answer my questions.

At the far end of the hall, I spied FitzAldelm. He was standing before the countess, she seated on her great chair. As we walked towards them, our boots scuffed the floor rushes, and the scent of fresh herbs filled my nostrils. Odd, is it not, how the mind retains small, irrelevant details in times of such turmoil?

FitzAldelm's fierce-eyed look reminded me of an alaunt about to grapple a wild boar. He was like his brother in that regard as well, I decided. Aoife's face, normally open and pleasant, was closed and hard.

My belly twisted. Nothing good could come from this meeting.

'I bring you Rufus, my lady,' said the steward, and stepped to one side, leaving me exposed to Aoife and FitzAldelm's scrutiny. I bowed, wishing to be anywhere else but where I stood. Given the impossibility of that wish, I straightened my back and tried not to show my fear.

'There is grave news from Ireland,' said Aoife in French.

If she spoke in Irish, FitzAldelm would not understand, I thought, but this was not her main reason. The choice of language was to show her disapproval of me. 'What news, my lady?'

'Your father and brothers rose in rebellion against the crown,' said FitzAldelm, regarding me as if I were a dog turd on the sole of his shoe.

Remembering my father's words, I struggled to believe what I was hearing. Ambushes and unexpected attacks, yes, but not this. I stared back at FitzAldelm. 'That is odd news. When did it happen, sir?' I almost choked on the last word.

'Last month. They attacked their lord's keep in some force. Burned several villages too. Two knights were killed, one a good friend of mine.'

'My father did that?' I retorted.

'Yes,' snapped FitzAldelm. There was a flicker in his eyes I did not like.

'I do not believe you.'

'My brother was correct, it seems. Are you calling me a liar, *boy*?'

Aoife was frowning at me. I had to tread with care.

I hesitated, then said, 'My father was beaten once, sir. He took an oath of allegiance afterwards, and sent me here as hostage to ensure his loyalty. That he should rise up makes no sense. It would fail – and place my life in danger.'

'Be that as it may,' FitzAldelm said with a sneer, 'rebel he did, and your brothers with him. The unrest continued for close to a month. A good number of men-at-arms and Irishmen allied to the English cause were slain. Not until troops were sent from Dublin was peace restored.'

I shook my head. 'And my father? My brothers?'

An evil smile. 'Your brothers died first.'

The shock hit me like a fist to the face. It was the norm for noblemen to be taken prisoner, not slain. My voice shaking, I said, *'First?'*

'Yes, in the battle that broke your father's forces. He retreated to his stronghold with the remnants of his men. Car-linn, I think?' He mangled the word, deliberately, I would say, and added with lasciviousness,

'He and your mother perished when the settlement burned to the ground.' He smiled, a wolf's smile, and whispered so that only I might hear, 'I set the torch in the thatch myself.'

My head spun. There was a roaring in my ears. 'They are *all* dead?'

'Traitors deserve no better. You are the last of the family yet living.' The threat behind FitzAdelm's words was unmistakable.

My mouth opened like a fish. Thrown completely off balance, I had not even considered my own position. My eyes darted to Aoife, and I said, 'I have committed no crimes, my lady.' Nor had my father and brothers, I wanted to scream after. Something happened to make them rebel – it must have.

'You have not,' said the countess, her tone stern. 'Yet the same traitor's blood runs in your veins.'

Uncaring of my fate, I retorted, 'Are you going to have me executed, my lady? It is plain as the nose on my face that *he* wants that.' I jerked my chin contemptuously at FitzAdelm.

Aoife's gaze met mine.

Neither of us spoke.

She has the spine to order it done, I realised with a thrill of fear.

'It is true that FitzAldelm wants your head parted from your shoulders at the earliest opportunity.' Aoife paused, then said, 'I, however, am the countess of Striguil. It is I who shall decide what to do with you.'

Dark visions of the cell beneath the hall loomed, and despite myself, my resolve wavered. 'Am I to be imprisoned again, my lady?' I laid emphasis on the third last word to remind her of the unjust treatment I had received from the other FitzAldelm, Robert, Boots and Fists.

'I see no need.' Aoife's voice softened a little.

'My lady—' began FitzAldelm.

The countess cut him off with a gesture. 'Ferdia swore not to leave without permission before, and he has kept his word. His entire family is dead; it is time to be merciful.'

'Yes, my lady.' Even as FitzAldelm made a stiff little bow, he contrived to throw me a look of pure venom.

'You may go, Rufus,' said Aoife. 'You have permission to visit the priory, should you so wish.'

Grief burst into scarlet flame within me. Tears sprang to my eyes. Unable to speak, I bowed to the countess and retreated with what dignity remained to me.

FitzAldelm's stare lay heavy on my back all the way to the door.

CHAPTER X

In the days that followed there was no time to grieve, save in my blankets at night, or on my knees in the church. At all other times, I walled it in. Word of my family's treachery had spread like the plague. Under suspicion from almost everyone in Striguil, constantly watched, and followed if I left the castle, I also had FitzAldelm to contend with. First he took to loitering near wherever I was working. Loud, derogatory comments rained down on me and my friends. Rhys got a kick if he chanced to stray too close. When FitzAldelm discovered that I had no master to care for, he was swift to appoint me as his de facto second squire. His own, the corpulent, fat-lipped youth I had seen on their arrival, was happy to burden me with the lion's share of his work.

I could have protested to the steward or the countess, but I had toiled for many knights, and with my situation more precarious than it had ever been, silence seemed the wisest choice. If FitzAldelm had beaten me unfairly, I would have had grounds to approach the countess, but he was too wily for that. Instead he made barbed comments about my family, and found fault with everything I did. He would knock over his cup at table as I reached in with the jug, or hide the knife I had laid by his platter, and deride me to his comrades as an Irish lackwit without the brains to lay a place setting. Oh, he was a fox, that one. Now and again, when there was an audience, he would offer praise, saying that perhaps not all men were the same as their traitorous kin.

I grew to hate him, deciding that he was worse than his brother. Every night I dreamed of murder, but in the dawn my desire would be cooled by the need to find out more about my family, and the knowledge that if I laid a finger on him, summary retribution would be mine. I raged about the injustice of it to Hugo and Reginald, declaring that my father would never have risen up without good reason, that

FitzAldelm had to be lying about something. Without proof, they told me wisely, I could do nothing.

I gritted my teeth, and prayed to God. Yet Striguil, of recent times a pleasant place to live, had turned into Purgatory. I existed only to serve FitzAldelm, who had been appointed to the mesnie by Aoife. Unless he died or left the castle, or I did the same, years of suffering awaited me. I could find out nothing about my parents' fate either.

If it had not been for Rhys, I think I might have killed myself during that harrowing time. I would stand atop the palisade at night, remembering FitzWarin, and wanting to let myself fall the same way. I felt responsible for the boy, however, and realising that my death would force him back to his previous miserable existence, I would step back, telling myself that I could endure.

Hugo and Reginald were a great solace. They were unable to prevent FitzAldelm from singling me out, but the malevolent knight was not always with us. Many's the day those two finished the tasks I had been set, lightening not just my load but my spirits. They would insist I went with them to the training ground, and order me to imagine each of them as FitzAldelm while we sparred together. I never had to open my purse in the taverns. In short, they treated me like a brother, which is why my conscience still pricks me when I think of the manner of our parting.

Days turned into weeks, and weeks to a month. Each dawn, birdsong filled the air. Rain showers came and went. The weather grew warmer. In the fields, lambs gambolled, and calves drowsed contentedly in the sunshine. Ships from Ireland arrived, but there was little fresh news from Leinster. As far as I understood it, 'peace' had been restored to what had been my family's territory. Seized in the name of the countess, it was now under direct English control.

I often imagined returning there, and raising an army to seize it back, but it was a fool's dream. The bulk of my father's warriors were dead, the rest no doubt dispersed to the four winds. Parts of Ireland remained free, it was true, but almost every king had sworn allegiance to Henry. No warm welcome would be mine at their tables, no men and swords offered. Although the king of Ulster had not bent the knee to Henry, his previous refusal to answer my father's call for aid made it improbable that he would help me, an orphan whose only follower was a Welsh urchin.

The bitter truth was that nothing remained for me in Ireland save my family's graves and the ignominy of seeking out my last living kin, relations of my mother in Meath. Even if they accepted me, which was by no means certain, I would be doomed to the life of a 'hearth knight', the term for a younger son with no land or inheritance, who was forced to stay at home and work for his keep.

Better the devil you know, the saying goes, and it is true. Striguil had become my home. FitzAldelm did his best to make my life a misery, but like a yoked ox beaten by his cruel master, I learned to trudge on regardless. My strength of will helped, and my desire for revenge. I had Rhys, Hugo and Reginald, and Isabelle too. The stout cook whose son I resembled continued to be kind; there were others as well, who had forgotten about my father's treachery, or who simply did not care about news from Ireland.

Odd as it may sound, I also wanted to stay close to FitzAldelm. Only through him could I discover what had happened in Cairlinn on the terrible day both my parents had perished. If I fled Striguil, our paths would never cross again. Stay, and some chance, however unlikely, existed for me to learn the truth.

Everything changed one fine evening in late April, when a messenger arrived. He bore another request from Duke Richard for troops, both knights and men-at-arms. Rich prizes could be had on campaign and on the tourney circuit over the Narrow Sea, so it was no surprise that FitzAldelm was among those petitioning the countess for permission to go. I decided to follow him, because to watch my parents' murderer ride away would be worse than eternal damnation. Somewhere along FitzAldelm's route to the port of Southampton, I thought, a chance would present itself to catch him off guard and force a confession. If that failed, I would follow him over the sea and wait for another opportunity. I gave no consideration to the cost of the passage for myself, Rhys and Liath Macha, or of how we would provide for ourselves in another land.

My departure had to be kept secret. Only Rhys could know, because I was taking him with me. Sad though it was, Hugo, Reginald and Isabelle must remain ignorant, in case they inadvertently gave me away. In truth I kept silent because they would have seen my strategy for what it was, that of someone whose wits have entirely left him.

A lackwit.

*

The countess gave Guy FitzAldelm leave to go a sennight after the arrival of Richard's summons. He and his squire left at once. I was anxious to go after them, but deciding it best to depart in a normal fashion, waited until the following day. I needed Liath Macha and my equipment, which meant a pretence of going to the tilting ground. Hugo and Reginald nearly always accompanied me there, so I had to wait until they were occupied and I was not. The revelation that I was not going to help – as they had so often done for me, I was reminded – did not impress my friends. Wishing I could tell them the truth, I promised both a few drinks by way of recompense, and took my leave.

Rhys and I were at the main gate when Isabelle called to me from the walkway above. Of her nurse there was no sign, as usual. She was forever running off on her own, fishing in the river, watching the young stock in the fields or as she was now, spying on the world from one of the best vantage points in Striguil.

Guilt swelled within me as I raised a hand. Despite the suspicion that had fallen on me, she had remained my friend. She even believed my hunch about FitzAldelm, and had, albeit unwillingly, accepted that her mother would disregard my claim. Leaving without saying farewell felt bad enough; now I would have to lie my way out of the castle. 'My lady.'

'Are you for the tilting ground?'

I nodded, praying that Rhys, transparent as the finest linen, did not give us away.

'Where are Hugo and Reginald?'

'Still at their labours, my lady.'

She frowned. 'Why are you not helping them?'

Ah, womenkind. Their nose for what is unspoken has ever amazed me. 'They are almost done, my lady.'

'You usually go down together.'

'We do, my lady, but today I grew impatient waiting for them.' Feeling awkward, worried that I would do or say something out of the ordinary, I took a step towards the gate.

'I will come with you then,' she declared, making for the stairs. 'Wait.'

Stricken, I shot a glance at Rhys and saw my horror mirrored in his face. I could not order Isabelle to stay behind, and I dared not risk her seeing me leave. There was no certainty that another chance would come my way either, and with each day that passed, FitzAldelm would draw further ahead. I *had* to leave now.

'Lady Isabelle!'

The nurse's summons could not have been more opportune.

As was her wont, however, Isabelle ignored it, and made her way towards us. Relief filled me when the nurse spied her from the door of the great hall, and hurled down a barrage of scolds and threats that could not be denied. Defeated, Isabelle made a point of coming to stroke Liath Macha before she turned tail. 'It is very warm to practise at the quintain in armour,' she said, glancing at the waxed leather roll containing my hauberk. Sharp-eyed, she had seen it lashed behind my saddle.

'Hugo, Reginald and I are to have a few bouts against each other on foot later,' I said, lying through my teeth.

'In this heat?' She gestured at the sun, which was directly overhead.

'Ah . . . yes, my lady.'

'Lady Isabelle!'

'If you are not careful, poor Liath Macha will get heatstroke.'

'I shall take care he does not, my lady, never fear.'

'Be sure you do, or I will never forgive you.'

'My lady.' I hid my sorrow by bowing my head, and thought, you will never forgive me anyway.

Half a month passed. I will not relate every twist and turn of the tale. Suffice it to say that Rhys and I had a hard time of it. We escaped Striguil simply enough, but thereafter good luck deserted us. Forced by my lack of coin to ride around the Severn estuary rather than take a ship across it as FitzAldelm had done, we made slow progress. Things were made no better on the second day when Liath Macha lost a shoe, necessitating a search for a forge. Sensing my desperation, the smith charged me the extortionate price of a silver penny to reshoe him. The weather turned, sending torrential downpours that drenched us to the skin, and turned the rough roads into quagmires. We battled on, sleeping in the woods, and existing on cheese and bacon that Rhys had stolen from the castle kitchen, and the occasional loaf I bought from a village bakery. The oats we had brought lasted Liath Macha for several days, but after that he had to rely on what grazing we could find, for my purse was almost empty.

Worst of all, we had seen neither hide nor hair of FitzAldelm and his squire. The lead they had on us was too great to make up. There was little chance of catching him before Southampton, but I did not turn back. Staying in the castle would have condemned me to a slow, living death. There could be no return, not even if the price was my own life.

Rhys, bless his heart, never questioned my leadership. To him the journey, difficult though it was, seemed a great adventure. His belief bolstered my own flagging confidence more than once. A great scavenger, he proved his worth over and again, stealing eggs from hen coops, and once a lump of smoked ham hanging in an outhouse. His finest prize, however, was a fresh-cooked beef pie lifted from a table just inside a baker's premises.

These successes were the exception rather than the rule, I regret to say, and by the time we neared Southampton, we were a sorry-looking pair. Gaunt-cheeked, I unshaven, and both of us in travel-stained clothing, we resembled vagabonds of the worst kind. Poor Liath Macha's ribs showed, and his coat had a staring quality to it, as if he were ill.

Our final camp was in a small glade, deep in the woods. It had not rained overnight, a blessing, and the fire I had lit the previous evening was easily rekindled when we climbed from our blankets. I knew from asking directions at a farm a day earlier that Southampton was about ten miles away. Breakfasting on a raw egg each, all that Rhys had managed to pilfer that morning, I took stock of our situation. A thought I had not even considered before leaving Striguil was weighing on my mind.

Ill-dressed, young to own a fine horse and war kit, I was liable to be taken for a thief when we reached Southampton. Suspicious looks had already been thrown my way by those we had encountered on the roads. If I were accused, telling the truth – that Duke Richard had rewarded my bravery at Usk with the armour and a heavy purse – would either meet with total disbelief, further questioning that would expose me as a fugitive, or both.

'Are you ready, sir?' Rhys's face was eager. His mind, no doubt, was on the hot food I had promised him later.

I did not answer, for my resolve was wavering. Perhaps there was no need to enter Southampton, I thought. FitzAldelm might be halfway to Aquitaine by now. Even if he had not embarked, there would be no chance of setting upon him in the crowded streets. I would have to follow him over the Narrow Sea. My fingers closed around my feather light purse, and I cursed. We could not afford the passage.

I looked at Rhys, waiting expectantly, and shame filled me. I was no kind of master. Penniless, purposeless, I felt like a rudderless ship in a storm. I cared little for myself, but Rhys deserved better.

'What is it, sir?'

'We need coin to cross the sea.'

'Can we steal it, sir? I am good at lifting things, as you know. Mayhap I can find silver in the farmhouses roundabout.'

'It is one thing to take food when we are hungry, Rhys, and another to rob coin. Before we knew it, the hue and cry would be raised, and if we were caught—' I made a chopping gesture over my right wrist, and then my ear, and Rhys winced. 'To be maimed like that would ruin your life and mine,' I finished.

'Could we work for a farmer? Liath Macha can pull a plough, and you and I will toil in the fields.'

'It would take a month or more to earn enough. FitzAldelm will be long gone.'

'But you know where he is bound, sir: Aquitaine. Can we not follow on after?'

I sucked on the marrow of that. Rhys had a point. Aquitaine was a large region, but presumably finding the duke's army would not prove over-hard. Another possibility, that of selling Liath Macha or my hauberk, was too painful to contemplate. Letting out a sigh of resignation, I said, 'I suppose that is our best course, for I can see no other way forward.'

Liath Macha, tethered on a long rope that he might graze, whickered.

Aware that I had been paying no attention to our surroundings, I glanced in his direction. He was pacing to and fro, stamping his hooves. Unease pricked me. 'To Liath Macha,' I said in a low voice. 'Quickly. Untie him and get on his back. I will be a step behind you.'

Sensing my urgency, Rhys obeyed without question. I lifted the heavy roll containing my hauberk, and scooped up my pot helm. Thanking God that my sword was on my belt, I hurried after Rhys, for the moment abandoning our blankets, my saddle and the rest of our poor possessions.

We had not quite reached my horse when a voice cried in English, then French, 'Hold!'

I looked over my shoulder and came to an abrupt halt. 'Rhys.'

He did not hear, or chose not to, and kept on towards Liath Macha.

'Take another step, boy, and I will put an arrow in your back,' said the voice, reverting to English.

The threat needed no translation. Rhys stopped. Three figures emerged from between the trees. They came singly, from different angles, each holding a drawn bow. It was the first time I had stared at the sharp ends of arrows, with unfriendly faces behind. I did not soil myself, but my bowels turned to liquid.

'Move when I say,' I said to Rhys in Irish, a language he understood. 'Do not run.'

'What barbarous tongue is that?' The nearest of the three was short, and cadaverously thin. His skin was stretched tight over his bones, so that he was all angles and joints, like an insect. 'It is not French.'

My English was poor, but I had some, learned from merchants who had come to Striguil's spring and harvest fairs. 'It was Irish. That is where I am from, friend. The boy is Welsh.'

'Irish and Welsh?' The first man cocked his head at his companions, one of whom was as fat as he was thin, and the other a pox-scarred youth with a cast in one eye. 'And here we was, thinking you was Norman, what with your fine horse and all.' He spat a great gob of phlegm, showing his opinion of those who ruled the land, and came prowling closer.

'We were just on our way,' I said, hoping against hope that we could extricate ourselves from the situation.

'Were 'ee indeed?' asked the fat one, gazing down his arrow at me.

'Aye,' I said. Without taking my gaze from the fat man, I added in Irish, 'Rhys, untie Liath Macha.'

Rhys took a step forward, and the thin man transferred his aim from me to him, and said in a silky tone quite at odds with his rough appearance, 'Move again, and you die.'

'Rhys, *stop*.' I glared at the thin man, and said, 'He is only a boy. Do not hurt him.'

'If he tries to loose the horse, I will slay him, as God is my witness.'

'Yon beast is worth a pretty sum.' The fat man had lowered his bow a fraction and was walking towards Liath Macha, who, not knowing him, pranced away as far as the rope would permit.

'The helmet will sell too, and your sword.' The youth spoke for the first time, English like his companions. His arrow tip moved to point at the leather roll over my shoulder. 'What is in there?'

It was irrelevant who we were, I decided, battling panic. They were going to take everything of worth; indeed, we would be lucky to escape with our lives.

'He asked you a question.' The thin man released the tension on his bowstring that he might grip bow and still-nocked arrow with his left hand, and reached out with his right to prod at my burden. Its weight was obvious at once, and his eyes lit up. 'He has a hauberk!'

His companions' gaze filled with greed – everyone knew the value of such armour – and the last of my hope teetered on a cliff edge of despair. Without horse, armour or weapon, I would be no better than a landless peasant. As for my pursuit of Guy FitzAldelm, well, it would become an even madder quest than it already was. Better to fight, I decided, than meekly to accept such a fate.

'I will have that,' said the thin man, tugging at the heavy leather bundle.

'Rhys, run!' I shouted in Irish. 'Save yourself!'

Trusting that he would obey, I jerked my shoulder, shoving the mail at the thin man. Unprepared for its great weight, he could not stop it falling on his foot, nor avoid my punch to the face. I hit him so hard his jaw clacked shut. He staggered back a step, and I made a lunge for his bow. It was a mistake; he somehow retained a fierce grip on it. We grappled; I punched him again, left and right, short but brutal blows to the belly. He bellowed like a wounded bull; still he would not release his bow. I grabbed for his dagger instead. Tugging it free, I planted it in his guts and let him fall, screaming now, to the ground.

Remembering the other ruffians, my guts churned. I threw myself on top of my victim. A shaft hissed overhead, through the space I had just been in. I felt no relief, just bubbling fear that the next arrow would spit me through and through. I squirmed over the moaning thin man, trying simultaneously to put him between me and whichever of his companions was shooting at me, and to divest him of his weapon.

An arrow thumped into the thin man, narrowly missing my hand, which had grasped his bow. He screamed, a high-pitched mewl that set my teeth on edge. I had the bow now, which was a start, and yet, flailing for a shaft, I knew it was all too slow. The next arrow was already being aimed at me. It would skewer my flesh long before I managed to get up, nock and loose.

An iron-tipped death did not arrive.

Instead I heard an impact, a crack such as a stone makes when it connects with bone, and an instant after, an outraged shriek. I had no idea who had been hit. I did not know if one, two, or even more ruffians were aiming at me. Utterly terrified, hoping that Rhys had run off, I threw myself up and looked around, at the same time fumbling an arrow onto the string of the thin man's bow.

Another crack, a second cry of pain.

I stared in astonishment at the pox-scarred youth, who clutched at the side of his head. Fifteen paces behind him, Rhys capered, his right arm drawing back to hurl another stone.

That enemy was occupied, momentarily at least. My head twisted. I took in the fat man, twenty paces away, arrow pointed straight at me. I swear my heart almost burst from my ribs, so great was my fear. Sure that Death was about to take me, I froze.

There was a rush of air, and the fat man let out a surprised gasp.

I blinked. A shaft feathered his chest – shot by whom, I had no idea.

He toppled, and I spun, desperate to save Rhys from the youth. I had not quite taken aim when another arrow punched my intended victim between the shoulder blades. He went down and did not move again. Beyond him, I spied Rhys, white-faced, but seemingly unhurt. I had never been so glad in my life.

'Did you see where those shafts came from?' I called.

Wordlessly, he pointed behind me.

Flesh crawling, for I did not know if the unseen bowman also meant us harm, I turned.

A tall, hooded figure stepped from behind a beech. He held a mighty war bow at full draw, an arrow ready to loose. 'There were but three?' he asked in French.

Confused, for I had not met a French speaker since leaving Striguil, I answered, 'I think so, friend.' Reverting to Irish, I said, 'Rhys, have you seen any others?'

'No, sir,' he answered, quick as a flash.

The tall man paced closer, gaze raking the trees and undergrowth. Only when he had satisfied himself did his weapon lower.

'The boy and I owe you our lives, sir,' I said. 'Thank you.'

Intense blue eyes regarded me from under the hood. 'I had hoped to hunt deer this day, not men.'

I felt an odd tickle of recognition. I peered closer. 'Might I know your name, sir?'

'God's legs – *you*!' The hood was swept back, revealing a familiar mane of reddish-gold hair. 'What are you doing in these woods, Rufus the Irishman?'

Robbed of speech, I dropped to one knee and bent my head. My life had been saved not by an English landowner, but by Duke Richard himself. I had thought him in Aquitaine, but here he was, larger than life.

A strong hand gripped my shoulder. 'Rise.'

I stood, gripping my bow. 'Thank you, sire.' A wave of emotion swept through me, and I added, 'But for you, we would both be dead.'

Richard's eyes creased at the corners. 'The boy is a fine shot with a stone. He was holding his own, which is more than I can say for you.'

Cheeks burning, I hung my head.

A warm laugh. 'I jest with you, Rufus. You had three enemies, all bowmen. That you were still breathing when I arrived is a testament to your determination.'

'Sire.' I ducked my head, feeling even more self-conscious.

'Sir!'

Rhys's cry made me look over Richard's shoulder. There, at the edge of the clearing, was another figure with a levelled bow. His arrow would take Richard in the back. I planted a shoulder in the duke's chest, who, unsuspecting, was unable to stop me driving him to the side. Unbalanced, we fell, I on top of Richard. He snarled with surprise and anger, even as I heard the shaft pass overhead. Oblivious to my own safety, desperate that the man who had saved my life should not die, I jerked upright. Somehow the bow remained in my left hand, and although the arrow had come off the string, I was still holding its far end against the stave.

I fumbled to nock the arrow, glanced up at the bowman, and for the second time in as many moments, stared at my own death.

Crack! A howl of pain, and my enemy staggered backwards.

God bless you, Rhys, I thought.

I drew. Took aim. Loosed.

It was one of the finest shots I ever made. My arrow deep in his left eye-socket, the bowman dropped. Worried there might be more ruffians, I helped the duke to his feet, begged a shaft of him, and together we patrolled the clearing. Rhys bobbed about beside us, a fresh stone in his fist.

Before long, it was clear that any remaining ruffians had fled. The duke's huntsmen arrived with a red-tongued, panting mob of hounds. Half a dozen knights and squires also appeared. The reason for Richard's presence in England became clear as I listened to his banter with the knights. Once again he had come from Aquitaine to find soldiers. Awaiting a northern lord who was marching to the coast, he had decided to spend the day hunting.

Richard ordered the hounds set on the ruffians' trail. When the barking and shouts of encouragement from the huntsmen had died away, he turned once more to me. 'It seems now that I am in *your* debt.' With a look at Rhys, he added, 'And yours, boy.'

Rhys puffed his chest up like a fighting cock. Embarrassed, I said, 'I did what any man would do, sire.'

'How many fights have you been in, apart from the fight in Wales?' Richard's expression was keen.

'One, sire.' Do not let him ask who it was I fought, I prayed, for it had been against the English, during the defence of my family's territory.

'I have taken part in a score and a half. Skirmishes and sieges for the most part, but also a set-piece battle. Let me tell you that not every man will risk his life for another. It takes rare courage.' Richard thrust out his hand. 'We are brothers now. Brothers-in-arms.'

I stared at his great paw. Even-cut nails. Fine blond hairs on its back. Callouses on palm and fingers from sword-use. No ring to mark his status. It was the hand of a warrior, not a duke. The fact that it belonged to the son of the man in whose name my family's lands had been taken, occurred to me not at all. Smiling from ear to ear, I took the grasp and said, 'Brothers-in-arms, sire.'

True knight that he was, Richard summoned Rhys and with great solemnity, shook his hand also.

'God's legs,' he declared – as I was to learn, this was one of his favourite sayings – 'but I am famished. There is nothing like a fight to whet a man's appetite. Are you hungry?'

'Yes, sire,' Rhys said before I could. He continued in his bad French, 'We have not eaten today. Rufus said we could fill our bellies in Southampton.'

'You shall do that and more, in my own tent. For now, there is bread and cheese,' said Richard with a laugh, calling to a servant that the boy was in need of food. Rhys vanished, his face alight with anticipation. And then it came, the inevitable question, the one I had been dreading. Frowning, the duke asked, 'What was your purpose in Southampton?'

Indecision, and not a little fear, battered me. Even if Richard believed my accusations, FitzAldelm would deny them, and he was the anointed knight, not I. For now at least, I decided, the duke must remain ignorant of my reason. That left but one option.

'I came to offer you my service, sire,' I said.

Those intense blue eyes bore down on me again. 'I thought as much. Did the countess Aoife grant you permission to seek my employ?'

I shook my head. 'No, sire.'

'Again you left Striguil without permission,' he said with a full-throated chuckle. 'Ah, the Irish. Strong-minded some would say. Bull-headed, others.'

My spirits fell, and I thought, he will send me back to Aoife, tail between my legs. Allowing me to join in the relief of Usk was one thing. To take me over the sea was quite another.

'Are you not a hostage for the good behaviour of your family in Ireland?'

'They are all dead, sire.' Before Richard could ask, terrified that the real reason would also see me sent away, I added, 'The plague took them.'

'That is a tragedy. You have my sympathy.'

'Thank you, sire.' I had risked everything by lying, and yet, I decided, there was no way to tell the truth without exposing myself as the last of a traitorous line. Now I had to continue the deception. 'Our lands were small, and there is nothing left for me there. In your service, sire, I hoped I might advance myself.'

'And so you might. I accept your offer, Rufus. Henceforth, you shall be one of my squires.'

Head spinning at my good fortune, I knelt again. Richard took my proffered hands within his. I swore to be faithful, and to follow his orders. In return he pledged his own loyalty and protection. Then he raised me to my feet, and gave me an approving nod.

I grinned like a fool. It did not seem real. In the course of an hour, I had gone from starveling fugitive to near death, and now I had taken service with the Duke of Aquitaine. Head spinning with delight, I imagined a glorious future. Knighted on the field, I would win glory and riches beyond measure.

'A knight from Striguil arrived some days hence,' said Richard. 'Were you following him?'

The realisation of what I had done hit me like an iron bar. God in Heaven, I thought, please, no. 'In a manner of speaking, sire.'

'No doubt you are friendly with his squire. Seek him out in the camp.'

'Yes, sire,' I said, trying to sound enthusiastic. Inside, however, I was close to panic.

FitzAldelm would denounce me the instant we locked eyes.

CHAPTER XI

A mile from the castle at Tours, William Marshal was standing on the threshold of an inn. One of the lower-class hostelries in the town, it went by the unoriginal name of The Sheaf of Wheat. A light drinker, Marshal was not fond of such establishments, but they formed an intimate part of soldiers' lives, and during his time in the Young King's service, he had spent many a night in one. His presence would not arouse suspicions, he told himself, lifting the latch. A leather hood covered his head, and his oldest tunic and hose turned him into any other tradesman.

The usual sounds filled his ears: loud voices, bursts of song, and the clatter of plates. Behind him, a dog barked in the stable yard, and an ostler shouted a curse in response. As the door creaked open, the smells came: wine and roasting meat, and underneath, a strong whiff of sweat. Marshal concealed his distaste. Gaze raking the dimly lit room for the messenger he hoped to meet, potential trouble, and the best place to sit, he weaved a path between the wooden tables and benches. Old strands of cut grass covered the floor, laced here and there with shards of broken crockery and half-eaten pork bones. Dogs, large and small, sprawled asleep by their owners' feet. Finding a table at the very back, he sat down with his back to the wall.

Marshal would have preferred the meeting to have been private, but that was easier said than done. He quartered with the Young King at the castle. Busy every hour of the day, with inquisitive eyes by the score, it was out of the question. In other towns there were merchants with whom he had done business, men who would turn a blind eye to a quiet gathering on their premises, but not, frustratingly, here. This place would have to do, he decided, careful not to let his attention linger on anyone. Already a pair of evil-looking types were staring.

Their designs, on his purse no doubt, were of less concern than that he might be recognised. It was vital that his business remained secret. Thankfully, he could be sure that the pair were not followers of the Young King. *He* had thrown a feast that afternoon, a reward for the many ransoms won at the Lagny-sur-Marne tourney, which meant that every knight, squire, man-at-arms, and archer who served him was within the castle. Apart from me, thought Marshal, amused. De Béthune had wanted to come as well, but they had agreed the risk was too great. One well-known knight might venture unseen into the town, but not two.

Ordering a jug of house wine from a sloe-eyed, once-attractive serving woman, he chuckled at her declaration it was the best vintage to be had in Tours, and pretended not to hear her throaty comment that she was also of fine quality. Often tavern women plied two trades, the first serving food and drink, the second customers' sexual needs. Even if Marshal had not had an important meeting, he would have avoided the opportunity. Unless a man paid, he risked disease, and this tavern was not home to such quality.

The wine arrived; it was both weak and sour, reminding Marshal of the king's court, famous for stuff so vile it had to be drank through clenched teeth. Raising the cup to his mouth in an impression of drinking, he monitored the room. Nothing was out of the ordinary. Men were playing dice, eating, throwing back drinks, holding shouted conversations. A florid-faced troubadour strummed popular tunes on a lute. Two alaunts squared up to each other. But for the roars of the keen-eyed landlord, which forced their sullen owners to leash them, a full-scale battle would have begun. Customers left; new ones entered. None seemed like the man he hoped to meet, one of Duke Richard's followers.

Not that he would recognise the fellow, thought Marshal with an uncharacteristic twist of his guts. If he came, that was: there was no certainty Richard would reply to his letter warning of the Young King's and Geoffrey's plot. Marshal's clerk had written it the very same evening the two had met Bertran de Born. Any answer was to be sent to this inn, this night or either of the following two. He would be sitting at the back of the room, with his hood up. The messenger was to ask for the man with one eye, and the correct answer was, 'He was my father.' Whether Richard knew of his father John's partial blinding by molten lead as he hid in a burning church tower during the civil war forty-odd years before, Marshal did not know, but it had amused him to insert the question in the letter.

Time passed. The bells of the nearby abbey tolled compline. It appeared likely that the messenger was not coming. Perhaps he would arrive on the morrow. Or not at all, Marshal's doubting side added. Richard wants no dealings with the likes of you, a close companion of the Young King. Marshal suppressed his concerns. He had done what he could, and the duke would respond – or not. Growing hungry, he ordered pottage, a staple dish in every tavern. His hunch that it would be good proved correct. Made with onions, leeks and spices, it even had a few lumps of pork. He set to with a will.

Floorboards creaked. A shadow darkened the table edge.

Alarmed, for his attention had been solely on his bowl, Marshal looked up.

A stocky man stood over him. Although his cloak was spattered with mud, it was triple-dyed, a mark of real quality. Bulges in its folds at waist level revealed the presence of a sword and dagger.

Uncomfortably aware that he had only his knife, Marshal dipped his chin in greeting. 'Do I know you, friend?'

'No, sir. I am seeking the man with one eye.'

Relief filled Marshal. 'He was my father.'

A part smile, and in a quiet tone, 'Then you are William Marshal.'

'I am. And you, sir?'

'John de Beaumont.'

They shook hands, and Marshal gestured at the bench on the opposite side of the table. 'Please, sit.' By his manners and dress, de Beaumont was a knight. That augured well, he hoped.

The newcomer eased himself down with a pleased sigh.

Marshal clicked his fingers and the sloe-eyed serving woman brought another cup, and a plate of bread and cheese. He said, 'My apologies for the wine. It is poor.'

'No matter. It was a long ride; I have not eaten or drunk since noon. The last two hours I rode in darkness, a hand ever on my sword.' De Beaumont drained the cup, then attacked the food.

Marshal burned to ask for his message, but courtesy held him back. When the other was done, he leaned over the table. 'You carry word from the duke?'

'I do.' De Beaumont's gaze was direct. 'When first he received your letter, he was inclined not to believe its contents. Reminded that Marshal had sent it, he considered the matter again. "He is a man of his word, it is well known," the duke said.'

'I am.' Not for the first time, Marshal was glad of the reputation he had worked years to build.

'The duke thanks you for your warning.'

De Beaumont did not elaborate, and Marshal thought, I am not to be told of his response to Geoffrey and the Young King's machinations. It was not surprising: he had revealed their purpose, but he was also in the enemy camp.

'He also asks why you would betray your master.' De Beaumont's tone was no longer friendly.

Marshal had been expecting this. 'A fair question, if betraying him is what I do.'

'I fail to see how else the Young King would view you meeting with one of Duke Richard's men in secret.'

'And yet here you are.'

'Indeed. Know, however, that I am full ready to get up and walk away if your answer proves unsatisfactory.'

'I remain loyal to the Young King,' said Marshal, careful to keep his tone even despite his rising temper. 'Gladly would I lay down my life in his defence. I will always act so, while there is breath in my body, or in his.'

'And yet?'

'And yet his current path is one of folly. A blind man could see it, but not he. If Aquitaine shears away, other parts of Henry's realm will follow. Brittany, the Vexin – who knows where it would end? And all the while, Philippe Capet will be circling, like a hawk over carrion. I seek merely to prevent that chaos.' Marshal's words had been heartfelt. If they did not convince de Beaumont, he thought, nothing would.

'I believe you.'

Relieved, Marshal threw back a mouthful of the wine, scarcely noticing its acidity.

'Have you any other news?'

Marshal had no qualms describing the events since his letter. Geoffrey was back in Brittany. De Born had set out on his mission, and sent back word that Count Aimar and the Taillefer brothers were already recruiting mercenaries.

'These are worrying tidings,' said de Beaumont. 'If there are further developments—'

'Anything that threatens the king's realm I will pass on,' said Marshal, laying emphasis on 'the king's'.

De Beaumont nodded his thanks. After a short silence, he said, looking a little uneasy, 'Rumours have reached the duke's ears.'

Irritation prickled Marshal. 'Make your meaning plain.'

'About you and the Young King's wife.'

Startled, for he had hoped the story was confined to the Young King's court, Marshal hissed, 'They are lies! Not a word is true!'

'I believe you, sir, and so does the duke, but if word of it has travelled to Aquitaine . . .'

'Gossip has ever spread faster than the plague,' said Marshal, shaking his head angrily. 'Queen Marguerite and I are on friendly terms, nothing more.' It was the truth. Although the queen was attractive, and the Young King often more interested in life on the tourney circuit than his wife, Marshal was far too shrewd to risk his position. He had little trouble deciding who might be behind the rumours: d'Yquebeuf and de Coulonces. It could not go unanswered, thought Marshal, worry nipping him. Quite how to respond, he was not sure. The lies his enemies were spreading would be precious hard to undo.

'If your place in the Young King's mesnie is threatened, you know where to come.' De Beaumont pushed back the bench and stood. 'The duke holds you in high regard.'

It was hard to imagine ever serving Richard – the Young King would take the throne when Henry died, and only a fool would throw away the opportunity to rise with him – but Marshal had never liked to shut a door that might be left ajar. 'Please thank the duke for his offer, and say that I will remember it.'

De Beaumont inclined his head. 'Until we meet again, sir.'

'Farewell,' Marshal replied.

De Beaumont called to one of the serving women. 'I need a room.' Catching her pouting look, he added, 'Just a room.'

Left alone, Marshal gave little consideration to the Young King's plotting with Geoffrey and de Born. Instead he brooded on his own position. It was a considerable shock that he should be so threatened.

He had personally trained the Young King to fight. Had knighted him, and with de Béthune, been one of his closest companions for more than a decade. Despite these strong bonds, Marshal knew that few barbs sank deeper into a man's heart than the accusation of a trusted friend conducting an affair with his wife.

Ribald laughter dragged him from his reverie. Still wary of being noticed, he glanced about the room. Loud guffaws two tables from his proved to be the source. He had not seen the men before; they must have arrived during his conversation with de Beaumont. Hard-faced, crop-haired, they were speaking in a guttural tongue he recognised as Flemish. Eyeing their gambesons and weapons, he judged them to be Brabançons, fierce mercenaries from east of Flanders.

Suspicious, for such men did not arrive in a place by accident, he tried to listen in on what they were saying. The clamour was too great. He sat for a short while, frustrated, considering his options. The wisest choice was to leave, and make his way back to the castle. Trying to eavesdrop risked being recognised. The Brabançons' presence deeply troubled him, however. Over the years, the Young King had often made use of them; Marshal had led, and fought beside the mercenaries.

He decided that with de Beaumont gone, the peril of discovery was worthwhile. Hood still up, he began a weaving path towards their table, that of the man who has had too much to drink and knows it, who is making every effort to appear sober while failing miserably.

Marshal had spent enough time around Brabançons to pick up some of their language. As he drew closer, he strained his ears. The talk was a mix of crude jokes, complaints about the wine, and predictions of the number of flea bites they would each have after a night spent at the inn. Coming alongside the table, he affected a stumble that took him to one knee. The closest Brabançons jeered. Keeping his gaze directed at the floor, he slurred an apology and 'struggled' to his feet.

Their attention moved on.

'They say the Young King will need thousands of us,' said one mercenary. 'Duke Richard's army may be small, but it is full of veterans. They will offer no easy victory.'

'He has no idea what is about to happen.' A second voice had joined in. 'Half of Aquitaine will be ablaze ere he has assembled his men.'

'The quicker the rebellion starts, the better, I say,' said a third. '*That* is when the real riches are to be had!'

Much laughter and pounding of cups on the table ensued.

Sick to the stomach, Marshal walked away. He knew from experience what the Brabançons did. Desecrators of churches and abbeys, defilers of women and girls, murderers of anyone who came within reach of their infamous long spears, they were the lowest form of humankind he had ever encountered.

Worse than their presence in the tavern, and the talk of rebellion, were the reasons behind. The Young King, or someone acting on his orders, had summoned them. No other explanation was possible, and Marshal felt a sharp sense of betrayal. This was the first time in years that his master had acted without telling him. Again suspicion pricked him that d'Yquebeuf and de Coulonces were behind it.

War was afoot, that was sure, for his master was already assembling his army. No doubt Geoffrey was doing the same in Brittany. John de Beaumont would have to be informed, so that Richard was aware, for these men could soon be ravaging Aquitaine.

Marshal had worries closer to home as well.

His position by the Young King's side had never felt more uncertain.

CHAPTER XII

It was getting on for evening when the duke ordered us back to Southampton. He was in fine mood, having shot a broad-shouldered stag with sixteen points on his antlers. Two more deer and a wild boar brought down by his knights added to the kill. Richard's catch was borne behind his horse by huntsmen, its hooves lashed to a branch. Drawn by the smell and the dripping blood, the hounds swarmed around it, whining and barking.

My brief time in the sunshine had gone. Richard now rode with André de Chauvigny and a handful of other knights, and I with the group of squires who followed close behind. No introduction had been made. Spying me after the end of the hunt, the duke had merely ordered me to find John de Mandeville, most senior of his squires. It was common for great lords to have several; until my arrival, Richard had had four.

Eager to get off on the right footing, for these men would be my comrades, I'd been respectful and humble to John. A sturdy type, he had middle-parted brown hair and a direct gaze. Surprised that Richard should have so unexpectedly taken on a new squire, he had listened to my abbreviated account of my first meetings with the duke, and of how I had been travelling to Southampton in the hope of entering his service. After a chance encounter in the woods, I told him, during which Richard had driven off some ruffians, he had offered me to be one of his squires. I could see John suspected there was more to it – I had made no mention of my own part in the fight – but not wanting to appear the braggart, I said no more, and John did not ask.

My position within the squires' hierarchy would be fifth, he told me. John himself was perhaps twenty-three, and had served the duke for five years. Second to him was another John, short, and sharp-featured as a weasel. The third in line was Louis, an arrogant-looking youth from Aquitaine. One rank above me was Philip, who was to prove the friendliest of my new comrades. Pleasant-faced, with a stocky build and a burn scar on the inside of his left forearm, he was the only one apart from John de Mandeville who bothered to shake my hand.

We rode behind Richard and the knights, and as befitted our status, at the front of the group of squires. John de Mandeville went first, his gaze fixed on the duke, alert for any summons. Weasel John, as I already thought of him, came after, then Louis, Philip and me. My presence had not gone unnoticed among the other squires, bunched to our rear. There were glances aplenty, most curious, but some openly hostile.

Louis saw me. 'They want to know who you are,' he said in a none-too-friendly voice. 'As do we.'

Philip gave me an encouraging nod. I could tell that Weasel John was listening too, so I spun the tale of how I had come to live at Striguil, avoiding mention of my father's fight against the English. I spoke of Isabelle, Rhys – running alongside, he pointed in delight at himself – Hugo, Walter and Reginald. Of the FitzAldelms, I made little mention, save to say that I had followed one to Southampton. The mere thought of the elder brother made my belly tie itself in knots, but with the squires impatient to hear my story, I had no time to dwell on it.

'You must have met the duke before,' said Philip, frowning. 'He would not take a stranger on as a squire, or I am no judge.'

I recounted my fight with Boots and Fists – the squires laughed at that, as I had hoped – and how Richard had intervened. I spoke of the march on Usk, my hope to save Walter, and of the fight with the Welsh at the stream. I indicated the hauberk, once again tied behind my saddle, and said, 'The duke's reward allowed me to buy this, and Liath Macha here.' I gave my mount an affectionate slap.

'Now I begin to understand Richard's purpose,' said Philip admiringly. 'We have a fighter here.'

Pleased, I gave him a grin of thanks.

Weasel John and Louis made no comment, but I did not worry overmuch. It is ever in men's natures to mistrust those who might be perceived as a threat. My father's warriors had competed for his favour; I had no doubt that Richard's squires and knights did too. God willing, I would find acceptance among them.

At last the incessant questioning came to an end, and the conversation moved on. Much was made of the feast that would be held that night, and some days later, the voyage to Normandy. After that, I learned, we would journey to Aquitaine, where unhappy nobles had risen against Richard's rule. I listened intently, noting names and places, trying to absorb every piece of information. At the same time, a dark realisation was taking hold in my mind. Of far greater concern than our lodgings that night, the ship we would sail in, or even the battles that might occur, was Guy FitzAldelm. If and when he saw me, it was impossible to think he would say nothing.

As Southampton's walls came into sight, I had three choices. The easiest was to make good my escape under the cover of darkness that night. I could ride to Bristol, from where ships sailed to Ireland. There I could take service with one of the provincial kings, or try to raise a force to fight the English. That both might be achieved seemed unlikely; the former would leave me unhappy, and the latter lead to a swift death.

The second choice was somehow to avoid FitzAldelm and his squire. Succeed in that until after we crossed the sea, and perhaps even Aquitaine, and prove myself to Richard. When the inevitable denouncement came, there would be hope of retaining my position. More probable, however, was that the duke would dismiss me from his service. Already I knew him as a man not to cross.

My last option was the most unpleasant. Disturbed, I thrust it away, but like a moth drawn to a candle, found myself returning to it over and again.

We lodged in a rich merchant's house in Southampton. The rest of Richard's household was scattered among a dozen dwellings through the town, while the men-at-arms and archers had to camp outside the walls. It was my first time attending the duke, and I paid close attention as the two Johns took charge of his horse, bow and quiver, and escorted him inside. Louis and Philip led the mount to the stables, and I followed, with Rhys at my back.

The two set about their business much as I had done in Striguil, stripping the horse of its tack, and providing it with water and a bucket of oats. I was ordered to rub him down, a task Rhys could help me with. I soon decided that the ducal squires' duties were little different to those who served ordinary knights, except that Richard was high nobility, and the king's son. Standards would be higher, and potential punishments more severe.

Our own horses had to be cared for afterwards, so it was some while before we entered the house itself. The wood-shingled roof and sprawling outbuildings told me the owner was wealthy, and my opinion was borne out in the grand solar, which lay on the first floor. Several of the windows were glazed, something not even Striguil possessed. The room was bright with candlelight and the glow from a blazing fire in the hearth. Embroidered hangings covered the walls, silken cushions adorned every chair. A painted wooden cupboard displayed an impressive array of silverware.

By the look of his damp hair, Richard had bathed. Seated at a cloth-covered trestle table, cup in hand, he was deep in conversation with a party of well-dressed men who had arrived while we had been in the yard. These, I learned from Philip, were the nobles who had come to answer his summons. We waited on them and the duke for hours, pouring drinks, cutting meat and clearing away plates. Rhys helped the servants, carrying dishes to the kitchen and fetching fresh jugs of wine.

The talk at table was all of Aquitaine, and the rebellion there. I listened in as best I could, but still confused by the names and places, and consumed with worry about FitzAldelm, it made little sense. It came as a considerable relief when John de Mandeville quietly told Philip and me that we could go to the kitchen in search of our own dinner.

My mind yet struggling with the dilemma before me, I ate little and drank even less. Philip set to with a will, however, devouring venison terrine on sliced bread followed by trout baked with almonds. Rhys ate as if it were his last meal. After a quick visit to the solar – we were no longer needed – Philip returned to our corner in the kitchen, and poured us each more wine. I made small talk as best I could, but was grateful when he accepted my intention to go and give thanks for my good fortune in the neighbouring church. 'It is not every day that a man is taken into service by the Duke of Aquitaine,' I joked.

Philip saluted me with his cup.

Faithful as a dog, Rhys slipped from his seat and came after me. I made to order him back, but had to stop myself, for it would seem odd to Philip that I should prevent the boy from worshipping with me. It was only then that I realised I had made my choice.

The third one.

Scourged by guilt that I should mention praying when my intention was altogether more sinful, I stole through the solar, unnoticed by Richard and his party.

At the foot of the stairs, I turned to Rhys. 'You are not coming.'

'Why not, sir?'

'I am not for the church.'

He looked confused, and I cursed inwardly, because I could not reveal my purpose. 'Philip must think you are with me, so you cannot go back to the kitchen. Choose a spot in the stables, and bed down there. I will find you in the morning.'

'Let me come with you, sir, please.' His tone could not have been more earnest.

I gripped his shoulder. 'Understand that it is not lack of faith that makes me leave you behind, Rhys. There is no one I trust more than you, but I must do this alone.'

There were tears in his eyes, but he made no further protest as I slipped out into the street.

Darkness had fallen. The air was laden with smells, some pleasant, others not so. Bursts of song and ribald laughter carried to me; the duke's men were enjoying themselves. I could not ask for FitzAldelm by name for fear of being remembered, which made my quest even more hopeless. Refusing to give in, I instead asked directions to taverns and eating houses. I picked a trail to the first inn, a stone's throw from the merchant's house. Peering in through the window like a thief, I spied several of Richard's knights, but with men's backs being turned to me, and the crowd within, I could not be sure that FitzAldelm was *not* inside. Heart thudding, I pulled open the door and entered.

A mug of beer later – one could scarcely linger in a tavern and not buy a drink – I emerged, relieved and frustrated in equal measure. FitzAldelm was nowhere to be found, which meant that my search must continue. It was that, or seek my bed and leave my fate in God's hands.

I headed for the next possible location, an eating house. FitzAldelm was not there either, nor was he in the dozen establishments I visited thereafter. I bought plenty of beer, but wary of getting drunk, left it unfinished on tables, or poured it quietly on floors. I had eaten half a chicken and raisin pasty, and picked at a bowl of pottage and a plate of bread and cheese. Frustrated, aware that I could not visit every premises in Southampton, I resumed my hunt.

Another hour passed in this manner. I had no luck. Cursing Fitz-Aldelm, I decided to drown my sorrows. By this point, I was in the stews. Narrow streets and alleyways ran hither and thither. The buildings were rundown, hovels. A mixture of mud and manure squelched underfoot. A rank smell indicated that something had died nearby, and was rotting.

The next inn I chanced upon did not deserve the name. Its thatch roof was mouldy, and stank to high heaven; the door hung from one hinge. On the dirt floor within lay a mixture of dead rushes, bones, broken cups and God knows what else. Long benches and rickety tables were its only furniture, and the customers as evil a set as I had ever seen. I saw none of the duke's soldiers. That the serving wenches were whores was evident; the plump, middle-aged woman who came to the table thrust her breasts into my face as she took my money.

I had no interest. Downing a mug of the beer she delivered in a rough clay jug – it was weak, sour and almost undrinkable – I poured myself another and wondered how soon FitzAldelm would realise I was part of the duke's household. A day, a sennight – any longer seemed unlikely – and the future I had earned by saving Richard's life would be snatched away. It was so unfair, I thought, drinking deep. The beer's bitter taste had lessened already, and I slurped another mouthful. Scratching a fingernail up and down my mug, oblivious to those around me, I decided that life was cruel. The best thing to do was drink until I forgot my worries. The morrow could wait.

A familiar sneering voice penetrated the fog of misery surrounding me. I looked up. To my amazement, FitzAldelm and his squire were emerging from a back room. Past them, I made out a low bed, and on it, a naked woman. My stomach turned to think of what the pair had been doing together. Sharing a joke, they pushed through to the door, and left. I decided that if there was ever a moment for me to seal my future, this was it.

Up I got, and followed. Outside, I stared after FitzAldelm, who was walking away, his squire a step behind. They were close, very close. With a grip on my dagger, I took a step after them, but then I hesitated. It was one thing to imagine stabbing a man in the back, and quite another to *do* it. Kill him and be done with it, a voice cried in my head.

I cannot, I thought. I am no murderer.

My hand fell to my side. I half turned, and my boot scraped a shard of pottery off another.

Alerted, FitzAldelm spun. In the gloom, it was impossible to see who I was, but in a place such as this in the depths of night, the likelihood was that I meant him no good. Ordering his squire to follow, he swept out a knife and paced towards me. 'Think you can rob us?' he cried.

I took a step back, desperately hoping not to be recognised.

He was already close enough to see my face. Shock twisted his handsome features. *'Rufus?'*

I dodged back further, realising that my presence made it seem as if I intended him harm. No one, least of all FitzAldelm, would believe that I *had* planned to kill him, but that my nerve had failed.

Slash. Had the blade connected, his powerful sideways rake would have disembowelled me.

I retreated again. Behind FitzAldelm, I glimpsed his squire. Sure my death was upon me, I pulled out my own dagger.

The struggle that followed was vicious. Grunts of effort came from both of us. My defensive parries barely stopped me being slain, while FitzAldelm's vicious lunges each came close to ending the matter. His breath reeked of beer and onions. The squire scrabbled to get around him, that he might also join in the attack. Forced into a continuous withdrawal, I felt a growing awareness – and terror – that however the brawl ended, I would lose.

Then FitzAldelm slipped. On what, I never found out, but one moment he was coming at me again, and the next, his leading foot slid out from under him, sending him, spread-legged, to the ground. Panicked, in fear of my own life, I stepped forward and without thinking, stabbed. He let out a horrible gasp, and his eyes went wide with shock. I stared at my blade, hilt deep in his chest, and thought, Jesu, what have I done?

An inarticulate cry of rage brought me crashing back to the alleyway. His squire loomed out of the darkness. I felt a stinging pain in my lower left arm. Weaponless – my dagger was still in FitzAldelm – I staggered backward. It was my turn to trip. One of my heels snagged on something underfoot, and I was falling. Winded, I flailed about, frantic to get up before the squire finished me off. I was slow, far too slow.

Oddly, no ball of agony erupted in my flesh as a knife slid deep into me. No punch to the face sent me sprawling back into the foul-smelling mire. I sucked in a ragged breath and managed to sit up. Where the squire had stood, I saw a shape, far too small to be a man. My gaze dropped. On top of FitzAldelm lay another body: his squire.

Sudden understanding came. Utter horror filled me. 'Rhys?' I whispered.

'I am here, sir. Are you hurt?' He darted to my side, the knife I had given him clutched in his fist.

'Not badly, I do not think,' I answered, probing with the fingers of my right hand. The left arm of my tunic had been slashed open, and under that, I felt a shallow cut. 'I will live.'

'Thank Christ,' Rhys said, solemn as an adult might. He helped me to my feet.

I kicked the squire, who did not move. Licking a finger, I placed it under his nostrils. I waited perhaps twenty heartbeats, but felt no air move. Beneath him, Guy FitzAldelm lay as still as a statue. My first emotion was that of fierce joy; my second, disappointment that any chance of discovering more about my family's fate had just vanished.

'Is he dead?' whispered Rhys.

'He is,' I said, the consequences of the killing already making my mind spin.

Rhys took my response for chastisement. 'He was going to murder you, sir.'

'Both of them were,' I answered wearily. No one would believe that FitzAldelm and his squire had attacked me first; I had slain the knight in self-defence, and Rhys had acted to save my life.

'Come, sir.' Rhys tugged at my arm.

A little addlepated, I gave him a blank look.

'There is not a soul about, sir. Leave now, and no one will be any the wiser that we were here.'

I glanced about. The door of the tavern remained shut. Not a sliver of light could I see up and down the alley. A yowling cat atop the near-est roof might have seen, but it could not tell its story. Hope flared in my breast. 'Aye,' I said, rolling over FitzAldelm to retrieve my dagger. 'Let us begone.'

Fear gripped me every step of the way back. Not knowing the place, we got lost several times, but at last the merchant's house hove into view. I had stripped off my torn, blood-stained tunic and buried it a hand's depth into the dunghill beside a stable. Rhys claimed to have no blood on him at all, so it was just my cut arm, wrapped in my undertunic, and my state of half-nakedness that we had to explain if anyone was up.

God and all His saints continued to smile on us, or perhaps, given what we had done, it was Lucifer who guided our path. I did not much care which it was. Rhys entered the yard first, returning to report that everyone was abed. The front door was unlocked, and the guard inside the threshold snoring. A jug by his feet told its own tale. Upstairs in the solar, which was warm and fuggy, snores rose to the rafters.

Finding our blankets, we lay down.

The pain from my arm hit me almost at once. I clenched my jaw, and breathed deep, telling myself it would ease. That I would find a surgeon to stitch it, and would somehow come up with a plausible reason for having such a wound.

'We should get up before dawn, sir,' whispered Rhys. 'You can pretend to teach me how to use a sword. I will catch you off guard, and cut your arm.'

I gazed at him in amazement. He was old enough to handle a blade, and accidents during training were common. 'You are a clever one and no mistake,' I whispered back. 'That is a fine plan.'

His teeth flashed white in the blackness.

I reached out with my good arm, and clasped his shoulder. 'You saved my life, Rhys. I shall not forget that.'

Again he smiled. 'I am your man, sir, always.'

My heart squeezed. I had never thought to see the void left by the loss of my family filled, but lying there in the merchant's house, I realised that I was not alone.

Remarkably, everything went well the following day. Kept awake by the discomfort from my arm, I woke Rhys when the first trace of light crept around the curtains. There was no one in the yard to see us commence our 'fight', which made it easy for him to land the blow that 'caused' my wound. To make it seem as fresh as possible, I had him hit my bad arm with the flat of the blade. The agony was so intense I almost passed out. When I regained my senses, there was a plentiful amount of blood, and a witness, one of the merchant's grooms. I cursed Rhys, and tried to cuff him around the ear. 'Fool,' I cried. 'Look what you've done!'

John de Mandeville was not impressed. 'This is a fine start to your service,' he said, inspecting the wound with suspicion. He turned to Rhys. 'How old are you, boy?'

'Twelve, sir, or maybe thirteen.'

'He will make a swordsman one day,' John said, directing me to a surgeon recommended by the merchant.

Some hours later, drowsy-headed from the mandrake I had inhaled before the cut was stitched, and my arm throbbing as if it was about to burst, I wove an unsteady path back to the merchant's house. Rhys was by my side, which allowed me to lean on his shoulder, a great relief, I must confess.

Philip was in the yard, currying the duke's horse. He enquired after my wound, but seemed little interested in my account of how it happened. 'Have you heard?' he asked the instant I had finished.

I felt a flutter of fear. 'What?'

'Two of the duke's men have been murdered. He is furious.'

'Murdered? Here in the town?' I threw a glance at Rhys, who had adopted a shocked expression.

'Aye. In the stews. A knight and his squire.'

'God rest their souls,' I said, thinking, rot in Hell, FitzAldelm. I felt a pang of regret for the squire, but if he had survived, he could have done me as much harm as his master. It was good that he was also dead. And yet it was not, my conscience replied. If it was discovered what Rhys and I had done, we were dead men.

Much of the day was spent seeking those who had slain FitzAldelm and his squire. Assisted by the town guard, Richard's soldiers turned the stews upside down. We squires remained at the merchant's house, preparing for our departure. It was a nervous time, for I could not be sure that no one had seen the fight. Someone in the inn might have remembered me. Two things were in my favour. Philip seemed none the wiser that I had not gone to the church, and the duke was ignorant of my injury. I hoped it would stay that way. It was not beyond the bounds of possibility that Richard might link the death of FitzAldelm – a knight from Striguil, whence I had just come – with my wound.

By nightfall, it appeared that our involvement would remain unknown. Two lowlifes had been named by the proprietor of the inn. Arrested and interrogated – for which, read, beaten within an inch of their lives – they had confessed. This news spread through Southampton faster than lightning. The two Johns, Philip and Louis went with the duke to watch them being hung. Ridden with as much guilt as relief, I was glad to be left behind. I lingered in the tack room, polishing Liath Macha's tack one-handed. I set Rhys to sweep the floor, but by his half-hearted efforts, it was clear that he was not happy either.

At length I caught his eye. 'What?'

'Those men are innocent, sir.'

'Quiet!' I jerked my head at the door, outside which anyone could be standing.

He shoved the broom forward, sending up a cloud of dust, and muttered, 'Well, they are.'

'Aye,' I growled. 'They did not do it. We did. Would you care to change places? Run to the square, and mayhap you will get there before they swing.'

He thrust the broom along the floor savagely.

Motes of dust spun and twirled in the uncomfortable silence that followed.

'We had the death of two men on our hands,' I said. 'God have mercy on us, now we have four.'

Rhys stared at me, mute.

'There is no turning back time, boy. No way to bring any of them back. We could confess—' Saying this, my heart pounded, for I did not know how deep Rhys's guilt ran '—but that would see us also on the end of a rope. Not for the criminals' deaths, you understand, but for those of FitzAldelm and his squire.'

'You only defended yourself, sir! And the squire would have knifed you on the ground had I not—'

'You saved my life, Rhys,' I said again. 'Should you hang for that?'

'No!' His voice was fierce.

'Nor should I die for fighting back against FitzAldelm.' I softened my tone. 'Let us to the church. We shall beg for forgiveness, and light a candle for each of the men in the square.'

He nodded.

We went and prayed.

Odd it is that of all the deaths in my life – in battle, in brawls, during tourneys, sieges and clashes at sea – the ones that trouble me most are of two men whom I never even met.

CHAPTER XIII

A sennight later, the bloody events of the night in Southampton and my miraculous escape from justice were fast being forgotten. Seizing the opportunity granted by a period of fine weather – storms had been common for a month – Richard was crossing the Narrow Sea with his household and the troops who had answered his call. My only previous voyage had been from Ireland to Wales, and I watched the English coastline vanish, wondering if I would ever see it again. Rhys, who had never been aboard a ship, varied between wide-eyed delight at the slap of the waves and the billowing sails, and green-faced nausea caused by the uneven motion.

Landing in Normandy, we rode to Caen first, where Richard was to take counsel with his father. I was as impressed with the castle there as I had been with Striguil. Built by the man who had conquered England over a hundred years before, Duke William, Caen had a large enclosing wall set atop a rocky outcrop. Behind the towered gate was a stout, square donjon; more towers dotted the perimeter. The space within the defences was far larger than the bailey at Striguil. It was as well, for the main part of Richard's force needed space to camp, the great hall being full of the king's mesnie.

I would not have minded sleeping in a tent, because the weather was altogether more pleasant than in England. Warm, early spring sunshine bathed the green landscape. The cherry blossoms were out, and in the fields, the wheat was close to knee high. Better it was that we squires were quartered with the duke in the great hall, however, for that is where the king was to be found, along with Richard's three brothers. At last I would latch eyes on the man in whose name Ireland had been invaded, and his other sons, about whom I had heard much.

Before the duke met with his father, he supervised his troops as they made camp in a spot allocated by the seneschal. I and the other squires tethered the horses, and fetched water from the cistern near the east wall – I favouring my left arm. It was healing fast, and although the other squires had given me a hard time about Rhys wounding me so easily, I appeared to have pulled the wool over everyone's eyes.

When we were done carrying buckets, we lounged about beside the horses. Rhys set to currying Liath Macha, as he liked to do at the end of each day. They had formed a bond, almost as close my own with the beast.

'See those?' Philip nodded at a set of tents close to the great hall, the largest of which was a grand affair striped in red and gold. 'They belong to Henry, the Young King. And those—' he indicated the ones a little further away, '—they are Geoffrey's.'

'Where are John's?' I asked.

Philip smiled. 'Lackland is too young yet to have his own retinue. He rides everywhere with his lord father.'

I still had much to learn. 'Lackland?'

'When Henry allocated various parts of his kingdom to his older sons some dozen years ago, he made no provision for John, who was a tiny child.'

'He is to become Lord of Ireland, is he not?' Yet has no right to be such, I thought darkly.

'Aye, but the name Lackland has long since stuck. Do not let him or any of his men hear you use it, unless you want a beating.'

I made another mental note. Since joining the duke's household, I had been soaking up information, and questioning Philip and John de Mandeville day and night. When they grew tired of my pestering, I had bought a costrel of wine and gone to Louis. Weasel John I had not bothered with; for no particular reason that I could ascertain, matters between us had soured. Sometimes there is no reason as to why men do not get along.

I knew that Richard's relationship with his brothers was volatile. With his father it was thorny at best, and liable to turn acrimonious in the blink of an eye. It had long been so. Nigh on a decade before, aided by their mother Alienor, he and his two older brothers had rebelled against Henry. Although the cracks had been plastered over, they had not gone away. Even now, Alienor remained a prisoner of the king, her cage in England gilded, but a cage, nonetheless.

'There you are.'

Surprised by the familiar voice, Philip and I took a knee. 'Sire,' we chorused.

'Rise, rise.' Richard's tone was light. 'You have never been to Caen before, Rufus?'

'I had never set foot in Normandy until a few days ago, sire.'

He smiled. 'What do you make of it thus far? And Caen, is it to your liking?'

'It seems a pleasant land, sire. The castle, well . . . Striguil is impressive, but Caen is even more so.' I stumbled over my words, unsure what to say, feeling he must think me the muddy-footed Irishman.

To my relief, Richard showed no disdain, or contempt. 'It is a sight to behold, that is true. However, I am not its master.' His usually open face became serious. 'You have not met my lord father, the king, or my brothers.'

'No, sire.'

'Today you shall. Come.'

'Yes, sire.' Leaving Philip open-mouthed behind me, I joined a surprised-looking John de Mandeville. Weasel John's glance at me was murderous, for I had taken his place. Since the fight with the outlaws in the woods, Richard had kept me close. We did not converse overmuch, but he appeared to enjoy my company. Louis, also more senior, seemed no less unhappy. I cared not, for it was I who walked behind the duke with his favoured advisers and knights, not they. Rhys stayed behind, accepting that he could not stroll into the royal presence uninvited.

A man-at-arms in royal livery stood on either side of the hall's arched doorway. They saluted the duke with a stamp of their feet. Despite myself, I basked in the recognition.

'See that my wine is well-watered down,' Richard said to John as we climbed the stair to the first floor. 'In this nest of vipers, I need my wits about me, and there is much afoot.'

Being told of the duke's problems had surprised me. Hearing the distrust fall from his lips rammed home that the camp gossip was true. Noticing Richard pause to take a deep breath and throw his shoulders back, I realised that it was no easy matter for him to meet his family.

A cluster of servants by the entrance watched us sidelong. An officer in a dark blue tunic bowed to Richard, and hurried away to alert the king of our coming. The duke did not wait, but strode forward, with us at his heel. At first glance, the hall was even grander than that at Striguil, but, wary of what might unfold, I did not gaze about me.

Close to the end of the room, Richard went on alone. He came to a halt in front of the dais, upon which five seats were arrayed, one before the rest. Four were occupied, the lead by the king, and three of the remainder by the duke's brothers. Henry's bastard son Geoffrey, who served as his chancellor, stood close by. Richard knelt, and bowed his head. A dozen paces behind, we did the same.

'Papa,' the duke said in a loud voice. 'I am come.'

'Welcome,' said Henry, his voice warm. 'Rise.'

Once as handsome as Richard and the Young King, those days were long gone. Silver-white rather than red-gold, Henry's mane of hair was thin, with patches of skull visible beneath. Folds of skin drooped from his jaw, giving him a ponderous look. Lines of veins scored his cheeks, the mark of a drinker, and there were heavy pouches under his eyes. There was nothing dull about his stare, however, which raked over Richard and on to us.

His attention passed on, and I breathed again.

Richard exchanged a few pleasantries with his father first, and then addressed his brothers. The Young King, attractive and tall like the duke, gave an impression of not caring. Geoffrey, of similar build and with a lustrous mane of hair, was all smiles. John's jowly nod was as solemn as if he were king and not the youngest son. Short and podgy with dark red hair, he appeared to have been cast from a different mould to his siblings. The second Geoffrey, older than all the rest, seemed quiet and reserved.

'Your letter said you are bound for Périgueux,' the king began. 'Those cursed barons are causing trouble again?'

'Yes, Papa. A quick assault there will catch them off guard. My intent is first to march through Poitou, gathering troops. After Périgueux, I will drive east into the Limousin.' Richard paused, and asked with a sardonic smile, 'Unless there have been fresh developments – a letter from William and Adémar, offering peace, perhaps?'

Henry snorted, and said, 'To think I forgave them for rebelling five years ago.'

The Young King added, 'Both are truly sons of their father the count.'

'They have sent no word then,' said Richard, unsurprised.

'War threatens again. My blood quickens at the thought,' said the Young King. 'Ha! Remember how you and I besieged the count at Châteauneuf, brother? The fortress fell after half a month.'

Richard's retort was instant. 'You left soon after, I recall, although the campaign had not ended. In the end, Hal, our lord father had to join me to bring the rebels to heel.'

The Young King coloured. 'I had my reasons. I have fought with you since. Just last year—'

'—you attended every tournament in the land?' John's tone was snide.

The Young King twisted around. 'Enough, you whelp!'

Henry lifted a hand. 'Peace.'

The Young King glared at John, who smirked.

A moment passed.

Into the silence, Richard said, 'It seems that I am indeed for Périgueux, sire. The rebellion must be stopped ere it spreads.'

Geoffrey sat forward in his chair. 'The rebels, as you term them, brother, maintain that their protest is against *your* rule. You oppress them with violence, and harry them brutally, they say.' He glanced at Henry and the Young King, adding, 'There have been accusations of rape against you *and* your knights.'

Richard levelled a contemptuous stare at Geoffrey. 'This is what the Aquitaine nobles say . . . when you meet with them?'

Henry frowned, and John chuckled, an unpleasant sound.

The Young King laughed, while Geoffrey glowered.

Richard spoke again. 'I would never dishonour any woman. Let anyone who says otherwise prove himself against my sword.' His hard gaze lingered on Geoffrey, who looked away. He continued, 'Every knight of mine will say the same thing. I cannot say that none of the fair sex have ever been violated by my ordinary soldiers, but if such crimes have occurred, they were against my orders. God's legs! Show me an army which never acts so, and I will show you the Gates of Heaven.'

No one argued the point, and Richard again regarded Geoffrey. 'There is a widespread rumour that you have met in secret with my rebellious subjects. What say you to this?'

Attention switched to the Count of Brittany.

'It is a lie. A damned lie.' Geoffrey's voice was blithe. 'I would never act so, brother.'

Richard made a derisive sound, and I noticed his eyes wander to the Young King, who affected not to notice. The duke seemed about to speak, but for a second time his father intervened. 'Unless you have proof of these meetings, Richard, I want to hear no more about them. As well you know, rumours tend to be campfire and street gossip, and as reliable as a leaking bucket.'

'Yes, Papa.' Richard clasped his hands behind his back. Only Philip and I saw how his fingers clenched together.

He trusts neither Geoffrey nor the Young King, I thought, or he knows more than he is admitting to. He also dislikes Henry wanting to keep the peace between them at all costs, but he will not say so. Richard's reasons for not arguing with his father were soon made clear.

'Regarding the rebellion, Papa. I have assembled five hundred archers and men-at-arms, and five score knights. This force should prove sufficient to subdue the rebels, but if it does not . . .' His voice died away.

'The matter needs to be settled,' the king declared. 'I will ride south should you need it.'

'My thanks.'

The disappointed look that Geoffrey and the Young King exchanged came and went so fast that I almost missed it. I glanced about, but it seemed no one else had seen.

Richard did his duty, dining with his father and brothers. The bastard Geoffrey had excused himself, citing a need to attend to important business. Philip and I remained to serve the duke. All manner of dishes were carried in, from fatted capons in lemon and oven-baked suckling rabbits, to roast swan, presented in its plumage and with a spicy, black blood sauce. At this, my stomach turned, and I was grateful not to be seated at table. My appetite returned, but busy with our duties, there was no chance to eat even a morsel. To keep my mind from my rumbling belly, I concentrated on Richard.

His manner remained bright and cheerful, but now and again, I caught his eyes slipping to Geoffrey or the Young King, who were thick as thieves, forever whispering in each other's ears.

I turned to Philip, who was standing beside me, and said quietly, 'Can any of the duke's brothers be trusted?'

An expressive 'Who knows?' shrug was his reply.

Philip's response did not weaken my opinion that Geoffrey was the one to be wary of. The conversation of earlier had also revealed that the Young King felt little loyalty to Richard. I did not like John's manner either; he varied between flattering the king and making sarcastic comments at his brothers' expense. Henry himself was hard to judge, speaking rarely while drinking plenty, and all the while his attention roving from one son to another. He resembled an old spider perched at the centre of his web, watching and waiting for the best moment to strike.

And yet it was John who noticed me.

'You have a new squire, brother.' He pointed with his table knife, a not altogether friendly gesture.

'I do.' Richard cast a half-glance at me over his shoulder. 'Rufus, they call him.'

John's snake eyes came to rest on me again, languid and black. It felt unpleasant, and I dropped my gaze.

'I can see why he is named so. Hair so red is uncommon in England. Is he Welsh?'

'Irish,' answered Richard.

'He is from *my* domain then,' said John, sounding pleased. 'I am to be Lord of Ireland.'

I bit the inside of my cheek so hard I tasted blood.

'What part?'

Staring at the floor, the best way to control my fury, I did not realise John's question had been aimed at me. A sideways kick from Philip made me look at him, and realising from the urgent jerk of his chin what had happened, I turned, stricken, towards the table. Both Richard and John were staring at me, the former bemused, the latter already annoyed.

'Your pardon, sire,' I said, bowing to John. 'I am from Cairlinn, in the north of Leinster.'

'I have never heard of it.'

'Sire.' There was no reason that he should have known of it, but irritated, I ignored the 'Shut up' stare Philip threw me, and continued, 'It stands at the mouth of a bay, sire, with a mountain at its back and more peaks across the water. Few people visit it, yet it is one of the most beautiful places in all of Ireland.'

At the time I knew not that my heartfelt description was a seed falling on fertile ground. It was a comment that would haunt me in later years.

John made a dismissive gesture, and said, 'No doubt it is full of unwashed Irish with cabbages sprouting from their ears, like you.'

The Young King laughed, and Geoffrey. Even Henry's lips twitched. Cheeks flaming, I could say nothing in reply.

'Rufus has no cabbages in his ears, brother, and he is as brave as an alaunt,' said Richard.

John's sly smile lessened, but he was not done. 'Does he bring down boars, then? 'Twould not surprise me, he being an Irish savage.'

Richard set down his cup, hard. Sensing an announcement, the musicians stopped playing. Heads turned further down the table, and the duke said, 'Rufus saved my life not a sennight since, you whelp. I doubt not that he will win his spurs one day.'

John was reduced to a humiliated silence, and it seemed that every eye in the room now turned upon me. More embarrassed than I had been in my life, I fidgeted like a small boy told to sit still.

'That is a story I want to hear,' said Henry to Richard.

The duke laid out the tale without adornment, making more of my actions than his own. As I was later to learn, this was a mark of his generous spirit. Finishing, he saluted me with his cup, and said to his father, 'If not for Rufus, you would have but three sons, Papa.'

The pair gazed at each other for several heartbeats, and then Henry raised his own cup in my direction.

Stunned by the recognition, momentarily forgetting how Richard had shamed John, I grinned and bowed from the waist.

The king's attention moved on; he and Richard began a muttered conversation. The chatter along the table resumed. Scarcely believing what had happened, I went back to my position against the wall.

Philip was on me in a flash, his expression eager. 'You saved the duke's life?' he whispered.

'I did.'

'You never said a word.'

'It would have served me ill to speak of it the first time we met. Imagine what Louis would have said, or Weasel John.'

'True enough, I suppose,' said Philip, giving me an almighty dunt with his elbow. 'Go on then, you dog. Tell me!'

He listened, rapt, as I recounted my version of the story. I emphasised how Richard had saved me from certain death, whereas I had merely knocked him to the ground. 'The arrow might have missed,' I said.

'He does not seem to think so,' whispered Philip with a little jerk of his head at the duke. 'You did well, my Irish friend. Know that I am also in your debt. But for your actions, I would be lordless, and forced to return home.' He had explained to me before his family circumstances, which were impoverished. Without Richard's patronage, a dull, rural life in Somerset beckoned.

Again embarrassed, yet also delighted, I protested that Philip would have acted in the same way. We gripped hands, and swore our undying comradeship.

A burst of laughter caught my attention, and I turned my head. The Young King had told a joke. His father nodded and smiled. Geoffrey had tears of mirth running down his cheeks. Richard was banging the table in appreciation. Only John had not joined in.

To my horror, he was staring at me, his eyes cold and dead.

I looked away, my heart pounding. It had not been the duke's intention, but his scold had set John against me, I was sure of it.

A moment later, when I dared to glance again, I was mightily relieved that John's attention had moved on. A nasty feeling lingered in my mind, however, that I had made a new enemy.

One far more powerful than either FitzAldelm.

CHAPTER XIV

Overhead, a hint of paleness marked the eastern sky. Dawn would not be long coming, but in the streets of Périgueux, darkness yet reigned. The townspeople were still abed, I thought, padding down the street with Rhys by my side. Even the dogs, prone to bark early in the night, were resting. Proud that we had gone to the river and back without being heard or seen, I led the way to the large house where Richard was waiting.

Half a month had passed since Caen. Hard riding it had been, through Anjou and Poitou, into the Limousin. The foot soldiers had had the worst of it, marching upwards of twenty-five miles each day. Forced in the end to let them rest, yet impatient to act, the duke had taken a score of knights the evening before and advanced in secret to Périgueux, there to spy out the situation. John de Mandeville and I accompanied the duke, much to the disgust of Philip, Louis and Weasel John.

In the days since meeting the king, Richard had had me act as his second squire. It was as if his public announcement of my saving his life had sparked him to acknowledge it on a daily basis. John de Mandeville had accepted my appointment without demur, but he worked me hard and rarely offered approval. I had decided I would have to prove myself to him, which was fair enough. Philip, being my friend, took it best. Louis acted as if the story were untrue – despite the duke having told it – and went about grumbling under his breath and refusing to speak to me. Second squire before my promotion, Weasel John saw Richard's actions as a personal slight. He could say nothing to our master, so, vindictive and sly, he took out his anger on me at every opportunity. One day, my costrel of wine had vanished, and another, my blankets were somehow pulled from our tent just as a rain shower began. Needing proof, I had set Rhys to watch my belongings. The 'weasel' had realised, and ceased for the moment.

At least I had no need to worry about him here, I thought, my eyes ever moving from house windows to their doors and on to the next building. Périgueux and its castle Puy-St-Front were held by troops loyal to the rebellious Count of Périgord; it was they I had had to watch out for down by the river, as well as the civilians who slumbered in the houses all around us.

We got back safely, my light coded rap on the portal seeing us admitted at once. The place belonged to a merchant loyal to the duke; a large courtyard surrounded by stables and storage rooms, it was perfect for concealing our force. I was taken to Richard, who was prowling about like a caged lion.

'What news?' he demanded.

'The bridge was clear of sentries, sire, and beyond on the rampart, I saw only one.'

Richard smiled. 'They know nothing of our presence here. And hiding places?'

'The street curves before the bridge, sire. We will be able to get very close.' I glanced at Rhys, who nodded in agreement.

'Let us to it,' said Richard, glancing at the nearest of his knights. Like him, they had already dressed in their hauberks and mail hose. Fierce grins met his words; men moved to don helmets and pick up shields.

I could not hold in my surprise. 'You mean to attack now, sire?' If I confess it, I was a little alarmed. Until this point, our purpose in the town had been to assess the alertness of the sentries before bringing up the rest of our force and making ready for a full-scale attack.

'The early bird catches the worm, Rufus,' he said, his eyes glinting with amusement. 'There will not be a better opportunity than this. Delay until the rest get here, and someone will see, and wake the garrison.' Letting me help him on with his helm, he strode off, issuing orders.

He might have been right, I thought, but to launch an attack with so few men was madness. Sheer gallant madness – and it had swept me up too. I went straight to John de Mandeville, who was putting a final edge on the duke's sword.

'Have you heard?' I asked.

John did not answer. He was sighting down the length of the oiled steel, looking for nicks or blemishes.

I moved from foot to foot, impatient. Richard would leave at any moment. 'John.'

He raised his eyes to mine. 'Squires are supposed to wait behind, until their masters return from battle.'

'There are twenty of them, and many times that number of Frenchmen in the fortress,' I hissed.

'In that case, what difference will the two of us make? Is your arm even healed?'

'It is!' I wanted to shout and rage further, but I held my peace. John was not an enemy of mine, but nor was he a friend. In the brief span since I had taken service with the duke, it had become clear that John was solid and loyal, but he did things as they were supposed to be done. He was not a risk taker, which explained in part why he was still a squire two years past the age many men were knighted.

'We could ask the duke,' I said.

'He would say no.'

I ground my teeth.

Soon after, John's words were borne out. The duke ordered we two to stay at the merchant's until it was clear who had emerged victorious. If things went badly, he said, we were to make our way back to the rest of his troops as best we could. If events unfolded as he hoped, he would send a messenger to find us. Without further ado, he led his knights onto the street. Their plan was to hide out of sight until the fortress gate was opened at dawn, and then to storm in before the guards had time to react.

I went to work on John that very instant. 'We have to go after him,' I said.

'We do not,' he replied stolidly. 'You heard the duke.'

'If anything happens to him—' I began.

'It will not.'

'You cannot be sure.'

'Nonsense. Have you seen him fight?'

'Even a giant can fall to a crossbow bolt,' I said, working the knife into the wound. 'How would you feel if the duke was hurt, and you had not been there to help?'

'God's eyes!' John made a gesture of exasperation. 'Anything to stop you bending my ear.'

I clouted him good-naturedly.

We helped each other don our hauberks. Neither of us had mail hose: we would have to trust to luck that no one aimed a cut – or a bolt – at our legs. We strapped on our swords. Arming caps on under our helmets, kite shields ready on our arms, we looked at each other.

'Know that his temper is fierce,' said John. 'You may be sorry yet.'

'Do you want to stay here?' I asked, ignoring the twinge from my recently healed wound.

A rare smile. 'I admit, I do not.'

'Nor I, which makes the risk worth it.' Through the door I went, checking to see that the duke was out of sight.

We moved fast, for dawn was upon us. The sky overhead was a glorious shade of pink. Traces of birdsong carried from the woods beyond the town. In a nearby street, I heard the sound of a wagon. No cry of alarm met our ears, however, and soon we had almost caught up with Richard and his knights. They were bunched together, waiting at the bend I had mentioned, with the duke at the front. None were looking behind them.

John and I slipped into the cover of an archway some hundred paces down the street, and set down our shields. From the acrid stink assailing our nostrils, the place was a tanner's yard. We took turns peering around the stonework. Focused on the task at hand, neither of us initially reacted to the sound of the bolt in the door at our backs. Then, horrified, we glanced at one another, and our gaze switched to the portal. The noise stopped; someone grunted and heaved, and with a screech of metal, the bolt moved.

I acted first. Sword out, the hilt raised high, I waited for the door to open inward. As it did, a yawning, hair-tousled-from-sleep, paunchy man was revealed. He stared at me in utter shock, then my pommel connected with his skull. His eyes rolled up to the whites, and he dropped. I seized his upper arm, managing to ease his fall. Laying him on the cobbles, I studied the yard, praying he had been the first to rise.

To my relief, peace reigned. The beams upon which the hides were scraped clean of hair stood abandoned. No apprentices were wielding long-handled paddles by the soaking pits. A trickle of smoke rose from the roof of the dwelling house off to the left, but the front door was closed. I could spy no dogs either. I put a finger to the man's throat, and felt a pulse. Gentle palpation told me his skull had not been broken either. I was glad. Killing the duke's enemies was one thing, an innocent civilian another.

John came in, his blade also drawn. 'That was well done,' he whispered.

'What should we do?' I hissed. 'He will not be living alone.'

With that, a baby cried in the house. Footsteps came from within. A soft voice began to croon, and we relaxed a fraction.

'Put the brute in there.' John aimed a thumb at the covered work area beside us.

We half lifted, half dragged the tanner behind a sturdy cart. It was not a good hiding place, but to linger risked discovery. A strip of cloth cut from the man's tunic served as a gag; his leather shoelaces acted as ties for his wrists.

'Denis!'

We started up. The woman's voice came from the house.

Peering around the wagon like two common thieves, we watched the door. The danger was averted thanks to the baby, which began to cry again. It was our opportunity to escape. Stealing to the gate, we pulled it quietly to, and glanced down the street.

Of Richard and his knights there was no sign. They could not have been gone long, however, because we could hear no clash of arms, nor any screams. That would soon change. Grabbing our shields, we ran. The shutters protecting a window were flung back as we passed. I caught a glimpse of a half-naked young woman. Her hand shot to her mouth in shock, and perhaps embarrassed by her state of undress, she did not cry out. At the corner, we halted, chests already heaving from the weight of our hauberks.

In the same moment I stuck my head around the corner of the last timber-framed building, I heard the sudden pounding of feet. Hearing it, John shoved in behind me, and together we watched the duke and his knights charging over the bridge. On the far bank, the fortress gate lay open.

It was a distance of perhaps two hundred paces.

As I mentioned, mail coats are heavy. Add mail hose, a helm and shield, and a man is carrying half his own bulk in armour. Fine physical specimen that he was, Richard almost managed to reach the portal before the lone sentry, who had spotted them, hurtled down the stairs and slammed it shut. The duke hit the door with a mighty crash, and I swear it opened a handspan. If anyone had been with him, they might have forced their way in, but as he drew back for a second attempt, the locking bar dropped into place with a solid thunk.

The knights arrived, and threw themselves in vain against the door. Sword hilts pounded on the planking. I could hear curses, and was muttering my own.

A trumpet shrilled an alarm.

'It is over,' I said to John. 'The duke *must* retreat.'

'That is not a word he understands,' John muttered.

He knew our master well. I stared in disbelief as Richard attacked the timbers. Even at a distance, I could see splinters flying. Encouraged, his knights began to do the same. Given enough time, I thought, they might eventually cut their way through, but the call to arms had been answered. Shouts and cries came from inside the wall. If the duke did not retreat, the enemy crossbowmen would shoot at them every step of the way back over the bridge. Mail afforded good protection, but at close range, the deadly square-ended bolts often punched through to cause terrible injuries.

Movement to the right, at the edge of my vision. I looked, and my stomach did a neat roll. From a sally gate that to an idle glance appeared to be part of the fortress wall, men were stealing. Many bore crossbows, and they were making for the small boats drawn up on the bank. The duke and his knights showed no signs of having seen, or of abandoning their mad attack on the gate. The French would cross in time to ambush them as they withdrew.

'Do you see?' I pointed.

John cursed long and hard, the first occasion I had ever heard him do so. 'How many crossbowmen do you count?' he asked. 'I make it—'

'Eight,' I said. 'And six men-at-arms.'

'Aye.' John swore again, and then, catching my eye, said, 'I suppose those French turds are the reason *we* came along, eh?'

My heart was beating against my ribs like that of a wild beast, but I grinned at him. 'Aye.'

It was forty paces to the bank where the crossbowmen would land. Run over too soon, and we risked being shot at ourselves – one man in every boat had cocked and loaded his weapon. Leave it too late, and we would advance into a hail of death-delivering bolts. We waited, dry-mouthed, as the last of the French clambered aboard and they began to row.

'What of the duke?' I asked.

'He still shows no sign of retreat,' said John. 'And there are cross-bowmen on the walls now.'

The news added to our woes. Notwithstanding the danger to Richard from the enemy atop the defences, we risked dying before any help arrived. To do nothing, however, placed the duke in even greater danger. I buried my fear as best I could, and told myself that God would watch over me. 'The boats are halfway across. We must move.'

'For the duke,' said John.

'For the duke,' I said, and charged.

It was a headlong rush, borne on the wings of sheer terror. Two of us against fourteen Frenchmen, more than half of whom had crossbows. Our only advantages were those of surprise and speed.

No one noticed us for the first ten or fifteen steps, but then a cross-bowman saw. Confusion filled his face. For all he knew, we were the leaders of a much larger group. We covered more ground. He raised his crossbow and shot. The bolt hissed over my shoulder. A second, loosed by one of his companions, flew past John. Holding up my shield, praying that my unprotected legs would not be noticed, I ran on. The distinctive click of the 'tickler' triggers on the Frenchmen's crossbows went off, twice more. I was not hit; I did not hear John cry out, and I rejoiced.

The crossbowmen had insufficient time to reload before we reached them.

We got to the river just as the boats bumped into the shallows. John went left towards the first, I went straight ahead at a second. Already ashore, a man-at-arms came at me, but my impetus was such that my shield-strike drove him backwards, into the man behind. They fell, colliding with a third. I turned my attention to the next boat along, for a burly man-at-arms was almost upon me. We traded blows, high, low, then high again, and battered at each other with our shields. He was skilled, and my worries surged. If I did not down him fast, I would take a crossbow bolt in the back.

Christ be thanked. An instant later, the man-at-arms slipped on a patch of mud. I rammed my sword into his mouth as he fell, and he died. I killed the crossbowman behind him – frantically trying to load his weapon – and I hacked off the left arm of another. Panicked by the spray of blood and their comrade's screams, the three remaining retreated, unbalancing the boat. One toppled into the river, and another dropped his crossbow.

'Rufus!'

John's shout came from behind me. I began to turn, and lucky I did. Instead of hitting me in the side, the bolt first struck the edge of my shield. It punched into me under the ribs next, and I stumbled, feeling as if I had been kicked by a horse. I was still on my feet, however, and very much alive. I laughed at the Frenchman's attempt to fend me off with his now useless crossbow, and stuck him in the belly. Bawling like a babe ripped from the tit, he dropped.

I do not know how many Frenchmen there were left at that point, but it was still enough to overwhelm us. The five remaining men-at-arms prepared to keep us at arm's length while the crossbowmen stood behind, ready to shoot whenever the chance arose. My spirits had been soaring, but now they sank. Our shields would not keep out their bolts; they could also aim at our legs.

Click, click went the crossbow triggers. Such an innocuous sound, yet it made my skin crawl. A bolt struck John's helm, making it chime like a church bell. I felt the wind of another passing over my left shoulder.

'We must attack,' I said.

John's wits were half-scrambled from the bolt that had hit him, but he heard, and knew what I meant. Close in, the crossbowmen would not be able to shoot for fear of hitting their comrades. 'I am with you,' he growled.

We charged. I say we charged; it was too short a distance for that. We lumbered forward, hiding behind our shields as much as possible. Click, click. Click, click. With a sickening thunk and a spray of splinters, a bolt punched through my shield, and on, into my helmet. Two inches higher, and it would have taken me through the eye, but it missed the slit and instead made a deep dent in the iron. Feeling as if I had been kicked in the mouth, but otherwise uninjured, I drove at the nearest man-at-arms.

To my surprise, he fell back. His conical helm afforded no protection for the face, which allowed me to see his expression of fear. I pressed forward, exhilarated but also confused. He had crossbowmen behind him, and I was not a terrifying figure like the duke, who towered a foot and more over everyone else.

Then I heard pounding feet, and the cry, from many throats, 'For Aquitaine!'

My heart leaped.

Richard, retreating at last, had come to our aid.

'Curse you for purblind fools!' The duke stamped about before us. 'Wastrels, the pair of you!'

I wanted to look at John, who stood beside me, but dared not.

Richard had taken off his hauberk and mail hose, and his sword. Huge sweat patches marked his tunic, and his hair was plastered to his skull. He stank of oil and leather, but by God's toes, he was every inch the warrior. I feared few men at that time, but I was scared of the duke.

He had said nothing to us after the French took flight, nor as we made our retreat from Périgueux. His curt manner made it clear, however, that we would not escape unchastised. We were summoned after he had met with his captains and issued orders to march on the town the next day, and here we stood, abashed as two boys caught stealing apples.

Richard rounded on me. 'Are you deaf?'

I met those blue eyes with difficulty. 'No, sire.'

'So you heard my order to stay at the merchant's.'

'I did, sire.'

'You at least should have known better,' said Richard, turning on John. 'Were you gilded this morn? Had you been at the wine?'

'Not a drop had passed my lips, sire,' replied John stolidly.

'And you?' Richard's stony gaze bore down on me.

'I had drunk nothing, sire.'

'Why did you do it then?'

John muttered something about twenty-one knights against an entire garrison, and how we had wanted to help. I nodded.

'And if you had been needed to carry word to the rest?' demanded the duke.

John looked at the ground.

Without thinking, I said, 'But we weren't, sire.'

Richard took a sideways step and suddenly, we were face to face.

I tensed, sure he was about to curse me to Hell, to strike me, or perhaps both.

To my amazement, he laughed. Not the mealy-mouthed effort of someone who pretends to be amused, but a full-throated belly laugh.

I shot a glance at John, but I could not read his expression.

Richard chuckled again. 'You speak the truth, Rufus – there is no denying it. If you had not attacked the crossbowmen, moreover, some of my knights would have been slain. I might have been injured myself. For that, I owe you my thanks.'

I could feel a smile tugging its way onto my lips. My eyes lifted to Richard's, which glinted like blue chips of ice, and my joy died a quick death.

'Disobey my orders again, and I will see the skin flogged from both your backs.'

'Yes, sire,' we chorused. I am not ashamed to say my knees were trembling. John was more composed, but he too seemed humbled.

'Fetch bread and meat. Cheese too,' said Richard. 'My belly feels as if my throat has been cut.'

Like that, it was over.

'Yes, sire,' said John.

Lost for words, I was still gaping like a fool, but John, more used to the duke, took my arm and steered me from the tent.

'Most men hold onto their ill temper the way a miser clutches at his gold, but some few are like a winter storm. Richard is one such,' John confided. 'His anger batters all before it, and threatens everything in its path, but when it dissipates, peace is restored.'

'So when we return, his mood will be good?' I asked, yet unsure.

'A silver penny says he is as sunny as a child offered a marchpane fancy,' John replied.

I took the wager, but lost it, gladly, upon our return.

Richard treated both of us as if nothing untoward had happened. If anything, he was warmer than usual, which bound me to him a little more.

Sweet Jesu, he was a leader of men.

We took Périgueux two days later, storming the walls at night with ladders. With the garrison survivors under lock and key, and a skeleton force left to man the fortress, the duke led us east at speed. Our enemies were numerous, and around the campfires each night, my understanding of their reasons for rebelling grew. John de Mandeville it was who provided much of the information. The shared experience at Périgueux had seen our relationship change for the better; Philip was no longer my only friend among the squires.

Count Vulgrin Taillefer of Angoulême had died the previous summer, John explained, leaving an infant daughter, Matilda, as his heir. Richard, Vulgrin's lord, had soon declared Matilda would come under his protection. The dead man's brothers, William and Adémar, whom the duke had referred to at Caen, saw things in a different light. In their minds, it was *they* who should be Matilda's guardians, not the duke, for he could keep the income from the child's substantial estates until she was wed.

With a dense network of inter-marriage and familial ties throughout the region, it had not been difficult for the disgruntled Taillefers to find allies. William and Adémar's half-brother, Aimar of Limoges, had rebelled against Henry and Richard previously; so too had the Viscount of Turenne. The count of Périgord, to whom Périgueux had belonged, and the Viscounts of Ventadour and Comborn, had also joined the cause, again not for the first time.

The duke's approach to the rebels was fast-moving and perilous. His strategy was to attack, attack, attack. He moved faster than his enemies thought possible. Appeared in their territory unexpectedly, or outside their fortress, and before their forces could be marshalled. Often, their only option was to surrender.

Castle after castle was stormed or opened its gates to us as we travelled east from Périgueux. Into the verdant country of the Limousin we went, the least populated area of the duke's huge realm. There were extensive areas of forest, oak and beech, from which I heard wolves howling at night. Rolling fields held glossy-flanked beef cattle, enormous creatures twice the size of those my family had owned.

How the local farmers and peasantry must have hated us. Richard ordered us not to take everything, for the man with an empty barn and no livestock starves in the winter, but taking half still sets a fire of hatred in people's hearts. To stand by as your crops are loaded into wagons and your stock rounded up would test a saint. Despite this, violence was rare. Thank God. Tunics do not compare to gambesons and mail, and pitchforks are no match for swords and shields.

Skirmishes were frequent, as the rebellious lords sought to weaken our forces and sap our morale. They ambushed us at every opportunity. From the woods. Out of valley mouths. As we forded rivers. At night. In the grey light that preceded dawn. Double strength patrols were essential, and we squires became fighters. We learned never to leave sentries on their own. To dig ditches around our camp. To look into wells, where the carcase of an animal might be lying, before we drank the water. We answered every call of nature with a comrade – this, to avoid having our throats slit, the fate of several unfortunate archers.

Nonetheless, we had advantages in most areas of battle. Crossbow-men, the missile troops used by the French, needed to be a lot closer to the enemy than our archers, whose range and skill was unparalleled. The duke also had more knights than individual rebel nobles, and at least as many men-at-arms. For these reasons, the French tried to avoid open battle; on the rare occasion it happened, we were invariably suc-cessful. Much was made of the cowardice of the French, but in my mind, it was hot air. Only an amadán fights a bigger, stronger man, as my father used to say. The intelligent thing to do is to hit the bastard on the back of the head with a stone, and when he stumbles, run in and hamstring him.

After a month, that is what the French began to do.

CHAPTER XV

It was late in Le Mans, and William Marshal was about to retire for the night. Servants had placed a chamber pot by the bed, folded back the covers and extinguished all but a few rush lights. The room seemed smaller and cosier now, a home from home. One day, God willing, he would sleep in his own castle, but until then he had everything needful: several changes of clothes, his armour and weapons, and safe in an iron chest, a heavy sack of coin.

Marshal knelt in prayer on the stone flags, asking for three things. That his sins be forgiven, and that both he and the Young King be granted guidance, so they might choose the right road. In truth, he thought ruefully, help was only needed with his master's path, because, oathbound, he would follow wherever the Young King led. Even if, as seemed likely from recent events, that meant joining the rebellion against Duke Richard.

All was not yet lost. Like his brother Geoffrey, the Young King had still not fully committed to the rebels' cause. In part this had been because the troubadour de Born's efforts had not borne as much fruit as hoped. Few noblemen apart from the barons of the Limousin and Périgord were prepared to commit to the fight, and if initial reports were accurate, they were faring badly in the struggle with Richard. This was not the Young King's sole reason for reticence. Counselled by Marshal at every turn against joining the rebels, concerned that his father would support Richard and not him and Geoffrey if it came to war, he could not reach a final decision.

Let him see the error of his ways, Marshal prayed. Move his attention away from conflict, towards amity and concord with his family.

Footsteps echoed in the corridor outside.

Ever alert, Marshal brought a swift end to his devotions, and stood. The feet came to a halt outside his chamber, and a fist rapped on the timbers.

One of his master's squires stood at the threshold.

'What is it?' demanded Marshal.

'The Young King wishes you to attend him, sir.'

Marshal was accustomed to such summons, which signified that his master was in his cups. Eager to influence the Young King away from the course of war, he donned his shoes and followed the squire. A short distance from their destination, the peace was broken by the sound of loud voices. Annoyance pricked Marshal; others were present. His hopes of success had diminished. Chances were also that the night might be long and tiresome.

Entering, he saw that the Young King's drinking companions were his friends Baldwin de Béthune and Simon de Marisco, as well as d'Yquebeuf and de Coulonces. Marshal was sure that the latter pair were behind the lies about him and the queen; being in their company was insufferable. None of this anger towards them could show, however, so he smoothed his face into an expression of pleasure.

Only de Marisco and de Béthune had noticed his arrival. The other three were engrossed in a heated conversation, their flushed cheeks and slurred speech revealing their level of inebriation.

'I tell you, sire,' said d'Yquebeuf loudly, 'your brother Richard is power mad. Nothing gives him more pleasure than dominating his subjects. Look at the way he took the child heiress Matilda into his care. By rights, she should have been surrendered to her uncles, the Taillefer brothers.'

'Richard has ever been high-handed,' muttered the Young King.

'He cares nothing for the girl, of course, sire,' said d'Yquebeuf. 'All he wants is the monies from her estates that will be his as her guardian.'

''Tis no wonder the Taillefers rebelled,' said the Young King.

'They needs must be cautious, sire,' said de Coulonces. 'Your brother is not called the soldier prince for nothing.'

De Béthune threw him a warning look, but it was too late.

The Young King's fist hammered the table. Spatters of wine flew. 'Hellfire, I know that!'

D'Yquebeuf, not renowned for his brains, continued owlishly, 'Two castles in the Limousin have already had their walls reduced, sire.'

'Indeed,' said de Béthune. 'It is none of our concern.'

'I am not interested in what Richard does. I too have taken fortresses by siege,' snarled the Young King.

'Even so, sire.' Giving d'Yquebeuf a jab in the ribs, de Coulonces added, 'You are a skilled tactician and courageous leader. Every man wants to be like you. In the battles you have fought, the world trembled.'

It was as if the Young King had not heard. He drank his cup to the lees and banged it down. As a squire hurried in with a brimming jug, he cried, 'Richard. Richard! Why do men talk so much about my cursed brother? *I* am the king's eldest son. *I* am the one who should be feared and respected.'

'You are, sire,' chorused d'Yquebeuf and de Coulonces like a pair of trained parrots.

It would have given Marshal huge pleasure to say 'lick arses', but he swallowed the insult and instead took the cup proffered by a squire. He sat down opposite de Béthune and de Marisco, giving them a friendly nod. His friends looked relieved by his arrival. 'Greetings, sire,' Marshal said in a loud voice.

The Young King twisted around, a smile easing his sour mien. 'Ah, Will. You are here.'

'It is a pleasure to join your company, Hal, as always.' Marshal raised his wine in salute, and ignored the hostile stares of d'Yquebeuf and de Coulonces.

The Young King launched straight back into his conversation. 'I am told that Richard will soon ask my lord father for aid to subdue the rebels. No doubt I will be summoned as well, and Geoffrey.'

'How will you respond, Hal?' asked Marshal, wondering how long his master could continue without declaring his loyalties.

'I will do as my lord father bids,' replied the Young King. 'Périgueux has fallen. I have no doubt that more castles will open their gates to my brother. I would be a fool to join with the rebels now, although their cause is just.'

'That would be the wiser choice.' Even as Marshal's heart leaped, he worried that his master's thwarted look meant the matter had not been laid to rest. But this for now he would take.

The Young King threw back another great mouthful. 'Nothing for it, eh? Back to the tournament circuit we shall go, while Geoffrey has

Brittany, and Richard rules Aquitaine. Even John, the whelp, can call himself Lord of Ireland, while I, title-less, landless, am forever condemned to prove my worth on the jousting field.' His lips twisted. 'Until my lord father dies, that is.'

'There are worse places, Hal,' said Marshal. 'The thrill of the tourney never quite goes away.' Almost a decade and a half had passed since his first contest, yet it was true.

'Remember the time you lost your helmet, Hal?' De Béthune was also eager to raise the mood.

'You were fighting on your own for a time, sire, and held off every knight who came at you,' said de Marisco.

The Young King's eyes brightened. 'Aye, so I did. You came then, Will, and sent them running.'

'We did it together, Hal,' said Marshal, embroidering the truth a little. 'That was a good day.'

'I suppose the tourney circuit will not be so bad.' The Young King did not sound convinced. He emptied his cup. 'More wine.'

From nowhere, de Coulonces pounced. 'It is said that you prefer to use your lance elsewhere of recent times, Marshal.'

The Young King's expression grew thunderous.

D'Yquebeuf started to snigger, and then thought better of it.

'Shut your lying mouth, de Coulonces,' grated Marshal. 'You too, d'Yquebeuf.'

His enemies glowered.

The Young King turned baleful eyes on Marshal. 'Are they both wrong?'

'If, sire, you refer to the vile rumours about me and the queen, then yes, they are. I swear it. May I be condemned to eternal damnation if I speak not the truth.' Marshal had never meant anything more, but to his dismay, the Young King's misery did not ease.

'You say one thing.' Glancing at d'Yquebeuf and de Coulonces, he continued, 'These men say another.'

'They are lying, sire,' said de Béthune. De Marisco added loud agreement.

The Young King's troubled gaze roved over them, one after another.

It is I who have been your loyal servant these many years, Marshal wanted to scream, not those faithless curs. 'Let the matter be settled on the contest field, Hal. I will fight both d'Yquebeuf and de Coulonces, one after another, and a third of their henchmen. Should I lose, hang me for an ordinary criminal. Emerge victorious, and I ask that my honour be restored.' Seeing the fear rise in his enemies' faces, his hopes rose.

The Young King breathed in and out through his nose, in the ponderous manner of the very drunk. He shook his head, as if to clear it. 'Far more important matters there are at hand, Will, than meaningless feats of arms. Have you forgotten my brother Richard?'

'I have not, Hal, but I thought—'

'Do you not see what he is doing? His territory forms the largest part of the king's continental dominions. Richard's intent has long been to break away, in order to rule Aquitaine himself, and call no man liege lord. He will *never* bend the knee when I am king. He must be chastened; taught a lesson.'

'You speak true, sire,' chorused d'Yquebeuf and de Coulonces.

To protest further would jeopardise his own position, Marshal decided. He nodded, as if accepting his master's opinion. 'How do you mean to combat the threat from Richard?'

'A hawk hovers in the sky, safe from danger, waiting for the perfect time to strike,' said the Young King. 'That is what I shall do.'

Frustration battered Marshal. The king would always cleave to those of his sons who seek to defend the realm, not to those hellbent on tearing it apart.

Disaster had not been avoided, but delayed.

A number of days later, Marshal was in Limoges. The Young King had taken it upon himself to travel south at speed, before his father had even done so. They had not taken the direct route towards Richard's forces, because, still uncommitted, the Young King intended to gauge the mood in the Limousin and Périgord. There had been little choice for Marshal but to follow.

Count Aimar was not at home – he was in the field, fighting Richard – but his wife had given the heir to the throne a warm welcome, and asked that he join her husband and his fellow rebels. Sly as a fox, the Young King had revealed he was on his way to meet Aimar's most powerful vassals. The stronghold of St Yrieix was to be first, with others to follow. After that, the intimation had been he would ride to join Aimar himself. Delighted, the countess had laid on a feast that had rivalled any in the royal court.

Bidding her farewell a few moments prior, they made their way out the main gate.

'She is a fine woman,' said the Young King.

From the glint in his master's eye, Marshal judged the Young King might have tried his luck with the countess had time not been pressing.

'Do you not think so?'

'I do, Hal, but she is married.'

'When the drake is away, the duck can play,' said d'Yquebeuf.

Sure that this was part-aimed at him, Marshal shot a furious glare at his enemy, who smirked; de Coulonces was chuckling in encouragement.

The Young King twisted in the saddle. 'I have half a mind to ride back.'

Let his master act like a randy squire and any chance of an alliance with Aimar and his fellows would vanish in a puff of smoke, thought Marshal. If the Young King did not join the rebels, the likelihood was Geoffrey would not either. It was tempting, but pricked by his conscience and sense of chivalry, he said, 'Imagine Count Aimar's reaction, sire, if he were to find out that you had bedded his wife.'

The Young King turned a hard stare on Marshal, and said, 'He would not be best pleased, Will, just as I was not to hear rumour about you and Marguerite.'

Sharp glances from d'Yquebeuf and de Coulonces.

'They are lies, Hal!' cried Marshal. 'I have ever been a faithful servant.'

The Young King gave no reply, but he did not wheel his horse and make for the castle.

Marshal suspected that he had unintentionally shamed his master into realising how Aimar might feel as *he* had when the stories about Queen Marguerite had first reached his ears. Wanting to be sure the Young King had been dissuaded, Marshal went on, 'The count of Limoges would be a powerful ally, Hal. He—'

'Yes, yes, I understand!'

An uncomfortable silence descended. Even d'Yquebeuf and de Coulonces knew better than to speak. They rode, letting the creak of saddle leather and the shouts of the serjeants fill the air.

To Marshal's dismay, the Young King slowed his horse only a short distance later. Christ Jesus, do not let him have changed his mind, he prayed. His master's purpose took him by surprise, however. They were within sight of the walls of the great Benedictine abbey of St Martial's, which lay close to the count's castle.

'I wish to visit,' said the Young King.

Marshal hid his surprise. The Young King was as religious as any other man, but he preferred a feasting hall to a church, and a troubadour's singing to the chant of monks. It was doubtful either that he wanted to see the library, famed for its collection of music scripts. He cast an appraising look at his master. 'To pray, sire?'

'Maybe, after.'

Marshal's curiosity grew. 'After what, sire?'

The Young King's expression grew smug. 'I have a gift for the abbot.'

It would not be a monetary donation, Marshal decided. His master's purse was ever light. Perhaps he means to make me pay – again – he thought. 'What is it, Hal?'

'A cloak.' Seeing Marshal's confusion, he laughed. 'You will see.'

Marshal nodded, wondering what he was playing at.

An hour later, as they took the road again, he had to admit that his master was no fool. The abbot of St Martial's had been impressed by and grateful for the show of royal affection: a magnificent blue cloak of Flemish wool, felted and thrice dyed, and edged with sable. On it, embroidered with gold thread, were the words 'Henricus Rex', 'King Henry'. Not just a present, Marshal decided, the garment had been a means to an end, to discover if the abbot of St Martial's, an influential figure, would offer any support.

A master of flattery when he chose, the Young King had pronounced the cloak to be but the beginning. Far richer donations would come, when he was king, when he controlled Aquitaine. Soon the cozened abbot had mentioned the widespread resentment towards Richard, who had imposed his own direct rule on the region for years. 'He pays no regard to local custom. And yet he is always generous towards the church.' The last words had been delivered with an ingratiating smile.

The Young King had sworn on the spot that a new jewelled cross for the main altar would be delivered before the winter's end, after which the abbot had blessed him and declared that he would make the best of kings.

Tellingly, however, he had not sworn to lend his support against Richard, something Marshal's master, his head swelled with images of sitting on the throne, had not noticed. Whatever the abbot's real loyalties, the Young King's intention to join the struggle against his brother Richard had been given a new lease of life.

It would have been better not to interfere, thought Marshal glumly. Let his master pursue the countess, and, his head filled with post-coital lust, he would have forgotten to lavish the embroidered cloak upon the abbot of St Martial's. Now, encouraged, he was holding forth about the lord of St Yrieix, and how many soldiers he might provide for the army that would defeat Richard.

What was done could not be undone, Marshal decided. More was the pity.

Richard needed to be sent a fresh message.

CHAPTER XVI

M id-May found Richard a long way north and east of Périgueux at Grandmont, known by the locals as the big mountain. I found the name strange, for it was only the same height as Sliabh Feá, a large hill. The previous days had been a trial. The duke had defeated the rebel noblemen time and again, but he lacked the strength to force them into submission, and like feral dogs gathering into a pack, they joined forces. Their attacks grew more frequent, and bolder. We began to lose men in numbers that mattered. Castles we had taken were abandoned, for fear of losing our under-strength garrisons. Retreat would have been most men's choice, but not the duke.

He sent word to his father the king, and fought on. Our tactics changed. Instead of riding through the countryside like princelings, we moved during the hours of darkness, from place of strength to place of strength. Ambushes and night attacks now became our tactic too. In this manner, a fortress we had seized and surrendered was taken again. Two days later, we abandoned the place for a second time. The process, said Philip, was like a madman's game of chess, and it was hard to disagree. In lands less fertile, we might have starved, but the Limousin was rich in cattle and sheep. True, the pickings grew leaner as we ravaged back and forth across the countryside, but we grew expert at sniffing out hidden cellars containing vegetables, cheeses and hams. Threats, and sometimes a little 'persuasion', saw farmers give up the secret hiding places for their livestock.

All the same, a wave of relief swept the camp when a messenger on a sweat-lathered horse rode in one afternoon, and soon after, word came that the king was journeying south in strength, with his son Geoffrey. Two hundred knights were with them, and a thousand each of archers and men-at-arms. United with this force, we told one another delightedly, we would force the rebels into submission.

Robert FitzAldelm – Boots and Fists – was also with Richard's force. There was little reason to suppose that he knew anything except the bare bones about his brother's death in Southampton, still less that I had slain him. And yet, worried I would give something away without realising, I had no wish to meet my old tormentor. I succeeded in avoiding his attention for a time, keeping my head down, and on the rare occasions he entered the duke's tent, making myself busy out of sight. Fool that I was, I began to think that we would never meet, that after three years, he might not recognise me, or that he would be slain in a skirmish with the rebels. The last, my preferred fate for him, did not happen, alas.

Inevitably, our paths crossed, but not in the way I might have imagined.

At the end of a long day, I was helping to water the duke's horses near our camp at Grandmont. Rhys, Philip and Louis were with me. It was no longer my place to care for the mounts, but the day was glorious, fresh yet warm, and the very air vibrant with the promise of summer. The evening before, a band of archers had passed the duke's tent, each carrying a line of sleek silver trout on slender twigs. When the smell of their frying had reached me, my belly was vociferous in its complaints. Today, I decided, Philip and I would also try our luck at fishing, and Louis might unstiffen himself enough to join us. When the French squire let down his guard, he was a pleasant individual, possessed of a sharp eye and a keen sense of humour.

Warmed by the sunshine, with the hobbled horses now cropping the grass, I supped from my costrel of wine, and passed it around. Everyone's mood was good. All was well with the world. The prospect of fresh-caught fish and after, a dip in the river, was mightily pleasing. The king would soon arrive. Alert to the danger, the rebels had pulled back. Rumour was that Henry would summon the nobles to a conference, and that, fearful of his retaliation, they would obey his call.

Oddly, the prospect of peace was not altogether welcome. No one spoke of it much, but each of us dreamed of knighthood, and war was the best way to achieve that goal. My gaze roved over Philip and

Louis, and I thought of John de Mandeville. Of the five, he wanted it most; anytime it *was* mentioned, a burning hunger lit in his eyes. It was unclear why he had not yet been knighted, but in my mind, it was because he was . . . in a word, dull. Dependable, yes. Dutiful, yes. Brave, undoubtedly, but he hesitated to act unless he was ordered to. He would not have come with me at Périgueux if I had not persuaded him.

Weasel John would earn his spurs eventually, but Richard was in no hurry to grant him that favour. It was common knowledge that the duke did not like him. My stare came to rest on Louis next. He was brave, rashly so. It would surprise no one if he was slain in an attempt to win his knighthood. My friend Philip nudged me, and I passed him the costrel. Philip was still young, I decided. At nineteen, he had a few more years of squiring until higher rank beckoned.

'Can I have another sup, sir?' asked Rhys.

I studied his rosy cheeks. 'How many have you already had?'

'Three, sir.'

Philip let out a snort.

I raised an eyebrow at Rhys, who grinned. 'Mayhap it was four, sir. Or five.'

'One more, and that is all,' I warned, and with a nod of thanks, Rhys reached out to Philip for the costrel. After a pull longer than I liked, he said, 'I will try my luck in the river next, sir.'

Glad, I nodded my approval as Rhys picked up one of our crude fishing poles. He made for the bank, a cup of worms in his other hand.

Philip, Louis and I fell to talking about the king's arrival, and the conference. Peace was likely, everyone agreed on that, but how long it would last was another. The nobles of Aquitaine, proud and independent-minded, had a history of bending the knee when forced to, only to rise up when the duke or the king had his back turned. Like as not, said Louis, the uprising would rekindle within the year.

If only the Irish kings were like that, I thought. It was a far-fetched hope, sadly. The French fought as knights in armour, like the English, while the Irish did not. Thus they were always destined to lose to the invaders, which made rebellion dangerous and unappealing. If I was ever to retake Cairlinn – my deep-harboured dream – I would have to win it as a grant from the king. To have any chance of that, I needed to become a knight. I smiled at myself, amused by the sea change which saw me desire the rank I would have once scorned.

The ground shook. Voices rang out. Horses whinnied. I glanced up. A conroi of knights was approaching the river. Dusty, their mounts clearly eager for water, they must have been on patrol. It was an ordinary sight; I paid them no heed. Senses a little blunted by the wine, made drowsy by the sun and the murmur of Philip and Louis's voices, I lay back on the warm grass and closed my eyes.

I dreamed of Cairlinn on a summer's day. Of Fionnuala, the laughing, freckle-cheeked carpenter's daughter whom I had tumbled twice, and remembered many times since. Strange it may seem, fit, strong youth that I was, but I had not lain with a woman after her. At first the chances had not come my way – fighting the English, being taken captive – but in Striguil, things were different, freer. Big Mary would have tupped me in the blink of an eye, but she had terrified me. There had been the tavern wench I fancied, and had never bedded. I could have futtered whores in the settlement as most squires did, but something held me back – a desire to rekindle what I had enjoyed with Fionnuala, perhaps.

Warm sun on my face, Fionnuala astride me – she had been forward – I let out a quiet moan.

Someone cried out.

I paid no heed, but gripped Fionnuala's hips, and smiled up at her.

An almighty clout in the ear smashed my dream into a thousand pieces. I glared at Philip. 'What?'

'Rhys is in trouble.'

I shoved Fionnuala from my mind, and sat up. The sound of a blow reached me, and after it, a cry. Recognising Rhys's voice, I stood, gaze searching the riverbank.

'I think some of the horses were drinking close to him,' said Philip. 'He was about to make a cast, and he nearly caught one in the cheek with his hook. A knight noticed, and—'

I did not hear the rest, for I was scrambling to the water's edge.

Rhys was about twenty-five paces away. He was in the grip of a knight who had his back to me, and from the man's swinging arm, was on the end of a drubbing. I ran, holding in the shout that rose to my lips. I was a squire, not a knight.

Drawing near, I said loudly, 'Good day, sir.'

The knight's blow did not fall. He turned, and with horror, I recognised the familiar block-head. It was Boots and Fists. He stared at me, a puzzled frown marking his brow, and said in disbelief, 'As I live and breathe – Rufus?'

'It is,' I said, forcing myself to add, 'sir.'

He cuffed Rhys, not seeing the boy's look of hatred, and said, 'Is this brat yours?'

'He is my page, sir, yes. Can I ask why you are beating him?'

'The purblind fool almost took out my destrier's eye with his hook,' replied FitzAldelm, giving no sign that he remembered Rhys from Striguil.

I glanced at the nearest horses, all of which were slurping greedily from the river. 'Was your steed wounded, sir?'

'That is beside the point,' said FitzAldelm, making to strike Rhys once more.

'Please stop, sir.' I took a step closer.

He hit Rhys again, and leered at me. 'Why should I?'

'Your horse is uninjured, sir. Rhys was careless, but I am sure he meant no harm. He has learned his lesson.'

FitzAldelm bunched a fist.

Raising my voice so that everyone within earshot could hear, I said, 'I am squire to Duke Richard, sir.'

The punch did not land. FitzAldelm's grip on Rhys slackened. He eyed me with suspicion. 'You jest.'

'I do not, sir, as Christ is my witness.' Remembering Philip, a few paces behind me, I gestured and said, 'This man also serves the duke.'

'That I do, sir, God bless him,' cried Philip.

'I may be wrong, sir,' I said to FitzAldelm, 'but I think the duke would look ill upon the knight who manhandles a boy in such manner.'

Drawn by the noise, others were watching now: Boots and Fists' companions, and a group of squires and men-at-arms.

With a black scowl, FitzAldelm flung Rhys away. 'Mind where you cast your line in future,' he growled.

Rhys scuttled to my side, throwing FitzAldelm a venomous glance. 'Are you hurt?' I asked quietly.

A savage shake of the head, and another furious glare at our enemy.

For *our* enemy he was, I thought. Rhys had had good reason to dislike Robert FitzAldelm before; now he possessed even more.

'How came you to be in the duke's service?' demanded FitzAldelm.

I could not help myself. 'I saved his life, sir.'

'He did, sir,' Philip put in. 'Ask anyone.'

Leaving FitzAldelm open-mouthed, I made my retreat while the advantage was still mine. 'Did you know he was here?' I asked Rhys.

'No, sir, on my life.' He gave me a reproving look. 'Even if I had, I have enough wits not to hurt his destrier. If I were to do anything, it would be to slit his saddle girth, as he did to de Lysle.'

'That is a sure path to the hangman's noose.' I knew Rhys's stubbornness well, and I shook him. 'Do you hear me? I was able to save you from a beating, but my hands would be tied if you did something like that. FitzAldelm will meet his fate one day, and God willing, we will be there to see it.'

'As we were in the alley, sir, with his brother?'

There had been no mention of the fight in Southampton since it happened. Discomfited, I replied, 'I would rather fight him man to man, and kill him that way.'

'He is a whoreson, sir,' Rhys snarled. 'I care not in what manner he dies.'

Wondering what my enemy's next move would be, I paid him little heed.

My concerns came to nothing. FitzAldelm came sniffing about the duke's tent that evening, and struck up a conversation with John de Mandeville, but John's confirmation of my status made him vanish back whence he had come. My own discreet investigations over the next day or two, made via Rhys and some of the squires I knew, revealed that FitzAldelm had made slight advancement in the three years since his departure from Striguil. He fought well enough, it seemed, but had taken no valuable prisoners – the swiftest path to wealth and status. He was no more important than a hundred other knights, I told myself, and I had little reason to fear him.

The king and Geoffrey arrived two days later. It was noticeable that Richard closeted himself frequently with his father, but not his brother. Rumours of the Young King's possible dealings with the rebel nobles were common knowledge in Richard's mesnie; it seemed now that he had the same suspicions about Geoffrey. If either brother was mentioned when the duke was alone, he would scowl. In public, he was the picture of equanimity, and I tried my hardest to emulate him.

It was the mark of a knight to refrain from showing emotion even in the presence of enemies, but to practise it was quite a skill. I had managed to keep my composure with FitzAldelm because Rhys had been in danger, but if the confrontation had been longer, I would have lost my temper. Richard, on the other hand, dealt with French nobles he had just defeated in battle in a friendly and courteous manner. Only in private did he express any bad feelings towards them. The man with an impenetrable public mask, I decided, had a real advantage over his enemies.

The conference took place a sennight later. It had taken time, but the noblemen of Aquitaine answered Henry's summons. On the appointed day, they rode into the designated field at Grandmont, neutral ground, with haughty expressions and backs stiff with resentment. I was there, with Richard, his father and Geoffrey. A large tent had been erected on the sward, a magnificent structure of red and gold fabric, the colours of the house of Anjou. A pennant hung from a pole by its entrance, the two snarling royal lions embroidered on it a clear warning of the king's presence. Two score knights in full armour stood guard outside – the rebel nobles were allowed a brace of men each as escort, and none of those were allowed to enter with their masters. It was a statement of force, made with a mailed fist.

In they came at the appointed hour, William and Adémar Taillefer, uncles to the child Matilda, Vulgrin's heiress. They were a pair of tough-looking men with righteous anger writ all over their faces. Their half-brother, Count Aimar of Limoges, was there, small and squat, and rumoured to be as fierce as a wild boar; so was the Viscount of Turenne, a strutting peacock with gold trim on his belt and scabbard. The Count of Périgord cut a fine figure despite his plain mail and worn scabbard, while the Viscounts of Ventadour and Comborn, effeminate and reeking of scent, stood so close to one another I judged them to be lovers. Bertran de Born the troubadour, a paunchy, self-important type, had brought his lute with him, as if to serenade the meeting. There were half a dozen more, but their names escape me.

Richard greeted the nobles in his father's stead, polite yet stern. I watched him, and again marvelled at his composure. Amazingly, the duke seemed to warm to the nobles as time passed. He ordered wine served, and even engaged several in conversation. We waited for the king. In another show of who was master, he did not make his entrance until at least an hour after the French had gathered. At last the heralds cried, 'Henry FitzEmpress, King of England, and Duke of Normandy.'

Geoffrey smirked.

I knew why. These titles would fall to the Young King eventually, but until his father died, he was an heir without power. Although younger, Geoffrey was for the moment more powerful. So too was Richard. Even John was Lord of Ireland. I began to understand the Young King's dissatisfaction better. Small wonder that he spent his time at tourneys, I thought, as a hush fell.

Henry limped as he came in, but his manner was confident, and the gem-studded crown on his head again made it plain who was lord. Taking a seat on the carved chair at the head of the tent, he waited.

Richard knelt, and Geoffrey, and so did we, and every man of the king's household.

Glances shot between the nobles from Aquitaine, none of whom had yet followed suit.

Henry's nostrils flared.

I watched with bated breath. Rebellion was bad, but if the French did not pay obeisance fast, the conference was as dead as a ten-day-old corpse.

William and Adémar went down on one knee together, but they did not look happy. It was enough, however, to make their companions do the same.

The tension that had sprung from nowhere eased but a fraction.

'Rise,' said Henry.

We stood.

'Well, messires?' Henry asked. 'I am come, because you have risen in arms against your rightful lord, the Duke of Aquitaine, my son. What have you to say?'

So angry were the nobles, they all began speaking at once. Accusations against Richard flew. Fingers were pointed at him. I heard insults muttered. Bertran hummed a tune under his breath.

The duke kept silent, but the point of one of his shoes tapped up and down, in the manner of a cat lashing the tip of its tail.

Henry waited for a brief pause in the commotion, and said acidly, 'I am reminded of a pack of squabbling children.'

A few nobles seemed ashamed. Most were annoyed still, but they did fall silent.

William, Adémar and Aimar exchanged words before Aimar stood forward, stiff-legged. 'Sire, we come to seek redress for the wrongs done to us by your son.'

'The Duke of Aquitaine, your lord,' replied Henry. 'Whom you have rebelled against previously.'

There were angry mutters aplenty at this, but the nobles managed to hold their peace. Aimar inclined his head, and said, 'In name he is our lord, sire, but he does not act like one.'

The snort Richard let out was meant to be heard.

'Explain,' Henry ordered.

It poured out, a torrent of bitterness and bile. Aimar claimed that Richard's great cruelty was the talk of France. He oppressed his subjects with unjustified demands and a regime of violence. He was wont to carry off his subjects' wives, daughters and kinswomen by force and make them his concubines. When he had sated his lust, Aimar declared, his voice rising, he handed them down for his soldiers to enjoy. These wrongs were just some of the many he inflicted on his subjects, and it was in defence of their people that the nobles had risen against him. When Aimar finished, his cheeks were flushed.

I shot a look at Richard, whose face was a complete mask, and another at Geoffrey. Now and again, his eyes became as calculating as those of a lion about to spring on its prey. I did not like it. He might be standing with his father and brother, but I wagered he was also engaged in secret dealings with the rebel noblemen.

Aimar's companions patted him on the back, and murmured encouragement. Bertran de Born strummed his lute, as if he were about to break into song about the duke.

Another silence fell.

I considered the allegations again, which were far-fetched, even fantastical. I had been with the duke for the previous month, or close to him, and seen no women at all. His soldiers had been ordered not to attack any females. I had heard of a few rapes, but not many. These lies, I decided, were designed purely to drum up bad feeling.

'If these accusations are true, they are heinous,' said Henry. 'What say you, Richard?'

'I have never heard such lies in my life,' answered the duke. 'I have never taken a woman by force, and nor shall I. My men have been commanded to leave the fair sex unharmed. Anyone proven to have violated a woman will receive swift justice. I swear this before God and His saints.'

Henry looked satisfied. He glanced at Aimar. 'There you have it.'

Aimar's jaw dropped. 'You discount my word entirely, sire?'

Bertran de Born was shaking his head in disbelief. Adémar had to hold back William, who had taken a step towards Richard.

'The duke has given his word that he has committed none of the atrocities you mention. He has sworn that any of his men who have done wrong will pay for it. Will you now call him a liar?' Henry's eyes resembled chips of flint.

Everyone's gaze moved to Aimar. He hesitated, then said, 'I will not, sire, but nor will I retract my words.'

'That presents us with a problem,' said Henry, looking at Richard and Geoffrey. Both moved closer, so they stood on either side of his chair, a triangle of Anjou power. All was not as it seemed, of course, for one – Geoffrey – could not be trusted.

Aimar turned to his half-brothers, who whispered something. He faced Henry again, and said, 'There is also the matter of Matilda, sire. Vulgrin's daughter.'

'The duke's ward, yes.' Henry's tone was off-hand. 'What of her?'

'The custom of Aquitaine dictates that she enter into the custody of her closest adult relatives, William and Adémar.'

The brothers stood a little taller, and glared at Richard.

'Local convention be what it may – Duke Richard is lord to the Taillefers. He has acted correctly in taking the child into his care. So say I, *his* lord.' Henry banged the arm of his chair for emphasis.

William Taillefer could take no more. 'Sire—' he began.

'Silence!' Richard's roar filled the tent.

'I have given my final word,' said Henry. 'Accept it, or consider your-selves still at war.' He sat, watching the French, as we all were.

The rebel nobles did not talk for long. Aimar addressed the king.

'We need to take counsel with each other, sire, in the comfort of our camp.'

Henry made an impatient gesture. 'Be gone.'

Richard bent to speak in his father's ear. The king nodded. Richard waited until the nobles were walking away before saying in a loud, confident tone, 'Send word of your answer by sundown, messires.'

Aimar looked back, and it was plain by the set of his jaw that they had already decided to reject Henry's ruling. 'We will, sire.'

'And so the war continues,' said Richard none too quietly.

I happened to glance at Geoffrey, who was watching the French with a speculative expression. Remembering the rumours that he had met with the rebel nobles, and Richard's accusation of the same, I decided Rhys should watch him. If there was treachery afoot, it was best the duke knew about it sooner rather than later.

With Rhys by my side, I stood looking up at Périgueux, remembering how I had almost lost my life during the duke's madcap attack. The world had changed. Instead of sentries, and crossbowmen intent on killing me, I saw dozens of labourers hard at work. The walls were slowly being enclosed by scaffolding. When that was complete, the defences would be dismantled, by the command of Richard himself.

Nigh on two months had passed since the conference at Grandmont. High summer was here, and with it came a prolonged period of fine weather. Perfect for campaigning, perfect for bringing the rebels to heel – for they had not accepted the king's directive, and fought on. Summoned to join us, the Young King had recently brought more troops. Henry, Geoffrey and Richard had been driving the French before them, but the arrival of the heir to the throne had seen their operations take on a new vigour. And despite the rumours of the Young King's and Geoffrey's dealings with the rebels, for the moment they appeared to be content to stand with their father and Richard.

'How many fortresses is that now, sir?' Rhys asked happily.

'Three. Four?' I glanced at him. Our plentiful diet and good living had seen Rhys fill out. He was no longer a torso with sticks for arms and legs. True, he would never be my size, but he had a wiry strength to him that promised much.

'Excideuil and St Yrieix,' Rhys began. These had been the first of Aimar's strongholds that the king had led us against.

'Pierre-Buffière,' I added.

'And this one,' said Rhys. 'Puy-St-Front.'

'Four then. A fine tally in less than a month.'

'The Frenchies deserve it.'

I remembered Aimar's insolence, and the bristling attitudes at Grandmont. 'They do. And with no walls to their castles, they will not be able to rise again – unless every one of them is a complete amadán.'

'Amadán. I like that word.'

I smiled. 'I have heard you use it many's the time. Take my advice, though. Say it quietly. Men do not have to speak a tongue to recognise an insult.'

Rhys nodded.

'Seen or heard anything?' Since Grandmont, Rhys had been spying on Geoffrey at every opportunity. Little of substance had come of it thus far, and busy with my duties, I had not yet had time to ask that morning.

'No, sir.' Rhys's gaze moved over my shoulder. 'The duke,' he whispered, and dropped to one knee.

Richard was almost upon us. Bowing my head, I also knelt. 'Sire.'

'Rufus. Rhys. Up, both of you.' My master was in a good mood. In a plain tunic of dark green, with orange hose and a plain belt, he could have passed for an off-duty soldier. Apart from his great size, of course – there was no hiding that. Men were used to the duke wandering his camp in plain attire, however, and knew to let him be.

'Sire.' We stood. If Rhys had had a tail, he would have wagged it off, so pleased was he to be recognised by name.

'How goes the spying?' Richard asked.

'We was just talking about it, sire.' Rhys's French was fluent now, but his grammar remained poor. 'I cannot get near enough to the count's tent. All I can do is watch.'

Richard grimaced. 'There are always too many sentries, non? Have there been fresh messengers?' Rhys *had* been able to confirm that plenty of men had come and gone from Geoffrey's tent over the previous day and night, some under the cover of darkness.

'There was one early this morning, sire,' said Rhys. 'He was French – I am certain.'

'You heard him speak?' asked the duke.

'Yes, sire. His accent was very strong.'

'What did he look like?'

'Fat, sire. Old.'

Richard chuckled. 'Plenty of men look like that.'

I gave Rhys a nudge. 'Nothing else?'

He paused, thinking, and said, 'He carried a lute, sire.'

'Bertran de Born, or I am a Saracen,' said Richard. 'Is he ever to be a thorn in my side?'

I cast my mind back to the conference, and the paunchy man with the lute. I had heard much of him since. He had taken part in the rebellion five years before, as well as the current one. His poetry praising the fight against the duke was immensely popular in the region. 'Which way did he go?' I asked.

'East, sir, on a horse.' Rhys made a frustrated gesture. 'I had to stay by the tent, so I could not follow him.'

'De Born must be taken, else the rot will spread, as it does with apples in a barrel,' Richard declared. 'Geoffrey and Hal I can do little about, but this, I can.'

To the east lay open countryside, and the entire Limousin – the troubadour could be anywhere. I glanced at the duke, and asked, 'Shall I keep watch with Rhys, sire? If de Born returns, I could seize him, or at the least, see where he goes.'

'It had been my intent to order my brother's tent watched by soldiers, but they would be seen, one way or another,' said Richard. 'It is a fine idea – yes, go to.'

Rhys grinned from ear to ear. Not wanting to seem childish, I hid my excitement, but inside I too was delighted.

Richard did not trust his own brother, but he had faith in me.

Several nights of watching, and being eaten alive by biting flies, and our patience paid off. It was a close thing in the end, for the rebellion was over. Aimar had come to make terms with the king. With the Count of Périgord, whose fortress of Puy-St-Front now lay defenceless, he had begged for forgiveness. Now the royal family was about to part ways. Henry was to return to Normandy with the Young King and Geoffrey, while we were to ride west again with the duke.

Fortune was with us, however, and we captured a very drunk Bertrand de Born after he had left Geoffrey's tent. Hauling him, indignant and spluttering, before Richard, we heard him reveal that Geoffrey was in league with almost every noble from Aquitaine who had rebelled against the duke, his brother. The Young King was also involved.

The odds were daunting, to say the least. Richard had enemies on every side.

His resolve did not waver even a fraction.

CHAPTER XVII

The smell of roast goose wafted through the chill air, and my belly grumbled. Almost six months had passed, and, wrapped in my cloak, I was standing in the enormous bailey of the castle at Caen, which was filled with tents. A gust of wind came from the other direction, and I smelled stewing beef. A moment later, the odour was of baking bread, and after that, I detected the tantalising aroma of capon. I thought of the breakfast I had wolfed down hours before, and regretted my decision not to take a savoury pastry for later, as I had seen Rhys do. If it came to the worst, I could demand half from him. Otherwise it would be a long wait until I ate again; once more we had been tasked with watching Geoffrey's tent.

Since Bertran de Born had revealed all in the summer, there had been little opportunity to watch over the Count of Brittany. The rebellion ended, he had returned to his own territory, as we had to Richard's. His efforts to turn Aquitaine against the duke had lessened, according to word sent by his spies, but it had not ceased. Frustratingly, there was no hard evidence to prove his treachery. Now, able to monitor him at close quarters once more, we were eager to catch him red-handed.

There would be little time to enjoy the festivities, for the duke also wanted us to keep an eye on his eldest brother, the Young King. Some months prior, having demanded Normandy or a territory of his own from his father, and being refused, he had gone in high dudgeon to the court of King Philip of France. There, by all accounts, he had been treated like a long-lost, much-loved brother. He had only just been wooed back by Henry. The price, much talked about, had been an allowance of a hundred pounds a day, a further ten pounds daily for his wife's expenses, and the monies to pay a hundred knights each year.

The vast sums involved were beyond my youthful comprehension. The Young King would surely be content, I said to Philip, who smiled and told me in a whisper that the heir to the throne's avarice knew no bounds.

It was rumoured that a thousand knights were encamped in the castle, summoned by the king to celebrate Christmas, which was almost upon us. Richard and his three brothers were here. So was every loyal noble of consequence in Normandy, Brittany, Anjou and Aquitaine. The duke was not happy about having to come, and had said as much on our journey, but he was honour-bound to obey his father's bidding. And, as he admitted, he could watch over Geoffrey and the Young King.

Philip, who was by my side, gave me a nudge. 'Look.'

I recognised Bertran de Born's rolling gait at once, and I glared across the bailey. In the half year since Rhys and I had ambushed him, the troubadour had been our captive. Silver-tongued, a talented poet, he had inveigled his way back into favour. Richard did not trust de Born enough to leave him behind, however, so had taken him with us to Caen. Like his father, the duke easily forgave those who had wronged him, and now de Born was allowed to come and go around the castle, more or less as he pleased.

'Into Geoffrey's tent he goes, bold as a cock,' I said angrily. I disliked seeing the troubadour strutting about the bailey when I would have slung him head-first into a dungeon and thrown away the key.

'It is the season of goodwill, of celebration. Mayhap he has been asked to play,' said Philip.

I knew he was trying for a response, so I gave him a dunt.

The delicate sound of a lute carried to us a moment later, and Philip smirked. 'What did I say?'

'A man can talk treason and play music at the same time.'

He pulled a face. 'True.'

The multitude of tents made it impossible to eavesdrop without being obvious, so we contented ourselves with keeping a sharp eye on the entrance, sustained by regular sups from my costrel of wine.

Hearing women's voices – a sound all too rare over the last year – my eyes roved the bailey. Good numbers of the visiting nobles had brought their wives, who in turn had ladies accompanying them. Unmarried, Richard kept a bachelor's court, and during our campaign we had had only male company. To my fellow squires and I, seeing so many members of the opposite sex in Caen felt like finding an oasis after a month in the desert. Our thirst went unslaked, however. Virtue was everything to young ladies, and carnal relations the devil's work. Weasel John claimed to have bedded one already, but none of us believed him. Louis spent his free hours pursuing a beauty in the employ of Geoffrey's wife; he spoke much of their trysts, and the kisses they shared. We hung off every word. Philip had been slapped, twice, by different women, and was now mooning after another. Stolid as ever, John de Mandeville contented himself with sly ogling of the ladies. For my part, I had yet to spy a woman attractive enough to warrant risking the embarrassment of being spurned.

Until that moment.

Blonde-haired she was, with blue eyes that were matched by her long dress, and curves that almost buckled my knees. Her skin was honey-golden, quite a contrast to the milky-white colour popular at the time, yet twice as alluring. She was in a group of other young women, none of whom I noticed.

The very breath caught in my chest.

As is so often the case when one watches another, she sensed my attention. Her face turned towards me, and our gaze met. The force of our connection hit me like a smith's hammer. I struggled to stop my mouth from falling open. Then, to my consternation and delight, she paused.

'It is rude to stare at a lady.' Her voice was light and melodious.

Light-headed, mortified, I was unable to answer.

Philip cleared his throat. 'I must apologise, my lady, for my friend's ill manners.'

She smiled at him, at me, and I lost my heart entirely.

'I am sorry, my lady.' Without thinking, I added, 'I could not help myself. Your beauty overcame me.'

Her friends tittered. She raised an eyebrow, but her eyes bore no mockery, and one corner of her mouth turned up. One of her companions, a striking girl with long chestnut tresses, whispered in her ear, and she made an apologetic gesture. 'Our lady awaits. I cannot stay.'

Again lost for words, I nodded and, suddenly miserable, watched them go.

'Fool!' Philip's elbow was sharp. 'Are you not going to ask her name?'

I wanted to, but I would rather have charged a line of French crossbowmen.

Lucky for me, Philip possessed more courage. Dancing light on his feet, he caught up with the young women and spoke to the girl with the chestnut hair. He was soon back, a broad grin splitting his face. 'Juvette.'

'The blonde is called Juvette?' It was not my favourite name.

A scornful look. 'Juvette is mine. The one you could not take your gaze from is called Alienor.'

'Where is she from?'

'I know not,' Philip retorted. 'But they both serve the duke's sister Matilda.'

My ears pricked. Richard was fond of his sister, and had visited her a few days before. Older than he by only a year, she was married to Heinrich der Löwe, former Duke of Saxony and Bavaria. Recently exiled from Germany, they had sought sanctuary at her father's court. I had accompanied Richard, but had not seen Alienor.

'Can we persuade the duke to call on his sister again?' Seeing Philip's look, I sighed. 'It is not our place to ask.'

'It is not.' Philip gave me a wink. 'But there is nothing to stop us from dropping by one evening, as if by chance.'

The mere idea set my confidence to ebbing. 'What would we say?'

Philip's glance was part-scornful, part-pitying. 'Have you never cozened a lady?'

'I have not,' I said, my cheeks aflame.

'You must pay her compliments, and plenty of them. Bringing a gift often helps.' He saw my curiosity, and said, 'Something small – a marchpane fancy or a trinket, say.'

I listened as he laid out the best tactics to win a woman's heart, unsure whether to believe him, but desperate to learn. If I was to have any success with Alienor, I would have to seem more than the dumb brute I had appeared to be a short time prior.

All thoughts of romance left my head as I caught sight of the Young King. I hissed at Philip, and together we watched him sidle into Geoffrey's tent. Clad in a dark blue tunic and brown hose, he was alone. This in itself was unusual. He was a gregarious type who liked to be surrounded by followers, but taken with his seeking out Geoffrey while Born was within, it screamed conspiracy.

We were about to abandon our post when the lute struck up a merry tune, and de Born began to sing. Curious, we approached Geoffrey's tent, our pace slow.

'Between Poitiers and l'Ile Bouchard and Mirebeau and Loudun and Chinon, someone has dared to build a fair castle at Clairvaux, in the midst of the plain.' De Born fell silent, allowing the lute to carry the tune, before continuing, 'I should not wish the Young King to know about it or see, for he would find it not to his liking; but I fear, so white is the stone, that he cannot fail to see it from Mathefelon.'

A laugh – made by Geoffrey? – was rapidly followed by an angry remark from the Young King.

Not understanding, I glanced at Philip, but he appeared as baffled as I.

One of the men-at-arms outside the tent was staring, so I waited until we had walked past before resuming our discussion.

'Richard has been building a castle at Clairvaux,' said Philip.

I had heard the duke talking about it. 'I know, in Poitou.'

'The local viscount is none too loyal, and he controls the Tours-Poitiers road. Richard's castle will force him to cede some of his power. Why would de Born write a song about it?'

'And why does the Young King care?' I asked.

Neither of us knew the answers.

Leaving Philip on watch, I sought out the duke at once, finding him in the great hall with his younger brother John. Feet close to the fire, red-faced from their proximity to the flames, or perhaps the wine they had drunk, both seemed in good spirits.

Spying me, Richard beckoned. 'It is cold outside. Warm your bones, Rufus.'

Eager to share my news, yet reluctant to speak in front of John, I shuffled closer to the glowing logs, bowing to both. Waves of heat met my approach. I welcomed them at first, but as John's lizard eyes fell upon me, I longed to return to the frosty air of the bailey. He had clearly not forgotten the occasion we had first met, when his older brother had rebuked him for mocking me.

'You came in search of me.' Richard was ever direct.

'Yes, sire,' I said.

'Well?'

Unable to stop myself, I glanced at John. He scowled, and Richard laughed.

'Speak freely in front of my brother.'

I told myself that my misgivings about John were based only on my gut reaction, and the way he stared. If the duke trusted him, that should be good enough for me. 'De Born entered Geoffrey's tent some time past, sire,' I said.

Richard's brows lowered. John's grew as bright as a fox about to pounce on a rabbit. 'Continue,' ordered the duke.

I explained how the Young King had arrived, and soon after, heard de Born singing his tune about the castle at Clairvaux. 'He did not seem best pleased, sire,' I said, faltering because Richard's face had grown thunderous.

A short angry bark of laughter. 'And Geoffrey?'

'He laughed, sire.'

'Of course he did. God's legs, are my brothers always to be a burr in my hose?' His eyes moved to John, whose expression had turned guarded. 'I do not mean you. It is Geoffrey I talk of in the main, and Hal also.'

John's smile of reply was thin. 'Why would Hal care about a castle in Poitou? Is that not where Clairvaux is?'

My gaze swivelled to Richard, who grimaced.

'It may be in Poitou, but it has lain under Anjou's sway these two hundred years. Hal seems to be taking its construction as a direct insult, or challenge to his power.'

'That was surely not your intention?'

'I gave it little thought, truth be told,' said Richard. 'I doubt Hal did either until that wine sack de Born composed his sirvente. The castle at Clairvaux matters not to Hal, but it is *vital* to me. Whatever Geoffrey might whisper in his ear, however feckless he is, Hal will see that. Of more import are Geoffrey's dealings with de Born, which from this point onward, shall be limited. I will order the troubadour's wings clipped.'

The matter resolved in his mind, the duke's black mood passed. He called for more wine. After sharing a cup with me, I was sent on my way, with orders to keep watch on Geoffrey's tent until the Young King and de Born had left.

Richard knew his brothers best, I told myself as I walked. The Young King was impetuous, but he was not naturally ill-disposed to the duke. Geoffrey could not be trusted, it was true, but far from Aquitaine, his ability to do harm would be destroyed once de Born had been confined to his quarters.

It all seemed simple enough, and my mind turned to a different, and far more attractive subject.

Alienor.

Philip was almost as obsessed with Juvette as I was with Alienor. We plotted together, but our first attempts to speak with the objects of our desire was a miserable failure. In retrospect, lurking about in the great hall near Matilda's quarters was not the wisest choice. We saw neither hide nor hair of either young lady, and were soon driven away by a prune-faced steward who knew lovesick squires when he saw them.

The two were present at the evening meal, but like us with Richard, were attending to their mistress. I cast meaningful glances aplenty at Alienor, and was encouraged that her eyes occasionally met mine. Each time they did, the brief contact made my colour rise, and my heart thump. God and all His saints, but she was a beauty. My concentration lapsed, and if it had not been for Philip's nudges, I would have repeatedly left Richard's cup unfilled.

The meal drew to a close. Servants removed the plates, and the musicians came forward, filling the air with festive music. We squires were no longer needed, and so retreated to the side wall. Naturally, our gaze fell at once on the young ladies, who now demurely kept theirs averted from us.

'Found your courage?' Philip whispered.

I looked across the room at Alienor, who was laughing at something Juvette had said. She was so beautiful I would have given my hauberk, or even Liath Macha, to have kissed her in that moment. Fear trampled down by desire, I said thickly, 'Aye.'

My opportunity came not long after, when Alienor made her way to the back of the hall, and, I assume, the garderobe. It would have been unseemly to encounter her in private, so rather than follow, I lingered by the servants, who were preparing to carry out sweetmeats and spiced wine. The instant I saw her blonde hair from the corner of my eye, all my fears resurged. Rather than confidently walk towards her and greet her with pleased – and feigned – surprise, as had been my intent, I stood there like a simpleton and stared.

To my good fortune, she had more composure than I.

'Rufus?' she asked, with a graceful inclination of her chin. 'Is that not your name?'

'Yes, my lady,' I said, mortified by the flush staining my face.

'Do you commonly stand with the servants?'

I knew by the twitch of her lips that she had intuited my reason for being here. Already she was playing with me. I threw caution to the wind. 'In truth, my lady, I do not. I saw you go down the hall, and seized my chance to talk with you.'

She moved a few steps away, looking back to show me that our conversation was not over. 'Walk with me,' she said.

My heart soared. 'Thank you, my lady.' To my delight, her pace was slower than that of an ancient. We had a little time until we drew near to the top table, and inquisitive eyes. 'You are the lady Alienor.'

'I am.'

Her smile was leg-weakening. I tried to unscramble my wits and asked, 'How long have you served Duchess Matilda?'

'Almost four years.'

I enquired where she was from.

'Near the town of Chester.' Her brow wrinkled. 'Your French is good, but you are no native speaker.'

'I am Irish, my lady.'

'Is Rufus your real name?'

'No, my lady. I was baptised Ferdia.' She seemed interested, so it all tumbled out. Cairlinn. My family. The Norman invasion. Being sent as a hostage to Striguil. Isabelle. Meeting Duke Richard. Entering his service, my passage over the sea and the events since. Naturally, I made no mention of Robert FitzAldelm. 'And you, my lady? You came here when your mistress's husband was exiled?' She nodded, and I asked, 'Were you in danger at any time?'

'Thank God, no. Emperor Heinrich is a humane man; he gave my mistress permission to remain in Saxony, but she chose to accompany her husband.'

'Right glad I am that you had to leave,' I said without thinking.

She arched an eyebrow, which made her even more lovely. 'My mistress left her home under duress.'

My colour deepened further, and I said hastily, 'I meant only that had you not come to Caen, we would never have met.'

'You are glad then?'

'So glad,' I said, grinning like an amadán.

She met my smile with a half one of her own. 'Shall we talk again?'

I realised with surprise and dismay that we were close to the end of the hall. Already our time was over, and my spirits sank. The dream of a kiss, which had seemed slight at the outset, was now an impossibility. 'I would like nothing more, my lady,' I said, half bowing.

By way of goodbye, she touched me lightly on the arm.

I swear I grew two feet taller.

Philip, who had seen us together, was all questions when I returned. 'Your swagger makes me think you fared well. Did you?'

I beamed until my cheeks hurt. 'I think she likes me.'

'A kiss?'

I glared. 'Of course not. Besides, there were too many people.'

Philip's look was knowing. 'You came nowhere near kissing her.'

'I did not,' I admitted ruefully. 'But she wants to see me again.'

Philip gave me a friendly nod. 'Where you lead, I follow,' he said, and walked off. He had keen eyes. Juvette was making her way along the hall.

'Good luck,' I hissed.

Christmas came and went. The feast held by the king was memorable, a spectacle grander than any I'd seen before or since. So numerous were the guests that fatted calves and pigs roasted in the bailey, and every baker in the town was kept busy for days to supply bread. De Born was confined to his room; on the rare occasion he was allowed out, an accompanying man-at-arms ensured he did not meet again with Geoffrey or the Young King. The flow of visitors to Geoffrey's tent slowed, but did not dry up. Richard was true to his word, and did not speak out or create a scene with his brothers. He busied himself with hunting in the countryside around Caen, which meant we squires were often absent from the castle from dawn to dusk.

Seeking out Alienor was therefore difficult, so I made the most of what chances I had. Despite my ever-present blush and awkward manner, she seemed to enjoy my company. She listened to tales of my childhood, of Cairlinn and my family, and even laughed at my poor attempts at jokes. For my part, I drank in her every word, and trembled if we happened to touch, or we drew near enough to imagine a kiss or an embrace.

Once she might have let our lips meet – we had drawn very close, and were staring into each other's eyes – but a summons from Matilda shattered the possibility more surely than a flagstone breaks a falling cup. Ardour fanned even higher by this failure, I slept little and dreamed of her much. Time was not on my side, however. The Christmas court would come to an end soon after the Epiphany. If I was to achieve any success, it would have to be before then.

New Year's Day, the year of our Lord 1183, dawned crisp and cold. I went about my duties as normal, but thoughts of Alienor kept distracting me from my purpose. Philip said something, but I paid him no heed. When John de Mandeville noticed, he brought me back to reality in no uncertain fashion.

'The duke may not have seen you mooning about yet, but I have,' he snarled in my ear. 'Unless you want a hiding later, wake up.'

Startled, for he had never spoken to me thus, I did as I was bade. With time, I grew to appreciate that tongue-lashing a great deal more. Love may be admirable, but not when it paralyses. If I had been in battle rather than serving the duke, I would have been slain by the first enemy I met.

It was not long before events drove Alienor from my mind, for a while at least.

Richard was at table with his father the king, Geoffrey and John. Of the Young King there was no sign, which was common. Fond of carousing with his knights, he often did not appear until after sext. The king was in good humour, declaring that the Christmas court had been an unparalleled success, and that his nobles had seen how unified his family was.

I saw Richard's eyes flicker to Geoffrey, who was whispering in John's ear, and I thought, the king says one thing, but the truth is another thing altogether. His sons were like a pack of dogs, constantly sizing one another up, and ever searching for advantages over their fellows.

'Stand together,' said Henry, raising his cup, 'and we are unbeatable. To the house of Anjou!'

Geoffrey's voice was loudest as father and sons toasted and drank.

The Young King made his entrance soon after, accompanied by a gaggle of clerks and priests. Wearing a gold circlet about his brow – unusual at this hour – he bowed deeply to Henry.

Richard made no comment at being ignored; John pouted, as was his wont, but said nothing. Geoffrey it was who spoke up.

'How now, brother!' he cried. 'Why do you spurn us?'

The Young King saluted Geoffrey with his cup. 'Good morrow, brother.' He did the same to John, who pretended not to notice. To Richard he again gave no sign.

I saw the duke's brows lower, but he held his peace.

'You have offered no greeting to Richard,' said Henry, ever the peacemaker.

'I have not, Papa, and for good reason,' the Young King replied.

Henry sighed. His expression calculating, Geoffrey ran a finger across his lips. John sat forward in his chair. Richard ripped open a hunk of bread and filled it with cheese, before tucking in with gusto.

'I find it early for such matters,' said the king. 'Can it not wait?'

'No, Papa.' The Young King directed his gaze at Richard, who was staring at him, chewing, and held out his hand. Given a bible by a waiting clerk, he turned his attention back to the king, and loudly swore loyalty now and for the rest of his life, and to give faithful service throughout.

'Your words are appreciated, Hal.' Henry looked pleased, but puzzled.

Richard joined in. 'There is more to this grandiose gesture than meets the eye. Is there not?' he asked the Young King, who ignored him and continued to address their father.

'I wish to have nothing preying on my mind, sire, no grudge or malice which might later offend you. I must therefore declare that I have pledged to support the barons of Aquitaine against the duke, my brother.'

Richard's nostrils flared. Only I was close enough to hear him mutter, 'At last, the truth.'

I studied Geoffrey and John sidelong. John seemed engrossed and curious, but he showed little sign of knowing what the Young King would say or do next. Geoffrey, on the other hand, was calm. Too calm. I thought of the meetings in his tent, and decided he and his eldest brother had deliberately engineered this situation.

'These are grave tidings, Hal,' said the king. 'I would know your motive.'

'I acted thus, because my brother has fortified the castle at Clair-vaux, which lies in Anjou.' The Young King's tone became deferential. 'It also forms part of my inheritance from you, our lord father.'

'So it does,' said the king, turning his attention to Richard. 'What have you to say?'

'Does this *really* matter to you, Hal?' replied the duke.

'It does.'

'Clairvaux is an insignificant place, of no importance to Anjou, and therefore to you or our lord father. A gold coin says you had not heard of it a twelvemonth ago,' said the duke.

'Come, brother,' Geoffrey reproached. 'That is churlish.'

'I resent the implication that I am unfamiliar with what is to be my realm,' said the Young King. 'Each and every place in it is dear to my heart.'

Richard said something under his breath. Again I was the only one to hear his words: this time, 'cursedly pompous'. His patience was wearing thin, I decided, and so was the trust he had expressed in his brother before Christmas.

'For my part I have no shame in admitting I have only a vague idea where Clairvaux is,' said Henry. 'Explain.'

'It lies near the Tours-Poitiers road, Papa, and the crossing of the River Vienne,' said Richard. 'Currently the Viscount of Châtellerault, no great friend to Aquitaine, holds sway over this strategically important area. My new stronghold will see that influence weaken, and reduce the unprovoked attacks on merchants heading south into Aquitaine. These were my concerns when I thought to order the castle's construction.'

'You must have known the land was our lord father's,' cried the Young King. 'Clairvaux has belonged to the house of Anjou these two hundred years and more!'

'So it has,' said Geoffrey.

'If I ever knew, Hal, I had forgotten,' said Richard casually.

My lord was shrewd, and also a good liar, for I had heard from his own lips of Clairvaux's links with Anjou. To admit this would have made him seem the villain, however, so he was playing ignorant. My gaze moved from his serene face to his elder brother's, which was taut with anger.

'Ignorant you might have been,' the Young King declared, 'but you cannot deny your crime now.'

'Crime? It was a mistake and nothing more,' Richard answered. 'Let us not argue over it.'

The Young King's lips twisted in disdain. Geoffrey tutted.

'This can be remedied without difficulty,' said Henry, intervening. 'Relinquish Clairvaux into my care, and we shall put this matter behind us.'

Richard made no reply.

'Come,' urged Henry. 'For the sake of family concord.'

'Our lord father speaks true,' said Geoffrey, his voice solicitous.

'Very well,' said Richard to the king. 'Clairvaux is yours. Dispose of it according to your good pleasure.'

'That was easy, was it not?' Henry directed a smile first at Richard, and then at his eldest son.

The Young King made a contemptuous noise, and I thought, he will not let this lie. Geoffrey's expression, cold and calculating, told the same story.

'There is the matter of homage, Papa,' said the Young King. 'The homage owed me, as your heir, by my brothers.'

'God's eyes!' exclaimed Henry. 'Your brothers are loyal.'

'I would have them pledge their allegiance again, if it please you.' The Young King's stare fell first on Geoffrey, who nodded acceptance, and lingered on Richard.

I saw the duke's hands, which were in his lap, form fists. He unclenched them a heartbeat later, but it was clear, to me at least, that the demand had angered him.

Henry let out a quiet sigh, such as a labourer tired of his load makes. He looked at Richard and Geoffrey. 'Do as he asks.'

Geoffrey rose at once, and bowed deeply to the Young King. 'Gladly do I offer you homage for Brittany, my lord.'

The Young King inclined his head. 'Right glad I am to accept it.'

So swift had this exchange been, I knew it had been arranged in advance. Glancing at Richard, I saw he had come to the same conclusion. His two brothers were working with one another, the losengers, the deceivers, and were trying to force my lord into a corner.

'Well?' asked the Young King of Richard.

'You grow unreasonable, Hal,' said the duke, placing his palms flat on the table. 'I will not pay you homage for Aquitaine, because I do not hold it from you. I inherited it from our mother Alienor, and so hold it independently, in my own right. For the nonce, you are no more nobly born than I. Why *should* I pay you homage?'

A shout of agreement rose to my lips. I swallowed it down.

The king looked dismayed, and all of a sudden, old.

Geoffrey, curse him, smirked. John, wide-eyed, watched in astonishment at the spiralling family dispute.

The Young King, cheeks rosy with anger, said, 'I am to be your lord, brother. If I demand it, you *must* pay me homage.'

Richard made a loud *phhhh* of contempt.

'He speaks the truth.' Henry's voice was weary. 'Say the words, Richard.'

Geoffrey echoed his father.

Again the duke ignored his brother. Fixing his attention on Henry, he said, 'I will not, Papa.'

The Young King hammered down his fists, rattling the cups. 'You tread on dangerous ground, brother.'

I followed Richard's intense blue eyes, malevolent as an angry lion's now. They bore down on the Young King. In a silky soft voice, laden with threat, he said, '*I* tread on dangerous ground?' His gaze flicked to Geoffrey, who paled a little.

The Young King's mouth opened for an angry rejoinder, but again Henry intervened. 'Peace, my sons. Peace.' Under his breath he muttered, 'The young of the eagle are my four sons, who will not cease to persecute me even unto death.'

A glowering silence fell.

Still new to the cut and thrust of the royal court, I had no idea what would unfold next. In my head, a battle was about to start against the Young King, and I was ready. Unpeeling my fingers from the hilt of my dagger, I told myself that cooler heads would decide. I looked at Philip, who seemed as unsure as I. Next I glanced at John de Mandeville, who must have seen many situations such as this. His expression was calm; he gave me a little shake of the head that said, this will not come to blows. Relieved, I took a deep breath and let it out again.

'Is it so hard to do what is right?' Henry asked Richard. 'Acknowledge Hal. In no way will this homage threaten you. As the throne is his birth-right, so the rule of Aquitaine is yours.'

'I and my heirs shall be lords of Aquitaine forever, sire?' Richard's tone was combative.

'You shall, and so shall they.' Henry's attention moved to the Young King.

An uncaring shrug, and a muttered, 'Aye.'

'If Aquitaine is always to be mine and my descendants', Hal, then my homage is yours.' Richard's voice was calm and measured, and sounded genuine. 'I swear this before Almighty God.'

I shot a look at Henry, whose face shone with relief.

'I cannot accept your homage,' declared the Young King.

'Richard has given you what you ask!' said Henry. 'Accept what he has offered, and all shall be well.'

'I will not, sire,' said the Young King, his tone rising.

'God's legs, brother. Our lord father has recognised you as his heir. Geoffrey is your man, and so am I. John here will swear also,' said Richard. 'What more do you want?'

'The nobles whose cause I am pledged to support will never agree to you and your descendants being the sole lords of Aquitaine,' said the Young King. 'Pay homage to me as your lord, making no mention of this, and I will accept it.'

'You favour men you scarcely know over your own flesh and blood. Shame on you, Hal.' Richard's voice was thick with contempt.

'I want only the rightful homage I am owed,' cried the Young King.

'And I have offered it, as long as you recognise my right and that of my heirs – granted to me by our mother Alienor – to be the lords of Aquitaine forever.' Richard's gaze moved to Henry, whose hopeful eyes slid to the Young King.

'That I cannot do.'

'Alas then, this meeting is over.' With a courteous bow to Henry, a nod to John, a dismissive look at Geoffrey, and no acknowledgement of the Young King, Richard walked away from the table.

John de Mandeville, Philip and I followed. I could not help but glance over my shoulder.

The Young King's expression was murderous. Geoffrey was whispering in his ear.

Richard was oblivious. 'Ready my horse,' he muttered.

'Yes, sire,' said John.

I summoned my courage, and asked, 'Where are we bound, sire?'

'I care not,' Richard replied. 'But I can stomach the sight of my brothers no longer.'

Shoes scuffed the floor, and I caught sight of John, who had come hurrying after the duke. Catching Richard's bitter words, his expression fell.

Something made the duke turn. Realising at once what had happened, he stretched out a hand. 'Brother. I did not mean you.'

John paid him no heed. His face twitching with emotion, he retreated to the table.

Richard let out a sigh, such as I had never heard from him, a great gusty sound of regret and sadness. His huge shoulders sagged. 'Must it ever be so?' he muttered.

Swallowing down my dislike of John, I asked, 'Shall I go after him, sire?'

For an instant Richard seemed as if he would say yes, but then with an emphatic shake of his head, he came back to himself. 'John need only think on it to know that he and I have no quarrel.'

I made no further argument, and we departed.

In later years, I would look back and wonder if it was then that John's malice towards his elder brother truly began.

CHAPTER XVIII

Wind whistled around the corner of the great hall, an eerie sound. Dirty yellow-tinged clouds hung over Mirebeau, threatening more snow. A thick layer had fallen the night before. The roofs were covered in glistening white, but servants with shovels had cleared paths through the bailey. Great mounds now stood in one corner, attracting every child in the castle. Inevitably, a fight had started, and now snowballs were hurtling back and forth between the warring sides. Proving he was not altogether a man, Rhys had joined in, throwing with the same accuracy that had saved my life in the woods outside Southampton.

Keeping well out of the way, I stamped to and fro, hands planted in my armpits, wishing I had a second, thicker cloak. Hours I had stood here, waiting for a messenger, one urgently expected by the duke. Whether he would appear today, no one knew. It was not for me to question my master, just to stand where I was told.

February was almost upon us. Soon after the argument on New Year's Day, the royal court had first moved to Angers, where Henry had convinced his three oldest sons to sign a pact of perpetual peace. This achieved – I knew not how, for the impasse between Richard and the Young King continued – Henry's next move was to order the malcontent nobles of Aquitaine to Mirebeau, where we now found ourselves. There had been no word from Limousin, where Geoffrey had been sent to deliver the royal summons.

With my master and the king's heir barely on speaking terms, tensions had been rising between their followers. We squires – John de Mandeville excluded – had already brawled once with those of the Young King; black eyes and bruised ribs had resulted on both sides. Matters had been more serious when it came to the ordinary soldiers. Not a sennight since, one of Richard's archers had died from a knife wound to the belly. An all-out war might have started if the duke had not intervened. Furious, he had spoken from the staircase overlooking the bailey, waving a fist to emphasise his words. Every man of us had been forced to take an oath. Keep the peace, Richard had ordered, or lose a hand.

Shrewd, calculating, he made certain news of the archer's fate reached the king. Incensed, Henry ordered the Young King to control his followers 'as his younger brother had'. This, whether meant deliberately or no, had poured fuel on the flames. A noticeable increase in the rivalry between the brothers and those who served them followed; despite the fragile peace, it continued still. Spying a man-at-arms who was reputed to have been involved in the archer's stabbing, I was minded to slip a pointed stone into a snowball and aim it at his head.

In the mayhem – the air thick with missiles and delighted children's screams – I would get away with it, but I held back. A cool head was preferable to a hot one. Duty came before desire. Desire.

An image of Alienor, left behind in Caen, entered my mind, and my heart twinged. Our goodbye had been all too brief. A fierce embrace, and the few kisses I had stolen, remained my most precious memory. Walking away, I had promised to wait for her; torturing me, she declared she would think about doing the same. Then, chasing after me, she had pressed into my hand a fillet, a strip of blue fabric she used to tie back her hair.

I reached into my tunic and touched the pouch hanging from a thong round my neck. In it was the neatly folded fillet, something I would rather die for than lose.

Hooves drummed on the packed snow. Two horses cantered through the gate. Recognising the lead rider, I waved and strode to meet him. A tall, sturdy man-at-arms by the name of Richard de Drune, whose brother had fought in the capture of Waterford town in Ireland, he had been sent by the duke to follow Geoffrey. Doing a rough calculation in my head, I judged de Drune's time in Limousin had been short – perhaps a day. That did not augur well.

'Well met.' I took the reins, noting the flecks of mud coating the horse from hooves to flanks, and the same on de Drune's legs. His companion was as bespattered. They had ridden hard. I glanced at him, seeing further evidence that his journey had not been easy. Dark hollows ringed his blue eyes; his long brown hair was lank and unkempt. 'Are you ill?'

A barked laugh. 'Not ill, my friend. Just tired. Famished. Saddle sore. Thirstier than I have ever been for an ale, or a cup of wine. This is the third horse I have ridden since leaving the Limousin four days since. In that time I have barely slept, and eaten little. My needs must wait, however. Where is the duke?'

'In the hall. Who is this with you?' I sized the fellow up and down. Receding hair, although he was young. Well-dressed, and a decent-looking sword at his belt. The leather-wrapped roll behind his saddle was a hauberk, or I was no judge. 'A knight?'

'I am,' said the young man politely. 'Owain ap Gruffydd. I used to serve Geoffrey.'

'Used to?' I asked, my voice sharp.

'He wishes to serve the duke,' said de Drune.

'The duke can be the judge of that,' I answered. 'I shall take you to him.' Whistling for Rhys, who happened to be close by, still battling in the snowball fight, I ordered him to care for the horses. To de Drune I said, 'Your haste in returning tells me the news is not good.'

De Drune shook his head. 'Rather than summon the discontented nobles here to Mirebeau, Geoffrey has joined their cause.'

'The duke will not be pleased,' I said, imagining the eruption. In a mutter, I added, 'And Owain? Is he just a common deserter?'

'No. He could not stomach joining with the rebels. He asked me to take him with me when I left.'

I looked at de Drune askance. 'And you believed his tale, as easy as that?'

'He is an honest type, or I am a nun,' said de Drune, although he did not sound as certain as his words made out.

'It is not the best time perhaps,' I said. 'The duke has been in foul temper of recent days.' I unslung the costrel that had been my fortification as I waited in the cold, took a long slug, and handed it over.

De Drune supped like a piglet on the teat. So did Owain.

We found Richard at table with his father, the Young King and John. Philip was there, and Louis, and squires who served the others. Platters and bowls had been laid in front of the king and his sons: squabs in wine sauce, aromatic frumenty, sliced roast mutton. There were richly crusted pies and loaves of fresh wheaten bread, pats of fresh-churned butter and bowls of clover honey. The tantalising smells made my belly rumble; I imagined poor de Drune's and Owain's were tying themselves in knots, before remembering they were more likely to be churning with anxiety.

Led by the king's steward, we drew close, our boots making little sound on the rush-strewn floor. The only conversation appeared to be between John and his father Henry, who was nodding and smiling at whatever was being said. Richard and the Young King, seated side by side opposite the king and their youngest brother, were entirely ignoring each other.

'Your pardon, sire, for the interruption.' The steward bowed.

John fell silent. Henry's sharp gaze fell on us. So did those of the Young King and Richard, whose expression grew sharp as a blade.

I retreated a step, and taking back my costrel, pushed de Drune forward.

'A messenger has come from the Limousin, sire,' said the steward. 'One of Duke Richard's men.'

De Drune dropped to a knee. Owain and I did the same.

'Rise,' ordered Henry. 'Speak.'

We stood, and de Drune laid out his tale. 'Geoffrey made no effort to deliver your command, sire, but joined the rebel barons forthwith and in right good cheer. He was greeted by some as if they had expected him.'

'This is a sorry story,' said Henry, shaking his head. 'Are you certain of what you saw?'

'Is it possible you mistook the meaning of Geoffrey's words?' asked the Young King. 'Perhaps the rebels merely want to discuss the terms we forced on them last summer?'

Intimidated, de Drune's eyes shot from Henry to the Young King and back again. 'There was no mention of discussing terms, messires, none. I swear it.' He glanced at the duke, who had as yet said nothing.

'Geoffrey would not play us false in this manner,' said the king. 'I cannot believe it so.'

Richard's chair screeched off the flagstones as he stood. 'God's legs!' he thundered. 'Am I the only one to recognise Geoffrey for the traitor that he is?'

The Young King coloured, and opened his mouth, but Richard was not done. 'Sire,' he said, speaking directly to Henry. 'De Drune here has been a man of mine these three years. Loyal and true he is, and no liar. Geoffrey *has* abandoned us, and furthermore, planted his standard with the rebels. These nobles do not recognise me as the ruler of Aquitaine, nor you as their king.'

To my astonishment, Owain stood forward. 'The duke speaks truly, sire. Geoffrey has willingly joined with the rebels.'

'*Who* is this?' Henry's icy stare roved from me to de Drune to Owain and back.

With the king and three princes staring at me, I lost my nerve, and said nothing.

'My name is Owain ap Gruffydd, sire.' His voice was low but firm. 'A knight, I am, from Wales. Until four days ago, I served Count Geoffrey.'

'You left without permission?' demanded Richard.

'I asked my lord for leave to go, sire, but he denied it. I know it was wrong to go against his word, but his actions are dishonourable. I do not wish to serve such a man.' Owain bent his head, and the Young King tutted.

'And you can corroborate what de Drune says?' As he spoke, Richard's eyes moved to his father and the Young King.

'I can, sire. I swear it.'

'Two men declare it is so,' said Richard. 'Are we to damn them both as liars, sire?'

Henry's lined face was troubled, that of an old man uncertain how to react. He glanced at the Young King, who gave him a broad smile. 'Richard is angry, sire. Anger clouds the mind, and prevents unbiased decision. Let us question the messenger again, and the traitor, to see perhaps if they were over-hasty in their assessment.'

Owain coloured at the accusation. De Drune shuffled his feet.

The room was thick with tension.

'That seems wise,' said the king.

Richard interrupted, his tone angry. 'Will you pay heed to weasel words, sire, rather than see what is in front of your nose?'

'Geoffrey is my son. He loves me,' said Henry almost plaintively.

'That has not prevented him from joining with our enemies, sire,' said Richard. 'We must act at once. Raise an army and crush the rebellion before it spreads. Before he and his allies have burned or sacked every farm and town in Poitou!'

'Your temper frays, brother,' said the Young King. 'And you are over-proud. It is not for you to tell our lord father how he should act.'

'That is not my intent, as well you know,' said Richard. 'Geoffrey's actions threaten all of us – including you.'

'You seek to tell me my business also?' The Young King rose to his feet, glaring at Richard. 'It is long past time for you to pay homage to me. Now, however, I would also have you swear an oath of fealty, on holy relics. Do that, brother, and I shall accompany you to subdue Geoffrey.'

In later years, I would come to recognise Richard's expression as killing rage. A tic worked on his left cheek; his jaw muscles bunched, and his fingers fell to the ivory-handled dagger at his belt.

'You insult my honour. This I cannot accept.' He ground out the words. His eyes moved to Henry. 'Will you ride with me to Limousin, sire, with force?'

The king did not answer.

With an exasperated cry, the duke stormed from the table.

'Richard!'

He ignored his father's call.

Philip and Louis hurried after our master. De Drune and Owain went next. With dragging feet, for I wanted to know what would happen, I came last.

Reaching the door, I heard the Young King's voice.

'Send me to the Limousin, sire. I shall clear up any misunderstanding. Geoffrey and I will return with the barons at our heels.'

Wearily, Henry muttered his assent.

I could not believe my ears. The Young King's intent was plain to me, even if it was not to his father. I hurried onto the staircase that led down to the bailey. Richard was already at its foot, and calling for his horse.

Eager to tell him what I had overheard, I clattered down after.

When I told him, the rage that had been hinted at in his expression burst free. A hair-whitening oath left his lips, and he swept out his dagger. 'I see his purpose, the damned losenger!' he roared, turning on his heel as if to return to the great hall. 'Rather than bring back Geoffrey, he will join him.'

It made sense, I thought. Why else would the Young King show so little interest in quelling a rebellion that could threaten the crown? Richard took a few steps towards the stairs, and my mouth opened to call Philip and the others, that we might support him when he stormed back in.

'Enter thus, and *I* shall be the traitor.' With a frustrated half-laugh, half-snarl, the duke slammed his blade back into the sheath. 'Instead I shall let Hal show himself as one.'

On our arrival from Mirebeau, there was little time to rest. Bands of mercenaries sent by Geoffrey from Brittany were on the loose to the north, in Poitou. We snatched a night's sleep and the following morning, rode to war. Although squires did not generally fight, we were so short of men that the duke had deployed us with his knights. I was glad of it; we all were, save Weasel John of course. De Drune came, and after swearing an oath of allegiance to Richard, so did Owain. Rhys wanted to join us too, but I forbade him. Be happy that you are with us, and guarding the camp, I said. He glowered and whetted his knife, but he obeyed.

Guided by locals, we fell on the invaders thrice in as many days, causing heavy casualties. Philip and I fought together, a pairing we came to relish. John de Mandeville conducted himself well. Louis was wounded badly in the first clash, and had to be left in camp thereafter. Weasel John played his part, but I never saw him bloody his sword, which made me doubt his courage. De Drune was a skilled fighter, but in those first skirmishes, he paled in significance to Owain, who fought like a man possessed – or one who is out to prove his worth. His tactic worked, I am glad to say.

We were more than a match for the mercenaries, who were used to attacking poorly armed, easily terrified villagers. They fled towards Brittany, but we gave no pursuit. What few prisoners had been taken were executed on the duke's orders, and the local farmers mobilised in case of further incursions. We could not stay to protect the area, for danger threatened Aquitaine from every side. Word had come of Gascon mercenaries, *routiers* as they were known, converging on Limoges. It was the city that Geoffrey had based himself in, and where the Young King had joined him. Richard's suspicion had been correct.

Pausing only long enough to let us fill our saddle bags with food, the duke led us south-east. This time Rhys, who had sworn to follow me if I did not give him leave to come, rode with us.

If I thought it had been cold standing in the bailey at Mirebeau, I had barely been tested. I was chilled to the bone every hour of the following two days and nights. So numb were my feet that only the stirrups prevented me from falling from the saddle. Fingers of one hand clenched in a death grip on my reins, I kept the other buried in the opposite armpit, and changed over when I began to lose control of Liath Macha.

Through wind, sleet and snow we travelled, a hundred and fifty riders led by Richard himself. We did not camp. We did not stop for food, but ate our way through our panniers' contents. Since that time, I have had an aversion to hard cheese: there is only so much of it, half-frozen, stinking of oiled leather, that a man can eat. With brief halts to feed and water our mounts, and to relieve ourselves, we journeyed at a steady pace, this to save the horses from foundering. Dawn to dusk we rode. Through the night, and into the following dawn. The second day was a little better, Christ be thanked. If it had been as bad as the first, many of us, man and beast, would have perished.

As it was, we were exhausted. Sagging in our saddles, lips cracked, gaunt-cheeked, we resembled a mob of starvelings. Being larger and stronger, Liath Macha had fared better than most of the mounts, but even he needed to rest. Rhys and his horse had been less affected, it because he was sparrow light, he thanks to his two cloaks, and a saddle bag that bulged with ill-gotten gains. When Rhys handed me hunks of bread or slices of ham during that ride, I did not ask their provenance.

Late afternoon saw us halt in a small settlement. Limoges was per-haps half a day's ride to the east, through dense forest. It was not our immediate objective, however. Thanks to a monk sent by the abbot of St Martial's, a local abbey famous for being loyal to Aquitaine, we knew a large force of routiers commanded by Viscount Aimar – the same man who had rebelled the previous summer – was advancing on the village of Gorre, not three miles distant. Their aim, Richard explained, would be to fall on the place, ransack its church and burn the village to the ground. It sounded barbaric, and was similar to what I had seen in Poitou, but a world apart from the war I had known in Ireland.

The duke spoke no more of our enemies that day, but cared for our physical needs. Sheltered overnight in a little church – the priest and villagers, grateful for the protection offered by our arrival, had made us welcome – fed as much pottage as we could eat, and supplied with warm, dry blankets, we lay down cheek by jowl and slept like the dead.

In the dark before dawn, we rose, mostly restored, and in better spirits. Everyone stood as the priest celebrated mass. It was an odd a service as I had ever witnessed: a bare church filled by scores of armoured men. The room reeked of sweat and unwashed bodies, and from outside came the whickering of our horses. Blessing us at the end, the priest called us angels of deliverance, led by the duke, but sent by God. Defeating and killing the routiers would see us go to Heaven, he said.

I heard similar things from the villagers who pressed around us as we rode away. 'Butcher them all,' cried a pleasant-faced matron. 'Blind them first!' roared her husband. A chorus filled our ears as we left the settlement behind. 'Death to the routiers!'

Richard, riding at the front with his cousin André de Chauvigny, smiled and gave loud promise that he would do as they asked.

Confused, I asked Philip about the locals' hatred of the mercenaries.

'Until the duke brought peace to Aquitaine,' he explained, 'the area had known nothing but war for years on end. The nobles quarrelled with each other, with Henry, and King Philippe Capet. Routiers were used by all sides, men whose only aim is to enrich themselves by whatever means is necessary. Soulless destroyers, they criss-crossed the land, burning and pillaging. No one was safe from their depredations. Even the children fell victim to their savagery. As for what did before they slew the women . . .'

'They are loathed by everyone,' said Philip after a pause. 'Do you understand?'

I nodded, imagining the terror experienced by my mother as Cairlinn was attacked, and feeling the first stirrings of hate for men I had never met.

Richard halted a mile from Gorre. He rode to and fro before us. He spoke quietly, but with passion. We were tired. We had endured a brutal journey from Poitou. There were nods, and a few chuckles. He declared we had done well, and deserved our night's rest in the church. Although the pottage had been simple, it had filled our bellies, and made us fart. 'Sweet Jesu, the smell last night!' he cried. Now we laughed. After we had finished our work today, Richard went on, he would see that we had meat aplenty, and wine enough to drink ourselves under the table. This made us cheer.

'First, however, you must follow me to Gorre,' the duke continued. 'There, the monk tells me, we shall find Viscount Aimar—' these last two words dripped with contempt '—and his band of routiers. They are scum. Lowlifes. The very dregs of humanity. Murderers, rapists and sodomites.' He raised his sword into the air. 'What shall we do with them?'

'Kill!' we thundered.

The duke smiled then, a smile sharp as an unsheathed dagger. 'Follow,' he commanded.

A pair of horsemen was spied half a mile from the village. Who they were: enemy messengers or outriders, or innocent travellers, no one knew. Richard did not hesitate. We increased our pace, and rode straight at them. If they fled, the duke called, we were to chase after them like the hounds of Hell. They could not be allowed to reach Gorre and raise the alarm. Strange though it was, with a mass of armoured riders closing in, the horsemen made no attempt to flee or even divert from their path. At fifty paces, both men reined in and waited. Their packhorse jerked its head to and fro, uneasy, but the rear rider held tight to the rope in his fist.

I could see the duke's eyes darting from left to right, suspecting an ambush. I was doing the same myself. The tree cover was light here, however, and no trace of danger could be seen.

'God's legs!' cried Richard as we drew closer. 'What are you doing here, Marshal?'

I stared, recognising the long-nosed, moustachioed knight I had seen with the Young King on a number of occasions. Renowned for his martial skills and his loyalty, he was a member of the heir to the throne's inner circle. I assumed the man with him to be his squire.

Puffs of snow rose as we came to a halt. Clouds of vapour rose skyward from the great mass of men and horses. Curious looks bore down on Marshal and his companion.

'Duke Richard.' Marshal bowed his head.

'Whither are you bound?'

'For Paris, sire.'

'By rights, I should take you prisoner.'

'I no longer serve your brother, sire.'

'How now, Marshal? Has the moon turned to cheese?'

'Lies and calumny were being spoken about me, sire – you heard these foul rumours – but I was not allowed to clear my name. Two members of my lord's mesnie, Adam d'Yquebeuf and Thomas de Coulonces, were responsible. I wanted to fight the treacherous caitiffs. When your brother forbade me from doing so for a second time, I renounced my service to him.'

'Did you, by God?' Something passed between them – I could not tell what, and then the duke asked, 'When was this?'

'Yesterday, sire.'

'Where is Hal?'

'The Young King is at Limoges, sire, with Count Geoffrey and the rebel nobles.'

The duke pointed down the track. 'And in Gorre?'

'Count Aimar is camped near there, sire, with a rabble of murderers and rapists.'

'Routiers?'

'The same, sire. I have heard they are set on attacking the church this very morning.'

'Are they indeed?' Richard eyed Marshal. 'Before I go, there is one thing. Do you recall the offer made you by John de Beaumont?'

'Yes, sire.'

'It still stands.'

'You do me much honour, sire, but I cannot accept. For now at least.'

I stared, amazed by a man with strength of will enough to deny the duke.

Richard shook his head, amused but also a little annoyed. 'You never change, Marshal.'

A wry shrug. 'I do my best not to, sire.'

'I have no quarrel with you, Marshal. You may go.'

'My thanks, sire.' Marshal clicked at his horse, and without another word, eased it down the side of our formation. Leading the packhorse, his squire followed.

'There, Rufus,' said Richard, 'goes one of the finest knights in Christendom. Pray that you never face the sharp end of his lance.'

'Yes, sire,' I said, thinking that to be regarded so highly, Marshal must be a fearsome warrior indeed.

The duke's expression hardened. 'And now to Gorre. Let us rain fury and death on those who would destroy the house of God.'

CHAPTER XIX

Fools that they were, the routiers in Gorre knew nothing of our approach until we were among them, hacking and slaughtering. Utterly panicked, few even fought back. They either ran and were cut down, or surrendered. I gave no thought to the prisoners' fate until later that day, when they stood by the River Vienne at Aixe, a nearby stronghold of Richard's. There we had dragged them, scores of unshaven, terrified-looking men in hauberks and ill-fitting gambesons, with their wrists bound. Aimar had escaped, but there were more than a dozen knights among them.

His face a cold mask, the duke told the defeated routiers that they would all receive the same fate as their victims in the surrounding area. He waved a hand, and his soldiers swarmed forward. I stood with the other squires, and watched, horrified, thankful I had not been ordered to join in. One thing it is to hear of men being blinded and drowned, or to talk of slitting throats, and quite another to witness it. A thick tang of shit and blood filled my nostrils, and my ears rang with screams. When silence finally fell, several priests, who had also witnessed the butchery, hurried forward to bless not just Richard but his red-handed men who stood there, bloodied swords yet in their fists. I could scarcely believe my eyes, but as Philip muttered to me, by ridding us of the routiers, the duke had just delivered many locals from the same fate.

In the end, I thought, God makes monsters or murderers of us all.

We rode for Limoges then, but the duke's hope that we might take the defenders by surprise came to naught. Despite the citadel's poor defences – Richard had ordered them demolished a twelvemonth before – we had not the strength to press home a meaningful attack. Setting pickets around the perimeter, we threw up a camp. Urgent messages were sent to Normandy asking the king to join us.

Henry rode south at once, with only a few supporters. A sennight later, in poor weather, with dark falling, they missed our camp and reached the ramshackle barricades surrounding Limoges. Thinking the citadel was under attack, a group of townsmen sallied forth. One of the king's party was wounded, and his own cloak pierced by an arrow before he was recognised and the shocked defenders retreated.

With Richard still unaware, Henry made for Aixe, which lay several miles to the west. Most of us had made our base there because of the foul conditions. A howling wind was blowing, and gusts of smoke kept blowing back down the chimney of the great hall, choking us. Undismayed, Richard, de Chauvigny and a dozen companions were sitting a distance from the fire, drinking and talking. I was close by, a jug of wine at the ready. Philip stood beside with another. Rhys, the rascal, was lurking about too, listening in for all he was worth.

Naturally, the talk was of the Young King and Geoffrey, their supporters, and how Limoges might be taken. Richard had been chafing since our arrival, but even he knew an assault with our small numbers would have been akin to suicide. He cast an eye at me. "Twould be even madder than my attempt to take Périgueux, eh, Rufus?'

I flushed and nodded.

Owain, who since his valour at Gorre and after, had been favoured by Richard, looked puzzled.

The duke explained what I and John de Mandeville had done. 'Headstrong Irishman he is, but there is no denying his bravery,' he said. 'I am lucky to have him.'

I felt like a dog with two tails, I was so pleased.

'Drink,' Richard ordered me.

Owain threw an encouraging grin; I grinned back as Philip poured the wine.

The duke and I clinked cups, and he raised his in salute. 'Long life and health to you, Ferdia.' He glanced around the room. 'To Ferdia — Rufus, as most call him!'

Cries of 'Ferdia' and 'Rufus' rang out, and my face turned as red as my hair. If Richard gave the order, I thought, I would follow him to Hell. The next instant, I remembered my dead father and mother, and wondered if they could have found it in their hearts to be proud of me, who served King Henry's son. I was not sure. Unsettled, I put their memory from my mind.

FitzAldelm chose that moment to come walking down the great hall. Excluded from the gathering, the acclamatory cries of my name would have burned him like rising bile in a man's throat. He shot me a poisonous stare, which I pretended not to see.

My mouth opened to return Richard's toast, but FitzAldelm interrupted.

'The king is here, sire,' he said in a loud voice. 'Even now he rides through the gate.'

'At this hour?' The duke was on his feet and calling for a cloak. Philip and I followed, and in the rainswept courtyard we witnessed the reunion of father and son.

'You are most welcome, sire.' Richard stepped to take the king's reins himself. 'I had not expected you for another sennight.'

'I came as fast as I might,' said Henry, slipping from the saddle with a grunt. 'God's eyes, but I am half frozen.'

'The fire inside is roaring, sire. Come.' Richard threw the reins to a stable boy and offered his arm to his father.

In we went. Everyone who had been sitting moved away. The king was given the best seat, and Richard sat alongside, offering him wine and food.

It all came out soon enough, how Henry had been attacked at Limoges. He showed the duke the rent in his cloak caused by the arrow. I swear the rafters shook with the duke's angry cry. 'They tried to murder you, sire!'

'It was a mistake, I think,' said Henry. He sighed, and drank deep.

'You *think*, sire?' I could see a vein pulsing in Richard's neck. 'A few inches higher, and you would have been sorely injured, or dead. And the man who did it fights for Hal and Geoffrey! This is evil work.'

'I would never give such an order,' cried a voice from the entrance to the great hall.

To my utter astonishment in came the Young King, cloak sodden with rain, hair plastered to his skull, and a sorrowful expression moulding his handsome features. A couple of equally bedraggled knights were at his heel.

'You have some gall, Hal!' shouted Richard. He motioned, and his men-at-arms stepped into the Young King's path.

'Let him approach,' said the king, glaring at his eldest son and heir.

Richard gestured again, and the Young King came on alone.

The king simply stared.

'Well, Hal?' demanded Richard. 'What have you to say for yourself?'

'I climbed on my horse the instant I heard what had happened, sire. The arrow, it was a mistake.' The Young King reached out his hands in entreaty. 'The sentries took you for men of the city, with whom the citadel is quarrelling.' Limoges was divided into two parts, with the city remaining loyal to the king.

'So you say,' snapped Henry. 'Why should I believe you?'

Richard seemed about to speak, but glancing at the king, held his peace.

I thought, he will be glad how angry his father is, and hoping that he will break off relations with the Young King without his, Richard's, influence.

'However things stand between us, sire, I would never wish you harmed! Nor would Geoffrey. I swear it.' The Young King's voice was pleading.

'Leave.' Henry turned his face from his eldest son.

'Sire—'

'You heard our lord father,' thundered Richard. He signalled to the men-at-arms. 'Escort my brother from the hall!'

To his credit, the Young King did not beg. Bidding his father farewell – Henry made no reply – he stalked back to his knights, and thence to the door, and a miserable, soaking ride to Limoges.

'Faithless rogue,' said Richard. 'At last his true colours emerge.'

Again the king did not speak, but hunched into himself, and clutched the cup of wine close to his chest.

Richard's hand reached out, as if to clasp his father's shoulder.

Henry, who had not seen, whispered, 'Ah, Hal. My dear Hal.'

I was close enough to hear – I and the duke.

His hand fell away, and he strode to the fire.

Only I saw the pain that filled Richard's eyes.

If the duke had hoped the incident with the arrow would convince his father of the Young King's and Geoffrey's treachery, he was mistaken. Two days later, seemingly forgetful of how close he had come to death, and ignoring Richard's advice, the king travelled to Limoges to speak with his recalcitrant sons. He was shot at again from the defences, this time with the Young King and Geoffrey watching. Only when the royal standard was waved in their direction did the arrows cease. Although his rebellious sons apologised, the bowmen who had targeted the king were not punished, which spoke volumes about the sincerity of the Young King's and Geoffrey's regrets. Unsurprisingly, the meeting did not continue.

The king was prepared to forgive almost anything that his rebellious sons did, however. A few days later, the Young King sought and was granted an audience with his father. This again was in spite of Richard's protests. Declaring he wanted to return to the fold, the Young King claimed he would demand the rebel nobles surrender. Mollified, the king gave his blessing, and the Young King rode back to Limoges to deliver the ultimatum to his erstwhile allies.

By nightfall he was back. His attempt had failed; begging forgiveness, he threw himself on his father's mercy. This was given willingly, once more despite Richard's objections. The Young King's part in the rebellion appeared to have ended, and peace descended over Aixe and our camps. Patrols were stood down, and we began to think of peace.

It was all a trick. The Young King returned to the citadel of Limoges, purportedly to gather his household. Several days passed without sign of him, and as reports came of routiers sacking and burning villages and churches in the surrounding countryside, it became clear that the Young King's intent had been to lower his father's defences so that Geoffrey's mercenaries could have a free rein.

Richard swore high and low he would hold his brothers to account, but when the Young King again came pleading to their father that Geoffrey had acted on his own, that he would never have sanctioned the routiers' brutality, incredibly he was believed. Furious though the duke was, he could not countermand the king's wishes. Nor could he remove the Young King from our camp. It was a strange few days, with Richard shunning his brother even as he played the model son to his doting father.

The Young King departed again, ostensibly to see if he could persuade Geoffrey to abandon the rebels' cause, but never returned. Matters worsened then as bad weather descended, making life in the tented camp brutally hard, and news came of fresh rebels in the south. Hugh, the Duke of Burgundy, and Count Raymond of Toulouse had entered the war on the Young King's side. Insult was added to injury by the revelation that Philippe of France had dispatched mercenaries to the aid of his brother-in-law the Young King. His apparent amity towards King Henry had been but a show. The two-month siege was abandoned without delay. As a furious Richard said, a besieging army which ignores the approach of relieving forces often meets a swift, unpleasant end.

The fate of Aquitaine and indeed the entire kingdom hung in the balance during that difficult time. The duke sent word to those of his nobles who had remained loyal – sad to say, the number was growing fewer – and recruited every mercenary to be found. Most were Brabançons, the very troops who formed the bulk of the Young King's and Geoffrey's forces. They were kept on a much tighter leash than those murderers, however, with execution threatened to any man caught raping or pillaging.

Despite the duke's best efforts, we would soon be greatly outnumbered. The month of May saw us crisscrossing the Limousin countryside, fighting skirmishes with our enemies that saw neither side gain victories, and awaiting the arrival of the Burgundians and the Count of Toulouse with increasing dread. We ate poorly, and drank less, and the news of monasteries sacked and strongholds lost saw our morale ebb little by little.

Thus it might have ended.

But God had not forgotten Richard.

Swifts arrowed to and fro above our camp, their piercing skirrs a sign that May was almost done, and June come upon us. I was currying Liath Macha in the sunshine. The simple, repetitive actions took my mind from my growling belly, and the privations of the previous weeks. Rhys stood by, trying not to look annoyed that I had taken his job. Philip lay on his back a short distance away, a strand of grass between his thumbs, and emitting, every now and again, a strangled whistling sound. John de Mandeville, Weasel John and Louis had gone scouting for food.

'A peaceful scene,' said a voice.

I heard Philip scramble to his feet. 'Sire!'

'Master,' called Rhys in an urgent tone.

I peered over Liath Macha's withers.

Richard was clad for war, as he had been every day since our abandonment of the siege at Limoges. His beard was longer than usual, and his eyes were red-rimmed, yet he still exuded a fierce, combative air. Whatever our situation, I thought, he was not about to give up. Stepping under Liath Macha's broad neck, I said, 'At your service, sire.'

'Give me the brush.'

Amazed, I stared at the duke, who laughed.

'You are not the only one to take pleasure from ordinary tasks, Rufus.'

'No, sire.' I thrust out my arm, and he took the brush.

Talking gently to Liath Macha, Richard stepped closer and began currying his back. The horse, enjoying it, stood calm and quiet.

'Ah, to be a stable lad. The simple life, eh?' The duke's voice was low.

Startled by his wistful tone, I cast a look at Philip, whose shrug told me he had no more idea than I had what was going on.

Richard moved on to Liath Macha's neck. 'This is a fine beast. You bought him with the coin I gave you after Usk?'

'I did, sire,' I replied, delighted he had remembered.

'It was money well spent.' The duke half glanced over his shoulder. 'Where's your Welsh boy?'

Rhys was by my side in a heartbeat. 'I am here, sire.'

A grunt. 'Do you recall de Born, that irksome troubadour, Rufus?' Concentrating on the brush strokes, he was talking with his back to us.

'I do sire, well.' Richard had released him before we had left Caen, accepting the silver-tongued rogue's word that he would cause no trouble. In one way at least, I thought again, the duke was like his father: over-trusting.

'Of recent days, he has contrived to retake his family castle at Hautfort. Much as I would like to ride thither and capture it, other matters are more pressing.'

'The Counts of Burgundy and Toulouse, sire?'

A barking, angry laugh. 'They are part of it, yes.'

My curiosity deepened. The duke had not come to discuss military matters with we squires and a Welsh tagalong.

'You did well with de Born,' said Richard.

'Thank you, sire.' Beside me, Rhys was grinning like a madman.

'I have a similar task for you. Not to abduct, but to spy, as you did on Geoffrey at Caen.'

'Whatever you command, sire,' I said eagerly. Rhys nodded so hard his head could have fallen off.

'News has reached me from Martel, a little town to the south of Limoges. It is there that my wretch of a brother Hal has taken himself.'

I was all ears. 'Sire.'

'He has been taken ill. It seems he might even die.' There was no sorrow in his voice, but nor was there satisfaction.

I, God forgive me, felt delight. Without the Young King, the rebellion would lose its focus. And, I thought, my master would become the heir to the throne.

'I want you and Rhys to ride to Martel and see if the news is true, or just a rumour started by Geoffrey, say, to weaken my purpose. You do not know the countryside, so de Drune, who does, will lead you. I will give you letters of safe conduct, as well as a message for my brother. Delivering it will be your apparent purpose.'

'Yes, sire. You want us to leave at once?'

'I do.' Finished with Liath Macha, Richard gave me back the brush. 'This task is not without risk. Not every routier or Brabançon will respect my letter.'

I could see Philip bobbing about behind the duke, pointing forcefully at himself. Taking his meaning, I asked, 'In that case, might we have another companion, sire?'

Richard's blue eyes held my own. 'Who?'

'Philip, sire.' I pointed.

The duke turned. Seeing Philip's enthusiasm, he chuckled. 'Let it be so.'

'Thank you, sire,' we cried, grinning at each other like fools.

Ah, the fervour of youth.

Several days' ride saw us reach the southern borders of the Limousin. Through thick forests we had ridden, up and down hills, and along the side of deep-flowing rivers. We camped at night, listening to wolves howl at the starry sky. Rhys did the cooking, and also cared for our horses. Philip, de Drune and I shared sentry duty, and stayed alert on the road. Routiers were not the only danger we faced. Law and order had broken down, and outside towns and villages, travellers often fell victim to outlaws and brigands. Twice, we spied figures watching from the trees, or flitting across the track in front of us. On another occasion, an arrow shot from nowhere, missing de Drune by less than a foot. Whoever loosed it did not possess the courage to take on three fully armoured soldiers, however, and after a tense time of watching the trees with raised swords and shields, we continued on our way. God was smiling on us, for the rest of our journey passed without hindrance.

I had only known Richard de Drune for a few months, but he was solid. Not solid as in stocky, for he was tall and lean, but reliable. If he said a thing would be done, it was done. I had fought beside him more than once, and been impressed by his skill with the sword. Possessed of a subtle sense of humour, he amused us each night with tales of his life before he had joined Richard's army. Strange though it seemed for a doughty man-at-arms, de Drune had once been a musician. 'Truth is, I am a better soldier than I ever was a lute player,' he admitted. 'I got tired of having the hard ends of loaves hurled at me, or worse. These days, if someone throws something at me, I can usually stick them with this.' He held up his sword, which ever lay across his lap as we sat by the fire, and everyone laughed.

We were still miles from Martel when an encounter on the road with a merchant changed our plans. Anxious-faced, leading a heavy-laden ox-drawn wagon in which sat his wife, children and his worldly goods, he came from Rocamadour, a shrine famed throughout France for the miracles that occurred there.

Although he quailed at the sight of our armour and weapons, he was put at ease by the disclosure that we were Duke Richard's men. Rocamadour, he told us, was about to be attacked by the Young King's soldiers. He was adamant that the heir himself was in charge of the force that had been seen approaching the village adjoining the shrine.

That was good enough for me and my companions.

We reached Rocamadour late in the afternoon. Perched on a limestone cliff, five hundred feet above a deep river gorge, the shrine was breath-taking. Scant chance we had even to admire the view. Shouts and cries reached our ears, and above the roofs, smoke was billowing.

'The merchant was right to leave,' I said, giving my companions a grim look. 'The routiers are already here.'

We donned our arming caps and helmets, and loosened our swords in our scabbards. I considered ordering Rhys to hide in the woods with the packhorses, but that in itself was not without risk. I had two stout companions and the duke's letter of safe conduct, and Rhys had his knife and his shabby, cut-down gambeson. Better we stayed together, I told myself.

'Ready?' I saw my own nerves mirrored in de Drune's and Philip's faces. 'Aye,' they muttered. Rhys was as pale as a winding sheet, but he gave me a fierce grin. The boy had more fight in him than most men three times his size, I swear.

A quarter mile from Rocamadour, we encountered the first body. A young man who had fled, I judged, but weak from the savage wound in his back, had fallen by the wayside and died.

Next came a tide of panicked villagers. I called out that we meant no harm, but they shrieked and jumped into the ditches, and then fled through the fields and after, the trees. I could not argue with de Drune's wry observation that their panic gave us a clear path into the village. Soon there were houses on each side, miserable, single-roomed affairs with thatched roofs such as one saw up and down the land. There were inns, and shops selling beer, food and pilgrim badges. A lame dog barked at us, but did not dare to approach. Not a soul was to be seen: everyone had fled. We rode on, heading for the base of the cliff, where a steep, winding track led up to the hospice, chapels and shrine.

We had still seen no sign of the routiers, yet my skin crawled as if a thousand ants were marching across it. I caught Rhys tugging out his knife, and shook my head, no. 'If they see naked blades, we will be slain.'

'We may be slain anyway,' muttered Philip, but he did not draw his weapon.

Our first encounter with the routiers passed off with relative ease. Three of them had loaded a cart with the contents of a butcher's shop. Caught up with their plundered half carcases of pigs, legs of lamb and haunches of beef, they paid us little attention. Those drinking themselves insensible outside a tavern did not care who we were either. I ordered Rhys not to look into the courtyard, where a screaming serving girl was being attacked. 'There are a dozen men in there, and we are four,' I said from the side of my mouth. 'Pray that her end is swift.' I hoped Rhys did not see through my lie.

By the time we were nearing the shrine, I had counted eight more bodies. Not a complete slaughter, not uncontrolled rape, but it felt truly vile. The soldiers here fought in the name of the man who stood to become ruler of England, Wales, Ireland and this land. My distaste for the Young King reached a new height, and the anger I felt towards the scum who followed him threatened to surge out of control.

'Halt!' The French was mangled by a Flemish accent. 'Declare yourselves.'

I stared at the Brabançon who had blocked my path. Shaven-headed, blood spattering his face, he wore a hauberk and carried a long spear. It was foolish to provoke him, but my temper was up. 'Declare yourself,' I replied.

'A mouthy one, eh?' Up came his crimson-tipped spear, pointing at my throat. 'You are not in our company – I recognise none of you.'

I darted forward, and his spear glanced off my ready shield. I drove it into his chest, and he went down like a sack of grain. 'Get up,' I cried, 'and I will gut you from arsehole to chin.'

He stayed on the ground, mouthing curses.

The din had brought several of his comrades out of the shadows. I snarled that I was a royal messenger, sent by Duke Richard with a message for the Young King. This revelation took their hands from weapons, and with a sullen jerk of his chin up the hill, one told me that his lord was above.

Much as I wanted to lay about me, and rid the world of the human filth clogging Rocamadour, I calmed myself. We had a purpose here, and I had lives to protect, in particular that of Rhys.

A shocking sight met us outside the shrine, which was dedicated to Saint Amadour. Routiers strolled in and out of the church and the religious buildings which stood on either side, carrying bags of coin, jewelled crosses and silver chalices. Monks stood about in tears, or prayed loudly for the saint's help. Pleas for the mercenaries not to plunder the house of God were met with laughter and curses. A braver monk tried to take back a magnificent, jewel-encrusted bible, and his reward was a punch in the face.

Almost as if he had sensed our coming, the Young King appeared in the doorway to the shrine. He was swaying from side to side, and a blade hung from his right fist.

Leaving Rhys and de Drune to guard the horses, Philip and I crossed the courtyard towards him. I had the letter of safe conduct gripped tight, a hand upon my sword.

The Young King paid us no heed until we were very close. Assuming we were his men, he said, brandishing the blade, 'This is reputed to belong to Roland, who died fighting the Saracens. Quite magnificent, is it not?'

'It is, sire,' I said, my contempt for him swelling. To pillage a shrine of its finest treasure was a crime of the lowest kind.

Whether it was my tone or my accent, I do not know, but his gaze switched from the sword to me. The news had been correct, I saw. The Young King's eyes were sunken in an ashen face. Red fever pricks marked his cheekbones, and a sheen of sweat coated his forehead.

'I know you,' he said, frowning. 'You are squires to Richard.'

'Yes, sire.'

His lip curled. 'What message do you carry?'

I offered the duke's letter. 'This, sire.'

Giving the sword to a servant, he unrolled the parchment.

I knew the duke had written a simple demand for his brother to lay down his arms, and disband his troops. He was to return to their father the king forthwith, and beg forgiveness for his actions.

The Young King had only read perhaps the first few lines when he doubled over suddenly, clutching at his belly and groaning. He staggered, and if the servants had not rushed in to catch him, would have fallen. 'The latrine,' he muttered. 'Take me to the latrine.'

With an arm draped over a servant on either side, he half-walked, was half-carried away, leaving us staring after him.

I stooped to pick up the letter, which had fallen to the cobbles. 'Did he read it, do you think?'

'I doubt it,' said Philip. 'He is very ill, right enough.'

'Good,' I said quietly.

Philip's eyebrows rose. 'You have changed, Ferdia.'

He was right, I thought. War and death do that to a man.

A little time passed. The Young King eventually reappeared, carried on a stretcher. He was borne into the monks' quarters, where a physician monk tended to him. We retreated to the safety of a nearby abandoned house, and kept watch from the window. Hours later, the Young King was loaded into a wagon, which set off down the hill. A handful of coin given to a servant revealed he was being taken back to Martel, where the priests would give him the last rites. I took counsel with Philip and de Drune, and we decided to head in the same direction the next day, giving the Brabançon rabble a good head start.

The Young King died before we got there.

Routiers clogged the road north from Martel, proof that his army was already falling apart. They were a real threat to our safety, and we agreed to return to Richard with all haste. Geoffrey would not continue the struggle unless the heir to the throne was by his side, and shorn of the magnetism of two royal brothers to aid their cause, the rebel nobles would do the same.

God forgive me. I felt no sorrow as I rode, only gratitude that the Young King was no more, and pride, that Duke Richard had won.

He was now the king's eldest son.

CHAPTER XX

High in the tower of Rouen cathedral, the bells tolled, deep and sonorous. They rang for the Young King, who lay in a lead coffin beside the vault that would hold his mortal remains until the end of days. William Marshal stood dry-eyed, watching the king weep for his feckless eldest son, and Geoffrey, who shed no tears, although he seemed sorrowful enough. Well he might be, thought Marshal, having lost his greatest ally. John did not even try to look sad. Instead, a bored expression shaping his podgy features, he picked at his fingernails and scuffed the point of his fine leather shoe off the flags. The king's bastard son Geoffrey was also present, a loyal, inconspicuous type who stayed close to Henry.

Marshal was the picture of composure. He still mourned, naturally, but the knife edge of his grief had been dulled by recent events. Recalled to the Young King's side after the fall from grace of d'Yquebeuf and de Coulonces, he had been reunited with his old friends de Béthune and de Marisco. Together they had unwillingly played their part in the chaos that had engulfed Aquitaine in May. When the Young King had been struck down by dysentery, it was Marshal who had summoned the physicians and leeches. Every sweat-filled, anguished moment of his master's last hours was etched on his memory. Matters had grown no easier after the Young King's death, over a month before. Marshal had had to fight, sometimes literally, to transport the body north to Rouen for burial.

Staring at the open lead coffin, and the waxen features of the man he had served for many years, a long breath escaped him. The ordeal was almost at an end. Alongside his sadness, he felt a sweeping sense of relief, as if a great burden was about to be lifted from his shoulders. There would be little chance to savour it, however, for the ground was shifting beneath his feet. Without a powerful master, his prospects were lean. Richard had previously offered to employ him, and he yet might, but the near success of the Young King's rebellion meant that the duke's position was a great deal weaker. Joining him guaranteed nothing. Marshal was thirty-six, and had little to show for half a lifetime of service. He needed security and definite prospects.

The priest came to stand over the coffin. Removing his chasuble, he handed it to an acolyte. Next, he censed the Young King's body and scattered it with holy water, before starting to recite the Lord's Prayer.

The congregation joined in.

His lips moving, Marshal studied the king sidelong. Henry's reddened face was blotchy with tears, and sobs racked his frame. Marshal stilled the sympathy rising in his chest, and decided he must strike now. While the king was mad with grief, his chance of success was greatest. It was vital that he did not appear over-eager, or Henry might divine his purpose.

To Marshal's good fortune, the king sought him out the moment the ceremony was over.

'You are here.' Henry's voice was grateful.

Marshal bowed. 'Of course, sire.'

'Walk with me.' The king limped for the opposite side chapel, which was empty of mourners.

Marshal followed, casting an eye at the main altar, and sending up an urgent prayer.

'They say Hal's end was difficult,' said the king.

'I cannot lie, sire, you have the truth of it. When it became clear he was dying, the Young King confessed in private, to the bishop of Cahors and an abbot.' Marshal saw that the king hung off his every word. 'I am told he did so naked, prostrating himself on the floor before the abbot's crucifix. He renounced his recent actions and was absolved.'

'He was sorry for what he had done.' Fresh tears rolled down Henry's cheeks.

'Be sure of it, sire. Four days later, he made another confession, this time in public. I was there to see him receive the last rites.' Marshal waited until the king regained a little composure, and signalled him to continue. 'Regretting his failure to go on crusade as he had promised, the Young King ordered a cross stitched to his cloak. He entrusted this to me, calling me his "most intimate friend", and asking that I take it to the Holy Sepulchre in Jerusalem.'

'You have the cloak still?' asked the king, his voice trembling.

'I do, sire. It is my intention to travel to Outremer as soon as my affairs are in order.'

Pleased, the king nodded. 'Did my sapphire ring arrive before he left this world?'

'Yes, sire. He cried to see it, and clutched it to him constantly.' Marshal decided not to mention the Young King's dismay that his father had sent a precious trinket by way of forgiveness instead of answering his request to come in person.

Henry seemed satisfied. 'Continue.'

'Wishing to show his complete repentance, the Young King ordered his clothes be removed. Donning a hair shirt, and placing a noose around his neck, he ordered us to drag him to the floor with it. There he lay, with ashes for a mattress and stones for a pillow and footrest.'

Henry's face was anguished. 'You were with him?'

'I never left his side, sire. Baldwin de Béthune and Simon de Marisco were there also.' It had been a piteous scene, one Marshal never wanted to witness again. 'When the end was near, the Young King raised your ring to his lips and kissed it. He closed his eyes then, sire, and never opened them again.'

'Ah, my son, my son.' Henry bent his head and wept. Tears spattered the flagstones.

Marshal's own grief surged back. He had loved the Young King like a younger brother. He had had many faults, it was true, but he had also been a person of huge charisma, immensely likeable, and capable of great kindness. These qualities were what Marshal would try to remember.

Henry palmed his brow, and turned his swollen eyes on Marshal. 'You are for the Holy Land?'

'I am, sire. There will be no rest for me until I have fulfilled the Young King's request.'

'That is well,' said the king. 'When will you come back?'

'I know not, sire. I may be called on to aid the fight against the Saracens. As you know, they have been pressing Outremer hard.'

'Even so.' Henry was silent for a moment, as if deciding something, and then he said, 'Know that there is a place in my household for you, whatever the date of your return.'

Marshal's heart leaped. This prize was precisely what he had hoped for, and like a ripe plum from the tree, it had just fallen into his lap. Truly, God had answered his prayer. 'I should be honoured, sire,' he said, dipping his head.

'And so it is settled.' A small smile appeared on the king's face.

Hoping to help his friends, Marshal threw the dice. 'De Béthune, sire, and de Marisco . . .'

'There is always room in my mesnie for loyal men.'

'Thank you, sire.'

They turned and began to walk towards the cathedral's main door.

'Recent tidings must please you, sire,' said Marshal. 'The Counts of Burgundy and Toulouse have skulked home. Aimar of Limoges has surrendered, and Philippe of France will think twice before interfering again. Geoffrey is soon to return to Brittany, and he will come to offer his allegiance at Angers, I am told. The rebellion is over.'

A heavy sigh. 'I suppose. And yet it is not.'

'Sire?'

'Richard has been Duke of Aquitaine these ten years, but the rebellion took hold like a spark falling on dry grass. His rule should have been more secure.'

If it had not been for the Young King and Geoffrey, thought Marshal, Richard could have contained the uprising himself. 'It is a little more complicated than that, sire, surely?'

'I think Aquitaine would benefit from a new duke.'

'Sire?' Marshal barely managed to conceal his shock.

'Richard will be my heir now, so he no longer needs to rule Aquitaine. I will not crown him joint king – after I did that with Hal, things went awry – but instead install him in Anjou.'

Marshal's eyes followed the king's, which had found John on the other side of the cathedral. Dread filled his belly. 'And Aquitaine, sire?'

'Why, John shall have it.' The king glanced at Marshal. 'In name only, of course. I will rule until he is man enough.'

Marshal bowed his head, relieved that he was to set sail for the Holy

Land. Realise it or not, he thought, the king had just laid the seeds for another rebellion.

Persist with this course, and Richard would be the son who rose against him.

PART THREE: 1187-1189

CHAPTER XXI

It was high summer, the twenty-second of June, and I was on a footing for war. Around me, close to the fortress of Châteauroux on the River Indre, was a massive camp. There were endless rows of tents and horse lines, hundreds of wagons, and thousands of men – the combined armies of Richard and his father the king. Around the fortress itself, which guarded the eastern border of Aquitaine and the kingdom of France, was a similarly sized army, that of King Philippe.

Four years had passed since the Young King's death. So much had changed, I thought, watching Rhys putting Liath Macha through his paces. He was no longer a stick-limbed urchin, but a strapping young man. I had seen to it that he was trained in arms, and he had loved every moment. Compare Rhys to a dog, and the only breed that fitted was the alaunt. Born to fight, he was, and I counted myself fortunate to have him in my service. Despite his youth, he had already been accepted as a man-at-arms by the duke, and fought at a number of sieges and minor battles.

There was Philip, sparring with Louis, both clad only in their hose, with leather guards on their blades to prevent injury. Philip was still the conscience to my devil, and the two of us continued to be thick as thieves. Louis had recovered from the wound sustained before Gorre, and never looked back. Gone was his stiffness and his arrogance; he had long since been one of us. Weasel John was no longer part of our company. Slain close to Toulouse during the duke's invasion two years prior, he had not been mourned for long.

Of John de Mandeville, there was no sign, for he had been knighted three summers past, during yet another round of fighting against the duke's brother Geoffrey. He had found position among Richard's soldiers. I saw him occasionally, and he never ceased to remind me how I had not yet been knighted. It was a sore point, like a wound that never healed. At squiring, I was expert. I had been in countless skirmishes, fights where every man had had to play his part. I was fluent in French. The reason for my lack of advancement was frustrating. Squires could be dubbed knights, but the duke liked to have a solid reason to do so. 'Your moment will come, Rufus,' he said now and again. I could only smile and grit my teeth, and tell myself that it was nothing to do with my being Irish.

A dozen paces from me, Richard de Drune squatted on his haunches, supping from a costrel; every now and again he called out advice to Philip and Louis. They listened, for his advice was golden. Since the journey to seek out the Young King at Martel, he had been a close comrade. Last in our group was Owain, who sat close to de Drune, running an oilstone along his sword blade. Some thought it odd for a knight to keep company with squires and men-at-arms, but to us it felt the most natural thing in the world. The lone Welsh knight in Richard's service, Owain was shunned because of it. He gravitated to our company little by little, and we got on well. I had no prejudices against his race, and like him, I was also not an Englishman or a Norman. In short, we were natural friends and allies.

Of FitzAldelm there was no sign, but the mongrel was in the camp. To my good fortune, he had been elsewhere in Aquitaine for much of the previous four years. During that time, however, his fortunes had changed utterly. After saving a conroi ambushed by the rebels, he had risen in the duke's esteem, and been given command of a small castle. Adept at organisation and leading men, he had proved a reliable deputy, conducting himself with some distinction in a number of sieges. Now, like almost every man under Richard's command, he was here, ready to fight King Philippe.

That rare thing, a full set piece battle, was imminent.

It did not seem real. I stretched luxuriously, enjoying the hot sun on my bare skin, and the cool, silky feeling of grass under me. Today we would train, and swim in the river, I thought; and in the evening, drink wine as we listened to the duke's musicians.

'How in God's name did it come to this?'

I squinted up at Louis, who had stumped over. 'You mean King Philippe being here with his army?' I asked.

'That, yes.' He waved an irritated hand. 'Did not Henry and Philippe become friends again after the Young King died?'

I rolled my eyes. Of all of us, Louis was the one who paid the least heed to what went on. As long as his belly was full, and there was coin in his purse, he did not much care for anything. In truth, he was not blessed with intelligence either, yet it was surprising that he had no understanding of why we were so close to war.

'They did,' I answered. 'Once the matter of Philippe's two sisters, Marguerite and Alys, had been settled, and an agreement reached on the Vexin.'

'Eh?'

I explained how Philippe's concern for Marguerite, the Young King's widow, had been allayed by Henry's provision of a substantial annual pension. The French king had also been troubled by the plight of Alys, betrothed to Richard and in Henry's care since her childhood. It was widely known that the duke opposed the match, and so it was suggested she might marry John, a proposal Philippe had agreed to. His sisters thus apparently provided for, he had allowed Henry to keep the Vexin, a sensitive border area between Anjou and France. 'The status quo lasted for almost three years,' I said. 'But the proposed betrothal of John and Alys came to naught.'

'And Richard continued to refuse to marry her,' said Louis. 'That was what started the argument again, eh?'

'He was wise to decline.' Owain lowered his voice and said, 'She looks like a horse.'

We all laughed, for he was right.

As we quietened, Louis asked, 'So is that why we are here – because the duke would not take Alys to be his wife?'

'It is more complicated than that.' I described how the previous year Geoffrey, unhappy at the freshly resurrected suggestion that Richard should wed Alys, had taken himself to Philippe's court. There the two had become fast friends, and Geoffrey was invested as seneschal of France. 'When that happened, many – Duke Richard included – thought that his appointment to a post with strong links to Anjou revealed designs on the English throne.'

'But Geoffrey was killed,' said Louis in confusion. 'Last August.'

'Trampled to death at a tourney,' said Rhys with malicious satisfaction.

'A fitting end,' added de Drune.

Owain looked a trifle upset, but said nothing.

Philip checked to see no one but we could hear. 'The son of perdition, he was, forever scheming and conniving.'

''Tis apt that he and Philippe should have shared a bed,' I said. 'The two were kindred spirits.'

'They say Philippe had to be held back at Geoffrey's funeral, else he would have thrown himself into the grave after. A pity he did not – he would have saved us from the need for this—' De Drune's wave took in the entire camp, and after, the fortress, '—and those French bastards over there.'

We muttered our agreement. For all our bravado, there was a real risk of dying or being maimed the following day.

'Geoffrey's death saw Philippe lose the last of his influence in Henry's court. He demanded custody of Geoffrey's children – which is his right as overlord of Brittany,' I said to Louis. 'When Henry refused, Philippe threatened to invade Normandy. He also demanded that Alys marry Richard at once, and if she did not, the Vexin was to be ceded to him.'

'Henry refused to hand it over,' said Owain.

'And the duke would not marry Alys,' added de Drune.

'Which made war inevitable. Even the arrival of a papal legate, sent here to negotiate a truce, did not help,' I finished. 'Do you see?'

Louis scratched his ear. 'I think so.'

I groaned, and Philip threw his sweaty arming cap at Louis, who scowled and leaped on him. A wrestling match ensued, while the rest of us egged the pair on with shouts and jeers.

'Sir.'

Noting the taut note in Rhys's voice, I turned my head. FitzAldelm was striding towards us. I fixed my face into a mask, hiding my hatred. If I confess it, I felt a little fear too. I gave my enemy a stiff nod.

There was no acknowledgement. His eyes flicked from mine to Louis and Philip, who continued to roll about. 'I am surprised not to see you down there as well. Dogs belong on the floor.'

A furious sound escaped Rhys. I gave him a sharp look.

FitzAldelm regarded Rhys as he might stare at something unpleasant he had stepped in. To me, he said, 'You still keep the company of churls, I see.'

He meant Rhys of course, but Owain had heard. 'I do not take kindly to insults, sir, in particular when they impugn my honour. Your name?'

'FitzAldelm. By your atrocious accent, you must be the Welsh knight.'

'I am he, sir.'

'You are as raggedy-arse as I expected.'

His colour rising, Owain took a couple of steps towards FitzAldelm. 'Apologise.'

I sensed de Drune on my right. If I knew him, he had a hand on his dagger. Behind FitzAldelm, Rhys waited, his eyes glittering. I could no longer hear Philip and Louis wrestling – they were watching as well. I had but to say the word, and we would fall upon my enemy. Tempting though it was, I knew it for pure folly, and a sure way to threaten my position with the duke.

'Apologise, to you?' It was incredible how much contempt the man could pack into three words.

Owain's fists bunched.

'Owain!'

He looked at me, his pleasant face twisted with anger. 'Aye?' he grated.

'This is not the time or place.' I did not want to say it aloud, but Owain probably did not have the beating of him, and I felt sure FitzAldelm would slip his knife into my friend given the slightest opportunity.

Turning back to FitzAldelm, who sneered, Owain said, 'I will have my satisfaction from you.' He added something guttural in Welsh.

'What did he say?' demanded FitzAldelm.

'I did not hear, sir, but I imagine it was similar to amadán,' I said, smirking.

FitzAldelm's lips pinched. 'Wastrels and turds, the lot of you.'

Delighted that my barb had sunk in, I enquired, 'Are you just here to be unpleasant, sir, or did you have another purpose?'

His cold gaze rested on mine. 'The duke wishes you to attend him.'

I hid my surprise. We squires spent hours in our master's company, not he. This command meant he had come straight from Richard. 'Now?'

'Now. You, the squire Philip, and the man-at-arms called de Drune.'

Owain looked stricken. Rhys had not been summoned, yet it did not prevent him from dogging our trail as FitzAldelm led us to the duke's tent.

In this part of the camp men were also preparing for battle. Squires were scrubbing mail with sand, a skin-ripping but effective way to make it shine. Pages polished belts, and horse harness. Knights discussed fighting methods, or sparred with each other. A serjeant led a group of men-at-arms towards the open ground beyond the tents, roaring that they would not be ready until he said so.

Richard was standing at the entrance to his pavilion, above which a red pennant adorned with golden Angevin lions fluttered. Spying us, a smile creased his lips. 'You found them, Robert.'

My gorge rose to hear FitzAldelm called by his first name. It was a salutary warning. The duke regarded my enemy as a friend. If I was ever to try to discredit him, I would need irrefutable proof.

'Yes, sire.'

We gathered inside Richard's tent, joining de Chauvigny and some of his captains. Serving we newcomers wine with his own hands – a high honour – the duke saluted us with his goblet.

'To victory over the French, sire,' I said, thinking to read his mood.

Philip and de Drune echoed the words at once, but FitzAldelm and the rest did not join in. My enemy returned the surprised look I gave him with an imperious one of his own. It galled me to realise that he knew something I did not.

'Battle should be avoided,' Richard declared. 'Do you know why, Rufus?'

I thought of the fights I had been in, and how they had often turned on a single moment, when victory or defeat were equally likely. Henry and Richard, I decided, could lose everything if they were defeated. There was also the chance – as had happened at Hastings a hundred and twenty-odd years before – that king or duke might fall.

'The risks are too great, sire,' I said.

'Just so. Much as it would please me – and you, I have no doubt – to fight tomorrow, it must not be allowed to happen.'

'But the talks were unsuccessful, sire. Even the papal legate could not break the impasse.' This had been the word sweeping the camp, as well as how in utter frustration, he had excommunicated the duke, and wild rumour of the crusade the pope wanted us all to join.

'They have failed. My lord father is set upon battle. My captains and

I want to make one more throw of the dice, however.' He indicated FitzAldelm, and said, 'Robert has made contact with the Count of Flanders.'

Hating FitzAldelm more than ever, I offered, 'If I can help, sire . . .?'

'Faithful heart,' said Richard, smiling. 'And your companions are possessed of the same. Will you ride with me to the French camp?'

There was only one response.

Dusk was falling when we took a circuitous route out of the camp, riding away from the fortress and the French positions around it so that suspicions would not be aroused. No one apart from Richard's inner circle knew what was afoot – not even the king. Our group to-talled ten: the duke, me, de Drune, Owain and Philip, FitzAldelm, and three of the latter's knights. These gave me contemptuous looks, no doubt because Boots and Fists had filled their ears with poison.

In a thick copse, under the heavy-leafed branches of a mighty beech, we met the Count of Flanders. Another Philippe, he was a dapper figure in a dark green Flemish tunic and brown hose. Greeting Richard cordially, and the rest of us with an appraising glance, he and a dozen knights accompanied us to the enemy camp. I was close enough to hear him and the duke talking.

'Are you certain there will be battle tomorrow, sire?' asked the count.

'No, but let that not seem like weakness,' said Richard. 'If it comes to a fight, we shall not turn away.'

'Your courage is unquestioned, sire.' Philippe hesitated, before adding, 'Can I speak my mind?'

'In times such as these, plain speech is always best. Go to, sir.'

'Many of us believe it foolish and ill-advised to bear arms against your lord the king of France. Think of the future, sire: why should he be well-disposed towards you, or confirm you in your expectations? Do not despise his youth either. The king may be young in years, but he has a mature mind, is far-seeing and determined in what he does. He is ever mindful of wrongs and does not forget services rendered. Believe those with experience; I too ranged myself against him, but after wasting much treasure I have come to repent of it. How splendid and useful it would be if you had the grace and favour of your lord.'

Half-expecting the duke to react angrily to Philippe's forthrightness, I watched with keen interest.

Making no reply, Richard stared into the shadow-bound trees.

The count did not press him, and I thought, he is shrewd.

'Thank you for your counsel, sir,' said Richard at length. 'Good relations between the houses of Anjou and Capet are ever to be desired. Your words have strengthened my desire for peace.'

Philippe's teeth flashed white. 'It is well. God willing, you and the king shall come to an agreement.'

There were curious stares aplenty from the French troops who saw us pass their tents, but in the poor light, with the duke's hood up, they did not guess our identity. Despite this, and the calm presence of the Count of Flanders, my unease swelled.

Sentries ringed King Philippe's tent, which was similar to Richard's, although a little larger. Hearing our arrival, he emerged, the torchlight revealing a well-built, ungainly young man with a shock of untidy brown hair. Dressed in a tradesman's drab tunic, he appeared to be blind in one eye. I was also struck by his youth.

'Not yet twenty-two,' Owain whispered in my ear.

Five years younger than me, and a king since he was fifteen, I thought. It was hard not to feel a sneaking admiration, for despite his slovenly appearance, the man was an astute politician.

The Count of Flanders bowed and introduced the duke, who slid from his saddle and paced forward.

'You are welcome, brother,' said Philippe, embracing Richard.

The pair gave each other the kiss of peace, and there was no sign of antagonism as the two entered the tent, their heads bent in discussion.

The Count of Flanders saw to it that we were offered food and wine, before also vanishing within. There was little conversation among us left outside. An hour dragged by. Word of our presence spread, and a large number of French knights and men-at-arms gathered. There was none of the apparent friendliness between the duke and Philippe. The air was tense, hostile even. When a towering man-at-arms spat in our direction, I ignored him, and ordered my companions to do the same. I assumed that as knights, FitzAldelm and his cronies would consider any reaction beneath their dignity.

The man-at-arms continued to bait us, swaggering up and down, making loud comments about parentage and lack of courage. There was much laughter, and ribald commentary.

FitzAldelm's expression grew more and more angry. He muttered to his knights, one of whom foolishly laid a hand to his weapon.

Seeing this, the Frenchman transferred his attentions to FitzAldelm.

Who responded in kind, with insults that would have whitened a bishop's hair.

This, of course, was what the Frenchman had been wanting. He demanded satisfaction on the instant.

FitzAldelm snarled his agreement, and stepped forward.

I could have stood by and done nothing, but it seemed clear from the bloodlust in the faces ringing us that my enemy would not be the only one to fall. A tide of French would overwhelm us. The duke himself might be threatened.

Raising my hands in a clear gesture of peace, I stepped in front of FitzAldelm. 'Your pardon, sir,' I said to the Frenchman. 'My companion is easily unsettled. There is no need for a quarrel.'

I received a string of obscenities in reply, and an order to move if I valued my life. Dry-mouthed, I told the Frenchman that he would have to strike down an unarmed man to clear his path.

FitzAldelm tried to shove by, but I anticipated his move, and managed to keep myself between him and the enraged Frenchman. He made another attempt, and again I prevented him.

'Out of my way, Irish churl,' he hissed.

'I will not, sir.'

'Stand aside, or the last thing you will feel is my dagger between your ribs.' The distinctive sound of a blade leaving the sheath followed.

Fear beat at me. Every instinct screamed that I should obey. I stayed put. 'You will not murder me in cold blood with so many witnesses, sir,' I said.

FitzAldelm swore. The Frenchman, who had seen him draw his knife, watched with narrowed eyes.

I felt like a mouse trapped between a pair of farm cats.

A roar of laughter came from inside the tent. A sign that things were perhaps going well, it broke the tension as effectively as a bucket of water thrown over two fighting boys.

'Robert,' said one of FitzAldelm's knights.

Snick went the dagger into its scabbard, and I heard him take a step back. With a sneer, the Frenchman rejoined his companions.

On legs that felt like jelly, I took my place among my friends once more. Philip gave me an encouraging nod. Owain clasped my hand. I had been a fool, de Drune told me, and close to being a dead one. A brave dead one, he added, with a wink. I glowered, and replied that we would probably all have been slain had I done nothing.

FitzAldelm was staring at me with pure hatred. Never give him another chance like that, I told myself. He might take it, and damn the consequences.

The confrontation with the French continued, although now both sides contented themselves with malevolent looks. To our relief, the duke materialised with Philippe a short time later. Both were wreathed in smiles. Neither appeared aware of what had gone on, and I was not going to mention it. I felt sure that as the person responsible for what had almost been a bloodbath, FitzAldelm would not either.

The French king, Richard told us during our return, had agreed to a truce on the condition that his father did the same. Battle would not be joined the following morning, he declared.

Owain clapped de Drune on the shoulder, and I whispered to Philip how, when the duke dismissed us, we would get drunk as lords, with no concerns for the morrow.

The church bells inside Châteauroux were tolling matins when Richard reached his father's tent. Again we were left outside as he entered to awake the king and deliver the good news. Philip and I held a muttered conversation about whether the impending truce meant there was any chance of wooing any ladies-in-waiting. I often thought of Alienor, and kept her fillet in the little bag around my neck, but like as not, I would never see her again. Although I felt guilty, my youthful attentions turned to other women, so when the rumour had begun that Richard's mother was to cross the Narrow Sea, a freedom granted her more regularly of recent years, I had been all ears. With her would come at least a score of women. The duke adored his mother, and would want to spend time with her. By our reasoning, wherever our lord went, we would too.

'WHAT?'

The roar must have woken half the camp. I stared at Philip in dismay, and listened to the king's enraged shouts.

'You went behind my back to Philippe?'

'I did so, Papa, in good faith, to prevent a battle—'

'Did you, by God? Or was it to talk about your succession, what you will do when I am gone?'

'No, I swear—'

'Hold your tongue! I see your purpose,' cried Henry. 'Good relations with the French king will be vital when you take the throne. A more golden opportunity to cement your relationship than this meeting, I cannot think of.'

'That was not why I met with Philippe!' At last Richard's volume equalled his father's. 'You speak of relationships. What of ours?'

'Ours?'

'Yes, Papa. True it is that we are father and son, but am I to be your heir? I have assumed until now that I am – the knowledge gave me strength during the talks with Philippe – but as the situation grows more turbulent, I would know your answer.' Richard's voice was strained.

'This is hardly the time or place,' said Henry.

'I can think of no better one, with our enemy the king of France close at hand, and an army at his back.'

'It is I who decides these things, not you,' snapped the king.

'When Hal and Geoffrey rose against you, Papa, I stayed true. The kingdom might have been lost else, yet your reward is to leave my future clouded with uncertainty.'

'I will name my successor when I please. Do not try to bury me before my time.'

'That is not my intention, Papa, as well you know.'

'Do I? You are the one scheming with Philippe,' came the snide reply.

'I talked with him of a truce, nothing more!'

An icy silence.

I felt a burning sense of injustice. The rumour I had refused to believe was true. Despite being the king's oldest living son, and the one who had remained loyal to him through thick and thin, my master had not been given what was his by right.

Henry spoke again, his tone strident. 'As for the matter at hand, there will be no truce. Let Philippe suck on the marrow of that, and we shall see how the morrow unfolds.'

Richard's protests were in vain, and soon after, FitzAldelm was charged by the duke with carrying the belligerent message to the French king.

He came back with a four word answer.

We fight at dawn.

CHAPTER XXII

Dismissed by the duke, my companions and I retired to our blankets, finding room alongside Rhys's snoring form. My mind whirled with images of battle, but I had been up since sunrise, and sleep took me almost at once. I dreamed of combat, the insult-shouting Frenchman, and FitzAldelm. It was not pleasant. When a hand shook me by the shoulder, I seized it in fright, taking the grasp for an enemy's.

'Sir, it is I, Rhys!'

I came awake with a jerk. Rhys crouched over me. Behind him, to my surprise, was the duke. 'Sire,' I whispered.

'Another foray into the French camp beckons, Rufus,' said Richard.

My heart leaped. 'You want me to accompany you, sire?'

'I do. Hurry. FitzAldelm is waiting.'

Curse him, I thought, why did he not pick de Chauvigny? There was nothing to be said of course, so dressing and arming myself as fast as I might, I joined the duke and my enemy outside the tent.

FitzAldelm and I stared at each other coldly. In the gloom, wrapped up with the business at hand, Richard did not see the sparking hatred between us.

'What is your purpose, sire?' I asked as we led our horses towards the edge of camp.

'The king has seen the error of his ways. He wants to accept Philippe's offer of a truce after all.'

'Will Philippe agree, sire?'

'Only God can answer that question, Rufus,' came the grim reply.

It was not a response that inspired hope. I prayed as we rode, asking the Divine to help my master persuade the French king to step back from the brink. Uncomfortable with FitzAldelm so close, shivering beneath an unseasonably cold breeze – in my haste, I had forgotten a cloak – I did my best to keep my spirits from sinking.

Close to the French lines, Richard had me light the torch I carried. A pair of astonished sentries greeted us at the perimeter. Their officer was just as surprised, but recognised the duke and had the initiative to guide him directly to Philippe. For the second time in less than a day, I found myself outside the French king's tent. On this occasion, however, Richard ordered me to enter. FitzAldelm came in as well. 'I want witnesses,' muttered the duke. 'So my lord father cannot gainsay what I tell him.'

We found Philippe up and dressed, clad in a glittering hauberk that reached to his knees. Around his waist was a belt of embossed, gilded leather; from that hung a sword in a magnificent gilt-edged scabbard. There was no embrace, no kiss of peace. Instead he gave Richard a cold nod. Us he ignored.

The duke delivered his father's request for a truce.

Philippe laughed. 'These are the same terms that I offered to your lord father a few hours ago, only to have them thrown in my face. You have a nerve even to come here.'

'I can do nothing about the day's events, sire, save apologise,' said Richard, his tone humble.

Anger filled me that the duke should have to act so; he had been placed in this position thanks only to his father's bull-headedness.

'I entreat you, sire, to accept the truce. Prevent blood being shed tomorrow,' said the duke. 'The loss of life on both sides will be considerable.'

Philippe stalked up and down, his expression thunderous.

Richard bowed his head.

If Philippe rejected Henry's offer, I thought nervously, many of us might lie dead on the field by sunset tomorrow.

Philippe broke the silence at last. 'The disrespect your lord father has shown me today has been unforgivable. I am the king of France!'

'Again, sire, I am deeply sorry that he should have treated you so.'

'Does he think me a child still, afraid of war?'

'No, sire.'

Philippe continued to rant and rave about Henry; it seemed that the situation was beyond salvage. I half-expected Richard to lose his temper and insult the French king, storm out. When I saw him un-buckle his belt, I did not quite understand. My confusion was mirrored in FitzAldelm's face.

'Sire,' said Richard.

Philippe stopped his pacing, and looked at the duke, who had knelt. He frowned. 'Yes?'

'The truce will be honoured, sire.' His head bent, Richard held up his sword and belt, which lay across his outstretched hands. 'If my lord father should break it, I will personally surrender to your judgement in Paris. This I swear before Almighty God.'

Richard's humility amazed me. Few men indeed had the strength of character to act so, and certainly not his father. I closed my eyes and prayed that Philippe possessed the magnanimity to agree.

'Rise, brother. Peace is preferable to war.'

I looked up.

'I accept your offer.' Smiling broadly, Philippe had taken Richard's sword and belt. As the duke stood, he handed them back. 'Let us hope now that your lord father sees sense.'

Richard bowed from the waist, as I had rarely seen him do, even to Henry, and said, 'With your leave, I would bring news of the truce to the king.'

'Go, with my blessing.' Philippe's bow was markedly shallower.

If Richard noticed, he gave no sign.

Dawn broke on the twenty-third of June, sunny and blue-skied. As news of the truce spread, it felt as if hope had been born anew. Thousands of men would not now die or be maimed in the nearby fields. Delighted that I had witnessed the crisis being averted, I woke my companions and regaled them with the tale. Philip and Rhys listened, wide-eyed. Louis yawned from his blankets and pretended not to be interested. Owain told me I was a lucky dog to have been there. De Drune made a joke at my expense, as was his wont.

When Richard appeared, we all jumped to our feet. FitzAldelm was at his back, curse him.

I was usually the one to greet the duke first, but disconcerted by the presence of my enemy, I allowed Philip to get in before me. 'Whither are we bound, sire? To Hautfort?'

My pulse quickened. The de Born family stronghold, this was where Bertran, the meddlesome troubadour, had ensconced himself after ousting his brother. Bringing him to heel was one of Richard's priorities.

The duke shook his head. 'Alas, that siege must wait.'

'South then, sire, to ensure the Count of Toulouse has truly retreated?' I asked.

His blue eyes turned to me, cold and hard. 'Not there either.'

Confused, unsure what I had done, I nodded.

'I am for Paris, with King Philippe,' he said. 'Robert is to accompany me.'

How had my enemy inveigled the duke so, I wondered, to climb so high in his esteem. I would have to work hard to keep my own favoured position. I nodded, as if pleased by the news. 'When are we to leave, sire?'

He gave me another icy stare. 'You are not to be part of the company, Rufus.'

My jaw dropped. 'Why not, sire?'

'Do not question your master!' FitzAldelm's voice cracked like a whip.

If looks could have killed, he would have fallen dead in that moment.

'Peace, Robert,' said Richard mildly. He turned back to me. 'You are being punished for your behaviour yesterday.' Into my astonishment, he continued, 'Abusing and insulting King Philippe's men. Spitting at them; challenging one to combat. All while I was incarcerated, engaged in talks of the utmost importance. If not for Robert here, who intervened, you would have jeopardised the very truce that came into force this morning. Such reckless actions needs punishment, Rufus. This shall be the start of it; upon my return, I shall consider how else you might make amends.'

Speechless, outraged that FitzAldelm should blame me for what he had done, I floundered for a response. 'Sire, it was not I!'

I saw my friends' faces, and knew they would corroborate my words. I saw the fear in FitzAldelm's eyes. I had not accounted for Richard's volcanic temper, however.

'Silence!' he thundered.

I shut my mouth.

'A belted knight, a man I know and trust, has sworn that you acted so,' shouted Richard. 'Be grateful that I do not seek to punish you further, Rufus.'

Seething but impotent, I gave way to his wrath. 'Yes, sire.'

'Philip, you are to come with me. Louis also.' He strode off without a backward glance.

I looked up to find FitzAldelm staring straight at me, his expression gloating.

So dispirited was I that I simply dropped my gaze to my boots.

The instant FitzAldelm had gone, my companions' outrage boiled over. Rhys was the angriest, threatening to steal after him with a ready knife. He subsided at my rebuke, and I listened to Philip's opinion, as well as those of Louis and Owain. De Drune held his counsel, as was his wont.

It would be a fool's errand to have each bear witness that FitzAldelm was a liar, I explained, because it would seem as if I had put them all up to it. In addition, FitzAldelm's knights would swear blind that their master's account was true, and their testimony outweighed ours.

'Wise words,' said de Drune.

'Besides, this is small punishment,' I said, remembering my incarceration at Striguil, and the beatings I had endured. 'God willing, Richard will have forgotten about it when he returns.'

'That will never happen with FitzAldelm by his side, sir,' declared Rhys, his eyes still alight with rage. In a hoarse whisper, he said, 'Let me find him tonight, sir, before they go.'

I remembered Rhys's remorse over the two ruffians who had hung in our stead, and thought, how men change. His ruthless suggestion was tempting. With FitzAldelm dead, I would soon return to the duke's affections.

'No,' I said firmly.

'He deserves nothing better, sir.'

'You are right, but murder is murder.' I hesitated, before adding, 'And it would have to be me, Rhys. Not this time, however. Understand?'

He gave me a savage grin, and let it go.

My fall from favour brought about an unexpected but altogether welcome consequence. Richard left orders that I was to join the king's court until his return. Part of a company that included Owain and de Drune, we travelled with Henry and his army back to Le Mans and after, to the castle at Angers, where to my delight, I met Beatrice. The rumours had been true: Richard's mother Queen Alienor had already arrived, and with her a great company of women. Chestnut-haired, voluptuous, possessed of a wicked smile, Beatrice was servant to one of the queen's ladies.

I fell for her, hard, but for every step forward I took in my pursuit, I took another back. Meetings were hard to arrange, and days could pass without a chance to talk. When an occasion did present itself, I was my own worst enemy. Thick-tongued when I wanted the voice of a poet, forever crimson-faced, so clumsy I tripped over my own feet, I must have seemed like a court jester. Despite my ineptitude, Beatrice bore with me, which gave me the fortitude to carry on. Little by little, my confidence grew, until I was able to steal a kiss from her most times we met.

Summer wore on. Whenever possible, I walked the castle ramparts with Beatrice as the sun went down, watching the swifts swoop and dive overhead, and as proud as any man alive. One evening in late July, I think it was, we halted by her favourite spot, which overlooked the River Maine. I was fond of the place too, but not because of the beautiful view. Defensively impregnable at this point, there were no sentry positions for a hundred paces in either direction, which meant – as long as there were no other courting couples – we could be alone.

Beatrice was watching for the otters she had spied on our last outing. 'Can you see them?'

'I cannot.' I was not even trying. Her rapt attention allowed me to stand very close and study *her*, which to my red-blooded mind, was a much more pleasing prospect than any sporting otter. I breathed in her perfume – rose-water – and, plucking up my courage, reached out to tuck a wayward strand of hair behind her ear.

Her sideways glance, through long eyelashes, made my heart pound. 'I know what you are up to, Rufus.' Her attention returned to the water below.

Encouraged, for she had not told me to stop, I traced a finger around the back of her ear and down her neck. She smiled, so I did it a second time. Once more I was not rebuffed, so I leaned in and kissed her cheek.

'We are here to see otters, sir.'

Although there was no heat in her voice, I was wary of being rebuffed. I made a pretence of studying the river, while my mind filled with any number of pleasant fantasies. All involved divesting Beatrice of her clothing, and shedding my own.

'Look, Rufus.' She pointed towards an overhanging willow on the opposite bank. I stared. A moment later, a dark shape slid out of the water, and vanished again. 'I see it!'

'There are two of them,' said Beatrice.

Mesmerised, we watched the sleek creatures sporting, batting with their forelegs and climbing on each other's backs. It was almost enough to take my mind from Beatrice. Almost.

To my relief, the otters' display did not last long. I begged a kiss of Beatrice, who with her usual show of reluctance, agreed. Her defences down, and we were soon locked in a passionate embrace. Steadying my nerves, I eased a hand down the front of her dress and cupped a breast. Instead of resistance, I heard a little moan.

It was all the encouragement I needed.

Ah, the ardour of youth.

Ah, the fickleness of fate.

'Beatrice!' A woman's voice from the courtyard.

I paid no heed, but Beatrice stiffened and pulled away. She listened. My ardour undaunted, I tried to kiss her again.

'Stop it, Rufus!' She was already pulling up her dress.

'Beatrice!'

I did well to win a last kiss from her before she answered the summons. Promising to see her again the next day, I went in search of de Drune and Owain and a costrel of wine. Both would tease me mercilessly, but I could give as good as I got, and had plenty of ammunition thanks to their oft-mentioned escapades in the stews outside the castle.

That was the last I saw of Beatrice for many days. Summoned by the king's steward the next morning, I was given a letter and told to ride to Paris and deliver it to Richard. 'Into his hands alone,' the steward repeated several times.

Given the company of de Drune and two more men-at-arms – Owain was disgusted at not being allowed to ride with us – I set out at once.

The content of the vellum parchment I bore was all we talked about. Well, that and Beatrice.

Since Richard's departure in June, rumours had swirled about the king's court like the eddying currents in a fast-moving river. He had sworn fealty and given homage to Philippe. The two had become fast friends, even sharing a bed. He was never going to return, unless it was at Philippe's side, leading an army against the king.

Although I did not want to wage war on Henry – I had come to know a good number of his men at Angers – I was Richard's man. Assuming he took me back, I would follow wherever he led.

The French court was even grander than Henry's. Richly embroidered tapestries hung from the walls; sunlight poured through the paned glass. An enormous dresser by the entrance to the great hall was filled top to bottom with silverware, and every window seat had cushions. Sweet flag had been mixed with the cut grass on the floor, filling the air with a pleasant smell.

Led by a steward through the crowded room, ignoring the curious stares of the courtiers, I found Richard at table with the French king. There was time before I was announced to nod a friendly greeting at my friends Philip and Louis, and to study the duke a little. I was pleased by what I saw. Gone were the lines of exhaustion that had marked his face during the rebellion and the days leading to the truce at Châteauroux. My master looked well, happy even.

Less welcome was the presence of FitzAldelm by his side.

Of course that snake saw me first, and whispered in Richard's ear.

To my horror, the expression he turned on me was cold. 'Rufus.'

I hid my disappointment. 'Sire.'

Philippe's head turned.

A little awed, I knelt at once. 'Sire.'

The steward mangled my name.

'Rise.' Philippe sounded amused.

'Sire, this is one of my squires,' said Richard. 'He has come, I suspect, with a message from my lord father.'

'Indeed, sire.'

'How is he?'

'He seems tired, sire. Irritable.' I could have added touchy and obstinate, and even lamer than before, but I did not dare.

Richard sighed, and beckoned.

I came closer, holding out the parchment. 'I am ordered to deliver this, sire.'

The duke all but grabbed it. Breaking the seal, he read the letter in silence.

'What does it say?' asked Philippe.

Yes, I wanted to shout. What does it say?

Richard threw down the parchment. 'I am begged to return to him. He says that I shall have whatever I want.'

'I see,' said Philippe. 'How shall you answer?'

It was a loaded question, but Richard did not hesitate. 'There will be no reply.'

Philippe's smile was self-contented, like the child given a whole plate of marchpane fancies and sweet wafers.

Do not trust him, I wanted to shout, but instead I merely asked, 'Sire?'

'Return to Angers, and if the king asks what I said, simply tell him that.' Richard's words were also a dismissal.

'Sire.' I bowed deeply, my hopes of regaining the duke's affections taking a second blow.

FitzAldelm smirked, and I longed to plant my fist in his face.

Instead I walked from the room with a heavy heart.

CHAPTER XXIII

According to the directions Marshal had been given by a farmer, the king's hunting lodge of Lyons-la-Forêt could not be much further. Daylight was fading from the sky; the summer air was cooling, and a heavy dew already glistened on the grass. If he was not to spend the night outdoors, he needed to find it soon. Directing his squires to seek directions from the inhabitants of a one-roomed cottage set back from the road, he took charge of the horses and pack mounts. His own, a spirited Spanish palfrey that had cost him as much as a trained destrier, nickered its hunger. Marshal patted her neck. Attracted by her spirit, uncaring of the price, he had bought her before leaving Outremer.

More than three years after leaving Henry's kingdom, he was back.

Whipcord lean, every inch of exposed skin tanned mahogany, and wearing a looser tunic than was common, he could have been taken for a Saracen. He sometimes was. Marshal smiled, remembering the rosy-cheeked proprietress of a cookstall in a town two days prior. Busy frying slices of pork, she had not seen him until the last moment. Her shriek could have raised the dead, and had caused one startled customer to drop his purchase, and then, furious, to demand a replacement.

'Just a little further, sir.' His oldest squire, a once round-faced, now knife-sharp-featured young man by the name of Joscelin, pointed down the road. 'There's a turn not a half mile further on.'

Marshal nodded, pleased by Joscelin's quiet confidence. As well as shedding weight, he had grown from boy to man in the time they had been away. It was in Marshal's mind to knight him soon. First, though, he had to find a new squire. A man of his stature needed two.

'Do not put the cart in front of the horse,' he muttered to himself. 'Let us see how the king greets me before making any decisions.'

A breeze shook the trees, and Joscelin shivered. 'In the heat of Outremer, sir, all I wanted was to be in Normandy, or Anjou. Now I am here, I am too cold.'

Marshal laughed. 'As they say, the far away hills are ever greener.'

'Hold!' A sturdy figure stepped into the road, a man-at-arms in a padded gambeson, and armed with a shield and spear. 'Who rides in the king's hunt?'

'William Marshal is my name.'

A scowl. 'Who may he be?'

'The greatest knight in Christendom, that is who,' cried Joscelin.

Marshal hid his amusement. The boy in Joscelin had not entirely gone.

'Never heard of him,' said the man-at-arms in a surly tone. Younger than Joscelin, he looked nervous.

'I judge you not for your ignorance,' said Marshal, riding closer. 'Know that I served the Young King for many a year. Now my master is King Henry. I hear he is close by, in his hunting lodge. I seek his company.'

The man-at-arms seemed about to protest further, but the arrival of a companion who was at least a decade older, and who recognised Marshal, saw the potential dispute ended. Cuffing the youth about the ear, and calling him a purblind fool, the older soldier apologised to Marshal. 'The king will be right glad to see you, sir. Needs his spirits raised, he does.'

'The hunting has been poor then?'

'No, sir.' The younger man-at-arms had sloped off in shame, but the other man glanced about anyway. In a low voice, he said, 'The king and Richard are on poor terms again, sir. The duke has been in Paris for almost a month.'

'With Philippe?'

'Even so, sir. The king has been in fearful humour since his departure.'

Marshal had not expected an easy life upon his return, but he had hoped that the tragic death of another of Henry's sons, Geoffrey, might have brought some accord between the father and his remaining sons. It seemed there was to be none of that. He rolled his shoulders, as he did before going into battle. So be it, he thought. I am not going to ride away now. Wry amusement took him, for he had nowhere else to go anyway. Thanking the man-at-arms, he rode through the deepening shadow to the tents and pavilions that sprawled around the hunting lodge.

Warm greetings rang out as Marshal was recognised. Rather than stop, he made brief reply or raised a hand in greeting. At the king's lodge, he left Joscelin and his second squire in charge of the horses, and made himself known to the sentries. He was ushered inside at once. The room was sparsely lit. Animal skulls decorated the walls: boar, deer, wolf. Hunting spears stood in racks, shields hung alongside. Rushes covered the floor, but by the dry, musty smell, it was past time for fresh herbs to be added.

The king was at table, a dozen or more barons and knights of his mesnie with him. Accompanying himself on a lute, a minstrel sang lays of hunting and battle. No one noticed Marshal immediately, and he took the chance to see who was present, and where they were sitting in relation to Henry. He was pleased by some of the faces. There sat his dear friends de Béthune and de Marisco. Peter FitzGuy was reliable and steady-headed, Gerard Talbot brave as an alaunt. It was frustrating that Thomas de Coulonces was three places from the king, but at least there was no sign of d'Yquebeuf. John, Henry's youngest son, sat beside his father, plump-cheeked and as sly-looking as he had ever been.

'Sire,' announced the captain in a loud voice. 'William Marshal is come.'

He might have declared the sun had fallen from the sky. Silence fell.

De Bethune grinned and nudged de Marisco.

Henry turned, surprised. Pleasure followed a heartbeat later. 'Marshal!'

'Sire.' Taking a knee, he bowed his head. The years had not been kind to the king, he thought. Henry's red-rimmed eyes, mottled complexion and sagging jowls spoke of heavy burdens, lack of sleep and an excess of wine, or perhaps all three.

'Rise, Marshal, rise.'

'Thank you, sire.' His gaze flickered over the others at the long table. De Béthune and de Marisco were beaming. Others wore welcoming expressions. Several were guarded, which was not unexpected, given the delight in the king's voice. De Coulonces stared daggers at Marshal, making it clear that their old enmity had not died during his absence.

'The Saracens could not kill you?' asked the king.

'They did their best, sire,' said Marshal with a lopsided grin.

'I am glad they did not succeed. Come, sit by me.' The king beckoned.

'Thank you, sire.' Marshal was pleased. John was on Henry's right, the most important place, but to be asked to attend him on the other side was a high honour, especially for someone returning from a lengthy absence.

'Did you reach Christ's tomb?' asked the king. His eyes darkening with emotion, he added, 'And lay Hal's cloak upon it?'

'I did, sire.' In a quiet voice, Marshal told his tale, of how the Young King's garment had been received with reverence, and of the candles he had lit in his memory, and the ones that he had paid for. 'They will be remembering him for many years, sire, in the holiest site in all Christendom.'

Henry's raddled face twitched. 'That is well.'

'I grieved to hear of Geoffrey's death, sire,' said Marshal, lying through his teeth. He had never liked the king's duplicitous third son.

'Thank you, Marshal.' Henry drank deep from his cup.

A silence fell: Marshal's respectful, the king's laden with grief.

It was unclear if John had heard. Either way, his timing could not have been worse. He leaned around his father, and asked with a smirk, 'You were not tempted to take the Templar oath, Marshal, and stay in Outremer to fight the Saracens?'

He held back his inclination to say that at least he had been to the Holy Land and played a small part in its defence. John, on the other hand, had never shown the tiniest inclination to take the cross – unlike Henry and Richard. 'It entered my head, sire, but I had sworn to return to your lord father's service. If he were to go on crusade, I would gladly follow him.'

John seemed about to make a sarcastic reply, but Henry nodded with pleasure. 'You would be first among my knights, Marshal. Did you know that while you were away, the Patriarch of Jerusalem came to request my help?'

'Yes, sire. His visit was much talked about in Outremer, where the Saracens threaten the Holy Land as they have not done these twenty-five years.' Patriarch Heraclius had laid all the hopes of Christendom at Henry's feet, including the keys to the city of Jerusalem, as well as those to the Tower of David and the Holy Sepulchre. The gesture had been grandiose, and deliberately so.

'It grieved me to reject Heraclius's offer, but the rule of my kingdom is of greater concern than that of one thousands of miles away,' said Henry. 'His proposal was not as simple as it appeared either. Like all who come to me, he was seeking his own advantage, not mine.'

Marshal caught John's pointed stare, and thought, the wretch. I like to be rewarded, but I am loyal, unlike you. Sufficiently stung to respond, he said, 'Whenever I am given recompense, sire, it is repaid with honest toil.'

'I do not mean you, Marshal. You are one of a kind,' said Henry with a smile. 'While we speak of reward, I would thank you for fulfilling Hal's dying wish.' He waved away Marshal's protest. 'The lordship of Cartmel in Lancashire is yours from this day forward.'

'I am honoured, sire. Thank you.' This was an excellent start, Marshal decided. Cartmel was not vast, but its revenue would see him comfortably off.

'You shall owe *me* homage for Cartmel, Marshal,' said John, his expression calculating. 'I hold it of my lord father.'

Marshal bowed his head, expertly hiding his mistrust of the king's youngest son. First he swore fealty to Henry, and then to John.

They drank a toast.

'What age are you, Marshal?' asked the king.

'Almost forty, sire.'

'And still not wed. It must be in your mind to start ploughing a furrow. A man should beget heirs while there is yet steel in his sword.' Henry leered.

'You read my mind, sire.' But for the Young King's death, Marshal would have been married years before. 'If the right woman appeared, I would not hesitate.'

'See what you make of Heloise of Kendal. You shall be her ward. Wed her if you wish,' said Henry, adding, 'In case you did not know, her lands are substantial. They also abut the borders of Cartmel.'

These windfalls were greater reward than Marshal had expected inside an hour of his return. Delighted about his new estates, but feeling uncomfortable about taking to wife a girl he knew nothing about, and had never met, he faltered. 'Sire, I—'

Interpreting his reticence for wariness, the king waved a hand. 'I do not insist you marry the wench. For all I know, she is as plain as a horse's rear end. Do as you see fit.'

Again Marshal expressed his gratitude. He felt relief too. If the swift improvement in his fortunes were to continue, he could aim even higher than the heiress of Kendal.

'Heloise is no beauty, but she is skittish,' said John with lecherous relish. 'If you do not plough her, Marshal, I shall.'

Marshal glanced at the king, who was affecting to listen to the minstrel. 'Thank you for the advice, sire,' he said to John, thinking, you will not lay hands on her while I have breath in my body.

Ordered then by Henry to speak of Outremer, Marshal painted a vivid picture of baking desert, massive crusading castles, and the sparkling blue sea. He spoke with reverence of the holy sites in Jerusalem, and with respect of the fighting orders, the Templars and Hospitallers. Far from those who would take offence, he was able to speak freely about the backstabbing politics that constantly weakened the Holy Land. Last, he mentioned Saladin, the great Saracen military leader whose armies threatened the very existence of the crusader kingdom.

Henry, who had listened keenly, was intrigued. 'God's bones, if I can ever settle with that rogue Philippe, I shall go there, and Richard with me. Ten thousand knights, men-at-arms and archers under our banners would send that devil Saladin on his merry way.'

Despite Marshal's reservations, his blood stirred. 'Lead, sire, and I will follow.'

Oblivious to John's scowl at the mention of Richard, Henry said fondly to his youngest son, 'You would stay here to guard the realm.'

In a heartbeat, John changed. ''Twould be my honour, sire,' he said, beaming.

A father's love is blinding, Marshal decided. John is a wastrel. News of his expedition to Ireland two years before had even reached Outremer. Mismanaging his men and money, he had alienated the native Irish and the Anglo-Irish settlers. Funds exhausted, John had been deserted by his mercenaries. Less than a twelvemonth after his arrival, he had been forced into an ignominious retreat. Glancing up and down the table, Marshal could see he was not alone in his reservations. Many men, de Béthune included, were taking a studious interest in the bottoms of their cups.

'Not that peace seems likely. War with France is a constant threat,' said Henry, his brows lowering. 'Philippe is as great a cozener and a schemer as I have ever met. He pours honey in Richard's ears, and poisons his mind against me.'

With the subject on the table, Marshal could mention the king's eldest son. 'Where is the duke, sire?'

'With Philippe in Paris,' growled the king. 'He left with him after Châteauroux.'

'I see, sire,' said Marshal, glad he had made sure to keep himself abreast of recent events, and knew what had happened there.

'It is said they share a bed,' John put in lasciviously.

His father glared. 'That does not make Richard a sodomite.'

'Of course not, sire.' John's eyes said otherwise.

'He will return soon.' Despite the king's words, a note of uncertainty was discernible in his voice.

'Let us hope so, sire,' said Marshal, although it was evident down the table that he was not alone in feeling doubt about that. He also noted the spiteful expression that flitted over John's face at the idea of his older brother coming back.

He decided to stay out of the family politics wherever possible. God willing, he would not be forced to take sides. In the meantime, he would serve Henry to the best of his ability, and hope to be rewarded for it. Heloise of Kendal was a decent catch, but there were wealthier wards in the king's care. An example was Isabelle de Clare, daughter of Earl Richard of Striguil. Owing to the recent death of her younger brother Gilbert, she was now one of the greatest heiresses in England. Marriage to her would elevate Marshal to the highest level of nobility.

'To the duke!' cried Henry.

Cup raised, Marshal echoed the toast, and decided, I deserve no less.

CHAPTER XXIV

Harvest-time came, and the road from Angers to Paris became as well known to me as the paths and tracks around Cairlinn. I carried letter after letter from the king to Richard, each one begging him to return. The duke wrote not a single word by way of reply, which encouraged his father all the more. The intervals between messages grew shorter, until it seemed that I was forever condemned to ride between the two kings' courts. I saw little of Beatrice, which fuelled my bad temper.

In the end, however, Richard decided to leave Paris. Whether it was because of his father's entreaties, or that his friendship with Philippe had cooled, I was unsure. I did not care, for the duke ordered me to stay by his side when I rode to the French royal court in mid-September, and soon after, to accompany him as he left it. I did not see him take his leave of King Philippe, but had no reason to think there had been an argument, for the duke showed no sign of unhappiness or discontent. He had also forgotten my crime at last, the one committed by FitzAldelm, and for that I was grateful. My enemy was ever at Richard's side, it was true, but the situation was better than it had been.

'Are we for Angers, sire?' I asked as we took the road west.

'No.'

I glanced at him in surprise, and was glad to see that FitzAldelm did not know his purpose either. My friends Philip and Louis, with whom I had been reunited, seemed equally in the dark.

Richard's chuckle was mischievous. 'We shall ride for Chinon.'

As we were to discover, the duke had no intention of returning to his father just yet.

In Chinon, we emptied the castle treasury. When the seneschal protested, Richard told him to stand aside or be strung up by his heels.

Purple with indignation, the official did the wise thing and obeyed. Wagon axles creaking under their load, we turned south and west a few hours later. The duke was in expansive mood, telling we squires that the monies taken at Chinon would fund much-needed repairs and improvements in his castles throughout Aquitaine.

'Will the king not be angry with you, sire?' I asked, delighted that my period out of favour had ended. In typical fashion, the duke was now treating me as if nothing had ever happened. FitzAldelm was unhappy – I could see it every time Richard addressed me – but could do nothing.

'Perhaps. I care not.' The duke shrugged. 'Besides, they are also his strongholds. The better their defences, the more secure his realm.'

Nonetheless, I noted a fleeting trace of regret – sadness? – in his eyes. I thought of my own father, who had ever been heavy-handed. Despite our stormy, troubled relationship, I had always loved and respected him. Richard was no different with the king, I reckoned. If it were possible, he would prefer to be on good terms.

My hunch was proven correct. Uncaring of the appropriation of the Chinon treasure, Henry continued to bombard Richard with letters. They arrived almost daily, no matter where we rode, and finally, the duke agreed to return to the fold. We travelled to Angers where father and son were reconciled, and I, heart pounding, reacquainted myself with Beatrice. To my relief, I had not been forgotten.

God was smiling on me during that time, for with Richard eager to see his mother, Queen Alienor, we stayed for weeks at the royal court in Angers. My enemy FitzAldelm disappeared, sent to check that the Chinon monies were being used wisely in the duke's castles throughout Aquitaine. Richard's malevolent brother John was also in Angers, but thankfully, I saw him little. With our master busy, we squires were often at liberty to do as we chose. I spent every moment possible in Beatrice's company. My comrades' ribbing was merciless; they called me a moonstruck calf, a lovelorn fool, and worse. I did not care, and as I told them, they were only jealous. A little forsaken, Rhys took up with a gang of urchins from the town, and vanished for days on end.

September arrived, and the farmers ploughed the stubble back into the ground. Every hedgerow was heavy with blackberries, and in the woods, mushrooms flourished. The swifts vanished, and in the vineyards, grapes hung in fat black clusters. Mornings were crisp and fresh, but in the evenings, a man needed a cloak against the chill – or to wrap his lady love in.

Many's the tender battle had been waged within the folds of mine, but despite my best efforts, Beatrice held firm. Her maidenhood was sacred, and not to be taken until the night of her wedding. I begged and pleaded to no avail. Wily vixen, she diverted my attention in the most pleasurable ways, and I, lust sated and purpose spent, would fall asleep with her in my arms.

It could not last forever. Life is ever a twisting trail of obstacles that have to be overcome. Level stretches tend to be few and far between, and of short duration. Much as I wanted our time at the royal court to continue, it was never Richard's intention to stay for long. To control his realm, the Duke of Aquitaine needed to be there. Only by the visible presence of ruling power could peace be maintained.

We set out a sennight after All Saints' Day, making first not for the south, but Tours. Richard had business in the city, I suspected with an agent of the French king. Cloaked and hooded messengers had come and gone during our stay at Angers, always late at night or early in the mornings. We were not told where they came from or who they served, but I had recognised one by the scar on his face from Philippe's court, and come to the conclusion that my master continued to follow the count of Flanders' advice. With Henry still refusing to name Richard as heir, the French king might yet prove a useful ally. I was minded of the old saying, told me by my father, never to shut a door behind me.

Mournful, clutching at the memories of my final tryst with Beatrice – again I had failed to persuade her to cross the final barrier – I rode at Richard's back with my head down. Philip, who had achieved a great deal less than I with Juvette, the object of his affections, was glad to be on the road once more. His efforts to lift my mood failed miserably, however, and he struck up a conversation with Louis, Owain and de Drune. Rhys, who had been reluctant to leave his new-found friends, scowled if I glanced in his direction. I had not been forgiven for neglecting him. There was time to win his affection again, I told myself.

'Oh, the shame!'

My gaze returned to the road ahead, which was empty apart from a priest on a sway-backed mule. The loud, groaning cry had been made by him. No sooner had I decided this than the priest let out another piteous cry.

'The shame!'

'Mayhap he has been robbed,' said Richard, his lips twitching.

'Shall we go to his aid?' asked de Chauvigny.

I peered into the distance, hopeful of bandits we could put to flight, but could see no one.

Richard spurred his horse forward, and was joined by de Chauvigny. Without thinking, I followed.

'How now, father,' the duke called as we drew near. 'Hast thou been set upon?'

A mirthless laugh. 'Would that I had, and left for dead, rather than have to carry such news. Oh, the shame!'

Richard's brows knotted; de Chauvigny and I were just as confused. His haircloth tunic and lack of head covering were evidence that he was repenting for something, but we had no idea what. I peered at the square of wood affixed to the pole the priest bore. The image it bore, a church, a mound of earth, and above, a strangely garbed rider on a horse that appeared to be pissing, made no sense to me.

'What news can be such a burden?' asked the duke.

The priest turned his red-rimmed eyes on Richard. 'Outremer is lost! The most precious relic in Christendom, a piece of the Holy Cross, has fallen into the hands of the infidel. Jerusalem lies at the enemy's feet.' He stabbed a finger at his crude standard. 'There you can see the Church of the Resurrection and above, the Messiah's tomb. Trampling it – defiling it – is a Saracen knight. These are the scenes in the Holy City even now. See, the infidel's horse urinates on the tomb of Our Lord. Oh, the shame.' The priest raked dirty fingernails down his cheek, and groaned.

I heard my own shock echoed by our companions, who had ridden up. This calamitous news had struck with the force of a lightning bolt. We none of us knew what to say.

'Outremer lost, you say? How?' cried Richard.

For all that his audience was on a windy road, with rain threatening, the priest held forth at length. We listened, captivated by the horror of his tale. Tensions had been rising steadily in Outremer, and the four-year truce between the Christians and the Saracens had lapsed in January. Around the same date we had faced King Philippe at Châteauroux, Saladin, the charismatic Saracen leader, and the King of Jerusalem, Guy of Lusignan, had assembled large armies.

It was said, the priest told us, that every Christian who could wield a sword had answered the call. When Saladin attacked the castle at Tiberias in Galilee, Guy had led his host to lift the siege. Crossing an area of desert in the height of summer and without sufficient water, he and his troops were ambushed by the Saracens at a mountainous place named the Horns of Hattin. Thousands of arrows rained down, injuring and killing many knights' horses. The enemy cleverly avoided direct combat, however, fearful of the havoc the heavily armed Christians could cause.

'Guy and his army were forced to camp overnight at a dry well. Thirsty, hungry, they had little rest, for the air was thick with fumes from the scrub set alight by the Saracens,' said the priest. 'Nonetheless, the Christians met the sunrise with stout hearts. They had a piece of the Holy Cross. God was on their side. Victory could yet be theirs!'

I glanced at Richard. Never had I seen him so rapt, so engrossed.

Licking his chapped lips, the priest went on, 'Battle commenced, and time and again, the Saracens were thrown back. Casualties were heavy, with as many men collapsing from the boiling temperatures and thirst as from blades and arrows. King Guy charged Saladin's position twice, knowing that success would see the heathens break and flee. Twice he was repulsed. Still they fought on, brave, desperate, inspired by the Holy Cross.' A long sigh. 'It was not enough. Saladin prevailed. Although some knights escaped, countless Christians were slain. Guy and thousands more were taken prisoner.'

'Did Saladin execute him?' demanded Richard.

'No. He was merciful to the king, and to all his followers, save for the Hospitallers and Templars. More than two hundred of them were killed. Decapitated,' added the priest with relish. 'Any ordinary soldiers who survived were sold into slavery.'

'And the piece of the Holy Cross?' I asked, hoping against hope.

'Taken, from the dead hand of the bishop of Jerusalem.'

'God's legs,' said Richard, his fists clenching and unclenching on the reins. 'What of the Holy City?'

'It lies virtually defenceless. It has in all likelihood fallen to Saladin by now, along with most cities in Outremer.' He jerked a thumb at his standard. 'Every sanctuary in Jerusalem will have been defiled.'

'God's legs!' Richard's voice rose to a shout.

'Such heinous crimes cannot go unanswered,' said de Chauvigny.

'They will not,' cried the duke.

As shocked as our master, we squires muttered to one another. Glancing at the duke, I sensed what might happen next. I had never sailed halfway across the world then, or seen a desert, or faced an enemy as implacable as Saladin, but the prospect made my heart leap with excitement.

'I must do my duty,' said Richard, calm and resolute.

The priest looked pleased. 'Will you take the cross, friend?'

'Yes!' Richard's eyes blazed bright. 'I will not rest until the Saracens have been defeated, and Outremer restored. André?'

'You know I will come, cousin,' said de Chauvigny, his eyes gleaming.

'I am with you, sire!' The words were out of my mouth before I had time to think. I forgot Beatrice, and Alienor. I forgot Cairlinn, God forgive me, so great was my fervour. The duke would lead us to Outremer, I thought, where we would defeat the Saracens, retake Jerusalem and win eternal glory.

He gave me a fierce nod. 'Good, Rufus.' His gaze moved past me, to Philip, Owain and de Drune, who were all saying the same thing. 'We shall go to war together.'

'When, sire?' I asked.

'I would leave tomorrow if I could,' said Richard with feeling. He shook his head. 'But preparations must be made. The spring, I would say.'

Only now did the priest, who had been wrapped up with the fervour of his message, realise that he had been talking to a high-born noble. In a quavering voice, he asked who the duke was. When I told him, the blood drained from his cheeks.

'Forgive me, sire,' he babbled. 'I did not recognise you.'

'Your news is what matters. Nothing else.' Richard gave him a warm smile, and pressed several silver pennies into his bony hand.

We rode away with the priest's blessings ringing in our ears.

At dawn the next day, the roads around Tours were thronged. The news of Saladin's victory had swept into the area, borne not just by the itinerant priest we had met, and others of his kind, but an official messenger from the Pope. Everyone for miles around wanted to see those who were about to take the cross, and in particular, Richard. Although no announcement of our coming had been made, word had spread.

Tours was separated into two parts. The castle and cathedral were separated from the marketplace and residential areas by vineyards and farms, and also an abbey, where we had stayed the night. Richard spent those hours on his knees, praying in the chapel, with de Chauvigny for company. We squires had taken turns to watch over them. I was bone-tired, and Philip and Louis could not stop yawning. The duke, however, was as energetic as if he had slept for a sennight. Fresh-bathed, his beard and hair oiled, he had refused all offers of food and donned his armour as if for battle.

Every man with him did the same. I had somehow found the time to burnish not just the duke's hauberk and helmet but my own gear. Rhys had polished Liath Macha's harness, and curried him until his coat shone. The instant we were ready, Richard gave the order to leave. A fine sight we made, the duke in the lead with de Chauvigny, we squires at his back, and Rhys, running alongside, followed by a score and a half of knights and twice that number of men-at-arms and archers. The onlookers cheered, and waved. Shouts of 'Jerusalem!' and 'Kill the Saracens!' filled the air. Faces alight with fervour, men and youths followed in our wake, their intent also to go on crusade.

The cathedral, which I had never seen before, took my breath away. At the south end of the bridge over the River Loire, two great towers reared towards the heavens, taller than any building I had ever seen. They gave the cathedral grandeur, yet behind the towers were low walls running to the south transept, covered by a temporary wooden roof. The remainder of the structure was still only an outline marked in the ground. According to Louis, the original building had burned down during the wars fought by Henry against King Philippe's father and the reconstruction was slow.

Eyes wide at the magnificent towers, I cared not.

The cathedral was packed tighter than a barrel of salted fish, and a powerful aroma of unwashed bodies assailed my nostrils as we walked to the front of the congregation. Mass began soon after. A bell tolled. Led by the archbishop, a procession of priests, members of the choir and clerks entered, their voices rising to the heavens in chant.

The archbishop's sermon concerned the dreadful events that had taken place in Outremer. Reading in its entirety the long, rambling letter sent by Pope Gregory, he thundered and raged, often pointing to Heaven to emphasise a point. It was deadly boring for the most part, but as his speech neared its climax, his excited tone attracted my interest.

'To those who with a contrite heart and humble spirit shall undertake the labour of this expedition—' by this, the archbishop meant to go on crusade, '—and shall die in repentance for their sins and in the true faith, we do promise plenary indulgence for their offences, and eternal life.'

I realised Rhys was staring at me, his face bright with hope. I had no need to ask what was in his mind, for the same thing was in my own. By taking the cross, our vile crime of letting two innocent men hang in Southampton would be forgiven. I smiled at Rhys. Until then I had not realised how much the men's deaths had plagued my conscience. Now, on a mission blessed by the Pope himself, with my sins washed away, I was to be offered a new beginning.

If only it were so easy to make one's black deeds vanish forever.

The archbishop was not finished. The rewards offered to every crusader did not end with entry into Heaven. All property of those on crusade would fall under the protection of the church, and outstanding loans did not have to be paid until after a man's return. With each announcement, the clamour from the congregation grew louder.

Glancing at Richard's ecstatic face, I knew that these considerations were not behind his desire to travel to Outremer. He was a born warrior, and this holy conflict, with its divine provenance and Saracen enemy, was his destiny. The duke could no more step aside from taking part than the sun fail to rise in the east.

At last the archbishop was done. He looked expectantly at Richard. What was about to happen had been agreed in advance.

A signal saw his knights form a solid line across the building's width, blocking access to the archbishop, pulpit and altar. Everyone who wished to join the crusade would be allowed to approach, but only after the duke had done so.

'Who will volunteer?' cried the archbishop.

A baying sound rose to the timber ceiling. It seemed every man and boy present wished to go.

Richard stepped forward, and I went with him, carrying the blue surcoat with the white cross I had stitched on the previous night. Jesu, but it was one of the proudest moments of my life to stand in that half-built cathedral with him. Philip and Louis were two paces behind.

Owain and de Chauvigny were standing with the knights; de Drune had managed to position himself there as well, although by rights he should have waited his turn. Rhys was just behind.

'Sire.' The archbishop's smile was wider than a money-lender whose debts have all been repaid at one pass. 'You honour us with your presence.'

Richard bowed deep. 'Your Grace. I am come to take the cross, if you will have me.'

Impossibly, the archbishop's grin broadened. 'I can think of few who would be more welcome on this holy crusade than you, sire.'

Richard knelt in front of the altar, where he made a quiet confession to the archbishop. He remained on his knees as I hurried forward and offered the surcoat to the archbishop.

Raising his right hand, upon one finger of which was a bright-jewelled ring, the archbishop blessed the surcoat, and the man who would wear it. Then, presenting it to Richard, who pulled it over his hauberk and stood, he proclaimed, 'The Duke of Aquitaine, God's warrior!'

Philip, Louis and I roared until our throats were hoarse, but our voices were lost in the tumult. I would wager a dozen silver pennies that the cheering was heard in Paris.

Priests filed in from the sides so that confession might be offered to as many as possible. I knelt with my friends, confessed, and was shriven. There had not been time to fashion surcoats for everyone, so we simply made the sign of the cross and pledged ourselves to the crusade.

Then, discharged by the duke, who was to take counsel with the archbishop, we went and got uproariously drunk.

CHAPTER XXV

The year of our Lord 1188 saw me not in a ship bound for Outremer, but beyond the southern border of Aquitaine. Cahors lay in the heart of the Quercy region, west of the county of Toulouse. A fresh breeze was blowing, carrying with it the pleasant scent of fresh-cut grass. Summer had not yet arrived, but in the fields beyond the town, farmers were taking advantage of the prolonged warm spell to make their hay early. Here on the open ground outside the walls, the weekly market was in full flow.

Booths and stalls stretched as far as the eye could see, selling food and drink, ironmongery and livestock, fabric and women's perfume. The place was crowded, and growing more so as people walked in from the surrounding countryside, or came trundling down the road in wagons.

Nothing stopped commerce, I thought, not even the proximity of an invading army. Richard's forces were perhaps twenty miles away, but the relaxed atmosphere gave no indication of this, or of the conflict that had raged in the area for six weeks. Count Raymond of Toulouse, a thorn in the duke's side since the Young King's rebellion and before, had pushed my master too far this spring, sanctioning attacks on merchants from Poitiers. If it had been robbery alone, war might have been avoided, but blinding, castration and murder could not go unanswered. Preparations for the crusade would have to wait. South from Aquitaine we had come, in force, raiding deep into territory that had been lost to Raymond during the troubles five years prior. More than a dozen castles had fallen already, Richard's fearsome reputation enough to see the majority open their gates within a day of our arrival outside their walls.

Cahors would be next, and rather than entrust his spies to bring reports from the town, the duke had decided to see it for himself. It was risky – some would have said foolhardy – but when Richard made up his mind, there was no swaying him. Six of us there were: the duke, me, Rhys, Owain, de Drune and FitzAldelm. Our pretence of being masterless soldiers from Angoulême, far to the north, had worked thus far. Nondescript clothing, serviceable weapons and average-looking mounts meant we appeared the same as any sellsword wandering the land. With God's blessing, said the duke, our disguises would see us through the day.

Much to their disgust, Rhys and de Drune were left in charge of the horses. 'Lose our mounts, and we shall be trapped here,' Richard had said. With glum nods, Rhys and de Drune accepted their lot. Surrounded by parked wagons, horses and mules, they would have a boring time of it.

The rest of us were to enter the town in pairs, our purpose to assess the strength and readiness of the garrison. Fluent speakers since childhood, Richard and FitzAldelm could pass for Frenchmen, whereas Owain and I could not. Even now the duke was unaware of the depth of hatred between FitzAldelm and me; thinking that we could set aside our differences, he ordered us to work together while he and Owain did the same. We were to meet again no later than none, mid-afternoon, and then begin the return journey towards our army. Orders given, Richard disappeared into the crowd with Owain.

FitzAldelm and I waited a short time before following, and like the duke, took only our daggers. At once we were into the market proper. A gaggle of children lingered by a stall selling gingerbread and almond marchpane fancies; the baker watched with folded arms and a disapproving expression. Young men jostled and examined the knives and swords on sale at a smith's booth. Lips pursed, a broad-bosomed matron unrolled a bolt of red-gold silk at a cloth stall. Her daughter stood at her shoulder, waxing lyrical about the beautiful dress it would make, and being told in return that the cost would see the family beggared. The stallholder leaped in, saying that the price was negotiable.

I smiled, thinking, merchants were the same everywhere, and deciding that the girl looked like Beatrice, whom I had not seen since the previous autumn. I had no idea if we would ever meet again, for Queen Alienor had been sent back to England by Henry. Remembering my Alienor then, I touched the pouch at my neck which contained her fillet, and wondered if she even recalled my name. Hers was burned on my heart.

An audience had gathered around a dancing bear, which was shambling about on its back legs as its master played a quavering tune on his flute. A stout chain ringed the unfortunate creature's neck; it led to a wooden pole that had been hammered into the ground. We watched for a moment, FitzAldelm with his lip curled in amusement, and I, thinking that the bear would be better off dead.

As we neared the town gate, it was clear that the commander of the garrison knew how close Richard's army was. There were twice as many sentries atop the walls as I would have expected, and only one of the two doors was open. A group of men-at-arms stood by, watching several of their fellows questioning everyone seeking to enter. My pulse quickened. Say the wrong thing, or arouse suspicion, and we could be taken prisoner. I told myself that if the duke and Owain could get through – as I assumed they had – so could we. I glanced at FitzAldelm, and was alarmed by the sweat on his face. His eyes were darting hither and thither too, in the manner of a criminal dragged before the justice.

'There are too many soldiers. We should return to the horses,' he said from the side of his mouth.

I bridled at his cowardice. 'The duke has gone in. So must we.'

'You cannot be sure. I say he will have turned back.'

I pretended not to have heard. FitzAldelm grabbed at my shoulder, but I kept walking. With a muttered curse, he made to follow, only for a wagon loaded with barrels of wine to rumble between us. A devil took me, and I increased my pace, keeping close to the rolling back wheel. The crowd, which had parted to allow the vehicle to pass, closed behind me. I looked over my shoulder, but could not see FitzAldelm. I smiled, sure that the faintheart would stop short of the gates without me by his side.

The wagon was almost at the entrance. My confidence suddenly seemed foolhardy. I dared not turn on my heel, though, for that would also draw attention.

A challenge rang out, and from the wagon's front, a man answered.

'Wine, plenty of wine, for the garrison. Straight to the quartermaster's store it goes, I was told, with no pilfering.'

A burst of laughter followed, which I judged was from the men-at-arms, and a voice ordered the driver to proceed. Still unsure how I would get through, my fortunes turned as the back wheel caught in a deep rut, and the wagon stalled. Setting my shoulder to the timber-framed back, I called out for the oxen to pull. Heaving with every ounce of my strength, I helped the wheel to ride up and out of the hole. Then, a hand resting on a barrel as if it were my own wine, and my heart racing, I simply walked past the sentries. They did not give me a second glance.

I slipped away from the wagon at the first opportunity, taking a side alley. Alone in an enemy city, I should have been scared, but delighted by my success and rid of FitzAldelm, I felt freer than a bird. Picking my way to the base of the walls, I walked the entire circumference of the town, counting soldiers. With growing confidence – looking back, I would say, cockiness – I decided next to spy out the citadel, which lay in the centre of Cahors.

Richard was of the same mind. Nearing the stronghold, I spied him and Owain drinking ale outside a tavern. Even with his hood up, the duke was easy to spot because of his great height. Remembering his orders to stay apart in case of discovery, I bought a wheaten loaf and took up a position on a corner diagonally opposite. The street was busy, so they did not notice me. Chewing happily, I studied the high walls of the citadel, but had no way of ascertaining how many soldiers were inside. The risks of entering were far too great – the sentries at the gate appeared alert and disciplined – leading me to decide that there was little point in lingering. When I saw Richard and Owain drain their beakers, I suspected they had reached the same decision.

Amusing myself, I kept my head down and slipped in behind them as they walked past. When the opportunity arose, I would make myself known.

As we passed another alehouse, a man-at-arms staggered out the door, followed by a companion. By some unhappy chance, his bleary-eyed gaze fell on the duke. He frowned, and belched, and looked again. 'Christ on the cross, there goes Duke Richard of Aquitaine,' he said.

His companion snorted. 'Pull the other one – it has bells on.'

'I tell you, it was him! I have seen the duke before.' His voice had risen to a shout, and heads were turning.

Ahead of me, I saw Richard hunch his shoulders. Owain glanced back, the wrong thing to do, and then he whispered in the duke's ear. They hurried on.

'You are even drunker than I thought, you fool,' said the man-at-arm's companion, trying to steer his friend back into the inn.

'Gilded I may be, but I am not blind.' His mouth opened to shout an alarm.

My dagger was out, and I was moving. The man-at-arms did not see me until I was on him. My blade sank deep into his chest, once, twice. Blood sprayed. He fell. I shoved my way back into the throng, his friend's cries filling my ears. A hand caught the back of my tunic; a fist swung at me. I twisted. Ducked. Elbowed. Make it to the other side of the street, I thought desperately, and I would be among people who had not seen me kill an innocent man.

I had not counted on my victim's friend being sober enough to give chase. Shouts of 'Murderer!' and 'Seize him!' filled the air. The faces that turned to regard me saw my blood-stained clothing, and soon I was surrounded by enemies. Only the threat of my dagger and the proximity of an alleyway saved me. Tunic ripped, head ringing from a punch, I threw myself into the narrow lane and ran.

Panic filled me as footsteps pounded at my back. If this ratline came to a dead end, I was a dead man. Twenty paces on, my worst fears were realised as I came to a sheer wall. Preparing to sell my life dearly, I spun, noticing as I did, an opening to my left. I took it. Left and right I turned, right and left, in my speed and panic losing all sense of direction. Cobwebs filled my hair. A projecting nail ripped a scarlet line down one arm. My boots were soaked through with what smelled like urine.

I stopped to listen. As I recovered my breath, I made out angry shouts, but they were far off. There were no approaching footsteps, no cries between pursuers. I felt little relief, for my predicament remained precarious. I had not the slightest idea where I was, and by the time I reached the gate, there was a good chance a watch would have been set upon it.

Fear swelled in my chest. I stood in the fetid gloom, indecision battering me.

'How often do I have to tell you? There is rain in the air. Take in the washing!'

I came to my senses. Shuffling in the direction of the voice, I peered into a small courtyard – the back of a business premises, I judged, with living quarters above. Hanging from a rope line stretched from wall to wall were two men's tunics and several sets of hose. I did not hesitate, for there were footsteps in the corridor that opened into the yard. In I darted, past a startled cat, and plucked free a tunic and a pair of hose, before vanishing whence I had come. No indignant cry followed me, and my heart leaped with joy. Not ten paces from the entrance, I undid my belt and stripped to my braies, and donned my ill-gotten new clothes. They had a musty smell, that of a greybeard, but I cared not. The tunic had no tell-tale scarlet marks on its front.

'I thought you said you had washed both my tunics,' said a man.

'I did,' replied a female voice.

'There is only one here.'

Biting my lip to stop myself from laughing, I padded away.

None was tolling as I reached the main gate. I had no way of knowing if Richard and Owain had escaped. If they were yet within the walls, I reasoned, I had slight hope of finding them, and a considerable risk of falling into French hands myself. Worry gnawed at me as I joined the back of a large group of peasants that was leaving the town.

Safely past the sentries, I broke free. Through the booths, now being taken down, I ran, uncaring who saw. To my immense relief, Richard and Owain were standing with Rhys, de Drune and FitzAldelm.

Grinning from ear to ear, I bent my head as I drew near. 'Sire,' I mouthed.

Richard beamed at me. Owain nodded happily. Rhys capered from foot to foot like the boy he had once been. FitzAldelm looked as if he had swallowed a wasp.

'We feared you were taken,' said the duke.

'I feared the same for you, sire,' I answered.

'It was a close-run thing.' Richard frowned. 'Were you there when the man-at-arms recognised me?'

'I was, sire.' I explained what I had done.

Richard glanced at Owain, and back to me. 'We are in your debt, Rufus.'

'I did what *any* of us would have done, sire,' I said. FitzAldelm would know the comment was aimed at him.

'You were lucky to escape at all,' said Richard. He regarded FitzAldelm, and then me again. 'Robert says that you were separated at the gate.'

I stared at FitzAldelm. His throat worked. He coughed.

Oh, I wanted that moment to last an eternity.

'Rufus?' asked the duke.

'Yes, sire, we were. I thought he was behind me when the sentries let me in. When I realised he was not, I had been carried a way into the town. I judged it dangerous to go back, in case the sentries grew suspicious.'

Richard's eyes lingered on FitzAldelm, who appeared most uncomfortable. 'Poor it is, Robert, when a squire succeeds where you have not, and moreover, saves me from certain capture.'

A hundred marks in silver would not have prevented me from witnessing my enemy's humiliation. The instant Richard's attention moved from him, however, he gave me a fresh look of loathing. I met it with one of my own, uncaring that our enmity had been made bitterer than ever.

'Rufus.' De Drune's voice.

I dragged my attention from FitzAldelm, who was apologising again to Richard. 'What is it?'

'Yon nobleman.' De Drune inclined his head. 'Do you know him?'

About to pass us by, unnoticed until now, I saw a fleshy-faced man in a crimson tunic on a pretty grey palfrey. Everything from his fine shoes to the gold ring on his left hand screamed wealth.

Memory tickled, I said, 'He was friendly with Geoffrey – I saw them talking years ago.'

De Drune grinned. 'I knew I recognised him.'

I caught Richard's attention. 'Sire. Do you see the palfrey, and who rides it?'

The duke stared. Smiled in disbelief. 'As I live and breathe. That is Peter Seillan, or I am an infidel.' Under his breath, he said, 'Seillan belongs to the family that governs Toulouse on Count Raymond's behalf. He is also one of his closest advisers, and the man behind much of the conflict between us. To horse!'

What Seillan was doing without an escort, I had no idea, but he paid for it a mile later when we caught up with him. Surrounded, threatened by ready blades, he allowed a grinning Rhys to take his reins without protest.

Richard's good mood grew expansive. He gave de Drune the purse of silver pennies that hung from his belt, and to me, he promised a destrier. Despite a couple of ransoms I had received for mid-ranking prisoners taken over the years, the cost of a trained war horse had remained beyond my reach. As I stammered my thanks, Richard saluted me with his costrel.

'You will need a proper steed where we are going, Rufus.'

It was a sober reminder that a war still waited for us, thousands of miles away, yet our mood was not dampened for long.

When the duke asked where I had got my clothes, everyone laughed. Except for FitzAldelm, riding at the back.

Within ten days, Cahors had fallen, and we were outside the walls of Toulouse. Richard demanded a meeting with Raymond, but things did not go as planned. Although we had Peter Seillan, Raymond had captured two of the duke's knights, passing through his territory as they returned from Compostella in Spain. Raymond agreed to release them on the condition that Seillan was set free. Richard refused, so Raymond held on to the pair of knights. The impasse continued for days, yet it could not last. The duke did not have the siege engines to prosecute a successful assault on the city of Toulouse, and everyone knew it.

Raymond asked the French king for help. When a letter to Richard met with failure, Philippe sent another declaring the duke's attack on Toulouse a breach of the truce agreed at Châteauroux the previous summer. Naturally, the duke disagreed, but that did not stop Philippe's army invading the north of Aquitaine soon after. The siege of Toulouse had to be abandoned in order to meet the new threat. Again we went on the march.

It seemed we would never go on crusade. Indeed by early July, when we found ourselves camped near Châteauroux for the second time in a year – the castle had fallen to one of Philippe's knights mere days before – it appeared our destiny was to be permanently engaged in conflict with the French.

After days of sitting on our hands, powerless to take Châteauroux without siege engines, and with its commander William des Barres unwilling to negotiate, Richard called a council of war. A dozen of his captains were present, including de Chauvigny and FitzAldelm.

The latter had been assiduous since Cahors in trying to work himself back into the duke's favours. Sad to say, he had succeeded, in the main because of his uncanny ability to find supplies. Whether he obeyed the order to pay for everything, I did not know; absorbed with trying to take Châteauroux, Richard did not enquire overmuch.

He began the meeting by demanding reports from elsewhere.

'As you know, sire, most of the duchy of Berry has fallen to Philippe,' said de Chauvigny.

Richard nodded. 'And Vendôme?' It was a strong border fortress west of Le Mans, on the River Loire.

De Chauvigny looked unhappy. 'A messenger arrived not an hour since, sire. The lord Buchard has surrendered his castle and lands to Philippe.'

The duke's mouth tightened. 'Loches?' he asked. This was another important castle, some miles down the Indre from our own position.

'It remains loyal, sire,' said FitzAldelm.

'That is because Philippe, the losenger, is carefully leaving alone the castles held in trust for my lord father,' said Richard in exasperation. 'And by attacking on such a broad front, he forces me to spread my army thinly. I cannot assail every stronghold of mine that he has taken. Ah, he is a shrewd one, for all his youth.' He glanced around the gathering. 'What say you, my lords?'

'Can Châteauroux be taken by trickery, sire?' Unsurprisingly to my mind, it was FitzAldelm who made this suggestion.

'It seems not. My spies have been busy inside the castle, and can find no one willing to open a gate,' said Richard. 'I am told des Basses has paid every man in the garrison three months in advance.'

'We could construct siege engines, sire,' said a balding knight.

The duke shook his head. 'Philippe will have threatened somewhere else before we had them finished.'

The assembled knights each found a fingernail to pick, or a buckle to toy with. FitzAldelm scuffed the point of his boot against a tuft of grass.

As the silence drew on, Richard's mien darkened.

'Your lord father, sire—' De Chauvigny hesitated. 'He has crossed the Narrow Sea with an army not a sennight since. Would he . . .?'

'His castles in Berry are not under threat, so he is likely to stay behind the borders of Normandy, protecting it alone,' answered the duke. 'He will not support me here, of that I am certain.'

Richard's tone was brusque, but a flicker of emotion in his blue eyes told me he yet desired to be reconciled with Henry, and not only so he could be named as his heir. The king had also taken the cross – at the same time as Philippe – which meant they all three were supposed to be going on crusade.

I had my own doubts. As time passed, the gulf between father and son was widening. The idea that they would go to Outremer together seemed impossible.

The duke and his companions bandied about ideas for a time, but could agree on nothing.

On impulse, I asked, 'Could we pretend to withdraw, sire, and when the enemy sends scouts after us, rush to take the gate?'

Every face turned towards me. The knights' expressions ranged from hostile – the majority, including FitzAldelm of course – to curious or surprised, that a squire should have the temerity to venture an opinion. Only de Chauvigny seemed interested, and most importantly, Richard.

'The old trick,' said the duke. 'Everyone knows it, and so no one uses it, because by definition, the deception is obvious.'

FitzAldelm sneered, and I wished I had kept my mouth shut.

'And yet, for that very reason, it might work.' Richard rubbed a finger to and fro across his lips, his habit when thinking. 'André?'

'I cannot see us entering Châteauroux any other way, sire. It may be worth a try.' De Chauvigny gave me a nod.

'Even so,' said the duke.

I grinned until my cheeks hurt.

I did not see the look FitzAldelm gave me. Rhys did, and told me after. Head swelled by Richard's recognition, I paid him no heed.

CHAPTER XXVI

The day was baking hot, even for July. It was late afternoon, and Marshal was hidden deep in the trees near the town of Chaumont-sur-Epte, which lay on the French side of the disputed border in the Vexin region. His one hundred soldiers, mostly men-at-arms, were similarly hidden. Their line stretched perhaps a quarter of a mile, crossing the main road, which led to Paris. Not wishing to escalate the situation into another Châteauroux, Henry had largely kept his troops confined to Normandy since their recent arrival from England. Forces like Marshal's were the exception, sent into Philippe's territory to sow terror and unease. Small, highly mobile and hard to find, they were capable of ravaging significant areas.

As yet, thought Marshal with some satisfaction, they had to encounter any of Philippe's soldiers. Six days of riding and raiding. Three villages burned, a town attacked, and one small keep taken. Scores of French troops had been taken prisoner at the keep, along with two knights and half a dozen men-at-arms. Civilian casualties had been acceptable thus far – at a guess, it was less than five score. Several hundred head of cattle and sheep had been seized and driven off. By now they were probably in Normandy, meat on the hoof for Henry's main army at Alençon.

Marshal's losses had been slight: one man slain, and two badly injured. At this rate, they could continue raiding until the autumn, but a preferable result would be for an agreement between the king and Philippe. Marshal was an expert at waging this kind of war, but he had no stomach for it. Burning barns and stealing farmers' food was routiers' work, not that of a knight. Henry had ordered it, however, and he was bound to obey. The town of Chaumont-sur-Epte, a larger target than any before, would send a sharp message to Philippe that nowhere was safe from attack.

'Marshal!' John's nasal voice.

He sighed. The burr in his hose was not the French, but the presence of the king's youngest son. Henry had insisted John be taken, telling Marshal the youth must learn some craft in war, because during his time in Ireland, he had missed all the fighting. It was plain as day to Marshal what that meant, but Henry could not see it. On one occasion, John's horse had been lame, he declared. On another, his favourite helmet could not be found. The string of excuses was endless. With Marshal to guide him, said the king, John would see action and God willing, win some glory.

'Marshal!'

He sighed. He had given instruction that noise was to be kept to a minimum, so the French did not hear, and yet John was bellowing like a fishwife. Marshal turned his horse in the direction of the prince's voice and wove a path between the men-at-arms and the trees. When he could see him, Marshal raised a hand. 'I am here, sire,' he called quietly.

John reined in, forcing Marshal to ride to him. His face was puce; sweat ran in streams from his brow. De Coulonces was by his side, similarly uncomfortable. 'When does the cursed attack begin?' demanded John.

Marshal curbed his temper. He had explained everything, twice; the first occasion had been the previous night, the second that morning. 'Sunset, sire. The light will be blinding from the west, allowing us to reach the gate before we are recognised.'

'I am boiling alive in this.' John slapped at his hauberk.

We did not leave camp until midday. You have spent the last two hours in the shade, thought Marshal. Try fighting in Outremer. 'It is very hot, sire, and uncomfortable,' he said in a solicitous tone. 'We must be prepared to move on the instant, in case we are discovered.'

'Yes, yes,' said John, his voice tetchy. 'But I see no need for such a long delay. Why are we not attacking now? Chaumont-sur-Epte is not a large town. Its garrison will be poorly trained, you said. The rabble should panic at the sight of us, surely?'

'Of course they will, sire,' agreed de Coulonces.

Marshal gave him a withering look, and in a patient tone, said to John, 'One or two men can shut a gate, sire, and it is a quarter mile from the edge of the trees to the town walls. Attack before sunset, and we could be recognised as enemies. Leave the assault until then, however, and our chances of success will be greater.'

John's scowl resembled that of a petulant child. 'I will wait around in my mail no longer. It can be put on again nearer the time.' He swung down from his destrier, and glanced up impatiently. 'Help me, Marshal.'

'It would be safer not to remove it, sire.'

John snorted and undid his sword belt. 'What is the worst that can happen? Some French peasant spies us and raises the alarm. I should have ample opportunity to don it before the enemy comes within a mile of us.'

'If a crossbowman were to see you, sire, and loose a bolt . . .'

'There is more chance of snow falling.'

This was patently untrue, but Marshal sensed the futility of further protest. He tried not to think of Henry's reaction if John were injured or killed.

John lifted the hem of his hauberk. 'Help me.' His tone was turning acerbic.

'Yes, sire,' said Marshal. By rights, John's squire should have performed the duty, but it looked rude to object. Letting Jean d'Earley, *his* new squire, take charge of his mount, Marshal obeyed. Catching de Coulonces smirking – something he did at every opportunity – he said curtly, 'You too, sir.'

John's shiny face turned towards de Coulonces, who quickly adopted a helpful expression. 'It will be my pleasure, sire.'

Together they soon had John out of the massively heavy coat. The padded gambeson he wore underneath was saturated with sweat. 'God's bones, but that is better,' said John. He began to unlace the gambeson.

'Please leave that on, sire,' said Marshal.

'I am too hot!'

As we all are, thought Marshal. 'Forgive me, sire, I must insist. Without it, you will have no protection against blade or arrow. I cannot take that risk so close to Chaumont-sur-Epte.'

'You carp like an old woman, Marshal.'

De Coulonces chuckled.

Marshal dipped his chin to hide his anger. Try as he might, the barbed comments and laughter were getting under his skin. De Coulonces was a troublesome enemy, and determined to twist the knife in the open wound of their relationship at every opportunity. Marshal took a deep breath and said to the prince, 'I am sorry you think so, sire. My concern is your safety.'

Walking away, John did not hear. Tugging at his hose, he unleashed a stream of urine against a tree.

'Guard your tongue, sir, and your humour,' Marshal warned de Coulonces. 'Or I will have satisfaction from you.'

De Coulonces sneered, but he made no further jibes.

John also left his gambeson on.

They were small victories, Marshal decided, but better than nothing. Tripling the number of men-at-arms around the prince, and sending more scouts to their front and rear in case anyone should come through the woods, he rode the entire length of the line. He had completed the same task a short time earlier, but anything that took him away from John and his lickspittle de Coulonces was to be welcomed.

His men were over-hot, and like their horses, plagued by clouds of horseflies. There was water, however, and food – Marshal had seen to that. They were also in the shade, and experienced enough to be grateful for such mercies. Stopping to talk with man after man, remembering this one's name and how that one had fought in a particular action, he told them the waiting would not last forever. Chaumont-sur-Epte was a fruit ripe for the plucking, and at sunset, it would fall into their laps. Women were to be left unravished, he warned, and menfolk killed only if they resisted. There would be wine, meat and bread for all. With luck, they would line their purses with silver as well. His words were plain and unvarnished, but soldiers who could soon face death liked nothing better.

Content that morale was high, that his captains and serjeants knew their orders, he made his way back to his original position. He had hoped John and de Coulonces might have gone; irritatingly, they had not. It *was* pleasing that the prince still wore his gambeson.

Marshal adopted an expression of pleasure. 'Sire.'

John's reply was an ill-tempered grunt.

'You will be pleased to hear, sire, that the men are ready, and eager for action.'

'I would expect no less.'

'As you say, sire.'

'I want to lead the attack.'

Startled, Marshal glanced at John. 'Sire?'

'I am the king's son. Chaumont-sur-Epte is an important prize. It is only right I should command.'

'I had thought for you to ride with the main body of men, sire,' said Marshal, again picturing John being hurt or slain, and the price he would pay for that.

'Richard often leads from the front.' This was said with a sour pursing of the lips.

'That he does, sire, but only when there is great need.' He also has considerable experience of battle, thought Marshal, unlike you.

'History does not remember soldiers who merely did as their fellows.'

Nor will it recall the men who took Chaumont-sur-Epte, Marshal decided. It is not Paris, or Toulouse. 'It is an unnecessary risk, sire.'

'I shall have you and de Coulonces with me, and therefore nothing to fear. Marshal, I insist.'

He nodded. 'Very well, sire.'

John saluted him with his costrel. 'To victory.'

'To victory, sire.' Marshal raised his waterskin.

John's throat worked as he drank. One, two, three swallows.

God's teeth, thought Marshal. If the man keeps that up, he will be completely gilded before sunset. Telling himself not to be presumptuous, Marshal bided his time, but to his alarm, John showed every sign of draining every last drop.

'Sire,' Marshal began.

'What now?'

'Might I beg a sup?' Marshal's smile was ingratiating.

With poor grace, John offered him the costrel.

'My thanks, sire.' Reaching out to take it, Marshal spurred his destrier with the heel John could not see. The horse jinked, and the costrel dropped to the ground.

'Clumsy oaf!' John cried.

De Coulonces's lip curled.

'A thousand apologies, sire.' Right hand by his waist, Marshal pulled down hard on the reins, forcing the destrier sideways. Annoyed by the rough treatment, it pranced back and forth as he 'struggled' to control it. As he had hoped, the costrel burst under the weight of an iron-shod hoof. Wine sprayed, and Marshal, his face anguished, made profuse apologies to an irate John.

'That contained the finest Pierrefitte, Marshal. You will pay for it.'

'Naturally, sire. An entire barrel will be yours the moment we return to Alençon,' said Marshal, thinking the price cheap to have prevented the king's son from drinking himself insensible.

John's scowl eased a little.

Seeing de Coulonces reach for his own costrel, Marshal thought, sweet Jesu, does the man want John to be killed? He threw a poisonous glare, and was relieved when de Coulonces's hand fell back to his side.

John returned to one of his favourite topics, that of his brother Richard. He had not a good word to say about him. Faithless and disloyal, the duke could not be trusted. He remained bosom companions with Philippe. It would not be that surprising, said John, if the pair joined forces against Henry. Everything he said had de Coulonces nodding his head like a puppet.

I see your purpose, thought Marshal. You seek to supplant Richard as the heir. It was not a prospect that filled him with happiness. Arrogant, self-serving, manipulative and ill-tempered, John would make a poor king. He had to act with care, though, for his reservations could never show.

'Are you with me?' asked John.

On the instant de Coulonces said, 'I am, sire.'

Marshal did not speak, leaving the loaded question hanging in the air.

John's beady gaze swivelled. 'Marshal?'

'I am the king's sworn man, sire. I stand with him in every regard, as you do.' He had evaded the question, and everyone knew it.

Sunset could not come too soon.

Marshal's attempts to improve the icy atmosphere failed. In the end he stopped trying, which meant his ears were filled with de Coulonces's sycophantic comments. He did not care. It was a relief not to have to make conversation. Peace between Henry and Richard, Marshal decided, was a necessity, and he resolved to do his best to see it come about.

The hours passed. The sun sank, an orange-red ball of fire, and as the bells in Chaumont-sur-Epte tolled compline, Marshal led his force to the treeline. There was a brief alarm when a hapless farmer driving an ox-drawn wagon appeared on the road, but calm was restored when a swift-thinking captain rode out of cover and took him captive.

Golden sunlight bathed the open, stubble-filled fields that lay between their position and the town walls. Atop the rampart, helmets winked, but there were not many. Peace reigned.

Marshal eyed John, and asked, 'Ready, sire?'

The tip of John's tongue circled his dry lips. 'I am.'

Marshal gave him an encouraging smile.

'We walk all the way if possible.'

'Correct, sire. With the sun behind us, they will see our shapes and not much else. Six horsemen do not pose a threat.' Marshal's tone was calm, as if he were describing a gentle morning ride.

'And if the alarm is raised?'

'We shall retreat here, sire. They will not pursue us.'

'The risk of crossbowmen?' They were not wearing helmets, because if any of the sentries noticed *that* detail, there was no chance of reaching the gate undetected.

'Once we are within a hundred and fifty paces of the wall, sire, it is there. I cannot deny it. Stay alert. Keep your shield high.' Once more, Marshal told himself that no harm would come to the king's son. 'If all goes to plan, we six shall take the gate. At my signal, the rest of our force will hasten to our aid, and the town will fall.'

'Thank you, Marshal.' The anxiety was plain in John's eyes. Nonetheless, he pricked his horse forward, onto the road.

Pleased, Marshal followed. De Coulonces and three other knights followed.

They rode towards Chaumont-sur-Epte, appearing to come from the direction of Paris. Dazzling light from the setting sun warmed their backs, and cast immense shadows on the ground before them. We look like giants, thought Marshal, childishly tempted to draw his sword and raise it aloft.

John was in the lead, as he had demanded. Marshal rode close behind, with de Coulonces – at the king's son's insistence – beside him. The three knights came last. Half a dozen riders. The right size for a French patrol or a group of scouts, seeking shelter for the night. Their pace was gentle, unhurried, that of approaching allies.

Two hundred and fifty paces they rode, over half the distance. On the sun-gilded ramparts, peace reigned. Marshal kept up a bland monologue, an amusing tale of a wagonload of wine taken as booty some years prior. The whole time he spoke, he watched John like a hawk. His back was stiff with tension, hands white-knuckled on the reins, but he did not turn from their path.

Taken from the archers by an unpopular serjeant, Marshal went on, the wagon had in turn been commandeered by a knight. He had lost it to a baron, only for the Young King to declare it his. When confronted, humbly of course, by the indignant archers, he had returned it to them with good humour. The esteem in which he was held had been augmented even further by his gift of an ox, 'some meat to accompany the wine,' he had said to deafening cheers. The memory was one of Marshal's favourites, with the Young King at his charismatic best, able to transform his soldiers' unhappiness into adulation.

'Someone is going to see us.' John's voice rippled with fear.

'No one will, until it is too late,' said Marshal. 'Stay calm, sire. Keep riding.'

John obeyed, and Marshal's tension eased a notch.

Fifty paces dragged past. A hundred more in front of them, the open gate loomed.

'Your intentions are made clear at last.' De Coulonces's voice was pitched for him alone.

'Sir?' Marshal truly had no idea what his enemy was talking about.

'You seek to replace me in the prince's affections.'

Incredulous, Marshal hissed, 'I try merely to keep him calm.'

'Cozener.'

'Desist. We have more important things to deal with,' said Marshal. De Coulonces fell silent.

Eighty paces. Seventy.

A sentry raised a hand to his eyes and stared in their direction.

John checked his destrier.

'Ride on, sire,' said Marshal quickly. 'He sees nothing suspicious.'

Encouraged, John rode on.

The sentry's hand came down. He walked several paces along the walkway.

Marshal breathed again.

Fifty paces.

The sentry stopped. Peered again.

Even with the sun at their backs, there was no concealing the size of their destriers at this distance. It was possible that half a dozen French knights would appear unannounced at the gates of Chaumont-sur-Epte, thought Marshal, but it was also out of the ordinary.

'Declare yourselves!' The sentry's shout was aimed at them.

'Now, sire!' said Marshal.

'Are you sure?'

'Yes, sire. Now!' Leaning forward in the saddle, Marshal gave John's mount a sharp slap. It sprang forward, reaching the gallop in a few strides. Marshal's destrier followed with a will; de Coulonces and the rest came after. In a thunder of hooves, drowning out the sentry's cries, they closed on the undefended gate.

Marshal had his spear already couched. John, inexperienced, had not. When the terrified guard in the gateway stepped from the king's son's path, he presented Marshal with an easy target. Punched backward by the impact, the spear deep in his chest, he went down like a sack of grain dropped from a height.

In they went, under the arch, and into Chaumont-sur-Epte.

'Halt, sire!' cried Marshal.

John, who had seemed about to ride off down the cobbled main street, reined in. His face was flushed, jubilant. 'We did it!'

'Victory is not yet certain, sire. Don your helmet, if you will.' Marshal seized the hunting horn at his belt, and blew a short series of blasts. That done, he had to trust his men had heard, and hold the gate until their arrival. His eyes went to the tower above the gate, and the walkway to either side. Four sentries, two armed with crossbows, and both within range. One had his weapon raised, and pointing at Marshal. He whipped up his shield.

Click. An innocuous, deadly sound.

The bolt struck the ground five paces from Marshal. Sparks flew. It clattered over the cobbles and was lost to sight.

'Into the gateway!' roared Marshal. There they would be safe from above, and could dismount. Form a line, and they could defend the entrance until the rest of his men reached them.

Click.

A strangled cry. One of the knights clutched at his lower leg, uncovered by mail. Managing to wheel his destrier, he made for the gate.

Marshal looked for John, and was relieved to see he had almost reached the entrance too, alongside a second knight. The last knight had already reached safety, while de Coulonces, still helmetless, was finishing off a spearman who had descended the nearest set of stairs. A second, halfway down, would soon join the fray.

Marshal stared upward again. His stomach twisted. A third crossbowman had appeared. He shot at de Coulonces, and missed. One of his companions also took aim at him, and the last pointed his crossbow at Marshal.

Who acted without thinking. Leaning forward to present as small a target as possible, he spurred his horse towards de Coulonces.

Click. The bolt shot into the space occupied by Marshal's destrier's hindquarters a heartbeat earlier.

'De Coulonces!' His enemy had killed the spearman, and was engaged with the second. While de Coulonces was occupied, he was easy prey for the crossbowmen. Marshal urged his mount to new effort, barged past de Coulonces, and with a massive downward slash, beheaded the spearman.

'He was mine!' De Coulonces was furious.

'God's toes, forget about him! Get back to the gate.' Marshal turned his horse, wishing he had had time to don his helmet, and bringing his kite shield in front of his body.

Click. The crossbowman had waited until his targets were clearer.

De Coulonces's mount squealed, a high-pitched sound of pure pain.

Marshal looked, saw the bolt protruding from its neck, and de Coulonces's face twisted with fear. The destrier staggered. Click. A second bolt took it in the chest. Mortally wounded, the destrier prinked sideways, then back. Its hindlegs gave way, and it collapsed. De Coulonces managed, just, to free his feet. Standing astride the corpse, he reached out a hand to Marshal. 'Help me!'

Click. Click. Two crossbow bolts hummed in. One hit de Coulonces's dying mount, the other drove into his shield.

Marshal's mouth was dry with fear. In all likelihood, the third man was now aiming at him. The other two were reloading. To ride for the gate was his best chance, perhaps his only one. He stared at the pleading de Coulonces and felt nothing.

'Marshal!' De Coulonces hurried towards him.

'Come on!' Marshal shouted for the benefit of John and the others. He ducked out of instinct, and a bolt shot over his head.

De Coulonces came lumbering in. His hands reached up for the cantle of Marshal's saddle.

Marshal was ready. His foot, already out of the stirrup, struck de Coulonces full in the chest. Side on to the gateway, no one there saw what he did. Mouth wide with shock, arms flailing, de Coulonces fell back, onto his rear end.

Click. A giant punched Marshal between the shoulder blades. Click. And hammered another blow into his left thigh. Half-winded, in agony, he drummed his right heel into the destrier's side, and aimed its head at the gate. 'Ha!'

His hope, that the crossbowmen would not be able to resist the easy target de Coulonces presented, was borne out. Reaching the safety of the gateway, Marshal glanced back. His enemy sprawled on his back, the feathered end of a bolt jutting from an eyesocket.

That will teach you to spread vicious rumour, thought Marshal coldly.

'Are you hurt?' asked John.

'I am not sure, sire.' Marshal half-slid, half-fell from the destrier. Laying down his sword, he probed the back of his neck and examined his thigh. His mail had held out against the bolt in the former, leaving him with what would be an impressive bruise. Several links had parted in the latter area, with the bolt driving through the gambeson with enough force to break the skin. 'I will be black and blue, sire, but that is the extent of it.'

'You had more luck than de Coulonces,' said John, his lips twitching.

'I did, sire.'

'You almost saved him.'

'If he hadn't slipped, sire . . .' Marshal shook his head in apparent regret.

They had no more time to talk. The three crossbowmen had come down from the walkway, and were about to attack. With John at the rear – Marshal insisted, and he did not protest – the four remaining knights donned their helmets and formed a short line. Shields high, they confronted the enemy soldiers. A volley landed. Two shields were hit, and a destrier injured.

Marshal wondered about charging the crossbowmen as they re-loaded, but decided the risk was too great. For all he knew, there were more of the enemy on the walkway. Reinforcements would soon arrive from within the town, and to leave the gateway risked seeing it taken. Staying where they were, however, provided the crossbowmen with targets as easy as bales of straw in the practice field.

The sound of galloping horses had never been sweeter to his ear.

Shouts of fear carried from the rampart.

The crossbowmen heard.

'A hundred riders!' Marshal shouted at them. 'A hundred!'

As one, the three men dropped their weapons and fled.

Marshal turned to John. 'The victory is yours, sire. Congratulations.'

The other knights joined in.

A smirk spread across John's face. 'I will not forget this, Marshal,' he said quietly.

'Sire.' Marshal dipped his chin, pleased. Whatever his opinion of John, it was better to have him as a friend than an enemy.

A town taken, a bitter enemy slain, and a debt owed to him by the king's youngest son, thought Marshal with some satisfaction. Today had been a good day.

CHAPTER XXVII

Two days after the duke's council of war, everything was in place. Half our army had left the previous morning. Des Barres' spies would already have confirmed that it was headed for Loches, making him assume – we hoped – that the rest of Richard's troops, now taking down their tents and setting off on the same road, would follow on behind. What des Barres did not know was that five score mounted men-at-arms had peeled away from yesterday's column in a stretch of nearby woodland, and spent the night hidden from sight.

Departing with the rest, leaving only trampled grass and black circles where the fires had been, the duke and his mesnie, and I among them, had left halfway between prime and terce. As news of our departure spread, our enemies lined the castle ramparts and filled the air with jeers and insults. We shouted back, showing our apparent frustration that the siege had failed.

A mile on, deep in the woods, Richard led a hundred knights off the road, while the rest of the troops marched on. The men-at-arms were waiting for us, eager-eyed. Dismounted and with our armour donned, we followed them through the trees in twos and threes, working our way back towards Châteauroux. It was slow work clad in full mail, and with no wind, desperately hot. Roots snagged our feet, branches whipped at our faces, and horseflies swarmed around us and the horses, biting any exposed flesh.

At last, however, we had reached the treeline that opened onto the fields where we had made camp, and a few hundred paces beyond that, the stronghold of Châteauroux. After a brief discussion with the duke, the officers in charge of the men-at-arms took them away, off to our right, where the woodland swung in a lot closer to the castle walls. Richard gave strict orders for silence. No one was to go within twenty paces of the open ground, for fear of a glint of mail giving us away.

With FitzAldelm, de Chauvigny and a couple of others, Richard stole forward of his men. Rhys and I followed.

The ramparts had emptied of the crowds who had seen us off so rudely. Here and there, sentries patrolled. To my disappointment, the gate was still closed.

Richard beckoned. 'Well, Rufus? Will they take the bait?'

My gaze raked the defences again, but they were quiet. I listened for sounds of horses, or marching men, and heard nothing. My hopes of surprising the enemy now seemed foolish. 'I do not know, sire.'

The duke leaned against a young oak. 'Let us wait, and we shall see.'

I slapped away a horsefly, and prayed for Divine intervention.

An hour dragged by. Hot air shimmered over the flattened grass. It was cooler under the trees, but not by much.

'Warm, Rufus?' Richard's brow was pricked with beads of sweat.

'A little, sire.' I smiled.

'They say the deserts of Outremer are twice as hot as the warmest summer day in Aquitaine.'

'It sounds like Hell on earth, sire,' I said with feeling.

'It does, and to reach Jerusalem, we shall have no option but to leave the coast behind and cross the sea of sand.'

'How far, sire?'

'Some thirty-five miles, I believe.'

'That is not so terrible, sire. With you to lead us, we shall cover the distance with ease.'

'I hope so,' Richard murmured, his eyes distant.

The unmistakable screech of unoiled hinges carried through the muggy air.

I stared at the castle, nervous excitement filling me as one of the great doors gradually swung wide.

'Des Barres grows curious,' said the duke. 'Let us see how much.'

A double file of riders emerged. Voices reached us: shouted commands.

My nerves grew taut. If the enemy horsemen were scouts, the party would not be large, and the gate would soon shut. Des Barres would not order it opened again. Holding Châteauroux was of far greater importance than losing a few soldiers.

If the Frenchman had been taken in, however, and was sending a larger force to shadow our army, then the duke would launch a frontal attack, while the men-at-arms drove in behind, their aim to cut the enemy off from the castle. Our plan – more a gamble – was that des Barres, desperate not to lose such a number of men, would keep the gate open so his men could either fight through our soldiers to safety, or so more troops could be committed to the battle. Both these possibilities would present an opportunity to seize the castle entrance.

That was the theory. Thinking about it now, my mouth went dry.

Twenty riders were in sight, and glancing at Richard, I saw his expression grow hawkish.

By the time two score of the enemy – a combination of knights and men-at-arms – had exited the gate, it was evident that des Barres believed we *had* retreated. Sixty riders, I counted, and then a hundred. Still they came riding out of Châteauroux. As the tally passed a hundred and fifty, I began to question the wisdom of launching an attack.

Richard, on the other hand, looked like a leashed hunting dog with the scent of a deer in its nostrils. As at Périgueux, he had only one intention. I wiped my palms on my hose, and hoped that we achieved a better outcome than that day.

At last the gate shut. Two hundred men had left Châteauroux, the same number we had.

'Such a strong force means des Barres intends not to shadow the army, but to engage our rearguard. *That* I had not foreseen,' the duke said, chuckling. 'We have no choice but to attack. If those Frenchmen reach the wagons, they will wreak fearful damage.'

And if, at the sight of us, des Barres sends out more troops, we will be sorely outnumbered, I wanted to say. I had spoken out of turn once already, however, and wary of rebuke, I kept quiet.

Richard sent a messenger to the men-at-arms, ordering them to be prepared. Swiftly, we rejoined the others, and prepared to clamber onto our horses. Squires checked saddle girths. Helmets were donned, and prayers muttered. When Rhys handed me my lance, as he had done at Striguil, reality truly sank in. This was no practice at the quintain.

I was about to ride at real enemies. Frenchmen, who would stick me with their spears if they could.

'God be with you, sir,' said Rhys. He looked nervous, which was even more unsettling.

I gave him a stiff nod, and eased Liath Macha in behind the duke's destrier, a massive black stallion. It entered my head that I should not be charging the enemy on a rouncy, but I could do nothing about it. There had been no time to find the war horse that Richard had promised. Liath Macha would do his duty, I told myself, as he always had.

'Ready, messires?' called the duke.

A rolling wave of assent followed.

'With me.' Richard pricked his spurs, and trotted out into the hot sunshine. He had us form a solid line, some three men deep, and then with a cry of 'For God and Aquitaine!' he urged the stallion into a gallop.

We thundered towards the French at an oblique angle. The narrow field of vision offered by the slit in my helmet meant I could see only the enemy. Perhaps a quarter of a mile separated us, and yet the charge seemed to take the blink of an eye. One instant we were leaving the safety of the trees, a warm breeze rushing past, and the next, the enemy were almost within range of our lances, and we of theirs.

'For God and Aquitaine!' Richard shouted.

The Frenchmen had turned in good order, and were cantering in our direction. Most appeared no different to us. They wore pot or conical helms, and long hauberks. Kite shields or variants thereof were their protection, lances their weapons. A few had crests on their helmets, as Richard had, or designs on their shields. Their line was a great deal longer than ours, which accentuated the difference in numbers.

I tried not to think about that. Instead, urging Liath Macha up alongside Richard's stallion, I couched my lance and picked a target, a man with a yellow-painted shield blazoned with thick red lines. To my good fortune, he was aiming at the duke, so he did not see me coming.

An almighty crash. Richard had struck an enemy. My Frenchman closed in, intent on reaching the duke, but instead my lance hit his shield. It was as near to a perfect strike as I ever made, punching the knight backward and out of the saddle. I was past him already, dropping my lance, which had been cracked by the force of the impact, and as I made to draw my sword, another French knight came at me. I sawed on the reins, and Liath Macha jinked to the side. The tip of my enemy's lance scraped across the face of my shield and was gone. Without a blade in my hand, I missed my chance to hack at the knight before we were pulled apart.

Out came my sword. I slowed Liath Macha, blinking away stinging sweat, and twisted my head to look around. I had not expected order, but nor had I appreciated the chaos of a cavalry fight. Horses thundered past; men yelled and screamed. From every side came the noise of lances and swords battering against shields and helmets. I recognised the duke's black stallion, and closer, the magnificent grey ridden by FitzAldelm, but could make out no other friend from foe.

Hooves pounded. My eyes swivelled. From nowhere, an enemy knight drove at me. His lance hit the top of my shield, slamming it into my chest. I reeled back in the saddle, and the lance tip skidded upward. I was lucky it did not find a home in my neck. Carried together by momentum, his destrier and Liath Macha collided. The massive difference in weight soon told. Poor Liath Macha staggered sideways, but he did not lose his footing, God be thanked. I was knee to knee with the Frenchman, and he still gripped his lance. I hammered at his head, and he met my blade with his shield, but the force of the blow split it in two. Scrabbling for his own sword, trying to fend me off with the sundered remnants of his shield, he could not stop my next thrust. I had spotted that his aventail was undone, exposing the base of his throat. A heartbeat later, he died.

'To me! To me!' Richard's voice was close.

Attacked by a Frenchman with a mace, I dared not look for the duke. In the brief bout that followed, I was lucky not to have my own shield smashed. Then, driven apart from the mace-wielder by the tide of battle, I spotted Richard off to my right. He was advancing, battering left and right with his sword, and his stallion biting at any enemy horses that came near. He had FitzAldelm with him. The French knights closest to them were falling back, and despite the presence of my enemy with the duke, I exulted.

I pricked Liath Macha, and we rode to join the fray.

There was no space on Richard's left, so I pushed in alongside FitzAldelm, who had the duke on *his* left. Many of our companions had also seen, and ridden after. We pressed the Frenchmen hard, cheering, and they flew from us. The walls of Châteauroux drew near. Deep in a swirling mass of knights and horses, it was impossible to know how our men-at-arms were faring, or if they had even attacked. We had the upper hand, I told myself. Catch the enemy knights between us and the foot soldiers, and victory would be ours. I tried not to worry about the foam flecking the corners of Liath Macha's mouth, and how his sides heaved under me.

Panicked shouts filled my ears. Disconcerted, because they came from behind me, I glanced over my shoulder. To my horror, scores of Frenchmen were riding straight at the side of our formation. As I discovered later, they had been splintered from their comrades by our first charge. Now, regrouped and led by des Barres himself, they were about to fall on us like a pack of ravening wolves.

'Sire!' I emptied my lungs into the shout.

Richard heard. Saw. Dragging his stallion to a halt and ordering us to do the same, he turned us about while the Frenchmen we had been harrying retreated beyond our reach.

'They are swarming out of the castle like rats!' FitzAldelm's voice.

The gap between our position and that of the French knights afforded us a previously denied glimpse of the battlefield. Our men-at-arms had never reached the gate, or if they had, were being beaten back from it. They had not broken, but were hard assailed. Enemy soldiers, mounted and on foot, were spilling from the entrance in an unstoppable tide. It was we who were caught now between the hammer and the anvil, not the knights we had chased.

I was at a loss. Where victory had stood, defeat and death now loomed. Fear's sharp claws tore at me, but I took courage from Richard's face, which was set and determined.

'We must withdraw, ere it is too late.' The duke cast a look at the gate, a hundred paces away, and barked a laugh. 'So near, and yet so far.'

Under the duke's command, we wheeled and rode for the open ground, away from the two bodies of Frenchmen, and parallel with the castle's walls. His intent, I realised, was to join the men-at-arms. Together we had a better chance of a fighting retreat.

Des Barres intuited Richard's purpose. Swiftly, the body of knights changed direction and thundered after us. I shouted a warning. The duke looked back, and urged his stallion to greater effort.

We were close to the men-at-arms when I could no longer deny Liath Macha's strain. Valiant heart though he was, he was not built to carry an armoured knight into battle for a prolonged period. Despite his best efforts, we were falling behind. Whether he would have carried me safely from the fray, I will never know, because his right front leg went into a rabbit hole, and he stumbled. Pitched over his head, I hit the ground with a sickening thud.

The world went black.

I came to, lying on my back, not knowing where I was. The din was incredible. Hooves pounded past, very close. Men shouted. Weapons rang. A horse leaped over me, and I flinched. Senses returning little by little, I decided that I could not have been unconscious for long. I remembered Liath Macha with a stab of horror. Gingerly, I lifted my head. He stood not a dozen paces from me, his nose touching the dirt. The shocking angle just above his right front hoof proved the leg was broken. My heart wrenched. There was not a surgeon or farrier on God's earth who could treat such a grievous injury.

The ground trembled. I threw myself down, and the sword cut that would have taken off my head parted only air. The enemy rider rode on, making no attempt to finish me off, and I remembered my companions, and the duke. When Liath Macha went down, I had been left behind. Fear gnawing my guts, I risked sitting up.

To my relief, Richard and the rest had reached the men-at-arms. Des Barres' knights had caught them, however, and a brutal mêlée was in full flow two hundred paces away. Clambering to my feet, I staggered to Liath Macha, who whickered in recognition. Sorrow overwhelmed me as I stroked his neck. There was only one solution, but I could not bring myself to do it.

Guttural shouts made me look towards the castle. Hundreds of the enemy were on the advance, the remnants of the column we had attacked and reinforcements from inside the walls. Stay, and I risked being taken captive, or more likely, slain. Poor Liath Macha would be left suffering and there was no certainty a Frenchman would end his suffering afterwards. The harsh realisation strengthened my resolve.

'Forgive me,' I whispered, drawing my dagger.

Liath Macha whinnied softly, and I cut his throat. Deep and deeper I took the blade, making sure that the great veins in his neck were cut.

Warm blood drenched my hands, and I was fleeing – like a murdering coward, my conscience screamed – even as he fell. Pausing only to snatch up my shield and sword, I aimed for the duke, clearly visible on his stallion.

I had never run from a mounted enemy before. I made the mistake of looking over my shoulder, and then, terrified, I could not stop myself from doing so every few paces. My wits still half-addled from being thrown, weighed down with half a man's body weight of armour, heart twisting with grief for Liath Macha, I hobbled towards the roiling mass of horsemen.

I never would have made it had the fighting not moved closer. At the time, my bowels churning at the thought of being trampled into the dirt, it felt like God had saved me. A moment later, surrounded by wheeling, bucking horses and riders hewing at one another, I found that I had been thrown from the frying pan into the fire. I was in mortal danger from both man and beast. Ducking and weaving, I struggled to reach the duke. Liath Macha's fate bright in my mind, I had not the heart to hamstring an enemy horse, or slide my blade into an easily presented haunch.

A Frenchman cut down at me. I took the blow on my shield, locking my knees not to fall. With a strength born of desperation, I stabbed him in the foot, my sword point punching through his mail. Screaming, he tried to pull his destrier away, out of my reach. Dropping my shield, I seized the reins and hewed at him sideways, a brutal swing that must have cracked every bone in his lower leg. Unhorsing him after that was easy. Suddenly, I had a mount. The destrier was well-trained, and let me climb astride its back even as its master lay screaming beside us.

I paid the Frenchman no more heed, but cast about, searching for the duke. He was further away than before, and making for the treeline where we had hidden what seemed so long ago. No longer concerned with fighting the enemy, I urged the destrier after him.

A mighty blow struck my shield. Turning in horror, I found Fitz-Aldelm coming at me. His grey nipped at my horse, which jinked to the side.

'I am no Frenchman,' I shouted. 'Rufus I am, squire to the duke!'

He made no answer, but through the slit in his helmet, his eyes glittered. The grey leaped forward, and FitzAldelm's right arm went back.

The whoreson knows me, I thought, and is intent on murder. Again I met his strike, but this time, I countered it with a swingeing cut that he did well to avoid. 'Desist!' I roared. 'I am also the duke's man!'

I might as well have asked Lucifer for mercy. I fought back, in my weakened state barely holding him off. The irony of my plight did not escape me. I was going to die in the shadow of Châteauroux, slain not by a Frenchman, but one of my own side.

'To the duke!' roared a voice. 'He has been thrown.'

FitzAldelm's attack checked, allowing me to see de Chauvigny riding past. It was he who had raised the alarm. 'I will help, sir,' I cried, adding quickly because of FitzAldelm, 'It is I, Rufus, the duke's squire.'

De Chauvigny dipped his chin, but gave no sign of having seen my enemy's attack. With a cry of 'To the duke!' he rode on.

Robbed, FitzAldelm could only join us as we galloped towards Richard.

He was fighting a pair of mounted knights alone. Killing one and putting the other to flight, we took the first man's horse for the duke, for of his black stallion there was no sign. Bleeding from a shallow facial wound, Richard was otherwise unharmed. 'Right glad I am to see you,' he told us. 'But you took your time.'

Even FitzAldelm laughed at that.

The duke rode to and fro, his calming influence steadying our men. Soon after, he ordered the retreat. In twos and threes, our men broke away from the French and rode for safety, led by de Chauvigny. The duke stayed behind, leading me, FitzAldelm and half a dozen others in short charges that prevented the as yet disorganised enemy from giving chase. Over and again, we were dragged into face-to-face clashes that could last for one or two blows, or twenty. Wherever the fighting was thickest, Richard was there.

In the end, des Barres let us go. We had inflicted heavy casualties on his men, but I decided that his response was a mark of respect to the duke's mad bravery. The general mood was sombre as we withdrew from the battlefield. Our own grievous losses had yet to be counted, and it was beyond fortunate that the duke had not been slain or taken. Châteauroux would stay in French hands for the foreseeable future, and the threat posed by Philippe remained considerable.

My own troubles weighed heavily on me also. Liath Macha, my faithful rouncy, who had borne me for so many years, was gone forever.

Rare though it was to bury one's horse, I would have willingly dug his grave, but with the field belonging to the enemy, that was an impossibility. Mixed with my grief was bitterness. But for de Chauvigny's unintentional arrival, FitzAldelm would have killed me, and to accuse my enemy would result in the plausible claim he had thought I was French. The destrier I had taken wore an overblanket decorated with the fleur-de-lis, symbol of the French royal family. I could say nothing.

But there had been no mistaken identity, of that I was certain.

FitzAldelm had tried to murder me.

CHAPTER XXVIII

Awakened from a bad dream about Liath Macha, I peered at the end of the tent. Through the flap, a dim light permeated. We had been on the move for so long that I had a little trouble remembering where I was. Three months had passed since my horse's death, and October had the land in its grip. Although we had been to Normandy and back, and up and down the Loire valley, we were only a few miles downstream from Châteauroux, at Châtillon-sur-Indre. Here Richard and his father were to meet Philippe in another attempt to find peace.

Knowing there would be no more rest, I climbed from my blankets and got dressed. Rhys, who slept at my feet, crosswise like a faithful hound, stirred. I whispered for him to go back to sleep, and donning a cloak, slipped outside. Dawn had arrived. The air was chill, and a heavy autumn dew coated the outside of the tent and the grass underfoot. In the nearby trees, rooks scolded and chattered quietly, preparing for the new day.

I padded to the horse lines, where I found the destrier I had taken at Châteauroux. He was grey like Liath Macha, and faithful. I called him Pommers, a French name instead of an Irish one. I had ridden him constantly since that defeat, and he had worked his way into my affections, and I into his. Pommers whickered at the sight of me, and reached out velvety lips for the apple I had in my hand. I let him have it, leaning in to stroke his nose.

I had discovered some time since that his previous owner was a first cousin of the French king. More concerned with FitzAldelm's attempt on my life, I had not dwelled on the lost opportunity, but my friends – conveniently forgetting that the battle's frantic nature had precluded the taking of captives – harped about it constantly. The ransom that had slipped between my fingers, they told me over and over, would have seen me die wealthy.

'You will do, Pommers,' I said. 'You are enough.'

He nudged at me, hoping for another apple, and I chuckled. 'I have no more, boy.' With a last pat, I checked on my second destrier, the reward promised by Richard. A deep chested bay with a white flash between his eyes, he was as stubborn as a mule. I had called him Oxhead, after the famous horse ridden by the famed Macedonian general, Alexander, and allowed a delighted Rhys to ride him.

All that I needed now was a pair of knight's spurs. If I alone had managed to save the duke when he was thrown at Châteauroux, it might have been the reward, but half a dozen of us had come to his rescue. Good things come to those who wait, I told myself.

Of more concern than a knighthood was FitzAldelm, whose friendship with Richard – and murderous intent towards me – continued. I had mentioned his attack to Rhys – but only after making him swear not to retaliate. As he glowered at me, I had emphasised that both of us would swing if FitzAldelm were murdered, and there was no point in that. One day, I said, our chance would come. Until then, we had to stay alert, and endure. I next sought the opinions of Philip, Owain and de Drune. Philip, the honest soul, wanted to go straight to the duke, while Owain favoured Rhys's choice of a dagger between the ribs one dark night. De Drune it was who thought my plan best. 'Do nothing. Watch and wait. FitzAldelm will make a fatal mistake eventually.' He had leered. 'Just stay alive until he does.'

That was how I had lived since. I rarely went anywhere alone. I kept a constant watch behind me, and slept with a blade by my hand. I partook of dishes only when others had eaten from them first. Unsurprisingly, my vigilance had started to take its toll. I was sleeping badly, and prone to irritability. Wine had become a crutch, something I reached out for more often than was healthy.

The horse at the end of the line stirred, and I grabbed my dagger hilt. Recognising the broad-shouldered figure of the duke, I relaxed.

'Rufus.' He sounded surprised.

'Sire.' I bowed.

'It is early to be tending your destriers. Does sleep evade you?'

'Yes, sire.'

'You look exhausted. What ails you?'

This was my opportunity, I thought, to tell him everything. How the younger FitzAldelm, Robert, had cruelly treated me on the voyage to Striguil and after. That his elder brother Guy had murdered my parents, and how I had slain him in self-defence down a Southampton alley. The enmity that had been rekindled with Robert FitzAldelm, and his mistreatment of Rhys. How he had tried to kill me in cold blood just a few months before.

'Rufus?' The duke's voice was concerned. 'Tell me.'

I panicked, and decided that the safest thing was to say nothing. I had no proof of Guy FitzAldelm's actions at Cairlinn, nor of Robert's attempt to murder me. The duke liked and trusted me, but I was still only a squire, and an Irishman at that. Robert FitzAldelm, in contrast, was English, a belted knight, and one of Richard's right-hand men. With his gaze heavy on me, I muttered, 'I am plagued by bad dreams, sire, of my horse. The grey which fell at Châteauroux.'

His expression softened. 'That I can understand. If Diablo were to die, I would be stricken with grief.' Diablo was his great black stallion, which had been found uninjured as we retreated that July day.

Hearing his name, Diablo nickered, and Richard's eyes grew soft. The stallion was as dear to him as a child, I had realised long since, much as Liath Macha had been to me. The duke stroked Diablo's neck, and said, 'One day we will ride together into Jerusalem.'

So much had gone on that I had given up thinking of the crusade. Hope pricked, in case Richard knew something I did not, I asked, 'Is there fresh news in that regard, sire?'

He sighed. 'No. Let us hope that the peace negotiations today go well. That would be a start.'

All of July we had marched to and fro, countering Philippe's moves against the duke. Henry had finally joined with his son, and in mid-August they had met with Philippe at Gisors. So unsuccessful was the conference that the enraged French king had hewn down the famous elm tree which marked the border and which was the traditional meeting place of kings of France and dukes of Normandy. Taking the initiative, Henry and Richard had invaded Philippe's domain soon after, and I went with them. There had been some successes, and plenty of booty, but no significant confrontation with the enemy, and no outright victory. Constrained by the need to take in the harvest and vintage, as Philippe also was, father and son had withdrawn beyond the border at the end of August. Little had happened in the month since.

'King Philippe asked for this meeting, did he not, sire?'

'He did. A good number of his nobles are unhappy that he should be warring with his fellow crusaders. They will fight against us no more, which weakens his position.'

Philippe had taken the cross not long after Richard; so too had Henry. In theory, all three would travel to Outremer to fight Saladin, a concept that still seemed destined to fail. 'Does that mean he needs peace more than you, sire?'

His eyes filled with amusement. 'I hope so, Rufus, else we shall be greybeards before we see the Holy Land.'

I smiled, and thought with a pang that reaching Outremer seemed more likely than ever returning to Cairlinn.

'There is also the small matter of who is heir to the throne,' said Richard, his tone growing serious.

'You are, sire,' I said fiercely. 'You are the eldest son, *and* the most deserving.'

He was pleased. 'Your loyalty is exemplary, Rufus. Would that I could say the same about mine own brother, the whelp.'

He meant John. Although relations between he and Richard were sour, I did not dare speak badly of the king's only other surviving son. Rumours had swept the camp of recent days, started by King Philippe it was said, of Henry naming John as his successor.

'You had brothers, is that not correct?'

'I did, sire. Two.' They were slain by men loyal to your father, I thought, the painful memories raked up again.

He gave me a sympathetic look. 'Were they younger? Older?'

'Both older, sire.'

'So you would probably never have inherited your family's lands?'

'No, sire.'

'Did you get on well?'

'We had our moments, sire, as brothers do. For the most part, however, we were friends.' In part, it had been because of the narrowness of the age gap between us. Only four years had separated us. Remembering how my father had said we were like a trio of wolf cubs from the same litter, my heart twinged.

'Would you ever have tried to seize power from either?'

'No, sire!' It was the truth.

'If you had been the eldest, and your father had named your young-est brother as heir, what would you have done?'

I stared at him aghast. It was an unpleasant idea, laden as it was with the implications of a family torn apart by rivalry. Unwilling to think evil of my dead brothers, I imagined John as my youngest sibling, and that he had been named as my father's successor. A righteous fury kindled in my breast.

'Speak your mind without fear, Rufus. I will not punish you.'

'I would seize power, sire, and take what was mine.'

He nodded.

Silence fell between us. The duke was deep in a reverie, and I was wondering if my opinion had helped him to reach a decision. When he spoke again, however, it was not of Henry or John.

'The plague took your brothers and parents, did it not?'

Christ on the cross, he remembers my lie, I thought. 'Yes, sire.'

'By rights, then, you should be lord of Cairlinn – that is its name?'

'Yes, sire, but the land was taken from us.' The truth had come out, despite my best efforts.

'By noblemen loyal to my lord father.'

'Yes, sire.' I could not look at him.

'God's legs, that is unfair.'

I wanted to shout my agreement, but I said only, 'If you say so, sire.'

'How now, Rufus. You *must* desire to be lord of your family's lands?'

I dragged my gaze up to his, and the lie died in my throat. 'I do, sire, yes.'

He clouted me on the shoulder, a blow which almost sent me stag-gering. 'Stay with me until I am king, and you shall be restored.' A pause, then he added, 'After the crusade, of course.'

'I am your man, sire,' I said, kneeling. 'As I have been since that day in the woods outside Southampton.'

He did not answer. Nervous suddenly, I looked up.

Richard stared down at me, an odd expression in his eyes. 'Fetch your sword and spurs.'

My pulse racing, wondering if I was in a dream, I obeyed.

'I should have done this a long time ago,' said the duke upon my return.

And so it was that one cold October morning in the year of our Lord 1188, my life changed forever. The ritual did not take place in a church or a great hall, but by the horselines in an army camp. There were no human witnesses, only Pommers, Diablo and their companions. I could not have cared a whit. The duke himself it was who buckled on my spurs and my belt, and gave me the colée, the open-handed slap that served as reminder of the knightly oath I took next.

Richard had made me a knight, and in return, I swore to be his liegeman until I died.

Bursting with happiness and pride, I went and woke Rhys, as well as Louis and Philip, who shared my tent. They were delighted all three, but Rhys it was who cried, and kissed my fingers. Laughing, I raised him to his feet and announced that he was now my squire. A broad grin was plastered across his face for the rest of the day. Owain shook my hand solemnly, welcoming me into the sacred brotherhood, and then he went to fetch a flagon of wine. De Drune wished me well but said little more, as was his wont at times, yet I could tell he was mightily pleased.

FitzAldelm had no idea what had happened, I hoped. When I chanced on him outside the duke's tent not an hour later, and he curled his lip at me, I could barely conceal my delight. 'Good morrow, sir,' I said.

He glanced at the massed banks of grey cloud. 'Is it?'

'I think so, sir.' He made to walk on, but I caught him by the arm. 'A moment, sir, if you will.'

He spun, eyes furious, reaching for his knife. 'Do not touch me, you Irish turd.'

My hatred of him rose up, hot and bubbling, but I said, 'It would be courteous, sir, to address me with the same manners I show you.'

His gaze narrowed; he had intuited the meaning behind my words. '*No.*'

'Yes.' God forgive me, I smirked. 'I am now a knight, like you, sir. Dubbed by the duke himself.'

Lost for words, he goggled at me.

'You are pleased, sir. Good.' I gave him a beatific smile and walked away.

That short exchange was one of the most satisfying of my life.

*

The conference got off on a bad footing. Philippe offered to return his conquests in the county of Berry – if Richard handed back to Raymond of Toulouse all his recently seized castles and territories. With far more to lose, the duke refused, but to his fury, his father agreed to the French king's suggestion. Richard protested, and soon the two were quarrelling in front of Philippe.

It was horrible to watch, and my temper frayed to see the French king watching, his fat lips twitching in amusement. The man was a schemer of the first order.

With the situation playing out to his advantage, it was odd when Philippe interrupted the disagreement to insist that Henry submit one of his local strongholds as security during the exchange of territory. The king lost his temper, and momentarily forgetting his differences with Richard, walked out of the conference with his son.

In my naïveté, I had hoped the duke and his father would be reconciled, with Philippe's actions bringing the two closer. I was wrong. Richard closeted himself with Henry and John, only to emerge, stormy-faced, and muttering that he could take no more.

As I gleaned in the days that followed, his father had been unprepared to support him against Philippe, stubbornly insisting that he should surrender the gains he had made against Count Raymond. John, who nowadays sat in on every discussion, had parrot-like repeated the king's words.

'Let my lord father surrender some of Normandy to Philippe, and the talks can continue,' Richard thundered.

That option was not on the table, however, and the conference broke up.

Less than a sennight later, we rode to meet the French king at Bourges, in the county of Berry, and there, in a heartfelt effort to break the deadlock, Richard offered to submit his quarrel with Raymond of Toulouse to the court in Paris. He would abide by their ruling, even if it meant returning all the territories he had gained during the spring and summer. Delighted to be recognised as the duke's overlord, Philippe agreed.

The news left Henry stricken by a fit of apoplexy that left him bedridden for several days. When he heard, Richard did not seem to care. The relationship between father and son had broken down, and when the king sent his rejection of the proposal, a new friendship had already sprung up between Richard and Philippe.

As October ran into November, letters between the two grew more frequent; those from Henry to Richard ebbed to a trickle. The duke did not reply to his father at all. He spent hours with his captains, and his scribes penned dozens of messages to his liegemen throughout Aquitaine.

I thought often of the conversation we had had by the horselines, and decided that Richard was set on becoming king, no matter what path he had to take.

I would be with him every step of the way.

And one day, Cairlinn would be mine again.

CHAPTER XXIX

I pulled my cloak tighter, frustrated by the ease with which the biting November wind stole in to find exposed flesh. It was a northerly, sweeping down from the Narrow Sea and across Normandy, where I found myself. The duke was just in front, in expansive conversation with Philippe. A twelvemonth before, it would have seemed odd to have been in the company of the French king, riding west towards Henry's territory, but the world had changed.

A month and a half had passed since the abortive conference at Châtillon-sur-Indre, and this time Richard had made the attempt to broker peace. In a concession to his ailing father, we were to gather at Bonsmoulins, close to the border between Normandy and France. Before that, however, we had ridden to meet Philippe. He and the duke would arrive together, a show of unity that would deliver a hammer blow to Henry's confidence.

I shot a glance over my shoulder. Rhys was behind on Oxhead, miserably hunched over in the saddle with his head down. Philip, the tip of his nose bright red, sneezed, and gave me a watery-eyed nod. Owain offered me his costrel. I shook my head, no. Of de Chauvigny and de Drune there was no sign: Richard had sent them ahead with the scouts, to ensure no ambush had been laid. Thankfully, FitzAldelm was also absent. He had taken a message to Henry a day earlier, and had not yet returned.

'When the time is ripe, I shall again offer to exchange the territories we have each taken,' said Philippe. 'Those in Berry for the ones you have taken from the Count of Toulouse.'

'And I shall refuse, naturally. The revenues from the Quercy total almost a thousand marks per year. I receive a fraction of that from my liegemen in Berry.' Despite his rebuttal, Richard did not sound in the least annoyed.

I pricked my ears. The two were deciding their strategy against Henry.

'A new offer might change your mind,' said Philippe. 'You may keep the lands seized from Count Raymond; I shall also return the castles and strongholds in Berry. The proviso shall be that you and my sister Alys will wed without delay, and for your lord father's barons to swear fealty to you as his heir.'

'That is an offer I would gladly accept,' said Richard.

No mention was made of the duke's long avoidance of marrying Alys. The sands of political and familial alliances could shift at will, I thought. On many occasions over the previous decade, these men had been at odds, but now their paths had aligned to the point of becoming kinsmen.

There was sense in the proposal for both men. Allied to Philippe by marriage and recognised as Henry's successor, the duke would secure not just lasting peace, but his own future and the freedom to leave for the Holy Land. Achieving similar ends for himself, Philippe would also ensure that the quarrel between Henry and Richard continued.

'John will not favour your offer, the whelp, but my lord father might see sense.' There was a wistful note in Richard's voice. 'Of his two sons, I am the only one suited to kingship. Despite his blinding love for John, he *must* see that.'

Even now, part of him still wants to be reconciled with Henry, I decided.

'I hope he does, but I am worried,' said Philippe solicitously. 'Why has John not taken the cross as you and your lord father have? As I have? The logical explanation is that Henry intends to make John his successor, and leave him behind to guard the realm when he joins us on crusade.'

Richard made no answer, but his back stiffened.

Whether the rumour was true, I was not sure, but Philippe had stabbed to the heart of the problem. Châteauroux and the other castles in Berry did not matter to the duke. Nor did the Quercy and its thousand marks. Even the Crusade paled into insignificance beside the fact that five years after the Young King's death, he had still not been named as his father's heir.

It was all he cared about.

Remembering Philippe's glee when the duke and Henry had quarrelled at Châtillon, I hoped Richard's burning desire did not make him blind to treachery.

I said as much to de Drune later, for he had a wise head on his shoulders. The man-at-arms snorted, and when I looked at him in confusion, said, 'The duke did not come down with the last rain shower, Rufus. Philippe is playing a game, sure, but so too is our master. The day he marries Alys will be the day I am beatified.' He steepled his hands as if about to pray.

I laughed. There was little else to do, and, I told myself, Richard knew what he was doing.

FitzAldelm had not rejoined us by the time we reached Bonsmoulins. The duke remarked on his absence at one point, but then, absorbed with the impending negotiations, did not mention it again. I gave the matter no further thought either as we rode on through worsening weather. The bells were tolling sext as, cold and wet, we reached the abbey where the conference was to take place. The area outside was full of horses and men; Henry and his entourage had already arrived.

FitzAldelm appeared, making loud apology to the duke. A fever had taken him the previous day, he explained, and the monk physician who had examined him had deemed it unwise to travel. He was much recovered now. Richard waved a dismissive hand, and enquired if there had been any reply to the letter FitzAldelm had borne to his father. My enemy shook his head regretfully, and the conversation moved on to the meeting itself.

I swung down from Pommers, intent on visiting the chapterhouse, where the two sides would meet. De Chauvigny, Owain and I had discussed it during the ride. Although a truce held, we did not trust Henry. The unfriendly stares bearing down on us since our arrival reinforced my desire to see the battlefield, as it were, in advance of any fighting.

A door closed, and I turned my head. Surprise filled me. Out of what I had taken to be the abbey's infirmary came none other than John, Richard's brother. It was the self-same doorway that FitzAldelm had emerged from a few moments earlier. There was no question of John also being ill. He looked as healthy as a trout, smug as a cat by a fire on a winter's night, and totally unsurprised by our arrival.

FitzAldelm and he had been talking, I decided, unease prickling my scalp. Summoned by the duke, I laid the idea aside before I could give it the consideration it deserved.

Of Henry there was no sign. We soon heard that he was unwell, and had come to Bonsmoulins in a litter, not astride a horse as a king should. He *would* be at the meeting, his messenger insisted.

'Let it be at the hour of none,' said the duke, showing no concern for his father. 'By then I shall be warm again, and dry, and had time to fill my belly.'

Philippe agreed, and the messenger bowed and departed.

Welcomed by the rotund abbot, who blessed both Richard and the French king, a group of us were taken by the cellarer to the west range, where the guest quarters were. As the duke was shown to his chamber, it was impossible to ignore the two knights guarding the entrance to the next room along the corridor. Disquietingly, it seemed this was where Henry had retired after his arrival. The monks understood nothing of what was at stake, I thought. Posting Owain and another knight on the door, I entered with the duke. A hacking cough carried through the walls, and Richard frowned.

'He really is ill.'

I nodded.

'Old fool. I hope his wits have not left him, even if his health has.' Years of quarrelling had seen the duke's attitude to his father harden to the point of callousness. I had a word with Philip as he set out fresh clothes for our master, and then joined Owain and his companion in the corridor.

Both looked furious. 'They are passing comments,' Owain whispered, with a roll of his eyes at Henry's knights.

'What kind?'

'They say the duke is a traitor.' Owain hesitated. 'That he and Philippe share more than a bed.'

My younger self would have drawn his sword and demanded an immediate apology, but the conference took precedence over name-calling. I snuffed out my anger, but before I left to investigate the chapterhouse, I needed to be sure that blood would not flow. I sauntered towards the pair, my hands nowhere near my sword hilt.

Even so, they both gripped their weapons. 'Come no further,' one warned.

'Does your lord the king know what you have been saying about his eldest son?' I asked. The dismay in their faces was instantaneous, and I continued, 'I shall see he hears it from the duke himself. Unless . . .' I let the word hang, watching them glance at one another, '. . . you stitch your flapping lips shut.'

Shamed, they muttered agreement.

Grinning, I walked back to Owain, who said, 'That was neatly done.'

Led by the abbot, Philippe and Richard stalked into the chapterhouse as the abbey bells rang none. A dozen knights in full mail accompanied each man. I was in Richard's party with Owain, de Chauvigny and eight others; FitzAldelm, curse him, was the twelfth. When the abbot, his face concerned, had queried the number of knights, no one answered. Perhaps realising for the first time the hag-ridden mistrust between the two sides, he wisely said no more.

Of Henry and his retinue there was no sign, but that did not stop my gaze from raking the chapterhouse again. Light spilled into the grand, rectangular chamber from high-positioned windows to left and right. Dominated by a central column and vaulted roof, the chapterhouse's walls were richly painted with biblical scene frescoes. Stone benches ran along the sides; here the monks sat for their daily gatherings and important meetings. A stepped dais at the far end had a triad of cushioned stools for the abbot, prior and dean.

The abbot gestured at the seats, two of which were arranged side by side on the lower level of the dais, and the last, the most richly wrought, positioned on the higher. 'You are welcome to use these, messires.' He cleared his throat. 'You must decide between you who sits where.'

Richard nodded his thanks. 'My lord father shall not have your stool, Father Abbot. I will not sit in it either, while it is raised up.' This was said with a courteous dip of his chin at Philippe.

'I will not be above you either,' replied Philippe.

'Let it be placed alongside the others,' said Richard with a mischievous look.

The abbot, discomfited, muttered that he had no objection. At once Owain and another knight lifted the heavy stool onto the lower level. Then, with their companions, they took up places to the left of the dais, separate from the French knights, but close to each other. Henry's followers would be outnumbered two to one.

A loud announcement came from the entrance, that entering was King Henry Fitzempress, of England, and with him, John, Lord of Ireland.

And so it begins, I thought, as Richard's mien became a mask. Philippe, in contrast, assumed a pleasant expression.

The stoop-shouldered king approached, the agreed dozen knights at his back. John paced beside him, languid and affected. His bastard son Geoffrey was also there. Rather than walk, Henry limped and shuffled, and not until the dais did he raise his head. The change since I had last seen him was shocking. He had become an old man. His jowls sagged; broken veins patterned his cheeks; deep pouches were carved below his rheumy eyes. Henry's gaze was still sharp, however. It went first to the duke, and after to Philippe. He seemed about to speak, but doubled over instead into a paroxysm of coughing.

With a long-suffering look, John lent the king a supporting arm. Geoffrey, his face more caring, also helped.

Richard made no visible reaction, but behind his back, one hand held the other in a white-knuckled grip. No matter how late the hour, I thought, it pains him to see his father so, and his youngest brother the leech.

At last Henry straightened. 'You are here.'

'*You* are late, sire,' said Richard.

John scowled. 'That is fine greeting to give your lord father and liege lord.'

The duke gave him a withering look. 'Still clinging to his hem, I see.'

Before John could reply, Philippe bowed to Henry. 'Welcome, sire.'

Henry's grimace might have been an attempt to smile – it was hard to be sure. With a grunt of effort, and John's help, he climbed onto the dais.

Richard and Philippe moved to stand behind the stool nearest to their men, and the one next to it, that of the abbot.

'The third seat is for me, I assume?' asked Henry, adding waspishly, 'Who is to sit on the abbot's?'

With a grand gesture, the duke offered it to Philippe, who made a show of refusing. After a second suggestion, he accepted, his alacrity a clear implication that he regarded himself the most important of the three. Henry scowled, but Richard did not react. He waited until his father was seated and then did the same. John, clearly furious that no stool had been provided for him, had to make do with the stone bench nearest the dais. Geoffrey joined him.

The abbot, who had been hovering anxiously, welcomed all four men to the abbey. Leading them in prayer, he asked God to help find a path to peace and concord. I doubted the efforts of every monk in the abbey would make much difference. The atmosphere had grown hostile since Henry and John's arrival. Our knights and Philippe's were glaring across the room at Henry's, who reciprocated their looks with equal venom.

'Let us to it, messires,' said Richard in a bluff tone.

Henry nodded. Philippe smiled.

'I am here to reclaim the castles in Berry – of which there are many – which have fallen into French hands.' The duke glanced at Philippe.

Henry said, 'That is also *my* purpose, but more important is that we should achieve a lasting peace. Constant war profits no one, save the devil.'

John's lips twitched. 'And the Brabançons.'

'If you have nothing useful to add, stay silent,' Richard snapped.

His face petulant as a slapped child's, John subsided.

'My purpose is first to retrieve the swathes of territory lost by Raymond of Toulouse.' Said Philippe.

Civilly enough, they began to bandy about the names of castles and strongholds in Berry and the county of Toulouse. An hour it lasted, without agreement. A second hour dragged by, and cracks started to appear. Henry raised his voice first. It was Philippe's turn next. Richard held his temper longest, but in the end even he was throwing barbed comments at his father and John.

The abbot intervened, briefly restoring the peace, but soon Henry was shouting at Philippe, accusing him of filling Richard's ears with lies. The duke responded, telling his father that the French king was a dear friend, who treated those close to him well – unlike Henry, who cared nothing for his own flesh and blood.

Philippe joined in, telling a spluttering Henry that he was no kind of father, that he never had been. 'Why else would your wife and three of your sons have risen up against you on so many occasions?' Philippe cried. His gaze moved to John. 'The one who has not remains loyal only to cozen what he can from you before the end.'

'You go too far, sire!' Henry was purple with rage.

Philippe shrugged. 'He speaks the truth,' said Richard.

John looked as spiteful as a cat deprived of a mouse, but he had either the wisdom not to join in, or not enough valour. I decided it was the latter.

'This is an outrage!' shouted Henry.

The pair of knights who had been in the corridor, hotheads, reached for their swords. FitzAldelm and a man beside him did the same, along with several of Philippe's knights. In the blink of an eye, Owain and I were two of only a handful who had not half-drawn their blades.

The abbot stepped onto the dais. 'This is a chapterhouse, messires, not a battlefield.' His voice quavered, but it was resolute.

Again Henry was consumed by a prolonged bout of coughing. No one was willing to start a fight with the king so unwell, and the enforced pause that followed allowed blood to cool and tempers to abate.

When Henry had regained his composure, if not his dignity, Philippe returned to his original suggestion of exchanging conquests. With an angry cry, Richard refused, mentioning the thousand marks income he had talked of during our ride to Bonsmoulins. If I had not witnessed their rehearsal, I would have believed the charade, and Henry's frustrated expression gave no impression that he suspected. Back and forth the argument went for some time, as it had before.

Philippe fell silent, as if deep in thought, and after a pause declared he would return the gains he had made in the previous year. Richard could also keep his acquisitions in the county of Toulouse. All this, he said, if Henry would marry his eldest son to Alys. It was, Philippe went on, a wedding long overdue.

I glanced at Henry. He did not look best pleased, but nor had he lost his temper again. I began to wonder if an agreement was possible.

Then Philippe added his final condition, that Henry's barons, in England and his continental dominions, should pay fealty to Richard as his heir. With a little smile at the duke, Philippe turned to Henry.

All eyes followed his.

The abbey bells rang vespers. Three hours had flown by.

'Sire?' Philippe asked.

'No.' Henry spat the word out.

'He is your eldest-born son, sire.'

'I need no reminding who he is!'

'He has been betrothed to my sister Alys these twenty years. He is your rightful heir.'

Both these statements were true, but Henry muttered, 'No. No. No!'

Philippe glanced at Richard, who shook his head as if to say, I knew this would be his answer.

The French king tried again. 'Come, sire, will you not think on it?'

'I will not act under pressure of this kind.' Henry's wrinkled fists thumped the arms of his stool. 'I will not be blackmailed!'

'That is not my intent, Papa,' said Richard.

'No?' Henry's face was ugly with anger.

'I ask only for what is mine by right. That I should be declared your lawful heir.'

John's mouth worked. His plump hand rose in protest.

Hard as stone, Richard's blue eyes bore down on him.

John's hand fell to his side again.

Henry was silent.

'Well, sire?' asked Richard. 'How will you answer?'

There came no reply, and my heart twisted for the duke, to be rejected so vilely.

'I will not beg,' Richard grated.

Again Henry did not answer.

'Then I have no choice but to believe the impossible to be true.' Unbuckling his belt, the duke knelt before Philippe and laid his scabbarded sword on the floor between them. Placing his hands between those of the French king, Richard paid him homage for all the continental dominions of the house of Anjou, from Normandy to Aquitaine. Finally, he swore allegiance to Philippe against all men save the fealty he owed his father Henry.

Philippe accepted Richard's homage with a broad smile.

'Lastly, sire, I beseech your aid,' the duke continued, 'should I be deprived of my rights as my lord father's heir.'

'Willingly shall I do so,' Philippe replied.

This was perhaps the deepest cut, I decided. Unless Henry agreed to Richard's demand on the instant, he faced a war against the combined armies of his eldest son and the French king.

Henry said nothing. He sat, looking utterly stunned, bewildered – lost.

He made no further contribution, other than to nod his agreement when a two-month truce was suggested. A table and stool were fetched, and a monk came to write out the peace treaty. The stilted silence was broken only by the scratch of quill on vellum and Henry's rasps.

Father and son did not speak a word to each other throughout.

When the meeting drew to a close, they did not even say farewell.

CHAPTER XXX

The sun was almost on the western horizon, its dying light tingeing the deep-lying snow orange. Rooks swooped and chattered, settling to their nests in the tallest trees. Marshal, who had been out hawking, came riding back to the king's castle at Saumur in fine humour. Between them the falcons had caught only a hare, yet his enjoyment had been none the less. To hunt with a friend on a crisp winter's day, he thought, was as fine a thing as a man could ask for.

The walls of Saumur hove into view, half a mile distant, and he felt the weight of responsibility bearing down again. Simple pleasures were not the only reason he had ridden out at first light.

'Once more into the fray, eh?' said Baldwin de Béthune. One of the Young King's most trusted friends, he had taken service with Henry. Also an old comrade of Marshal, he had welcomed him back from Outremer with open arms.

'You sense my mood,' said Marshal.

'Mine own is the same. Heaven be thanked that Christmas is over, and the New Year begun. I could not bear another Yuletide feast like the one just past.'

Marshal laughed. 'God's teeth, but it was dreary!'

They rode on.

Remembering the Christmas at Caen in 1182, when a thousand knights had been in attendance, Marshal decided the contrast with this festive period could not have been starker. For company, Henry had only him, Béthune, and a handful of others from his mesnie. Perhaps two score retainers attended them. Their small number had been lost in the vastness of the castle. By rights the place should have been full, but the barons and nobles invited by Henry had sent excuses and stayed away. The message behind their absence was plain: the balance of power had shifted towards Richard and Philippe. The king's mood, already low, had sunk further. Old and tired, he had rarely come out of his private chambers, and since falling ill on New Year's Day, had been confined to bed.

Seeking a topic that would not drag their mood into the frozen mud, Marshal said, 'Tell me again about the heiress of Châteauroux.'

De Béthune's eyes lit up.

Of vital strategic importance given its proximity to the border with France, and encompassing a large, wealthy area, the lordship of Châteauroux was an enviable prize. It was made even more so by the young lady in question, who was pretty and well-mannered. De Béthune had been pursuing her for six months, mostly by letter.

After an account of what seemed every message, he drew breath.

'I wish you luck,' said Marshal. 'You deserve this match.'

De Béthune cast a keen look at Marshal. 'And what of the lady Heloise of Kendal?'

'I am not minded to marry her. You know that. She is not comely.'

'Since when has that stopped a man making the right match? My gut tells me that rather than seeking greater beauty, you have set your sights on greater position.'

'You know me well,' admitted Marshal with a rueful nod. 'Truth be told, I want more than Heloise can offer. A decade and a half I have spent in loyal service to the house of Anjou, and all I have to show for it is Cartmel. Why should I not receive greater reward than Kendal?'

'Have you someone in mind?'

'Yes.' Marshal's ears picked out the distinctive sound of galloping hoofs. He stared towards Saumur, but could see nothing.

'Who?'

'Isabelle de Clare.'

'Her estates are not as valuable as those of Châteauroux,' de Béthune joked.

'They are large, and *not* on the French border,' said Marshal quick as a flash. 'The Welsh are also less troublesome than Philippe.'

De Béthune smiled in agreement. 'Her mother is feisty. The girl may be too.'

'I have heard she is. All the better.' Marshal did not like coquetry and fluttering eyelashes.

'Let us hope the king's humour returns with his health, that he may grant us both what we desire,' said de Béthune.

'I will drink to that,' said Marshal, lifting the costrel that hung from a leather loop around his saddle pommel. Pulling its stopper, he drank a mouthful and passed the skin to de Béthune. His friend drank, and saluted him.

This time, the sound of hooves could not be denied.

'Do you hear?' Marshal put a hand to his eyes and squinted. Dusk was falling hard and fast now, blurring the landscape.

'There.' De Béthune pointed.

The rider was on the main road, which led to, among other places, Paris.

Marshal could feel his good mood evaporating. 'A messenger from Richard or Philippe, do you think?'

De Béthune took another pull from the costrel, and said dourly, 'Like as not.'

'I need another drink,' said Marshal. 'Give it here.'

Marshal's new squire, Jean d'Earley, was waiting as they clattered into the bailey. A thin, nervous type, he had been entrusted to Marshal by Henry himself. Taking the reins Marshal tossed at him, Jean said, 'Th-the king orders you both a-attend him, sir.'

He dismounted. 'Now?'

Jean looked abashed. 'Y-yes, sir.'

Marshal turned to de Béthune. 'The news cannot be good.'

'I fear you are right, my friend.' Leaving his horse in the care of his own squire, de Béthune walked with Marshal to the wooden staircase that led to the great hall.

They found Henry propped up in his curtained bed, still attended by the cowed-looking messenger. A chamber pot stood close at hand, and two servants hovered unobtrusively by the door. Waves of heat radiated from the blazing fire. A cloying smell of incense hung in the fuggy air. Thick quilts covered the king's lower half, and a fur coverlet was draped around his shoulders. Red blotches marked his cheeks, and his eyes were closed. Wheezes and rasps accompanied every breath.

Marshal and de Béthune approached. 'Sire.'

Henry blinked, focused. 'What took you so long?' His voice was querulous.

'We came the instant your summons reached us, sire,' said Marshal.

'I have had word from Richard.' Henry coughed, a wet phlegmy sound. He glowered at the messenger, who stared at his muddied shoes.

'Is it good news, sire?' asked de Béthune. The truce agreed at Bonsmoulins was almost over, and the three parties had agreed to meet again. Too ill to travel, the king had requested a delay until he had recovered.

'It is not. I am a liar, says my son. Philippe agrees with him.' Henry brandished the letter which had been lying in his lap. 'They will recommence hostilities the day after the truce ends.'

Marshal and de Béthune exchanged a dismayed look. Neither had expected this. The forces available to the king were small in number, and given the barons' refusal to spend Christmas with Henry, unlikely to increase.

'Another messenger arrived earlier, when you were not here,' said the king to Marshal. 'Where were you?'

'I went hawking, sire, with de Béthune. We came to see you this morning, and you wished us good fortune,' said Marshal, worried now not just about the king's health, but his state of mind.

'He came from Brittany, from a minor baron who yet remains loyal.' Henry's eyes grew bright for the first time, with anger. 'Rebellion threatens, apparently. As in Aquitaine, the nobles seek to assert their independence.'

The great stag weakens, thought Marshal. Wolves gather. Soon a circle will form, out of which there is no escape. It was hard not to think that refusing Henry's offer before his own departure to Outremer would have been a wiser choice than to accept. When the king was defeated, Marshal's fortunes would plummet. He shoved the notion away. Oaths had been taken, and he would not break them. His fate was bound to the king's, for good or ill. All the more reason to seek Henry's permission for a match with Isabelle de Clare, he thought. 'That is unfortunate, sire. Can you negotiate with the Bretons?'

'Why should I?' cried Henry, adding in a furious mutter, 'I am their rightful lord.'

'No one is questioning that, sire,' said Marshal. 'But their unhappiness and the letter in your hand raise the concern of a war on two fronts.'

'That, sire, is a conflict you could not win,' added de Béthune gently.

Henry's suspicious gaze darted from Marshal to de Béthune and back.

'You do not have soldiers to send to Brittany as well as against Philippe and Richard, sire,' said Marshal, thinking, you barely have enough to do the latter.

'I will order the barons to raise a levy,' the king retorted.

'They did not come here for Christmas, sire,' said de Béthune. 'I doubt many will send you troops.'

Henry glared at them both. 'Have you lost the stomach for a fight? There is no place in my mesnie for fainthearts.'

Marshal drew his sword and bowing, held it out to the king. 'This blade is yours, sire, as is my loyalty. But say the word and I will ride, alone if needs be, against any enemy you name.'

'He will not be alone, sire. I shall go with him.' De Béthune jutted his chin.

Henry's distrust eased. He sank back on his pillows, looking drained, and closed his eyes. 'Yes, yes, all right. There is no need for such grandiosity.'

Marshal tried again. 'Regarding the Bretons, sire . . .'

'I will not deal with traitors! Those nobles in Brittany who remain loyal must deal with the problem as best they may.' The king waved a veined hand. 'See to it that the clerk sends word to that effect.'

'Of course, sire,' said Marshal. 'What of the duke and Philippe?'

'I will dictate a letter to my son.'

Unless you acknowledge him as heir, he will ignore its contents, as he has the last one, and the many that went before it, thought Marshal. A blind man can see that. He should have been named as your successor years ago. 'Sire, the duke—'

'*You* will carry it to him in Paris, Marshal. He is visiting Philippe there.' The king's eyes remained shut. His voice was quiet. Calm. 'That matters not. He will listen to the greatest knight.'

It was high praise, but Marshal remembered Richard's determination and fury at Bonsmoulins, and decided, my being the messenger will make no difference at all. God himself could not change that man's mind. He looked at de Béthune, who gave a helpless shrug.

'Do you hear me, Marshal?' said the king.

'I do, sire. Your will is my command. I shall bear your letter to the duke, and speak to him as you wish.'

'He must abandon his alliance with Philippe, and return to my side. Together we will bring the Capet upstart to heel.'

As your heir, Richard would do that willingly, thought Marshal. Again he glanced at de Béthune, and mouthed, I *must* mention the succession. To his relief, his friend nodded. Steeling his resolve, Marshal said, 'I would never presume to know your mind, sire, but through this difficult time, you have never spoken of John as heir. Some might suppose this is because you *do* mean to name Richard when the moment is right. If that is the case, sire, I would urge you to do it now. I believe that path is the only way to avoid further conflict.'

Rage filled Henry's face.

The door opened, and someone entered. Aware that by questioning the king's actions, his own fate hung in the balance, Marshal paid the newcomer no heed.

'And if that is not my intention?' Henry's voice was sibilant with menace. 'If I wish John to succeed me?'

'Why, then, sire, I will support him.' Although Marshal was telling the truth, he felt a fresh stab of regret to have so willingly taken service with Henry. If John became king, Richard would fight him for the crown, and he would win. The aftermath would see Marshal's fortunes suffer badly.

'Am I to be king after you, sire?' asked a voice.

Startled – it was John who had come into the room – Marshal turned. He bowed. 'Sire.' Beside him, de Béthune muttered the same.

John made no acknowledgement, but shoved past, to his father's side. He was clad in a dark green tunic, embroidered at the cuff and neck with gold thread. His hose was of a lighter green, his boots shiny and new. A belt of gilded leather circled his waist; from it hung an ornate, sheathed dagger.

He looked like a fat merchant, Marshal decided, not a prince.

'Papa?' said John.

Henry softened at once. 'My son. I have missed you.'

'And I you, sire.' John took his father's right hand and kissed it. 'I heard you talking as I entered. There was mention of my becoming your heir.' His voice was light, but there was no mistaking the naked desire within it.

'I have not made my decision,' said Henry.

Fury sparked in John's eyes, but he forced a smile. 'When will you, sire?'

'It ruined Hal to be named heir so early. I will not do the same again.' There was a note of sorrow in Henry's voice.

Christ on the cross, thought Marshal, if he waits much longer, the decision will be taken from him, and we shall all be damned. To speak, however, risked angering the king – and alienating John, who might yet become his liege lord – so Marshal kept his mouth firmly shut.

'I would speak with my son. Leave us,' Henry ordered. 'The letter will be with you by nightfall, Marshal. You will depart in the morning.'

'Yes, sire.' He and de Béthune bowed to both men and made for the door.

'*Another* letter to Richard?' John's voice was spiteful.

'Try not to be so jealous,' said Henry. 'I need him by my side as well.'

John's reply was indiscernible, but his tone was unhappy.

'I trust him less than a mad dog,' Marshal whispered to de Béthune.

His friend's nod of agreement was grim.

Footsteps behind them. 'Marshal, a word?'

His stomach did a neat somersault. Could John have heard? He turned, and was heartily relieved to see no trace of suspicion in John's pudgy features. 'Sire?'

'You ride to my brother on the morrow.'

'Yes, sire. Your lord father the king has commanded me to bear him a letter.'

'Remember me to Richard. Tell him he is dear to me, and I hope we may see each other soon.' John's snake eyes fixed Marshal's.

'I will, sire.' He cozens Henry and Richard at the same time, thought Marshal. He is a losenger and a paltoner both, a deceiver and a traitor.

'See that you do.' John turned on his heel and re-entered his father's bedchamber without another word.

Marshal looked at de Béthune. 'Let us hope that one never becomes king.'

His friend's answering grimace spoke volumes.

A sennight passed, one of enduring cold and long hours in the saddle. Reaching the French royal court in Paris, Marshal made himself known to the guards. After a captain was summoned, he was allowed to enter. His exhausted horse was led away to the stables, and he was guided to the great hall. The captain who dealt with him, also a knight, was courteous, but there was no friendliness in his manner. The veiled hostility was no coincidence. Before entering Philippe's hall, Marshal was forced to surrender his sword and dagger. Although furious, he made no protest.

Feeling like Daniel entering the lion's den, he followed the captain through the iron-studded doors. In complete contrast to the solar at Saumur, which had lain empty for most of the festive period, Philippe's great hall was thronged with noblemen and women. The hum of conversation mixed with the music of lute and harp. Surrounded by a circle of laughing onlookers, two jesters capered about, one pretending to beat the other. Each kick to his fellow's rear was accompanied by a loud noise from his bladder-slapstick, and a fresh burst of hilarity from the audience.

No one paid Marshal any heed, and his disquiet eased as they wove a path towards the end of the hall. There, under a pair of banners, one deep blue and emblazoned with golden fleur-de-lis, the other red as blood and marked with the Angevin lions, he found Philippe and Richard seated side by side on a dais. Their heads were bent together in discussion, so neither saw him approach.

Marshal's hope, that their friendship might have soured, faded. He composed himself as the knight climbed onto the dais and announced his name.

Philippe's head turned first, but he did not speak.

Hoping the duke's reaction would be more favourable, Marshal knelt.

'God's legs!' cried Richard. 'Marshal?'

'It is I, sire.' He raised his head, and although his face remained impassive, his concern redoubled. The duke's expression was stony.

'You come from my lord father?'

'Yes, sire.'

'You serve him yet then.'

'I do, sire. I am his man unto death.'

'His death,' said the duke, adding the menace, 'or yours?'

'Whichever comes first, sire,' said Marshal, resolute despite his chilly reception.

Richard's eyes were appraising. 'It is true what they say about your loyalty.'

'My word is my bond, sire. Without it I would be nothing.'

'You bear a message, I assume?'

'Indeed, sire.' He fumbled with his purse, and held up the letter.

A gesture from Richard, and the knight who had escorted Marshal took it to him.

By now, those nearby had realised something important was going on. A hush fell; the skin on the back of Marshal's neck prickled as many pairs of eyes bore down on it.

Philippe watched as the duke read the letter. As Richard laid it in his lap, he broke the silence. 'Well?'

'He offers nothing new. I am to abandon your company, and return to his side that we might be reconciled. Only then can the threat posed to his kingdom by you be addressed.' Richard's lips twitched. 'There is no mention of who will be heir, or of your sister Alys.'

'It is the same letter he has sent a dozen times.' Philippe's lips twitched. 'I have to commend your lord father's perseverance.'

Richard snorted.

The task set him by Henry had about as much chance of success as a single knight winning a team tourney, Marshal decided, but he had to discharge his duty. Catching the duke's attention, he said, 'Your lord father misses you sorely, sire.' Henry had not uttered these words, but they were the truth, thought Marshal. Encouraged by what he hoped was a trace of sadness in Richard's eyes, he went on, 'Might I speak with you alone?'

'You may not.'

Marshal cursed inwardly. He had two choices, each as unappealing as the other. Give up and return to Henry, or plead the king's part as he had been ordered – in public.

'Have you anything further to say?' demanded Richard.

Marshal rolled his tongue around a dry mouth, and said, before he could stop himself, 'Sire, the French king is not your friend.'

'Is that so?' asked Philippe, his voice icy. 'Yet here Duke Richard sits as guest of honour, treated with the same love and courtesy as if he were my own flesh and blood.'

Marshal kept his gaze fixed on the duke. 'Philippe seeks only to divide the house of Anjou, sire. The dissent he has sown benefits him, not you or your family. It threatens your lord father's realm as no other danger has these many years.'

'Lies,' said Philippe, his cheeks growing pink. 'All lies.'

I speak the truth, thought Marshal, praying that Richard saw what he did – fear – in the French king's face.

'I will not be accused like this in my own court!' cried Philippe. He signalled to his men-at-arms, who stepped towards Marshal.

'Spare the messenger, sire,' said Richard.

Philippe nodded stiffly. 'As long as he holds his tongue forthwith.'

'I will say no more,' said Marshal.

A wave of Philippe's hand saw the men-at-arms retreat to their positions.

'My lord father is old and confused,' said the duke. 'Philippe is my friend, and has proven himself so many times.'

The French king's smile was possessive, and predatory.

Despite his promise to stay silent, Marshal did not want to give up. 'Sire—'

Richard cut him off. 'Tell me, did the king speak to you of his heir, of who will succeed him?'

Defeated, Marshal replied, 'He did not, sire.'

A bitter laugh. 'In that case, you have had a wasted journey, Marshal.'

'Will you make any reply, sire?'

Another laugh. 'I will not. Return to him with nothing.'

With a heavy heart, Marshal bowed.

Henry's fate was sealed.

CHAPTER XXXI

Emerging from the forest at the head of the column, I stared at the castle of Montfort through the clear summer air. I had never seen it before, yet it lay only a few miles from the larger one at La Ferté-Bernard in Maine, where I had attended the duke's recent Whitsun conference with King Henry. My memories of that meeting were unpleasant. Despite the presence of a papal legate, sent to salvage the crusade, and no less than four archbishops, it had been a miserable failure, laced with acrimony and accusations. There had been confrontations with the king's retainers too; bloodshed had been narrowly avoided. FitzAldelm had been at the heart of it all. Frustratingly, Richard believed his lies that Henry's men had started the quarrel. At least, I told myself, I had not been blamed this time.

After the failed conference, and the duke's excommunication by the infuriated papal legate, the king had travelled from La Ferté-Bernard to the nearby town of Le Mans. Rather than return to their respective territories, Richard and Philippe had launched an immediate attack into Maine. The duke was no longer prepared to wait for his father to change his mind. La Ferté-Bernard had fallen to our surprise assault, and we travelled to the next castle, Montfort.

The offensive was set to continue.

A signal from the duke, and we resumed our advance. The army was not over large – a hundred and fifty knights, twice that number of men-at-arms, and almost six hundred archers – but was sufficiently big to besiege poorly garrisoned castles. When combined with Philippe's two thousand troops, it was doubly so. It also outnumbered the forces available to Henry by a considerable margin.

The village surrounding Montfort appeared no different to a host of others I had seen on this side of the Narrow Sea. Miserable one-roomed, wattle and daub hovels lined the road. Snot-nosed children in rags stared from doorways, or ran alongside our horses, their grimy paws held out. We smiled, and threw them the hunks of bread given to us for just this purpose. To the adults who watched, we called out polite greetings. Mindful of the peasantry's terror of armies, Richard had given strict orders to show his troops came in peace.

At the centre of the village was a green, upon which a flock of sheep grazed. The boy guarding them took one look at our column, and whistled to his dog. In no time he was shepherding his charges off down a muddy lane, away from what he saw as men who would eat the lot.

A squat church with a small bell tower stood opposite the tithe barn, behind which ran a stream. Smoke rose in a trickle from the forge. The tantalising aroma of baking bread reached my nose, and my belly rumbled. At the end of the main street loomed the castle, our destination. The gate was closed, and I could see men's heads atop the battlements, watching us. It was not a massive stronghold like Caen, but the stone-built wall and the ditch were imposing, nonetheless. Taking the place by storm would prove costly.

The houses ended two hundred paces from the castle, a sign that the local lord paid some attention to his security. Dirt crunched beneath our destriers' hooves. Tramp, tramp went the foot soldiers. Overhead, a buzzard called, its insistent shrill cry seemingly aimed at us. The defenders watched us in silence. The duke ordered the halt, and rode on with only half a dozen companions, I included.

Closer we rode, until we were within crossbow range. 'Sire,' warned de Chauvigny. 'They might shoot.'

Richard chuckled. 'Let them try.'

I glanced at FitzAldelm. For once, I thought, we were at one. His face also showed concern. As it grew pale as a three-day-old corpse, I felt a savage glee. He was terrified of being shot.

'Sire,' said FitzAldelm. 'It is dangerous to go any closer.'

Richard laughed. 'Go back if you wish, Robert.'

FitzAldelm flushed, and God forgive me, I delighted in his shame.

Fifty paces from the ditch, Richard reined in.

I spied the ends of crossbows jutting from the parapet, and my guts churned. I had seen what a bolt could do to a man. FitzAldelm was right to be afraid, I realised, hoping that my own fear did not show.

Raising a hand to his mouth, the duke shouted, 'Let the lord of Montfort make himself known! Richard of Aquitaine is at his door.'

A scurry of activity atop the walls followed. Footsteps clattered down a ladder.

Richard sat, hands resting on his pommel, his stance relaxed. He might have been a man out hunting who pauses to take in the landscape, not a warlord within killing range of his enemies. He glanced up at the sky, the spiralling buzzard, and the lambswool clouds far above. 'A fine day, is it not, Rufus?'

'It is, sire,' I said, my unease lessened by his devil-may-care attitude. 'Do you not think so, sir?' I asked FitzAldelm.

A little behind Richard as we were, and still pale, he glared, managing a polite, 'Indeed.'

'Sire,' called a voice from the ramparts.

We turned. A podgy red face regarded us. 'I am Jean le Gros, sire.'

'He is well named,' said Richard under his breath, and we tried to hide our amusement. 'You know who I am, sir,' the duke went on.

'I do, sire,' answered le Gros, his voice nervous.

'Doubtless you have heard of the fate of La Ferté-Bernard?'

'Yes, sire.'

'If you do not wish to see your castle stormed as it was, I would open your gate.' This was bending the truth, for La Ferté-Bernard had fallen to a surprise attack, while Montfort's defenders stood ready to repel our assault. Our forces, however, were more than enough to prosecute a successful attack, and both men knew it.

With indecent haste, le Gros asked, 'What are your terms, sire?'

Grinning fiercely, I clasped hands with de Chauvigny. FitzAldelm let out a long, hissing sigh.

Richard did not look surprised. 'You shall surrender, and swear oaths of fealty to me, and to King Philippe as your overlord. Do this and see yourself remain lord of Montfort.'

'I accept, sire.' Le Gros sounded as thankful as a man with his head on the executioner's block who is granted a reprieve. He shouted an order, and a moment later, both gates were pulled inward.

'Praise God,' said Richard.

'Amen,' FitzAldelm replied.

I kept to myself the thought that our success had more to do with the duke's aura than any divine help. He seemed invincible.

A sennight later, and Richard and Philippe had seized three more castles north-east of Le Mans: Maletable, Beaumont and Ballon. Each was given over by its lord, eager not to fall afoul of the duke and the French king. More would have followed, but Richard had received information from his spies in Le Mans. His father was still within the citadel there. It was time for a change of tactic, he declared, and Philippe agreed.

Under the cover of heavy fog on the eleventh of June, we marched around Le Mans, approaching it from the south. Pitching tents along the banks of the River Huisne, a long bowshot from the city walls, we set up camp. Spirits were high – buoyant, even. Come the morning, we would attack. Richard knew the town like the back of his hand, having stayed here on numerous occasions when he was growing up. There was only one bridge across the Huisne, but he had told us where the fording places were. Rather than assault the main gate, we would focus on a number of weak points, holes or gaps in the walls caused by subsidence and lack of upkeep.

Everyone was under strict orders not to drink too much. Clear heads were needed for the impending battle, the duke had said. Seeing the men-at-arms' dejected faces, he promised them double the normal ration the following night. Instead of cheering, for they did not want to alert Henry's soldiers, they shook their clenched fists in the air and grinned at him like idiots.

The moon rose, and men retired to their blankets. I was still wide awake, however, my mind full of what might happen on the morrow. Until now, most of the fighting had consisted of clashes or short sieges; this promised to be a good deal larger. Henry had at least seven hundred knights, and perhaps one and a half times that number of men-at-arms and archers. With the king in no mood to surrender, they would put up a vigorous resistance. Men I knew would die. Owain, perhaps, or de Drune. Rhys. The last was the worst to imagine. I closed my eyes, and asked God to protect all of us. If anyone had to be slain, I asked it was me. Or FitzAldelm, a little devil in my head added.

Restless, unable to settle, I went for a walk. My feet took me down to the Huisne, where I found Rhys on sentry duty. Alert, he heard me coming. His teeth flashed white in the darkness.

'Anyone stirring on the other side?' Through the thinning fog I discerned the outline of the stone and timber bridge, and beyond it, the town walls.

'There has been barely a sound since before matins, sir. A silver penny says the sentries are fast asleep.'

'They will get the shock of their lives at dawn.'

'I hope so. What happens after we capture Le Mans, sir?'

'That depends on the king. If he should be taken, the war will be over. If he escapes, it may continue for some time.'

'Will we ever leave for Outremer?' Rhys grumbled. 'We took the cross at Tours a year and a half ago.'

'It has been an age,' I agreed. The bitter dispute between Richard and his father meant little to me, and even less to Rhys. I knew from previous conversations that his head was full of exotic, kohl-eyed women and fierce Saracen warriors, and of tales of the fabled cities of Constantinople and Jerusalem. Although I had explained the reasons for the delay, he could not see them. Closer to Richard, witness to his confrontations with his father, I did. 'The duke would leave for the Holy Land tomorrow, but he cannot go without being named as Henry's heir.'

'Else John will take his place.'

'Or Arthur, his two-year-old nephew by Geoffrey.' He *had* been listening, I thought.

Rhys sighed. 'God grant we take Henry prisoner then.'

I nodded, amazed at how normal it sounded to be talking of capturing a king.

'They say John is a liar and a rogue. Is it true, sir?'

I remembered John's snake eyes on me after I had mentioned Cairlinn, and of the times since, when he had given me similar looks. 'I do not know, Rhys, but he gives me a bad feeling.' Even though there was no one near, I lowered my voice further. 'Let us hope that he never takes the throne.'

I got little sleep that night, yet when the dawn came, I leaped from my blankets. Today Richard would defeat his father, and I wanted to be part of it. As the last of the fog vanished beneath the rising sun, I returned to the bank of the Huisne to gaze upon Le Mans. Dressed in my hauberk, needing only to don my helmet and clamber astride Pommers, I was ready for battle.

Incredibly, the enemy sentries had still not spotted our camp. All I could spy on the ramparts was a solitary figure, unarmoured and helmetless. Finding him vaguely familiar, I studied him. Wrapped in thought, he paced along the walkway, vanishing every moment or two between crenellations. Amused, I was minded to attract his attention with a shout, but decided against it.

A horse whinnied behind me. Too late, its rider muttered soothing words.

The figure I was watching stopped. Turned. Saw. A hand went to his mouth in shock. He stared. I back, wondering who he was, and how soon he would raise the alarm. To my surprise, he stayed put, unable to tear himself away from the sight of our large camp.

I stirred. I could hear men mounting up, and the men-at-arms' captains ordering them to make ready.

A second figure stepped up beside the first. It too seemed familiar. I squinted. He had an old-fashioned short haircut, and a moustache. Few men sported such an appearance. William Marshal, I wondered – could it be? I looked again, and decided it was, and that the man he was talking to with some urgency might be King Henry himself. Finally, Marshal seemed to persuade his master to accompany him, for the pair vanished from sight.

At last a voice bellowed the alarm. The cry was taken up by others. Church bells began to toll. Shouts rose inside the town, and hooves rang off cobbles.

'To horse!' Richard had arrived. He was not clad for war – for the nonce, he would command from the camp. 'To horse!'

I ran for Pommers. Joining a group that included de Chauvigny, Owain and to my disgust, FitzAldelm, we made for the bridge. Seize that, the duke had told us, and we would take Le Mans before terce. Destriers thundering over the grass, we reached it at the same time as a party of Henry's knights and men-at-arms, who, by their half-dressed appearance, had come straight from their beds. The latter bore bundles of faggots that had been soaked in oil, and as the knights rode onto the bridge to defy us the passage, they set fire to the structure.

'Madmen,' said de Chauvigny, but he was laughing. 'But if they are prepared to fight on a burning bridge, so must we be. Follow!'

Flames licked at the timber planking on the far side. Smoke billowed, and through it, four knights came riding abreast.

De Chauvigny couched his lance and charged. My heart in my mouth, I did the same. Owain was on my right side, FitzAldelm on my right. The rest came pounding after.

We met in midstream, with a thunderous clash. Ahead of us, de Chauvigny had already downed his man, and sword in hand, was battering at another. I took aim at a third, but my lance splintered against my enemy's shield, while his struck mine fair and square. The impact was like being hit in the chest with a smith's hammer. Feet by a miracle in my stirrups, and Pommers still galloping, I shot past the knight even as he dropped the lance and reached for his blade.

I dodged a second lance, just, and was then enveloped in smoke from the burning bridge. Well-trained, Pommers did not stop. Coughing, eyes smarting and half-stunned, I found myself on the wrong side of the Huisne. Surrounded by enemies – there were knights and men-at-arms everywhere I looked, I panicked. Wheeling Pommers in preparation for a desperate attempt to recross the river, I realised no one was attacking me. 'Lost control of your destrier?' shouted a voice. A manic laugh bubbled up my throat. My arrival, straight after the attack by the four knights, had seen my enemies assume I was one of *them*, and that Pommers had fled the fighting.

'Aye,' I cried, and charged back through the smoke.

Catching the enemy knights on the bridge unaware, I snatched at the bridle of a man with a flat-topped kite shield, and dragged him with me. Recognising Pommers by his colour, or the Angevin lions on my shield, de Chauvigny waved me towards his little line, which spanned the halfway point. The fighting, I realised, had lulled.

'How is it on the other side, Rufus?' he asked gaily.

'Busy, sir,' I replied. 'We will need more men.'

'They are here.' He gestured to our right, and I saw knights probing the shallows with their lances, seeking the best way across on their destriers. 'You had best hand your prize into Rhys's care,' said de Chauvigny, 'or you will soon lose him again.'

'Leave some for me,' I said, pulling my prisoner onto our side of the Huisne. Rhys looked less than impressed by my order to remain in the camp, guarding the captive. Things changed when the knight made himself known as Geoffrey de Brûlon, a wealthy landowner from Somerset. He gave his word to stay in my tent. Although he seemed a trifle pompous, I liked his forthright manner, and accepted.

'Back to the rest of the squires,' I said to Rhys. They were waiting by the bridge with replacement horses and equipment for their masters.

'He will run away the moment we are gone, sir,' said Rhys, glaring at de Brûlon.

'No, he will not,' I answered. 'A knight's honour is his most important possession.'

Rhys was unconvinced. Under his breath he asked, 'And FitzAldelm, sir?'

It was a fair point, but with Richard bellowing for every man to ride to the attack, and smoke rising from the buildings outside the walls of Le Mans, this was no time for debate. I told Rhys so in no uncertain manner.

He shrugged. 'Very well, sir.'

'Your squire is impudent,' said de Brûlon.

'Mind your business, sir,' I snapped. 'And be sure to stay here, or I will come looking for you.' Leaving my prisoner with his mouth hanging open, we returned to the battle.

Where the bridge had stood, I found a smouldering ruin of pilings. Fearing for de Chauvigny and Owain, I called out to a group of knights who were riding into the Huisne.

'One man drowned when it collapsed, but those two are on the far bank. I saw them not long since,' came the reply.

Praying that the lone casualty was FitzAldelm, not either of my friends, I too began to ford the river. The knights told me that the city's defenders had apparently fired the buildings now ablaze. They had not counted on the wind, I thought, seeing flames licking at the very roofs of several that lay close to the castle walls.

The far bank was a mass of riders and men-at-arms, swirling about in a maelstrom of violence. I heard shouts, curses, screams. The deafening ring of weapons hammering against each other. Churned to mud by hooves, the ground was everywhere stained with the blood of the dead and injured. The king's men were outnumbered by some margin, however, and the tide of battle was flowing our way. Foot by foot, the enemy was being driven back.

'I see de Chauvigny,' cried one knight, pointing. 'Sweet Jesu, he is fighting Marshal!'

My gaze followed his outstretched arm. There was de Chauvigny's dun destrier, charging a knight bearing a shield with a green and gold pattern. It was a sight to behold. The pair rode at each other with such élan they might have been the only men on the field. Both struck well; neither was unhorsed, but both their lances shattered. Smartly turning their mounts, they drew swords and went at one another again.

Pommers reached the shallows. I reined in, mesmerised by the duel. I had a healthy respect for de Chauvigny, who was a skilled knight. Much of the time he would have beaten me in individual combat; I had still not reached my potential. Marshal was an altogether more dangerous opponent, however, and his destrier could turn on a silver penny. I would have no chance against him. To and fro the combat flowed, with de Chauvigny constantly on the defensive. He tried charging his mount into Marshal's, and the old trick of slamming his shield against that of one's opponent. But Marshal anticipated or evaded his every move, and in return launched a deadly counterattack.

In the end, de Chauvigny was undone by the simplest of moves.

Sheathing his sword as he cantered away from an exchange of blows, Marshal wheeled his destrier about and pricked it to the canter. Riding past de Chauvigny's left side – making him a hard-to-reach target – he leaned out and seized the dun's reins, dragging its head around and forcing it to follow.

To see a warrior of de Chauvigny's stature taken captive with such ease was incredible. I shook my head in disbelief.

The knight who had seen the contest first chuckled. 'Marshal is quite the master, eh?'

'That he is,' I replied, grateful not to have been in de Chauvigny's place.

'How now, Rufus!' roared a familiar voice. 'Art taking thy ease while the battle yet rages?'

Richard jested, but I coloured, nonetheless. 'I was watching de Chauvigny fight Marshal, sire. He is taken.'

Richard was riding Diablo, but to my astonishment, his only protection was a simple iron helmet. He bore no blade either. Urging the stallion out of the water, and alongside Pommers, he took in the scene. 'Ha! They are flying – look!'

In the time I had watched de Chauvigny and Marshal, the king's men had taken to their heels. Some had fled along the riverbank, but most had retreated into the town. Our knights charged after. Howling like wolves, the men-at-arms followed.

'De Chauvigny will soon be released. Meanwhile, the city is ours,' said the duke with satisfaction. 'Even my lord father will see that. We must press home the advantage. With me!' Diablo plunged forward.

I swallowed my protest about Richard's lack of armour and weapons, and urged Pommers after him.

Attacking a burning city is madness, yet that is what we did that day in June. Richard led, uncaring of the danger, and seemingly invulnerable. Inspired by his mad courage and terrified that he would be slain, I and a score of others followed, constantly trying to form a protective screen around him. Narrow, cobbled streets and beaten earth alleys were the battleground, spaces which two men standing abreast could hold with ease, all the more so because of the smoke blanketing the city. Yet fear had kindled in Henry's soldiers' hearts, and that is a flame hard to put out. We advanced from the main gate, our mere presence driving the enemy before us.

Almost at once we met Owain at a corner, bloodied but grinning. To my surprise, he had a white-faced de Chauvigny with him. Cradling his left arm, he explained how a stone thrown from the walls had struck him as Marshal made for the gate. Terrified by other stones which were landing around them, de Chauvigny's destrier had reared, ripping the reins from Marshal's hand. Despite the pain of his broken arm, de Chauvigny had regained control of his mount, and ridden for the bridge. There he had met Owain, who had protected him since. The pair joined our group, riding in the middle with the duke, where it was safest.

Abandoned carts and overturned wagons blocked some streets, and burning buildings others. We worked our way into a small square dominated by a church, and found a band of Henry's knights gathered to make a stand. They fought bravely, holding off our first charge, but with no foot soldiers to support them, were outflanked by our men-at-arms. A second attack broke them. Half were taken prisoner, and most of the rest slain or injured. Only a handful made good their escape. Our greater numbers continued to tell as we encountered knights in twos and threes. Forced to retreat, at times ambushed from side alleys by our men who had managed to get ahead, the enemy's fighting withdrawal soon developed into a rout. Sadly, the panicked townspeople, trying to escape with whatever possessions they could, were often caught in the middle. Women and children screamed, babies wailed. Men died.

Everywhere we went, Richard demanded knowledge of the king. The answers that came were confused, that Henry had not been seen since the morning, or that he was in the areas we had already ridden through. Undeterred, the duke pressed on, and before the bells had rung terce, we had entered the northern part of the city. There an injured knight of Henry's, propped up in the doorway of a house, his bleeding leg stretched in front of him, gave us better news. The king had ridden past not long since, accompanied by several hundred of his knights, among them Marshal. They were heading for Alençon, which lay some fifty miles away on the border with Normandy.

'If he reaches Alençon, the Norman barons will stand with him,' said Richard, urging Diablo towards the nearest gate. 'Failing that, he can sail for England, and I will never catch him.'

Urgency throbbed from the duke's voice, and I remembered talk of the nobles of Normandy, who had answered Henry's summons, but halted at Alençon until it became clear who would win the struggle, he or Richard and Philippe. It was one thing not to answer when called, I thought, and another to defy the king face-to-face. To take his father prisoner, as Richard seemed intent on doing, would force them to commit one way or another.

Out of the northern gate we went. Free of the crowds and the burning buildings, our destriers willingly galloped towards Fresnay, and beyond, Alençon. It was a blessing to escape the smoke and breathe clean air again. We soon overtook a wain laden down with furniture. Its owner, a pasty-cheeked merchant, stared at us in terror, but we paid him no heed. Hearing us come, the townspeople on foot moved to the roadsides, leaving a clear passage. Not everyone heard. A second merchant, this one astride a horse, with two pack animals on a lead rope, panicked as we came pounding along behind him, and charged off into a field of not-quite-ripe wheat. It was a comic sight, and I laughed until my sides hurt.

'There!' yelled Richard.

In the distance, I saw horses. The puffs of dust told me they were being ridden hard. I spurred Pommers, who answered with a will. Despite the fact that I was in armour, and the duke was not, he outstripped Diablo. Any time the stallion pressed him, he put on a fresh burst of speed. Somehow Owain's horse kept up too; so did that of a knight called Philippe de Colombiers. Diablo did well to stay within fifty paces of us. All became clear when I heard the duke's frustrated shout that his stallion was going lame. As for the others in the group, well, they were left far behind. God and all His saints, but I was proud of Pommers that day.

The countryside flew past on either side. Hedges, lush with summer growth. Fields of barley and wheat. Sheep grazing a sward of grass. Alder and birch trees on the banks of a stream. A thatched farmhouse, with outbuildings and a walled garden. A pig nosing in the earth for worms.

I drew nearer to our quarry; Owain was half a length behind me. The group numbered fifty riders, I guessed. In their midst was a hunched shape on a steady bay. A man rode to his left and right, close enough to support him if needs be. It was Henry, I was sure. Imagining the duke's pleasure if *I* captured his father, and unthinking of the danger, I urged Pommers to new efforts. The gap narrowed to a hundred paces. Wind whistled in my ears. Beneath me, Pommers' hooves beat a frenetic, rapid rhythm. I prepared to throw away my lance, that I would have a free hand to seize the king's reins. Then the foolishness of what I was about to try sank in, and my guts twisted. On my own, I had no chance.

From nowhere, Philippe de Colombiers overtook me.

'Rufus! Owain!' Richard's voice was faint. 'Philippe! Come back!'

Two of the horses ahead slowed, and then turned. Without hesitation, their riders couched their lances and rode at me and Philippe. I cursed. To obey the duke risked a spear in the back. We had to ignore his command – and Philippe showed no sign of reining in his destrier. Grateful now that I had not discarded my lance, I tucked it under my elbow and aimed at my opponent's shield. Both at the full gallop, we closed in the blink of an eye. For the second time in as many hours, a lance hit me straight and true. The shield punched into my chest; blinding pain erupted from my ribcage. I was driven back in the saddle, and lost both stirrups. Tumbled feet over head like a doll tossed down a staircase, I landed on the flat of my back and knew no more.

Pounding hooves woke me, as they had at Châteauroux. Later, I realised that perhaps only a dozen heartbeats had passed. I took a breath, and needles stabbed me in the chest. Wheezing, I rolled onto my side and with a hand in the dirt, managed to push myself into a sitting position. I saw Pommers first – he appeared to be unhurt, which gave me heart. Next I spied the knight who had unhorsed me lay in the grass thirty feet away, unconscious or dead. I had done to him what he had done to me. Philippe was sprawled close by, cursing loudly, while his opponent rode away, clutching the shattered stump of his lance.

Hooves rang on the road. My head turned. Now Marshal had ridden back – I recognised the green and gold insignia on his shield – and was blocking the road. In full armour, helmeted, he had his lance at the ready. It was not aimed at me, I was glad to realise. Then I followed the direction of its tip and my heart skipped a beat.

His target was Richard, who had slowed Diablo to a walk. Never had his lack of armour and shield been more obvious.

Marshal pricked spurs to his destrier, and charged.

'God's legs, man, kill me not!' shouted the duke at the top of his voice. 'That would be wrong, for I am unarmed.'

Marshal slowed not a fraction.

Nausea washed the back of my throat. Richard was about to be skewered, and I could not react in time. Fast as I could, I heaved myself into a standing position. Drew my sword. Staggered, wobbly-legged, towards him.

'Let the devil kill you, for I will not,' Marshal cried, dropping the lance tip. His aim was unerring. Spitting poor Diablo through the chest, he killed him with one blow. Galloping close enough that I – had I not still been addlepated – could have reached out and struck him, he wheeled his destrier and without even glancing at Richard, rode after the king.

Sure that the duke would be badly injured, or worse, I hobbled to his side. He had been thrown clear of Diablo, who lay prone, blood already pooling beneath him.

'Sire!' I dropped to my knees, and rolled Richard over. He took a breath, and coughed and his eyelids flickered. I could have cried. 'You are alive, sire!'

'I appear to be.' He grimaced. 'Diablo?'

'Dead, sire.'

Richard closed his eyes.

Fresh terror assailed me. 'Are you hurt, sire?'

'No. I grieve for Diablo.' The duke sighed. 'Help me up.'

Ignoring the pain from my broken ribs, I draped Richard's arm around my shoulders and gripped his hand with my own. 'Ready, sire?'

He grunted.

We stood, and gazed after Marshal, who was visible a distance down the road. I glanced back in the direction of Le Mans. 'Our companions are almost on us, sire. They can give chase.'

'No. Let them go.' The finality in his voice was absolute. Slipping free of my grasp, he limped to Diablo's carcase and stood over it in silence.

Calling to Philippe de Colombiers, who shouted he was unhurt, I walked towards the knight I had unhorsed. Another ransom was about to be mine. It was then that I saw a prone form, a little way along the road. I could not see who it was, but I recognised the destrier which stood nearby.

'Owain!' I broke into a stumbling run.

He was dead. Neck broken by the fall, perhaps, or his internal organs crushed by the lance that had punched a hole in his mail at chest level, he lay on his back, arms spread-eagled. Forever still. Gone.

I forgot Marshal. I forgot Henry. I forgot Richard, and Diablo. Grief consumed me. Sitting down, I pulled Owain's body into an embrace and wept.

He was the first close comrade I had lost.

Would that he had been the last.

CHAPTER XXXII

Marshal's heart was heavy as he rode away. If there had been any chances of resurrecting his fortunes when the duke took the throne, he had just burned them to ash. His had been the devil's choice, however. To have slain Richard would have made him all but a regicide, and to let the duke past seen his name dishonoured forever. Killing the duke's horse had been his only option.

The knowledge did little to sweeten Marshal's mood. It had been buoyant, thanks to the king's recent agreement that he should marry Isabelle de Clare. Now his actions meant that match was doomed ere it had even been arranged.

Rejoining the party, he made his way to Henry's side. To his alarm, the king's face was ashen, and beaded with sweat. Doubled over with pain, he was breathing through his mouth, laboured, sawing efforts. But for his bastard son Geoffrey, who rode close beside him, supporting Henry with one arm, Marshal judged he would have fallen from the saddle. 'Sire?'

Henry's bloodshot eyes swivelled. 'Ah, Marshal. Where have you been?'

'Fighting a rearguard action, sire.' He decided that mention of his clash with Richard would benefit the king not at all. 'We are no longer being pursued, I am happy to say.'

Henry seemed not to hear. 'We make for Chinon.'

'Sire?' Chinon had long been dear to the king, thought Marshal, but it lay two hundred miles to the south, through territory controlled, or soon-to-be-controlled, by Richard and Philippe. 'Alençon is much nearer, sire, and closer to Normandy, where you have many loyal barons.'

'Marshal is right, sire,' said Geoffrey. A curly haired man in early middle age still with the good looks of his half-brothers, he continued to serve as Henry's chancellor. 'If we are to raise a fresh army, Normandy is the place to do it, not Chinon.'

'You will ride there, Geoff, and rally those who remain loyal.' The king swallowed, and dry-retched.

Alarmed, Marshal beckoned to the physician, who persuaded the king to drink a little ginger tisane.

Henry appeared moderately restored, so Marshal tried again. 'You said Chinon, sire?'

'Yes. You will attend me. Choose five men to accompany us.'

'Of course, sire.' Marshal caught Geoffrey's eyes, and saw his own disquiet mirrored there. 'Are you sure that is where we should go, sire?'

'I am yet king,' snarled Henry. 'Am I not?'

'You are, sire,' Marshal replied, the weight of his service heavy as a leaden ingot on his back.

'Then obey.'

'You are unwell, sire. At least let us make for Fresnay, where you may rest.'

Henry waved an accepting hand. 'Very well.'

As they rode, Geoffrey tried to change his father's mind, but Henry was obdurate. They stayed that night in Fresnay, and once more Marshal ventured the opinion that they should make for Alençon. The king flew into a rage, and was sick. After, when he had recovered somewhat, he told Marshal and Geoffrey not to broach the subject again. His mind was made up.

The following morning, while the main body of men prepared to ride north, Marshal and Henry set off southwards with five knights, one of whom was Maurice de Craon, a trusted lieutenant of long standing. They took smaller roads and byways, in the hope of avoiding an encounter with troops loyal to the duke or Philippe. They succeeded, but the long and hazardous journey took half a month. If the king had been in better health, they could have ridden a great deal faster, but with each passing day, Henry grew weaker. Vomiting regularly, unable to keep liquids down, and in continuous pain, he shrank until he was only a husk of his former self. Too weak to ride, he travelled in a covered wagon, like a farmer or merchant. On occasion Marshal was convinced that he would die before they reached Chinon, but the king had lost none of his stubbornness, and somehow endured.

When the massive castle came into sight, he smiled for the first time in days. 'Chinon,' he said. 'I am home.'

Marshal had visited it often, but the fortress never failed to impress. Built on a long limestone outcrop over the River Vienne, it had natural defences on three sides and a massive ditch on the fourth. First built more than two centuries earlier, Chinon had been Henry's from almost the start of his reign, when he had seized it from his rebellious brother. During the thirty-plus years that had followed, the king had overseen a vast building project, turning the castle into an impregnable stronghold with luxurious living quarters for the royal family, and accommodation for a large garrison.

'At least you will be comfortable here, sire.' Marshal could think of little else to say. All the news was bad. In the time since they had fled Le Mans, Richard and Philippe's forces had overrun the entire area. Rumour had it that Tours, which had remained loyal to Henry, was about to be attacked. When it fell, his realm would lie open and vulnerable. It would not be long before a summons arrived, he thought, or even the duke himself, at the head of an army. The king would have no choice but to agree to his son's terms. What would befall *him*, Marshal worried, only God knew.

His head turned towards the litter. 'Sire?'

Again there was no answer.

Peering inside, Marshal saw that Henry had fallen unconscious. He could not be roused.

'To the castle,' Marshal ordered, worry nipping at him. 'Now!'

His worst fears were realised. The king grew more ill by the day. Treatments of wormwood and mint prescribed by the physician who had accompanied them from Le Mans relieved his pain a little, but did not improve his condition. A second physician summoned by Marshal diagnosed an excess of blood, and bled Henry. Weakened further, the king slept for an entire night and day. Finally wakening in the afternoon, lucid and in better spirits, he demanded from his bed to be kept informed of every piece of information that reached Chinon.

'Tours has fallen this very day, sire,' said Marshal, not knowing how to leaven the blow.

Henry's face sagged. 'Tours? How?'

'The river is low, sire, thanks to the dry weather. Knowing this, Richard's men carried ladders to the walls on the bank – the defences are not as high there – and launched an attack.' Next Marshal named a litany of castles that had gone over to the duke and Philippe.

'God's bones, am I to have no respite?' muttered Henry. 'Is there aught else? More messages from my son?' Two had come in the previous days, demanding he meet Richard and Philippe to make terms. Nobles from the French court had visited the previous afternoon, offering to mediate. Henry had given answer to no one.

'Right sorry am I to say so, sire, but there is.' Marshal held out the letter that had arrived a short time before.

Henry's head sank back on the pillow. 'Read it to me.'

Cracking the seal, Marshal unrolled the parchment. With great care, for he was no friend of the written word, he read the message in silence.

'Marshal?' The king's voice was weak but querulous.

'You are summoned to Ballan, sire, to meet with the duke and King Philippe.'

'When?'

'Tomorrow, sire.'

Surprisingly, a husky laugh. 'I am too ill to travel that distance.'

'We shall ask for a delay, sire,' said Marshal, a long-building anger towards Richard finding voice at last. 'That is reasonable.'

'No. I will attend. What are the terms?'

'You are to place yourself wholly at the will of King Philippe, sire. You must do homage to him for your continental possessions. His sister Alys is to be given up to a guardian named by the duke; he will marry her upon his return from Jerusalem. Richard is to receive the fealty of your subjects on both sides of the Narrow Sea as lawful heir to all your lands. You will pay King Philippe an indemnity of twenty thousand marks. The starting date of the crusade is to be Lent next year, when you, King Philippe and Duke Richard will muster at Vézelay. Until the terms have been fulfilled, three castles in the Vexin or Anjou—' Marshal listed them '—are to be handed over as a pledge of good faith.'

Henry did not speak.

In the distance, the abbey bells tolled vespers. Sunlight spilled in through the window, warm and golden, but could not dispel the wintry atmosphere.

The king's eyes were closed. He lay still as a corpse. Dreading the worst might already have come to pass, Marshal leaned in, and was relieved to see his nostrils move with a breath. 'Sire?' he whispered.

Henry's voice was barely audible. 'We shall set out at dawn. Order the litter prepared.'

'Sire.'

'Leave me.' Two words, laden with grief and lost opportunity.

'Yes, sire.' Heavy-hearted, Marshal padded from the room. He hoped his own fate would not be as humiliating as the following day's meeting promised to be for the king.

Half a mile from the meeting place at Ballan, Henry called a halt. Insistent that he would ride the final distance, he had to be helped onto his horse. Wracked by fever, his face flushed and eyes sunken, he was so weak that Marshal had to support him from one side and de Béthune from the other. A suggestion that the king travel all the way in the litter was ignored. Their pace slowed to that of an ox-drawn cart, and it was past the appointed hour of none when they caught sight of Richard and Philippe. A large crowd had gathered. Barons, knights, bishops and priests, ordinary soldiers and peasantry, all were eager to witness the final clash between the enemies.

The duke made no greeting to his father; he simply stared. Cold. Remote. Unforgiving.

Philippe looked shocked by Henry's appearance. Calling for a cloak, he offered to help the king from his horse that he might sit upon the ground.

Henry, his cheekbones marked by red fever pricks, refused. 'I have not come to sit and talk with you, sire, but to hear what is demanded of me.'

Philippe bowed his head. 'Very well, sire.'

Marshal and de Béthune, now on foot, remained on either side of the king, holding him in the saddle. It was the most shameful, degrading thing Marshal had ever seen someone of Henry's rank subjected to. He was the loser, however, and had to listen to his son's and Philippe's demands.

One of the French king's barons read out the terms, slowly and deliberately. When he had finished, Henry nodded his assent.

'You agree to everything, sire?' It was the first time Richard had spoken.

Robbed of his voice, again Henry nodded.

Richard and Philippe exchanged a glance.

Overhead, dark clouds had been gathering. Riveted by the unfolding drama, few had noticed. An unexpected peal of thunder rang out, startling the audience. Superstitious, Marshal crossed himself. He was not alone.

Unsettled by the thunderclap, Henry's horse jinked about. Weak and semi-conscious, the king toppled sideways. It took all of Marshal's strength to heave him back into the saddle. De Béthune seized a handful of Henry's tunic for a better grip, and together they propped him upright. The indignities heaped on the king would not be added to, Marshal decided. He ordered the litter fetched. It mattered not if Richard and Philippe saw Henry leaving in that rather than on the back of a horse.

'The litter is coming, sire,' he whispered. 'It will not be long.'

The king groaned.

Pity filled Marshal, that someone so high could be brought so low. At least it was done, he decided. Henry had received his justice.

'One thing remains,' said Richard.

Henry seemed oblivious, so Marshal replied for him. 'Yes, sire?'

'My lord father must give me the kiss of peace.'

Will it never end? Marshal thought. He shook the king's arm gently. 'Sire.' Henry came to, and he explained the duke's demand.

'Very well,' croaked Henry, a flash of emotion rising in his face. From somewhere deep inside, he found strength, and stiffened his back.

Richard climbed onto his horse and rode towards them. He did not look at his father; Henry ignored him. The duke bent over, close enough for the kiss.

Henry leaned sideways and pursed his lips, but did not quite touch his son's cheek. He hissed, 'God grant that I may not die until I have had my revenge on you.'

Richard jerked back in surprise.

Henry leered at him, a wolf's smile.

Richard's mask slipped back into place and he rode away without another word.

Henry gasped. His eyes rolled in his head, and he slumped down, unconscious. But for Marshal and de Béthune, he would have tumbled to the ground.

*

An even crueller blow struck Henry the next day. He had asked at Ballan for a list of the nobles who had deserted him to join with Richard and Philippe. A letter arrived, detailing the traitors. Marshal tried to keep it from him, but the king insisted on having it read aloud. At the very top was his son John's name.

Hearing this, the last of the colour left Henry's cheeks. 'No,' he moaned. 'Not John.'

'His name is there, sire,' said Marshal.

'No. No.'

Stricken, Marshal could find nothing to say. It was common knowledge that John had left early that morning, taking his possessions and the few retainers who called him lord.

'Marshal,' croaked the king.

'Sire?'

'Search every room. John is yet in the castle – I know it.'

Which was worse, Marshal wondered, the quick, deadly blow, or the one that is delayed? It was no choice at all. 'Sire, he is gone. I saw him depart myself.'

Henry's red-rimmed eyes filled with tears. 'Did you not stop him?'

Marshal continued with the lie – he had to. 'I could not, sire. He ordered me to stand aside.'

'He has gone to Richard?'

'I believe so, sire.'

'Ah, John.' A long, rattling sigh left Henry's scabbed lips.

Betrayed by his favourite son, the king lost the will to live. Refusing food and water, he lapsed in and out of delirium. During his brief periods of lucidity, he cursed the day he was born, and his sons. Once he asked to be carried to the chapel. There he confessed his sins to the priest, and received communion. In this fashion, he lingered for another three days. There was no way of knowing when it would end. Marshal had letters sent to Richard, informing him that his father was close to death, but there was no reply.

Exhausted by his constant vigil at Henry's side, and surprised how the king's wasted body continued to fight its losing battle with death, Marshal left him in the care of his servants late on the evening of the fifth of July. De Craon and the others were already abed. He slept deeply, awaking refreshed and in better spirit. Reality crashed in soon. Dressing, Marshal hurried to the king's chamber.

The door was ajar, which was unusual. Not a sound came from within. He told himself not to worry – Henry was asleep, and the servants watching over him.

He stepped inside. Horror-struck, for the room had been stripped – wall hangings, enamelled chests for valuables, silver tableware, all were gone – he glanced at Henry, who lay naked and still on the bare mattress of his bed. Limbs splayed like a discarded doll, his flesh grey, he was dead.

'Christ Jesus, no,' Marshal cried.

The king's nostrils and mouth were caked in black blood, the result of a final paroxysm. His bloodshot eyes stared at the ceiling, dull forever. Averting his gaze, to afford his master a shred of dignity, Marshal hurried to the corridor and roared for someone, anyone, to attend him. William de Trihan, one of the five who had accompanied the king from Fresnay, was the first to arrive. Ordering him to take off his cloak and guard the door with his life, Marshal went back in to cover the king's corpse. Guilt and shame battered him.

'Forgive me, sire. I should have stayed, spared you from such indignity. This would not have happened.' Marshal studied the room. The servants had been thorough. Not an item of value remained. Flies seek honey, wolves the carcase, and ants wheat, he thought bitterly, and so it is with humans. Rather than let his fury at the faithless servants, he set it aside. There was much to do. The king had to be washed and dressed in fine robes. Tomorrow he would be borne to the abbey of Fontevraud, some twelve miles down the Loire valley. A house of nuns particularly favoured by Henry, it was where he had requested to be laid to rest.

One other task, the least appealing, also remained.

Word must be sent to Richard of his father's death.

Occupying himself with the business at hand, Marshal did his best not to think about his next meeting with the duke – the new king.

It was peaceful in the church of Fontevraud. Fat candles burned in stands, bathing the interior with golden light. Henry's body lay on a bier before the altar. Dressed in the finest of robes, his eyes were closed with silver pennies, fingers folded in prayer over his chest. Dressed in full mail, with drawn swords, Marshal, de Craon and their companions stood guard around the king. So they had remained all the previous night, as the nuns, many weeping, had filled the air with plain chant, and through the day. Mass had been celebrated, Henry's body blessed. Now they waited for Richard to arrive, and John.

Marshal had not joined in, but there had been much muttered conversation in the dark hours of the night. Everyone, from the knights to the barons that had come to pay their respects, was worried about the treatment they would receive from Richard. The general consensus was that submitting to his authority, and offering fealty and their swords in service, would suffice. Marshal's case, having killed the new king's horse under him, was different. He had lost count of the well-intentioned offers of loans, destriers and weapons; in the end, growing irritated, Marshal had said he was not sorry for his actions. God had looked after him all his life, he went on, and His will would be done.

Marshal's rejoinder had seen him left alone, but his inner turmoil continued to rage. Being stripped of his lands and banished from the royal court seemed likely. Imprisonment was possible, even probable. Noblemen were not often executed, but neither did they commonly act as he had on the road from Le Mans to Fresnay. There was nothing to stop him from fleeing – the idea had crossed his mind more than once – but to do so would be the act of a coward, a man without honour. Marshal had a longstanding, well-earned reputation for honour; it meant everything to him. Rather than run, he would await Richard's justice.

Even if it meant his own life.

Time passed. The tide of mourners died away to a trickle. Nuns brought draughts of water for those standing watch over the king. The abbey bells rang vespers, and an hour later compline. It would be another long night, thought Marshal, his hips and knees complaining. It mattered not, nor how tired he might be come the dawn. When Richard arrived, he would be ready.

Hoofbeats carried from outside, then voices. A challenge, and an answer.

All eyes turned to the entrance.

Jean d'Earley came hurrying in, worried. 'Sir,' he called. 'The duke is here!'

Christ on the cross, Marshal prayed. Help me now.

A moment later, preceded by several knights, Richard strode in. Head to toe, he appeared the king. His lustrous mane of hair was fresh-combed and oiled. Gold Angevin lions patterned his plum tunic; his belt, scabbard and shoes were gilded. His face could have been that of a statue, however, so fixed was his expression. A step behind him was his snake-eyed brother John; there were others too, but Marshal paid them no heed.

More nervous than he had been in years, he knelt and bowed his head. The others around the bier did the same.

Richard halted a few steps from his father's body. 'Rise.'

Marshal and his companions obeyed.

'By your leave, sirs.' That Richard wanted privacy was plain.

They moved back a respectable distance and watched the duke stand in silence over the bier. After a short time he moved next to its head, that he might gaze upon Henry for the last time. Still his emotions were indiscernible: not joy or sadness, sorrow and grief or gladness. He knelt in brief prayer, then stood. Turning his back on his father's corpse, he made straight for Marshal.

'A word.' He crooked a finger at Maurice de Craon. 'You also.'

And so it comes, thought Marshal, feeling an odd relief.

Outside, the sun was nearing the horizon. Its gold-red light bathed the countryside, colouring everything it touched. Swifts banked and dived overhead, their high-pitched skirrs a gentle reminder of summer.

'Let us ride.' Richard indicated that Marshal and de Craon should take horses belonging to knights of his mesnie. His own mount was a magnificent dun with a bristling mane, broad chest and heavily mus-cled hindquarters.

The three mounted, and rode out of the courtyard. Marshal turned to de Craon, who rolled his eyes as if to say, I have no idea what he will do or say. Of the same opinion, Marshal could do nothing but pray. That is what he did, silently and fervently.

'I had to find a new destrier,' Richard mocked. 'After what you did to poor Diablo.'

'He was a fine steed, sire,' said Marshal.

'Ha! You intended to kill me the other day, and you would have, without a doubt, if I had not deflected your lance with my arm.'

He twists the truth to make himself look better, thought Marshal, indignation pricking. It would not aid his cause to say so, however. 'My intention was never to kill you, sire. I am still strong enough to direct a lance. If I had wanted, I could have driven it through your body, just as I did with that horse of yours. And I do not consider it wicked to have killed it, nor am I sorry for doing so. I was oath sworn to your lord father, and he was in danger.' Marshal glanced at the duke, but turned away again, dreading his response.

'I forgive you', said Richard. 'Moreover, I bear you no ill will.'

'Thank you, sire.' Marshal's voice trembled. He waited, for there was more.

'It was as fine a strike as was ever seen at a tourney, or a battlefield for that matter.'

'I have had plenty of practice, sire, down the years.' Get to the point, he thought.

'Indeed, serving my brother, and then my father. Most loyal of servants, you have been, staying to the very end, when lesser men have fled.' Lowering his voice, Richard added, 'And yet you made approaches to me some years since.'

It was impossible that the duke would have forgotten this, thought Marshal, nor that he would bring the matter up. 'I did so only to protect my master's interests, sire. Moreover, my actions never posed a direct threat to the Young King. Splintering the realm would have left him with far less when he assumed the throne. Preventing that was my only motive.'

Richard studied him for longer than felt comfortable, and although Marshal had spoken the truth, he felt his colour rise.

'I believe you, Marshal.'

'Thank you, sire.'

'How would it be for you to serve me?'

Praise God, thought Marshal. I have passed the test. A daring thought took hold. He hesitated, then decided that this was his best chance. 'A short while before he died, sire, your lord father gave me the hand of Isabelle de Clare, heiress to Striguil. I would see that match completed.'

'He did not *give* you her hand, but merely promised it to you.' Richard's tone was sharp, the inference clear that without his blessing, the union would never take place.

Marshal held his composure, and said, 'That is true, sire. Nonetheless, the girl was to be mine.'

'There is steel in your sword yet, I see!' Richard broke into a booming laugh. 'You also have a keen eye. Her lands are extensive – far greater in area and wealth than Kendal, say.'

Discomfited by the ease with which Richard had slid inside his guard, Marshal did not reply.

Richard dealt him a great buffet. 'Come now! Take her as your wife, and have done. I do not promise – I give her to you.'

'My thanks, sire,' said Marshal, joy kindling in his breast. Here at last, he thought, was a reward that befitted his long service to the house of Anjou. Remembering de Béthune, and knowing the iron would never be hotter, he struck. 'If I might mention a friend, sire. He was to wed the heiress of Châteauroux.'

'God's legs, but you are persistent!' cried Richard. 'And yet de Béthune is a worthy man, and loyal. He shall not have Châteauroux – that I have promised to André de Chauvigny – but he will have suitable recompense.' He eyed Marshal keenly. 'Will that satisfy you?'

'It will, sire,' said Marshal with a deep bow. 'If you will have me, I am your man.'

CHAPTER XXXIII

August saw Richard arrive in Southampton, the port from which we had left seven years before. A month had passed since his father's death. He had been invested as duke of Normandy, seen his excommunication revoked, and met with Philippe of France at Gisors. There Philippe had laid fresh claim to the Vexin, but had set this aside in recognition of Richard's promise to wed his sister Alys upon his return from Outremer. He was also to receive the twenty thousand marks indemnity that Henry had agreed to pay, and a further four thousand to defray his costs in the recent campaign. In reciprocation, Philippe gave up Châteauroux and other territory he had seized. The two kings had agreed to set out on crusade the following spring, and parted as friends. Matters settled abroad, Richard had finally been ready to sail for England.

I travelled with him, but in contrast to his joyous return, mine was bittersweet. There was no denying that my position as a trusted knight of his mesnie was far greater reward than I could ever have hoped for in Cairlinn. My future also looked bright. I was wealthy, thanks to the ransoms I had won – that of de Brûlon in particular had yielded a huge sum of silver. I had Rhys as my squire. Owain was dead, God rest his soul, but Philip and de Drune, also good friends, were not.

Nonetheless, a decade had passed since my being taken hostage and sent to Striguil. My parents and brothers were now bones mouldering beneath the turf, in graves that might never be found. The man who had murdered my mother and father was dead, it was true, but his brother Robert still haunted my life as a trusted adviser to Richard. I consoled myself with the duke's promise, that he would restore the lordship of Cairlinn to me when the time was right. When we had come back from crusade.

Troubled by dark memories of the two innocent men who had hung for the murder of the elder FitzAldelm and his squire, I was glad to leave Southampton. This was not my only reason. On the evening before our departure, I had seen Robert FitzAldelm deep in conversation with a man-at-arms whom I did not know. Noticing my gaze, my enemy smirked; the man-at-arms had muttered again in his ear. What it was they were talking about, I had no idea, but it disturbed me. I was grateful not to see the soldier again, and when FitzAldelm made no attempt to speak with me thereafter, I told myself I was worrying about nothing.

Rhys's mood grew lighter as we rode north, towards Winchester, and mine did too. Our destination was the royal palace, where Richard was to be reunited with his mother Queen Alienor. I had high hopes of seeing Beatrice. After that, we would travel to Gloucester for John's wedding, and then to London for the duke's coronation. William Marshal would be at both ceremonies with his new bride Isabelle de Clare. This knowledge saw an odd sensation steal over me.

I had never harboured romantic feelings for Isabelle during my stay at Striguil – she had been a tiny child, I a grown man – yet there had been real friendship between us. It rankled that Marshal, a man old enough to have a daughter of Isabelle's age, had been allowed to wed her. Telling myself that I was a fool, that Richard would never have even considered me for such a match, that I had Beatrice to pursue and Alienor to dream about, I turned my mind back to the celebrations that would surround the coronation.

'They will last for days. There will be more wine than we can drink – and good wine at that. Once our heads have stopped pounding,' I said to Rhys, 'the real preparations for the crusade can begin.' He muttered something in Welsh, and I said, 'The waiting is almost over.'

'I will not be happy until the coast of Outremer is in sight, sir,' he replied.

'It has been a long time, and that is the truth,' I agreed, feeling much the same way. Between constant rebellions in Aquitaine and the interminable quarrelling of Richard's family, I was bone weary. A friend today could be an enemy tomorrow, and vice versa. At least in Outremer we would have a common foe, the Saracens. I threw a mischievous glance at Rhys. 'If you are so eager to take ship, it would be no great hardship to miss the duke's coronation, surely?'

His face grew indignant. 'I have fought for the duke these last seven years, sir. I want to see the crown on his head.'

'I jest, Rhys.' I winked.

He grumbled again, but there was a smile too.

Arriving at the royal palace at Winchester, Richard threw himself from his palfrey, a sleek golden-coloured beast. Startled, Philip jumped off his own horse and seized the duke's reins.

'Attend me, John,' Richard called. 'You also, Robert and Rufus.'

Delighted by the honour, resentful of FitzAldelm – as he clearly was of me – I left Rhys in charge of Pommers, and hastened after Richard and John, who were already halfway down a corridor, preceded by a portly, out-of-breath steward. Our shoes made little sound on the stone floor as we made our way to the queen's chambers. This had been one of her gilded cages, where Henry had kept her, but since his death and the letters Richard had sent, she was free again.

'Here, sire,' said the steward, making to knock.

Pushing past, Richard rapped once and opened the door. 'Mama?'

'Sweet Jesu,' said a musical voice. 'Richard?'

'Mama,' he cried, his expression of pure joy. He stepped inside.

John hurried after him. 'He is not alone, Mother. I am here also.'

'John, my dear.' There was less warmth this time.

'After you, sir,' I said to FitzAldelm with exaggerated courtesy.

'We need to talk,' he said, glowering, and walked in.

Uneasy, but powerless to make any kind of rejoinder, I followed. The instant I entered the light and airy living area, my concerns fell away.

Richard and John were kneeling before their mother Alienor, beautiful and straight-backed despite her advancing years. Hair caught up in a gold beaded net, dressed in a robe of the deepest purple, with a magnificent brooch on her breast, she was the picture of a queen.

'Rise,' she said, laughing. 'I cannot have both the future king *and* the Lord of Ireland on bended knee.'

'I will always show you such respect, Mama,' said Richard, kissing her right hand.

'And I,' added John, his tone eager to please.

She threw Richard a look of pure adoration. 'Stand, sire, please.' Turning to John, she bade him get up also. 'My heart is warmed to see you both so well.'

'As mine is to see you,' said Richard.

Her smile was radiant. 'And now you are king. At last.'

Pleasure filled Richard's face. 'At last, Mama.'

John looked as if he had bitten into a rancid piece of meat.

Noticing, Alienor asked, 'How was the voyage from Normandy?'

'Passable, Mama,' said John.

Richard winked. 'My brother spent most of it staring at the bottom of a bucket.'

'It is not my fault that the sea makes me feel nauseous,' objected John.

Richard snorted. 'You had best get used to it. You will be returning there soon enough.'

John pouted.

I had heard the duke's plans for John and his bastard brother, Geoffrey. Both were to be forbidden from entering England while we were on crusade – this, to prevent any attempt to take the throne.

'Peace,' said Alienor.

The brothers subsided, and I hid a smile. Both grown men, yet she could calm them with a single word.

'I have been busy, Mama, but you have been busier,' said Richard. 'I am grateful.'

'As one who has been long confined, I know well the joy of being set free,' she said. 'It was a pleasure to order the prisons emptied. The charitable act will help ease Henry's soul into Heaven too. Your lord father has been buried?'

'Yes. In Fontevraud, as he requested.' Richard's tone was matter-of-fact.

A shadow passed across her face. 'It scarce seems real that he is gone at last.'

She has feelings for him yet, I thought, amazed. Vestiges only, perhaps, but something of their love remains.

Richard caught her hand again. 'You are free now. Once more you are Queen!'

'Until you wed.'

'Even then you will be loved and revered, Mama.'

Her eyes brightened. 'John being with you makes me think you took my advice.'

'After much consideration, I did. The counties of Somerset, Dorset,

Devon and Cornwall are to be his, and also Nottingham and Derby. They will provide an annual revenue of four thousand pounds – suitable recompense for a royal prince.'

'That is well,' said Alienor.

'I am grateful, sire,' said John.

Richard gave him a stern glance. 'It is a rich prize for unfaithful service.'

John's cheeks coloured, and his gaze fell away.

'Blood is blood,' said Alienor. 'We must cleave to our own.'

The duke's actions made little sense to me. He valued steadfastness and loyalty like no other. Rewards had been given to those of Henry's nobles and knights who had stayed with him to the end: Marshal was the foremost example. Those who had been less faithful had been stripped of their office, fined or both. The thieving seneschal of Anjou had even been chained hand and foot and thrown into prison. Craven John, abandoning his dying father when it was clear his cause was lost, was to suffer no punishment at all. Quite the opposite: he had been granted the lordship of swathes of England, and would receive a vast yearly income. It was a sweetener, as de Drune told me, because John had not been named heir. That honour had gone to Arthur, son of Geoffrey, Richard and John's dead brother. It was a calculated move, for a two-year-old boy posed little threat to the throne while Richard was away on crusade. John, an adult man, was an altogether different – and dangerous – proposition.

'Let us put the past behind us,' said Richard to John. 'You are my only remaining brother, and I would have us friends.'

'That is my heartfelt wish also,' said John, his tone earnest.

As Alienor watched in approval, the two brothers exchanged the kiss of peace.

I did not believe a word that had come out of John's fat-lipped mouth, but a furtive look at FitzAldelm told me that my enemy was delighted by this new amity. Unhappy that this should be so, I set to thinking. Busy with our duties since Henry's death, FitzAldelm and I had had little to do with each other. If I pondered on it, however, I could recall seeing him and John in conversation more than once. Their possible meeting at Bonsmoulins the previous November sprang to mind. Christ on the cross, I thought, the pair were in league. It was troubling that I had no idea to what purpose.

'I would introduce two of my most loyal men, Mama,' said Richard. Again I shoved my concerns aside.

The duke called FitzAldelm, who approached the queen and knelt. Much was made of his service in Aquitaine; without him, Richard declared, a great deal of territory would have been lost to the rebels. Hard-working, dedicated, FitzAldelm had become indispensable.

Alienor let FitzAldelm kiss her hand; they spoke together for a short time.

John looked on with clear delight.

I felt sick to my stomach. My enemy now had two powerful allies, Richard and his brother. My hopes of seeing justice wrought on him appeared fainter than ever.

'Rufus.' Richard's voice was warm.

I walked past FitzAldelm, who was returning to our position by the door. We ignored each other completely. I knelt before Alienor and the duke, and bowed my head. 'Sire. Madam.'

'Rise, Rufus.' The duke's strong grip helped me stand. 'Mama, meet Rufus, a former squire of mine, an Irishman, and now a knight in my mesnie. He has the heart of a lion, and is fierce in battle. Stout-hearted, steadfast and loyal, I can think of no one finer to have beside me when I face Saladin.'

'My son does not give praise lightly, Rufus,' said Alienor. 'My heart gladdens to know you will be with him on the crusade.'

'I will never leave his side, madam, unless he orders it,' I said, my voice hoarse with emotion.

'The duke might have something to say in that regard when it comes to his matrimonial bed.' Alienor's voice tinkled with amusement.

'Madam?' Confused and embarrassed – I thought Richard was to wed Alys upon his return from Outremer, not before – I glanced from him to his mother.

'I am not even crowned, and you are stirring the pot, Mama,' he said, raising an eyebrow. 'Who have you in mind, if it not be Alys?'

Alienor's gaze flickered to me, and on to FitzAldelm.

Understanding, Richard nodded. 'My thanks, Robert, Rufus. Leave us.'

Curiosity filled me as I took my leave with FitzAldelm. To my satisfaction, he also seemed completely in the dark. He seemed about to speak to me, but then a short way down the corridor, I spied Beatrice.

Surprised, delighted, I hurried forward. 'My lady.'

Her hand went to her mouth. 'Rufus?'

I bowed, my curiosity about the duke and his possible bride and my worries about FitzAldelm forgotten. Now my heart pounded, and straightening, I felt my still-crimson cheeks suffuse with even more colour. 'It has been too long.'

Her eyes were warm. 'I have remembered you often.'

And I you, I thought, but I could not say it in front of FitzAldelm, who had followed me. Already I sensed an unhealthy interest in her.

'You have not introduced me to your friend,' she said, unsuspecting.

'My lady.' He bowed, even deeper than he had to Alienor.

No, I wanted to scream. He is an evil monster. Stiffly, I said, 'Lady Beatrice, Sir Robert FitzAldelm, a knight of the duke's mesnie.'

He gave her a second bow, the losenger, and said, 'Your beauty is beyond compare, my lady. Rufus should have mentioned it when he spoke of you.'

She murmured her thanks, and a heartbeat later gave me a sharp look.

I had never mentioned her to FitzAldelm for obvious reasons, but to protest would make me appear the fool. Raging with fury, I said nothing.

Meanwhile, her expression grew waspish. 'You do not find me beautiful?' Beatrice's voice was full of hurt, and anger.

'Of course I do,' I whispered.

Movement at the corner of my eye. I stopped.

'Your pardon, my lady,' said FitzAldelm. He gave Beatrice an apologetic look. 'I must tell Rufus something.'

'Can it not wait?' I demanded.

'No.' One word, laden with ominousness.

Smiling an apology at Beatrice, furious at FitzAldelm, I walked a few steps with him. '*What?*'

'When we passed through Southampton, it was not the first time you had been there. Was it?'

I battled to conceal my shock. '*This* is the reason for your rude interruption?'

His reply was as fast as a sword thrust. 'Do I speak true, or no?'

'I sailed from there just after taking service with our lord the duke,' I answered in a bluff tone. 'What has that to do with anything?'

'My brother was supposed to cross the Narrow Sea with Richard,' said FitzAldelm, never taking his gaze from mine. 'He was known to you.'

'He was.' I did not like where this was going, nor could I see any way of pretending not to have known about his brother's fate. 'A pair of lowlifes swung for his murder, if I recall aright.'

'The wrong men!' Spittle flew from FitzAldelm's lips.

My laugh sounded high, and to my ear, false. 'Richard himself oversaw their interrogation. He would not make such a mistake.'

'And yet you were in the inn my brother was just before he died. So the man-at-arms I spoke with in Southampton swore. You see, Rufus, I used our time there to make enquiries. It has never rested well with me that you were in the same town as my brother the night he died. At last I have proof of your involvement.'

'Proof?' I cried, even as sweat prickled my spine. All this time, I thought, FitzAldelm has known I was in Southampton, and said nothing. He had merely been waiting for his chance. To my ill-fortune, he had struck gold with the man-at-arms whom I had seen in his company. I briefly considered admitting my part in his brother's death, but he would never believe my claim of self-defence. There was only one way to respond. 'I was in the town. So were a thousand more of the duke's men,' I said belligerently. 'Do you believe the word of every drunkard? When your brother met his end in the stews, I was not drinking in a rat-infested hovel, no. I was on my knees in a chapel, giving thanks to God.'

'You *were* in the inn, and you followed my brother onto the street, where he was done to death. You had a hand in his murder, I know it.' FitzAldelm's face was in mine now. His breath stank. 'I can smell a liar a mile away. The man-at-arms told me the truth, but *you* are lying.'

Bile washed the back of my throat, so great was my fear. It *was* possible that the man-at-arms remembered me from the inn. I swallowed, and said with a curl of my lip, 'Mind your tongue, sir! This fellow, is he of good character? Has he men who will corroborate his word?' FitzAldelm hesitated, and I cried, 'I thought not. Whereas my squire Rhys, whose loyalty to the duke is long-proven, will swear that he was with me in the chapel until dawn.'

FitzAldelm's jaw worked.

I locked eyes with him, aware that the slightest hint of fear would reinforce his suspicion. 'Bring this *man-at-arms*—' I loaded the phrase with contempt '—before the duke, and I will fetch Rhys. Let us see who is believed.'

The struggle as we stared at each other was invisible, yet titanic.

'There were other witnesses,' he hissed.

'But the man-at-arms could not produce them,' I threw back.

He did not answer, which proved I was right.

'Were there not a lady present, I would beat the truth out of you.'

Relief filled me. I had slipped under his guard. 'How ungallant, sir. What Queen Alienor would make of such behaviour, I know not. As for the duke . . .'

He stepped back, his expression still bright with malice. 'This is not over.'

'Nor is it, FitzAldelm.' I made sure he saw my fingers trail across my dagger hilt.

With an oath, he spun on his heel and made off down the corridor.

When he was gone, a long breath escaped me. I had had the better of him, but only just. At the first opportunity, he would return to Southampton and seek out the man-at-arms. If further witnesses were found, I was undone. My one consolation was that this had not already happened, which either meant that the man-at-arms was lying about having companions, or that they were vanished or dead.

I too needed to go to Southampton, although the chance of being released from the duke's company was slight. This was a task for Rhys, I decided. He had as much reason as I to see the matter – or more exactly, the man-at-arms – buried forever. Revulsion soon took the place of ruthlessness. Resort to cold-blooded murder, I thought, and I might as well have deliberately slain FitzAldelm's brother.

'Rufus?'

Beatrice's touch made me start. I glanced at her, managing a smile of sorts. 'Your pardon, my lady.'

'That sounded like an argument.' Her face was full of concern. 'I thought FitzAldelm was your friend.'

'He is no friend of mine!' Quickly, I laid out my history with Fitz-Aldelm, from his brutality on the voyage from Ireland to his recent attempt to kill me.

She regarded me with horror. 'Can you not tell the duke?'

'Richard thinks he is a fine fellow. Only a moment ago, he was singing FitzAldelm's praises to Queen Alienor.'

'And what happened just now?'

I flailed for a plausible lie, and could find none. 'He blames me for the death of his brother.' I began to explain about the other Fitz-Aldelm, but she interrupted.

'Had you anything to do with it?' Her eyes were wide, and so alluring.

Pathetically glad to find an answer that did not involve lying, I said, 'I did *not* murder him.'

'I believe you.' She came closer, took my hand in her little one.

I gazed at her, my fear and rage lessening with each beat of my heart. I could not help, however, from glancing over her shoulder in the direction whence FitzAldelm had vanished.

'Put him from your mind.'

'It is hard.' The battle was far from won. The evidence from the man-at-arms might not be convincing enough to bring the matter before the duke, but FitzAldelm would not give up. From this point on, I would have to sleep with one eye open.

'This might help.' Suddenly, she was very close. I could smell her favourite perfume, could feel her body pressing against mine. Our lips brushed.

'Is this not better than worrying about him?' she whispered.

I could barely speak, so overcome with passion was I. 'Yes.'

'Kiss me, Rufus.'

So I did.

The last days of August passed in a glorious spell of hot weather. Prince John married Hawise of Gloucester, an arrangement made soon after Richard had become the new king. Richard's reason was simple. He was yet unmarried and childless. John was second-in-line to the throne after the child Arthur, and therefore needed a son as fast as possible. Hawise was a pretty little thing, but dull as ditch water: the kind of woman who seemed to take John's fancy. Eager to avoid any trouble with the duke's brother or FitzAldelm, I kept my head down at the celebrations. I had no idea if my enemy had asked Richard for leave to travel to Southampton. He remained with the court, which was some respite, and I heard nothing about his brother's death. Nonetheless, I slept badly, and had frequent nightmares about him. If Beatrice had not accompanied Alienor, providing me with plenty of diversion, I would have been in a much darker place.

Gloucester's population turned out in its entirety to see Richard. It was the same everywhere we went: adoring crowds, rapturous applause, priests calling down the blessings of God. Ordinary people had good reason to love their new monarch. In addition to the pardoning of prisoners, and the easing of penalties on those in debt, Richard had repealed the forest laws. With much of England covered by woodland, wherein dwelt a rich variety of wildlife and potential source of food, they had long been hated by the entire population.

From Gloucester we went to London, arriving at the palace of Westminster in the first week of September. A sennight later, on the thirteenth, Richard was to be crowned king. The days passed in a flurry of activity. Tailors, jewellers and armourers swarmed through the court. Wains and wagons beyond counting trundled through the gates, laden with provisions for the feast that would take place after the coronation. Serjeants paced the route to Westminster Abbey, from where the sound of chants carried. The monks were preparing too.

Richard himself was busy from dawn to dusk, stuck in endless meetings with barons and bishops. Thankfully, Philip it was who had to endure these, not I. Free of formal duties until the coronation, de Drune and I did more drinking than was good for us. I drank to forget FitzAldelm, and de Drune drank, well, because he could. Rhys, unaware of my enemy's threats – I worried he might do something rash if I told him – joined in with gusto. Whenever the opportunity allowed, I enjoyed trysts with Beatrice. Still she would not lie with me, a torment which, God forgive me for saying so, became my cross to bear.

The day itself arrived. It was given to de Chauvigny, the Marshal and de Béthune to dress the duke. I could not feel resentful of the two latter newcomers to our camp; they were steadfast men who had been knights since I was a boy. There was little chance to talk to Richard either; preoccupied, he bade me good morning and nothing more. Again it mattered not to me – this was his day – and FitzAldelm, also in the room, was also ignored. I busied myself with helping Philip, not a knight's task, but a welcome distraction from my worries.

The religious came for Richard at the appointed hour, summoning him to the door of his chambers with a series of loud knocks. Uttering a prayer, his face calm, he opened the portal. Waiting was a vast crowd, at the front of which were priests, abbots and bishops, almost everyone in the realm, it seemed. After a ritual exchange of words between Richard and the senior bishops, the priests led off, carrying the cross, holy water, and burning tapers. In silken hoods, the rest followed.

In their midst walked a quartet of barons, each bearing a gold candlestick, and then a noble carrying the king's cap. With them was John Marshal, William's elder brother, carrying two massive gold spurs. Marshal himself walked alongside, in his hands the royal golden sceptre. More nobles followed, carrying golden swords, the king's arms and robes, and the crown, which was studded on every side with precious stones. Richard came next, a bishop to his left and right, with a silken canopy held over his head by four barons.

In descending order of rank, earls, barons, knights and clergy, the rest of us walked after, our feet silent on the woollen cloth that had been laid down early that morning. Huge crowds lined the entire route, cheering, and calling down blessings on Richard. I saw women openly weeping, and more than a few men. Small boys perched on rooftops, whistling. It was impossible not to be infected by the excitement. Forgetting about FitzAldelm, three steps from me, I began to enjoy myself, and to imagine the glories of Richard's reign.

The procession entered Westminster Abbey, which rang with chants of praise. As a knight, I was to stand halfway down the nave, a long way from the duke. Wise to this, I saw to it that I was nearest the central passage, with a view of the ritual. FitzAldelm, two men in, would not. He was furious, but powerless. It would further stoke his hatred, but caught up with the general excitement, I was able to set aside my concerns.

At the altar, Richard took many vows, among them to observe peace, honour and reverence to God and the Holy Church. He would exercise true justice, and care for his subjects. These pledges made, the bishops undressed him to his shirt and braies. The shirt was unbuttoned, and slipped from his shoulders, and gold-embroidered sandals placed on his feet. At this point the silence, which had been complete, somehow deepened. Mesmerised, I could not take my gaze from my lord and master.

Baldwin, the archbishop of Canterbury, anointed Richard as king with holy oil in three places, his head, chest and arms. These, I knew from the more learned Philip, represented glory, valour and knowledge. Richard was dressed in royal robes, and given the sword of rule, with which to crush enemies of the Church, and the golden spurs were attached. Robed last in a magnificent fur-lined mantle, he was led to the altar to confirm his oaths. Taking the crown from the altar, and handing it to the archbishop, Richard was then crowned.

He took his seat on the throne, and a murmur of appreciation and happiness rippled through the congregation.

The choir burst into a soul-stirring rendition of the *Te Deum Laudamus*.

Moisture pricked my eyes.

Head full of the battles we would win in Outremer, and of our glorious entrance into Jerusalem, I remember little of the mass that followed. At its end, Richard offered a mark of pure gold at the altar, before the procession we had made began in reverse. My attention sharpened as down the aisle came the clergy, the abbots and bishops, and the barons carrying the silken canopy over the new monarch's head.

My vision narrowed. All I could see was Richard. Tall he was, broad in the chest and handsome. Anointed as God's ruler over England, Wales, Normandy, Brittany, Anjou and Aquitaine, girded with a sword that would smite the Saracens, he looked every part the ruler. The warrior. The king.

As Richard came alongside, his head turned, and our gaze met. His chin dipped in recognition, just a little, and then he was gone.

His acknowledgement meant more to me than all the riches in Christendom.

AUTHOR'S NOTE

F ew figures stand out from British history like Richard Coeur de
Lion, the Lionheart. Asked by my publishers to move into a non-
Roman period (shock, horror!), I seized the chance to write about
someone I have been interested in since childhood.

Some have called Richard fearless, and a great leader, but he has also
been depicted as a poor king and brutal warrior. It was fashionable for
a time to call him gay. I tried to address all these possibilities in this
novel, with the exception of the last theory, because Richard's possible
homosexuality has, in my opinion, now largely been discounted. In the
main this is thanks to a re-appreciation of the medieval custom of men
who were friendly sharing the same bed. As is now recognised, this was
done with no sexual connotation. Proof comes from several sources,
not least the depiction of the practice in the stained-glass window of
a medieval church, a location that would never have been used for
anything considered immoral or scandalous. Much has also been made
of Richard's repenting of his sins in Sicily in 1190, and another occasion in 1195, when a hermit told him to remember the destruction of
Sodom. In modern parlance, this refers to homosexuality, but eight
hundred years ago, it did not have this implication. What constituted
sin in medieval times was a much broader subject than our narrowed
idea of it.

The character of Ferdia/Rufus sprang from my long-held desire to
pen a leading Irish character. For those of you who still don't know,
I am Irish! Ferdia and his best friend Cúchulainn (pronounced 'Koo-
hullen') are characters in the mythical tale The Táin. Ferdia is also my
son's name. To hell with it, I thought after a week or two of writing
Lionheart, I might as well give him our surname as well. Ó Catháin
is Kane in Irish. I went the whole hog then, and made Ferdia come
from Cairlinn (Carlingford) a beautiful village in County Louth near

where I grew up. There you can find a medieval ruin called King John's Castle, which I hope will feature in later books. Sliabh Feá is Slieve Foy, the tallest of the Cooley Mountains, and a great climb!

I fictitiously placed Cairlinn in Leinster; until the late 16th century, it was actually in Ulster. It was also not conquered by the English until the 1180s. The Ó Catháin family never ruled Cairlinn either, but it was commonplace in medieval times for hostages to be taken as guarantees of good behaviour. Richard de Clare, 'Strongbow', was the leading noble in the invasion of Ireland in 1169, and parts of his stronghold at Striguil (Chepstow in Wales) still stand today. They are well worth a visit, as is the nearby Caldicot Castle. It is not certain that de Clare's widow Aoife was resident in Striguil with her children in 1179, but is by no means impossible. To clear up any confusion, the twelfth century Norman invaders of Ireland were known by the Irish as 'English'. They were also called the 'grey foreigners', perhaps because of their long mail shirts. In England itself, a hundred years of conquest had seen the Norman ruling class also termed 'English', although I suspect the native English would have strongly disagreed with this terminology (hence my use of the term when Rufus is ambushed in the woods near Southampton). By this time, only those who came from Normandy were known as Normans.

Henry II was a remarkable man, whose empire stretched from the Scottish border almost to Spain, but despite his political ability, he had little luck with his family. Condemned to perpetual conflict, he experienced not only his wife Alienor (as she would have been called) turning against him, but at various times all of his four sons. No matter what his children did, Henry always seemed prepared to forgive them. He was less lenient with Alienor. I have done my best to convey the scale of the family feuding, but its fine details lie beyond the scope of this novel. I have used historical descriptions of the Young King, Richard, Geoffrey and John wherever possible, and quotes from medieval texts. 'Son of perdition', for example, was a name given to Geoffrey, and Henry's whispered curse to Richard at Ballan is attested. So too is his savage description of his four sons (in the chapter set at Christmas in Caen). Bertran de Born's quoted poems are original. The advice Richard received from the Court of Flanders I reproduced verbatim.

The scabs that Ferdia placed inside FitzAldelm's clothing were ringworm, a contagious fungal condition that can pass from cattle to in-contact humans. The names I used for cats and horses are medieval; readers may also know the book Sir Nigel by Sir Arthur Conan Doyle, and the main character's horse Pommers. I made up the attack on Usk, but Welsh border raids were frequent at the time. A mark was not a coin, but a weight of silver or gold, about two-thirds of a pound.

Richard's whereabouts in 1179 are little known; it was my invention to have him visit Striguil. He spent much of the 1170s and 1180s putting down rebellions in Aquitaine and beyond, honing his skills in warfare and siege craft. His strained relationship with the Young King and Geoffrey is documented, and no surprise, given how the latter two behaved towards him as the years passed. It is to Richard's credit that he remained loyal to his father for so long, despite Henry's refusal to acknowledge him as heir after the Young King's death. Whether Richard quite realised the level of Philippe Capet's deviousness, we cannot be sure, but from the mid-1180s, the French king was no friend to the house of Anjou.

Tall, handsome and endowed with natural dignity, Richard was a born leader. He was famous for his sense of right and wrong, and his determination to forge the correct path. His brevity earned him the nickname in the Occitan language of 'Yes and No'. His favourite curse was 'God's legs'! When needed, he was ruthless, as his treatment of the routiers in Gorre proved, but like his father, he could also be astonishingly generous to those who had wronged him, cf. his forgiveness of Bertran de Born when the war in Aquitaine was finally over. Richard's relationship with his father is a definite exception to this propensity for forgiveness. As for the crusade – an all-out war halfway across the world against the formidable Saladin – Richard could have been born for it. The term 'Crusade' would not have been around in the twelfth century, instead men spoke of 'taking the cross'. I judged it too confusing for modern readers not to use 'crusade', however. As Duke of Aquitaine, Richard will probably have used two lions as his heraldic device, like his father. He adopted one lion on accession to the throne, however. Later in his reign, this was changed to three. It was a marketing decision to have three on the book's cover – I hope readers will forgive this!

Sir William Marshal was a fascinating character. Much has been written about him in recent years; see the list of texts later on for more details. Servant to first the heir to the throne (the Young King) and then four kings (Henry II, Richard, John and Henry III), he was a consummate politician as well as loyal follower. In my opinion, he must also have possessed a keen instinct for opportunity as well as a ruthless streak; this is how I tried to portray him. I can hear the objections from some quarters already. Wrongly accused of adultery with the Young King's wife, he left his master's service during the Christmas court at Caen in 1182, earlier than I described. Most historians believe his mission to the Holy Land lasted two years; I chose to use the older theory of three. He was not at Gorre, and his attack on Chaumont-sur-Epte is my invention, as is John's involvement. The fate of d'Yquebeuf and de Coulonces is also unclear.

The historical record is silent as to John's whereabouts in summer and winter 1182, which meant I could place him in Caen. The apple of his father's eye until the very end of Henry's life, he seems to have been a devious but intelligent character. Alienor is a fascinating woman; she was one of the most powerful and influential women in medieval Europe. Her confinement by Henry was immensely frustrating to my plans, because I wanted to include her as a major player. If I had, however, I would still be writing this book.

Richard never went to Cahors in secret as far as we know, but his alliance with Philippe Capet and the final set of clashes and abortive peace conferences between him and his father unfolded as I described. Bonsmoulins may well have been held in a field, as was the norm, rather than in an abbey. It also lasted three days, not three hours! The audacious attack on Le Mans, the battles therein, and Richard's pursuit of his father all happened, as did Marshal's killing of the duke's horse. The fact that Richard was willing to forgive this later on is therefore a mark of his regard for Marshal, and no doubt, his famed loyalty.

Rufus's and Richard's adventures will also continue in book two, working title Lionheart: Crusade. It should hit the bookshops in May/June 2021.

Researching a new period in history is both fascinating and intimidating. I spent three months reading about the medieval world before beginning *Lionheart*, and have spent hundreds of hours during the writing of the book doing the same. I consulted medieval accounts by

Roger of Howden, Gerald of Wales and Ralph of Diss, and read again and again the incredible document that is the History of William Marshal. The texts that never left my side were *Richard the Lionheart* by A. Bridge, *William Marshal* by David Crouch, *Richard the Lionheart* by J. Gillingham, *Saladin* by P.H. Newby, and *Henry II* and *King John*, both by W.L. Warren. Also indispensable were *Life in a Medieval City, Life in a Medieval Village* and *Life in a Medieval Castle* by J. and F. Gies, *The Normans* by Gravett and Nicolle, *Food and Feast in Medieval England* by P.W. Hammond, *Knight* by R. Jones, *The Medieval Kitchen* by H. Klemettilä, *Medieval Warfare* by H. W. Koch, *Chepstow Castle* by Turner and Johnston, numerous Osprey texts and articles in *Medieval Warfare* magazine.

I am deeply indebted to Dr Michael Staunton of the School of History in University College Dublin, Ireland, for his generosity and time. A specialist in the twelfth century and the House of Anjou, he kindly answered my many questions throughout the writing of the book. When it was done, he read the entire thing, checking for inconsistencies and errors. Go raibh míle maith agat, a Mhícheál.

I have visited quite a number of the sites in the novel, including Chepstow, Limoges, Gorre, Aixe, Chinon, Vendôme, Rocamadour and Fontevraud, as well as Châlus, where Richard took his death wound in 1199. I recommend a tour of these and other amazing medieval sites in Britain and France.

I do many things apart from writing novels. Look out for my recent digital short stories, which include 'The March' (it follows on from The Forgotten Legion, and reveals what happened to Brennus), 'Eagles in the Wilderness' and 'Eagles in the East' (both featuring Centurion Tullus of the Eagles trilogy). Don't own an e-reader? Simply download the free Kindle app from Amazon, and you can read the stories on a phone, tablet or computer. If you would like to visit Pompeii and Herculaneum with me as a guide, Google Andante Tours (tinyurl.com/yc4uze85). If you enjoy cycling with an historical twist, take a look at Bike Odyssey (bikeodyssey.cc) and Ride and Seek Bicycle Adventures (rideandseek.com). Both these companies run epic trips (Hannibal, Lionheart, Venetians, Napoleon, Julius Caesar) that I am involved with as an historical guide.

I support the charities Combat Stress, which helps British veterans with PTSD, and Médecins Sans Frontières (MSF), which sends medical staff into disaster and war zones worldwide. If you'd like to know more about one of the money-raising efforts I made with author friends Anthony Riches and Russell Whitfield, look up 'Romani walk' on YouTube. In 2014 we walked 210 kilometres in Italy, wearing full Roman armour, and finishing at the Colosseum in Rome. The documentary is narrated by Sir Ian McKellen – Gandalf! Find the film here: tinyurl.com/h4n8h6g – and please tell your friends about it.

I also help Park in the Past, a community-interest company which plans to build a Roman marching fort near Chester, in north-west England. Its website is: parkinthepast.org.uk. Thanks to everyone who has contributed to the fundraising thus far. Three readers who have been especially supportive appear in this book: Philip, Rufus's friend, is based on the wonderful Bruce Phillips, one of life's true gentlemen. Richard West is the man behind Richard de Drune, and Taff James is the real Owain. Thank you, all three. (Bets are off regarding the survival of Philip and de Drune in book two! Apologies, Taff, but you had a glorious end at least!) Hugo is based on my nephew, Hugo Ryan-Kane, with much affection.

Every writer needs a good editor, and I have been blessed in that regard. Big thanks to Ben Willis and more recently, Francesca Pathak, both at Orion Publishing. Thank you also to Craig Lye. I'm indebted to my foreign publishers, and in particular Aranzazu Sumalla and the Ediciones B team in Spain – gracias! – and Magdalena Madej-Reputakowska and the Znak team in Poland – dziękuję ci! Thank you, Charlie Viney, my fantastic agent and friend, and Chris Vick, masseuse extraordinaire.

And so to my wonderful readers. I have been a full-time author for more than ten years, thanks to you. I love your emails and comments/messages on Facebook and Twitter! Look out for the signed books and goodies I give away and auction for charity via these media. After you've read my books, leaving a short review on Amazon, Goodreads, Waterstones.com or iTunes (or all of the above!) really helps. In fact, it has never been more important. Historical fiction is currently a shrinking market, sad to say. Times are tougher than they were when I was first published, and an author lives and dies on their reviews. Just a few minutes of your time helps a great deal – thank you in advance.

Last but not least, lots of love and thanks to Sair, Ferdia and Pippa for simply being who they are. Life would not be the same without you.

Ways to get in touch:
Email: ben@benkane.net
Facebook: facebook.com/benkanebooks
Twitter: @BenKaneAuthor
Also, my website: benkane.net
YouTube (my short documentary-style videos): tinyurl.com/y7chqhgo

Turn the page to see what happens next in

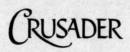

CHAPTER I

Near Southampton, November 1189 . . .

It was a filthy day. A biting wind had lashed us since morning; rain-filled clouds pursued us at every step. Patches of woodland, which afforded some relief from the weather, were few and far between. Stubbled fields ran along both sides of the road, which was a quagmire. Mud sucked at Pommers' hooves and flicked up onto my sodden lower legs. My woollen mantle – still damp that morn from the previous day's soaking – weighed heavily on my chilled shoulders. Rivulets of water ran down my face and dripped onto my red-knuckled hands, clenched on the reins. Moisture trickled down my back. If there was any part of me that was dry, I could not feel it.

'This is worse than the ride to Gorre, sir.' Hunched over in the saddle like an old man, hood pulled low over his face, Rhys was riding on my left.

'Sweet Jesu, I had forgotten about that.' Despite the grim images dragged up by his words – two brutal days and nights of riding through snow and ice, a short, sharp fight and then the slaughter of hundreds of prisoners – I laughed. There *had* been other times in my life when I was as miserable. 'It was colder then, true, but I have never been so wet as I am now.'

'Being frozen is better than this, sir.'

'Aye, well, we are more than halfway there. With a little luck, we should make Southampton by nightfall. I see little point in turning our horses and making for London again.'

Rhys grumbled under his breath.

'Would you rather be back at court, running errands, and listening to the lawyers drone?' Since Richard's coronation in September, his only focus had been to raise money for his long-planned crusade. The joke went that everything in his kingdom was for sale: powers, lordships, earldoms, sheriffdoms, castles, towns and manors. 'I would sell

London, if I could find a buyer for it,' the king had memorably said. Not a day passed without his palace being thronged with lords and bishops seeking to retain what they already had, or eagerly trying to better themselves. As a household knight with little to do but stand guard over Richard, I had been bored to tears. Rhys, part of the mesnie but lower in status, had been reduced to messenger boy, a role he had performed with ill-concealed resentment.

'Well?' I asked.

He groaned.

'There might come a day in Outremer when we long for weather like this.'

'I cannot see it, sir.'

Damp, cold and uncomfortable, I too could not imagine the blistering temperatures and burning sands described to me by Richard. I wiped a large drop of water off the end of my nose, and comforted myself with thoughts of the warm, dry inn where we would spend the night. My spirits were further raised a short time later as the road wound into a large copse of oaks and beeches, protecting us from the driving rain.

Inevitably, my mind turned to my purpose in Southampton, and the name of FitzAldelm. Since being taken hostage a decade prior in Leinster, my Irish home, I had been tormented at various times by two brothers. The first, Robert, lived still, and was my bitterest enemy. High in the king's favour, he was currently part of an embassy sent north to meet the new Scottish king, William. The second, Guy, was long dead, God rot his bones. During a confrontation in a dark alleyway years before, I had slain him in self-defence in the very town I was riding towards.

Robert FitzAldelm had known nothing of the fight; indeed we had never spoken of his brother's demise. He had long harboured suspicion, however, because when the royal party had recently passed through Southampton, he had somehow found a witness – a man-at-arms – who claimed to have seen me in the inn last frequented by his brother Guy. This by no means proved my guilt. If I was accused, Rhys – who had been with me in the alley and had killed Guy's squire – would swear blind he and I had spent that night on our knees in a chapel, but since FitzAldelm's shocking revelation, worry had nipped at me like a dog worrying a trespasser's heels. If the man-at-arm's testimony was plausible, if, as my enemy had implied, other witnesses might be found, my entire future was in jeopardy.

It was fortunate that FitzAldelm had been kept busy with his duties since the coronation; he had had no chance to continue his investigations. Richard's decisions, to send him to the Scottish border, and to charge me with delivering an important message to his ships' captains at Southampton, had come as welcome relief. With my enemy out of the way, *I* had a chance to find the man-at-arms, and silence him by one means or another.

A heavy purse of silver nestled at my waist, my first means of persuasion. More than three years' pay for an ordinary soldier, it was a sum that would seal most men's lips. Loath though I was to admit it, I knew that coin alone would not guarantee my safety. Only the bollock dagger hanging from my right hip could do that. My mood darkened. I was a wretch. I may not have murdered Guy FitzAldelm, but two innocent men had hung for the crime while I stood by. Now I was prepared to slay another just to keep my good name.

'Sir.'

Rhys's voice stirred me from my brooding. I cast him a look, and seeing his gaze fixed on the road, turned my head.

Around a slight bend, the road had been blocked by a fallen decent-sized beech. Bare of foliage, its branches stuck out in every direction. 'That is no storm damage,' I said, suspicion pricking me. 'The trunk has been cut through over to the left. See the stump, there.'

'They will have bows, like as not, sir,' said Rhys with not a flicker of emotion.

'They will, curse them.' Rhys had a padded gambeson on under his mantle, but along with my hauberk, mine was rolled up tight upon the packhorse's back. Those who had felled the beech would show themselves long before I could don either. I came to an instant, if galling, decision. 'Let us retrace our steps. There was a left turn a mile or so back.'

Young though he was, Rhys also knew that discretion is the better part of valour. It did not stop him from complaining. 'Does that track even lead to Southampton, sir? For all you know, it might take us to Rye.' That port lay a good distance further along the coast.

'Better to end up there than riddled with arrows,' I said, pulling on the reins so Pommers began to wheel.

'Aye.' It was incredible how much frustration could emanate from one word.

I threw him a look. Few knights would have permitted their squires such freedom, but Rhys and I had long history.

Almost as if it discerned our about turn, the wind changed direction, tugging hungrily at our mantles. Rain sheeted down. Miserable, I tucked my chin into my chest, fixing my gaze on Pommers' withers. He would follow the road.

'Stop!' The order came from behind us. It was given in English, not French, as I had expected, but to my surprise, the voice was thin, reedy – a boy's.

I glanced at Rhys. He was staring in front of us. 'There's another there, sir,' he said quietly. 'Two of them in fact.'

A pair of youths blocked our path, twenty paces away. Clad in ragged tunics and patched hose, they were barefoot. Faces chapped, cheeks hollow, they were as fine a pair of starvelings as I had seen since leaving London. Each had an arrow nocked on the string of his bow, however. One was aimed at Rhys, the other at me.

'Off your horses,' shouted the taller of the two, a spike-haired lad of perhaps fourteen years.

I ignored him, and glanced over my shoulder. Two more scarecrows, both also armed with bows, one no more than ten, the other maybe sixteen, were clambering over the felled beech. We had a little time before they closed the trap.

'Sir?' Rhys had a hand on his sword.

I shook my head. 'Two more are coming up behind us.'

'I said, off your damned horses!'

'On my word, charge,' I muttered. 'God willing, we will escape unharmed. Try not to lose the packhorse.'

There was fear in Rhys's eyes – boys or no, there was a real chance that one of us or our horses would be hit by an arrow, or worse – but he nodded his assent.

Tugging back my mantle, I swept out my sword. 'For the king!' I shouted, squeezing my knees against Pommers' chest.

Well-trained, he went from a walk to the full charge in two paces. Rhys's mount Oxhead, my second destrier, matched him, and the packhorse followed its companions' lead. Close enough to reach out and clasp hands, Rhys and I pounded at the two churls. Mud spattered, water sprayed, and I bellowed again, 'For the king!'

Rhys echoed my cry.

The youths raised their bows, but one was shaking so badly he could scarce direct the arrow at me. The other, the older, was made of sterner stuff. 'Stop, or I will loose!' he cried.

My guts tightened, and if I confess it, naked fear took me. He did not have the strength of a grown man, but at such close range, his iron-tipped arrow would slice deep into Pommers' flesh, or mine.

'HA!' I tugged the reins a fraction, aiming Pommers straight at him. Leaning low on my destrier's great neck, trying to make myself as small a target as possible, I shouted again, 'HA!'

Pommers increased his speed. By God, he could move. The ground below me was a blur. We covered the distance to the youths in another heartbeat. With a cry of terror, the younger one dropped his bow and threw himself off the road. The other, aware he would be smashed into the mud by Pommers, loosed early. His arrow went past the side of my head, and was gone. The wind of its passing made me want to piss. I was unhurt, however, and the youth had fallen onto his arse in the mud. Eyes wide with terror, he stared up at me.

I could have ridden over him – Pommers was a destrier, and used to this – but pity took me. I jerked the reins a little to the right, and left him staring after us, his mouth gaping.

We rode a hundred paces before slowing.

Rhys's face was covered in mud, but he was grinning from ear to ear. 'We made it, sir!'

'Aye,' I said, relief washing over me. The packhorse had not broken free either. 'Thank God.'

He stared back down the track. Four figures stood watching us. One, the smallest, shook a fist. His reedy voice carried to us. 'Another day!'

I saluted him. 'Another day,' I shouted back.

Rhys scowled. 'Cheeky little bastard. Maybe we should go back and teach them a lesson.'

'Let the wretches be. They were starving, or near as.' I had no desire to injure or kill children. 'You were not so different ten years ago.'

Rhys scowled. 'I never robbed anyone.'

'Not with a weapon, maybe, but you stole.'

The beginnings of a smile. 'I was hungry!'

I cast my eyes down the track, at our would-be ambushers. 'And they are not?'

'Aye, sir, all right.'

'This was the wiser choice as well. We might not be so lucky a second time.'

'True enough.' Bows were the great leveller on the battlefield, especially to men without armour.

'Come on. Southampton is not getting any closer.'

Keeping an even warier eye on the road, we rode back whence we had come.

A log moved; crackles came from the hearth. Waves of warmth radiated out, baking me, but I luxuriated in the heat. Washed, dry, in my second-best tunic and hose, I was perched on a stool in front of the blaze. Not every room in the inn had a fireplace, but after the travails of our journey, the extra expense had seemed cheap. As I said to Rhys, he or I could have been lying in the mud, an arrow skewering our flesh. A dead man cannot spend his silver, let alone enjoy a bath and a roaring fire.

Rhys, who had used the tub after me, was drying himself with a cloth.

'Better?' I asked, supping my ale.

'Aye, sir. I can feel my toes again.'

I chuckled, inching my own feet a little closer to the fire.

The diversion forced on us by the ambush had added at least an hour to our journey. Night had fallen before the walls of Southampton loomed before us. We were here now, though. Pommers, Oxhead and the packhorse were in a comfortable stable, being tended to by the ostler. Our baggage, armour and weapons were piled in the corner. Clouds of moisture rose from our sodden clothing, which was draped on stools near the hearth. A platter of roast meat, bread and cheese delivered by a servant awaited our attention. A pair of straw lined pallets with rough woollen blankets would be our beds.

With our bellies full, and our jug of ale drained, I decided to make for the inn's public room. We would find out nothing on our own. The door had no lock, so I eased up a floorboard and hid my purse between the rafters, afterwards sliding the clothes chest on top. Thus prepared, we went down the creaking staircase to the ground floor.

'Less ale, more listening and watching,' I warned Rhys.

He nodded.

Slipping into the dimly lit, fuggy room, which was half full, I found us a quiet table along one side wall. A few heads turned, but this was a place full of travellers, so no one paid us any heed, apart from a tail-waving gazehound which ambled over to stick its nose into my hand. A rosy-cheeked wench brought us two mugs of ale, which was drinkable but not much more. I cast a casual eye about, appraising the other customers, a mixture of traders, merchants and respectable tradesmen. There was also a tonsured cleric who sat alone, reading a parchment.

'We will not find him here,' I said, stroking the gazehound's head. 'Not a man here save the innkeeper is from the town, I would wager.'

'Aye, sir. They are all like us – blow-ins.'

This brought me to the nub of my problem. I was in Southampton, but I might as well have been in Outremer. All I had to go on was the fact that the man-at-arms had a beard shaped like the end of a spade. I did not know his name or anything about him. The chance of finding him, as I had, incredibly, with Guy FitzAldelm, was infinitesimally small. Start asking questions, moreover, and I would be more likely to send him to ground than discover his whereabouts. Rhys, with his Welsh-accented French, stood little better chance than I of success. We had to try, however, or our mission here would be wasted.

The serving wench had batted her eyes at Rhys, so I got him to ask her where soldiers drank. Armed with a list as long as a bow stave – I judged we would not remember half of them – we set out to investigate the nearest, which was further down the unpaved street. Eyes peeled for cutpurses and ruffians, we found the place easily enough, thanks to the raucous singing and gaggle of drunks outside. One, singing tunelessly to himself, weaved towards us, ale pot in hand. Seeing a dog skulking by the entrance to an alley, he clicked his tongue at it. 'Here, boy!'

It growled.

Ignoring this warning, he walked towards it, still clicking his tongue. Hackles raised, rumbling in its throat, it took a step towards him.

'Leave the creature alone, you fool,' I muttered.

'Come on, boy,' said the drunkard.

The dog lunged at him, teeth bared.

A shouted curse, a yelp of pain. Bitten in his left leg, the man tried to throw a kick with his other. Instead, unbalanced, he toppled on his arse in the mud. The dog scuttled into the alleyway, and the onlookers jeered with laughter.

'Get yourself to a doctor lest that bite turn bad,' I said, walking by.

All I got back was an earful of abuse.

Shrugging at Rhys, I put my shoulder to the door of the alehouse, and shoved.

Inside, I was astonished to be recognised within half a dozen paces by a man-at-arms who had fought for Richard in Aquitaine. I had stood beside Somerset John in more than one skirmish against the French, which meant I could hardly refuse his offer of a drink. Balding and paunchy now, with a drinker's red nose, he sat by a corner table, his rough-carved wooden leg propped on a stool before him.

Rhys and I sat opposite, both of us uncomfortable that we had our backs to the room.

Somerset John clapped me on the shoulder again. 'God's bones, but it is good to see you, Rufus. And you, lad,' he said to Rhys.

'How long has it been?' I asked, smiling my thanks as he poured us generous measures of the local cider.

'Six year, I reckon.' He raised his wooden beaker. 'To old times, and death to the French!'

We drank.

'To King Richard, God bless him,' I said next.

'Aye, to the king!' cried John.

As the men who had heard gave a cheer, we clinked our cups and took another swallow. The cider was strong, and sweet. I did not like it overmuch, but Rhys had finished his already, and was helping himself to another draught. I threw him a warning look, and answered John's questions about life in Richard's service. I told him of the campaigns we had fought after his injury, the Young King's death, and the night-time bargaining that had resulted in the truce at Chateauroux. I explained how Richard had taken the cross, and related his struggle to seize control of the kingdom from his father Henry, and the last confrontation between them. John drank it all in, his eyes glistening. Last I spoke of the king's recent coronation, and the feasting afterwards. We toasted Richard's health again, and his good fortune on the crusade.

'So you are for Outremer?' John's tone was wistful.

'Come the spring.' I nodded at John's wooden leg, remembering the brutal wound made by a mace that had necessitated the amputation of his limb. 'But for that, you would come with us, I have no doubt.'

He gave me a sad smile. 'I would like nothing better, Rufus. As I am, though, I would be nothing but a hindrance.'

'Not at all,' I protested. ''Twas a rebel from Aquitaine who gave you that, was it not?'

'Aye,' came the sour reply. 'A big bastard of a knight he was, on the largest destrier I ever saw. He smote me to the ground and rode away, laughing.'

'Still. You are here, and many others are not, God rest their souls.'

We fell to talking about the battle, a vicious little affair a day or two before the peace conference at Grandmont. Somerset John had been fortunate, because the gathering called by King Henry had meant that after the clash Richard's soldiers, we among them, had set up camp. Attended by the surgeon, his leg amputated the same day, John had had the time to recuperate from the life-threatening operation in one place. Others who had taken similar wounds while we were on the march had not been so lucky. Lying on blood-soaked straw in the backs of wagons, jolted about from dawn to dusk, many had succumbed. We drank to their memory.

'Most are rotting in Hell, like as not,' said John. 'Keeping the Devil on his toes.'

'Let it be many years before we join them,' I said with a chuckle. 'You are getting by, I hope?'

He grimaced. 'You find me in here drinking, right enough, but I should not be. Times are hard. I – who was once a man-at-arms to the Duke – sell gewgaws to women. Bronze and enamelled brooches, you know the type. Glass and ceramic to fashion necklaces or rosary beads. It is a low vocation, and many's the night I go to bed hungry. It is only fortunate that I have no wife and children.' He put his head in his hands.

I silently indicated that Rhys should order more cider. 'No old comrade of mine shall go wanting,' I said.

John's eyes, half hopeful, half fearful, rose to meet mine. 'What mean you, Rufus?'

'A belted knight I am now,' I said in his ear. 'And many's the ransom

I have won in Normandy and Aquitaine. A heavy purse is yours, to do with what you will. It is the least I can do.'

Lost for words, he stared at me. A tear rolled down his unshaven cheek.

'I ask but one boon. Nay, nay, do not fear,' I said, as his expression grew wary. 'It is not your soul I ask for, but your help in finding a man.'

CREDITS

Orion Fiction would like to thank everyone at Orion who worked on the publication of *Lionheart* in the UK.

Editorial
Francesca Pathak
Lucy Frederick

Copy editor
Steve O'Gorman

Proof reader
Linda Joyce

Contracts
Anne Goddard
Paul Bulos
Jake Alderson

Design
Rabab Adams
Tomas Almeida
Joanna Ridley
Nick May

Editorial Management
Charlie Panayiotou
Jane Hughes
Alice Davis

Rights
Susan Howe
Krystyna Kujawinska
Jessica Purdue
Richard King
Louise Henderson

Finance
Jasdip Nandra
Afeera Ahmed
Elizabeth Beaumont
Sue Baker

Audio
Paul Stark
Amber Bates

Production
Hannah Cox

Publicity
Virginia Woolstencroft

Marketing
Cait Davies
Lucy Cameron

Sales
Jen Wilson
Esther Waters
Victoria Laws
Rachael Hum
Ellie Kyrke-Smith
Frances Doyle
Georgina Cutler

Operations
Jo Jacobs
Sharon Willis
Lisa Pryde
Lucy Brem

Help us make the next generation of readers

We – both author and publisher – hope you enjoyed this book. We believe that you can become a reader at any time in your life, but we'd love your help to give the next generation a head start.

Did you know that 9% of children don't have a book of their own in their home, rising to 13% in disadvantaged families*? We'd like to try to change that by asking you to consider the role you could play in helping to build readers of the future.

We'd love you to think of sharing, borrowing, reading, buying or talking about a book with a child in your life and spreading the love of reading. We want to make sure the next generation continue to have access to books, wherever they come from.

And if you would like to consider donating to charities that help fund literacy projects, find out more at **www.literacytrust.org.uk** and **www.booktrust.org.uk**.

THANK YOU

*As reported by the National Literacy Trust